VAN DOREN
LOREN

LOREN
VAN DOREN

CREA REITAN

DRAGON FIRE FANTASY

Loren

Van Doren | Book 1

Copyright © 2024 by Amber Reitan writing as Crea Reitan

www.facebook.com/LadyCreaAuthor

Cover Copyright © 2024 Rebeca Covers

Editing by Lindsay Hamilton

Proofreading by Chaotic Creatives

Alpha Readers: Lindsay H, Cassandra F, Carrie F

Beta Readers: Sarah Jane, Amanda B, Suzanne B, Chelsi F, Michelle R

Patreon pretties: Melaney, Melissa, Heather P, Jessica S, Jordan, Joanna, Cora, Nicole C, Ashley D, Isabella, Mel, Darcy, Amy, Kimberly, Ashley, Nicole I, Taylor K, Annissa, Rachel, Heather F, Anthia, Megan, Tamara, Suzanne, Gina, Jennifer B, Terriann, Fawn, Miriam, Ay Bee, Carrie F, Jennifer M, Sarah Jane, Lauren

All Rights Reserved. No part of this publication may be reproduced, distributed, or transmitted in any form or by any means, including photocopying, recording, or other electronic or mechanical methods, without the prior written permission of the publisher, except in the case of brief quotations for review purposes.

This book is sold subject to the condition that it shall not, by way of trade or otherwise, be circulated without the author's prior consent *in any form of binding or cover other than that which it is published* and without a similar condition including this condition being imposed on the subsequent purchaser.

No generative artificial intelligence (AI) was used in drafting, editing, design, or production of this work of fiction. The author expressly prohibits any entity from using this publication to train AI technologies to generate text including but not limited to technologies capable of generating works in the same style or genre as this publication. The author reserves all rights to licensed uses of this work for generative AI training and development of machine learning language models. None of this content, internal and cover, may be used for or in connection with AI producing material.

This is a work of fiction - all characters and events portrayed in this book are fictitious. Any resemblance to actual persons, living or dead, places, or events is purely coincidental and not intended by the author.

Dragon Fire Fantasy, Inc.

dragonfirefantasy@gmail.com

Version 2024.06.29 - P.NA

Created with Vellum

I have had these characters in my head far before I broke into the MM side of romance. They've been percolating for *years* and I finally get to introduce them to you in more than just a side character! I know I've hinted at Loren specifically a few times but it's because he's just a lovable sociopath that I couldn't help myself.

I'm going to tell you this up front - Loren is a serial killer. Not one that picks victims on his own but one that does so by contract. He and his eldest brother are contract killers - hired assassins. Because of his occupation, you will find *brief mentions* of some serious topics, such as domestic violence, sexual assault, child abuse, murdering puppies, etc. Please note that these are *brief* mentions, rarely more than a line.

There is the beginning of an abusive relationship - NOT between main characters. You will find stalking in this book - by a character who will be killed and by a main character.

Please note that there are a few scenes of somewhat graphic murder. Once you meet Loren, you will understand why. Especially with the murders on page.

This story features a broad cast of characters which is partially because books live like soap operas in my mind and you *know* there are characters out the wazoo in a soap opera! Some of them will end up in other books. For this series specifically, I have already introduced and/or mentioned every character in the Van Doren series! Oakley's friend group meet the Van Doren family!

As with most things I write, this story is also about friendship. Friendship comes in all forms and different configurations. Different colors. It doesn't need to fit into a mold. Again, if this isn't something you can accept, find something else to read. You're not my audience.

And of course, this is a love story.

You'll also find insta-possession, sociopathy, touch aversion, stalker, bi-awakening, obsession, contract killer, dirty talk, biting, and murder, sex toys, touch him and die. This is a slow burn but there's a decent amount of spice... I think.

If anything you just read bothers you, makes you uneasy, or isn't what you're looking for, please do not read this book. Indie authors don't deserve bad reviews because readers read the warnings and ignore them. I'm not for everyone and I'll be the first to tell you to go read something else if this doesn't sound like something you're going to enjoy. Otherwise, enjoy this story filled with just a few red flags.

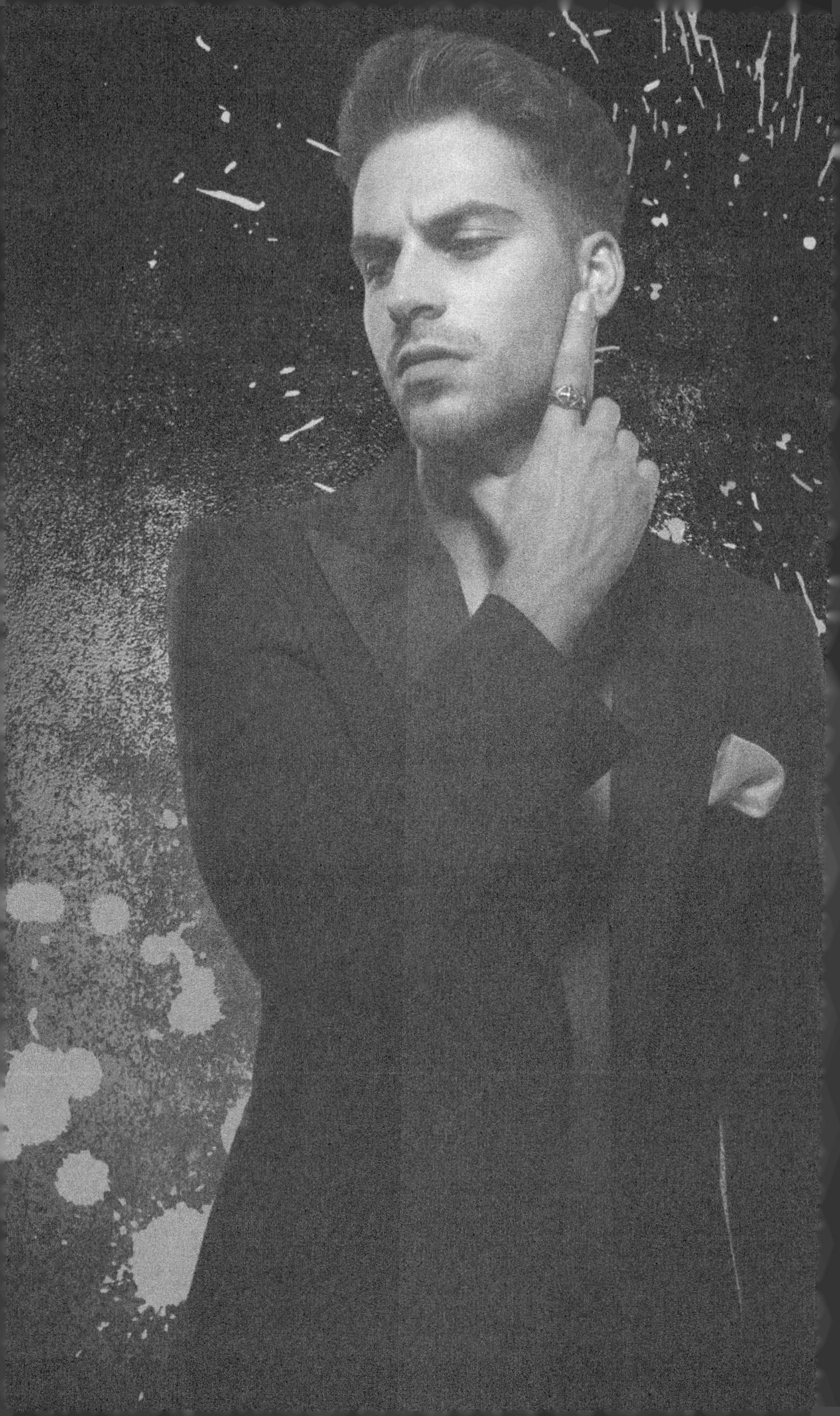

1
LOREN

"What you're saying is I should have killed him last summer," I clarify.

Myro studies me. Behind him on the big screen is the picture of Daniel Rollins-Alabaster, a man who has gone by many names and left a long trail behind him. Not one of broken hearts, but one of emotional manipulation, verbal and mental abuse, and men who often dropped out of school because of the state this man left them in.

I'd flown out to California last summer when my friend Noah mentioned him to me. It still makes me smile that he did. His awkwardness was really kind of cute. I tried so hard not to smile when he was telling me about this guy over the phone.

It took me some time to find him, since the name we initially had was a lie. I hadn't been sure if he'd been excellent about covering his trail or if I just hadn't gotten an accurate read on him right away. But once I tracked this asshole down, we had words. He landed in the hospital.

"He's been quiet for some time," Myro says. "But he's recently moved to Tucson close to Eastern State University, where he's once more looking for his next victim."

Myro goes on to tell me what Imry has found in detail—complete with pictures, call logs, and his new identities. Yes, plural. I stare, not because I'm entirely interested in what he's saying. Not even because I'm *not* interested in what he's saying. I'm just irritated because I wanted to kill him six months ago and Myro talked me out of it.

Imry is sitting across from me. I know it's Imry because of the way he's trying not to smirk. Also, he'd been the one to help me track down Daniel last summer. It was already his assignment and when I don't kill my target, he makes a habit of keeping tabs on them.

Just in case.

In case of situations like this where my target hasn't smartened the fuck up. I'm confident he'll stay away from Roux Kipler, but that he's still preying on more men is unacceptable.

The only other person in the conference room is our father. Even though he is the president of Van Doren Technologies, he almost exclusively works remotely from our home. And while all us kids might be well into adulthood, I think we enjoy each other's company and it's comfortable.

Besides, we're well spread out on the big Van Doren estate. For instance, this conference room is in our lab—a completely separate building from our living and playing quarters.

I look at Myro again when he appears to have concluded his briefing. He's waiting expectantly as he watches me.

"That's a lot of words to confirm that I should have killed him last summer," I say.

Imry raises his hand to cover his mouth and looks away. At the other end of the table, our father smirks but doesn't say anything.

Myro sighs. Placing his hands on the table, he leans forward toward me. "I know you feel zero remorse, which makes you a very good killer, Loren. But sometimes I think you kill *too* easily. I was trying to... I don't know, prevent you from turning into a cold-blooded murderer."

"That's what I am," I say. "That's my job. And *yours.*"

"Yes, and that's why I give you the jobs that don't sit well with me because *I do* feel remorse and I rather like sleeping at night."

"I don't have that issue," I tell him.

"Yes, I know. And maybe I should have let you deal with it on your own, in your own way because I know despite your inability to sympathize, you do think things through. I was putting my personal concerns on you and I shouldn't have," Myro admitted.

"That's very grown up of you, Myro," I say.

He huffs, standing upright. His hand ruffles my hair and I smirk.

"Always protecting us," Imry says quietly.

"Yes," Myro agrees. "Even when I don't need to." He looks at me again. "This is back in your hands. Deal with him however you'd like to, preferably before he causes too much more damage."

I nod just as the door opens and the rest of our brothers join us. Voss drops into a chair beside me with his computer, setting it on the shiny surface of the table. The remaining two-thirds of the triplets take chairs next to Imry, rolling them close until the armrests are against each other.

"Why are you always starting meetings without us?" Avory asks.

"You only missed Myro telling me I should have killed one of my previous targets instead of landing him in the hospital," I inform them.

"Which?" Avory asks.

"There haven't been that many," Ellory says. "He's a perfect killer."

"This is what I wanted to prevent," Myro insists.

"Why?" the triplets ask in unison.

Voss looks up when they speak as one and grins. As does our father, while Myro chuckles.

"As we've just established, I'm always trying to protect my baby brothers," Myro answers. "Loren will take care of Alabaster and now we'll move on."

"Where is he?" Avory asks.

"Conveniently, he's moved to Arizona. Not quite so convenient, he's about four hours south," Imry says. "We'll head down later today." His gaze meets mine and I nod, entirely unsurprised that he's joining me.

I listen to them for a while as they talk about the projects that they're working on. Van Doren Technologies is a very large umbrella company that has a lot of tentacles in nearly every industry around the world. Name it and it's likely that, if nothing else, we hold substantial stock in it.

Most of what we do is completely legal. Those are the things the world sees. Everyone knows our father's face as the kingpin, mob boss, mafia king—all of the above—of Van Doren. He has truly revolutionized the company since taking it over from his father twenty years ago.

But every big company has a darker underbelly that the pretty lights and big bank accounts are protecting. Van Doren has several. Myro and I are part of clean-up. We take out the trash through contracts. Most of the time, this means we're just causing accidents for our targets to die. There are times when we have to take matters into our own hands and kill them outright.

Some people just have all the luck and somehow miss the accidents.

I don't do it for the money. I don't have some hero complex and think I'm cleaning up the streets of those who slip through the law's fingers. There's no sense of doing good for me.

Quite frankly, I kill people because I enjoy it. Watching their life drain from their bodies and knowing that I did that? It's a very satisfying feeling.

Myro does it for the 'right' reasons. Which is why when we get a contract that makes him uneasy, he gives it to me. My sense of right and wrong is slightly skewed, according to studies of people like me.

Voss doesn't kill. He's a computer genius, and there's not a damn thing he can't do online. He works for the tech side of Van Doren, but his contributions to the dark underbelly are leaking the scandals of assholes so they receive some comeuppance and covering Van Doren's tracks. Rather unironically, his handle is always some form of 'karma.'

Then there are the triplets who work for the law offices of Van Doren. While Voss can find anything online that there is to find, the triplets can find everything that's *not* online.

There are other shadows that Van Doren hides. Dad likes to say that we're doing good work. The things that can't be done legally but should be. In a broken world, someone needs to fix all the cracks or everything will just fall apart.

One of the most common debates growing up was whether we *should* let it all fall apart or not, meaning the government, the police, the law. All the crooked shit that's going on. He likes to say that we're picking up the pieces they can't *legally* take care of.

But we're all aware of how broken our political system is. And it's not just the political system—there's the school system, big pharma companies and the entire health care system, plus the way organized religion *still* holds sway where it shouldn't.

Most of the time, I just listen and absorb. My answer is almost always, *let's start over.* Myro says my first kill was a really bad idea because now I have a taste for it, and I think it's the answer to everything.

I suppose I understand his point. I'm of the opinion that we need to get rid of all the old, white men in office—*all* offices. Not just in the government, but also school boards, medical boards, etc. *Everywhere.* And start over.

There's been this habit in human history where some people get rich from the labor and suffering of others. I don't need a conscience to know that it's wrong. It's just that my way of fixing it is apparently unappetizing.

"Loren."

I look up from admiring the way the lights reflect off the shiny surface of the table. Myro's shaking his head. "It didn't concern me," I say, shrugging.

"How do you know that?" he asks, crossing his arms.

We all know I'm right. I have an eerie knack for tuning in when something *does* concern me, and we all know that.

LOREN

Once again, Imry is trying to hide his amusement.

"I'm considering ways to kill Alabaster," I offer.

The way Myro studies me, I can tell he's trying to determine if I'm lying. I know for a fact that it's nearly impossible for most people because I don't have any of the usual tells. That's not how I'm built.

He sighs. "Be careful."

I nod and look around the table. Are we dismissed?

Dad is watching me, too. He's in business mode right now, though. Very laid back and listening. Like me, he's absorbing. He's leaning back in his chair, one of his arms on the armrest and his hand under his chin as he thoughtfully studies me.

While I don't get sentimental over anything, I often acknowledge how lucky I am to have been born into this family. All things considered, I think we had a pretty good childhood because of our dad. Especially when he finally took us away from Mom.

My gaze touches on two-thirds of the triplets. As if they know what I'm thinking, their eyes flicker to mine and I receive small matching smiles. Just hints. As if we share a secret.

Nothing was ever a secret, though. The day Dad came home to find Myro, Voss, and Imry protecting me, Avory, and Ellory from Mom yelling at us—*again*—for me being a sociopath and our brothers not being appropriate, Dad finally had enough. He forced Mom to leave and then moved us all to Arizona.

Thankfully, Dad had the foresight not to let Mom know anything about the true workings of Van Doren. He also had her sign a prenup so… too bad for her. You shouldn't just love and approve of three of your six kids. No matter how many times Dad told her that she needed to love us all equally, some of us just didn't fit into what she considered acceptable human beings.

Me because she wanted me to be something I'm not. Mom insisted I pretend to be like everyone else. Studies say that my particular antisocial disorder means I can blend seamlessly into society if I choose. To her, that was the only option I had.

Dad and my older brothers disagreed. Dad said my only obligation was to be whatever version of myself that I was proud of. That I was comfortable with.

Avory and Ellory, well? Mom also doesn't believe that you should be able to love who you want to love. Apparently, there are lines you aren't supposed to cross with certain types of love.

It all seems rather nitpicky to me, but I guess my idea of love is different from what many people think. Noah once told me we can define what love is for ourselves. Everyone is unique, with individual personalities and emotions. As with love languages, the way someone loves is distinctively their own. To me, that means Avory and Ellory can love who they want in whatever way they want.

Besides, it's not bothering me. Why should I care?

Which is why I never understood why Mom was so upset all the time.

Doesn't matter now. Mom is gone. I'm confident she's still alive, but I have no idea where she is. Though I'm sure the triplets or Voss could tell me if I cared to know.

Looking at Dad again, I *know* I don't care. Dad is the only one who's loved us all, just as we are. He's never said that anything we do, though maybe not accepted by society, is wrong or inappropriate. He's always said that we need to be true and authentic to ourselves.

"How many people have you terminated, Loren?" Dad asks.

My eyes are locked with his. We both know I know the answer, and I'm at least 87% sure he knows the answer. What I don't know is why he's asking.

"One hundred and thirteen," I say. "About to be one hundred and fourteen."

He nods. "Remember what we agreed upon when I accepted your employment in this particular position?"

"I'm not allowed to go above twenty kills a year," I answer.

"Mmhmm. What else?"

Really, I always hope he's forgotten about the second part of the agreement. "When I reach five hundred, I retire and need to find something else to do with my life," I say.

He nods, then removes his hand from where he had it against his chin as he listened to us. Mostly, he was listening to Myro. He's our talker.

When his hand comes down, I can almost visibly see the switch in him from Boss Dad to just Dad. He smiles. "Good. Forty-three will come quickly."

I frown. I'm only twenty-four, so I have almost twenty years before I reach 500. Besides, I usually bank some to roll over into the next year, which means I can likely keep killing people until I'm fifty.

Okay, maybe forty-five.

"Okay," I say.

He chuckles. "Go get packed. Be careful. Don't draw attention to yourself."

I look at Imry. When I have to stalk for a bit, Imry is always at my side. Because I have *never* attempted to assimilate to society and therefore, I tend to stick out unless someone is actively coaching me on what's making me draw attention.

"All right," I agree.

"Get this man off the street," Myro says. "Just as I should have encouraged you to do last summer."

My gaze drifts back to Myro and he's smiling. I return it and nod. This man won't see another week alive.

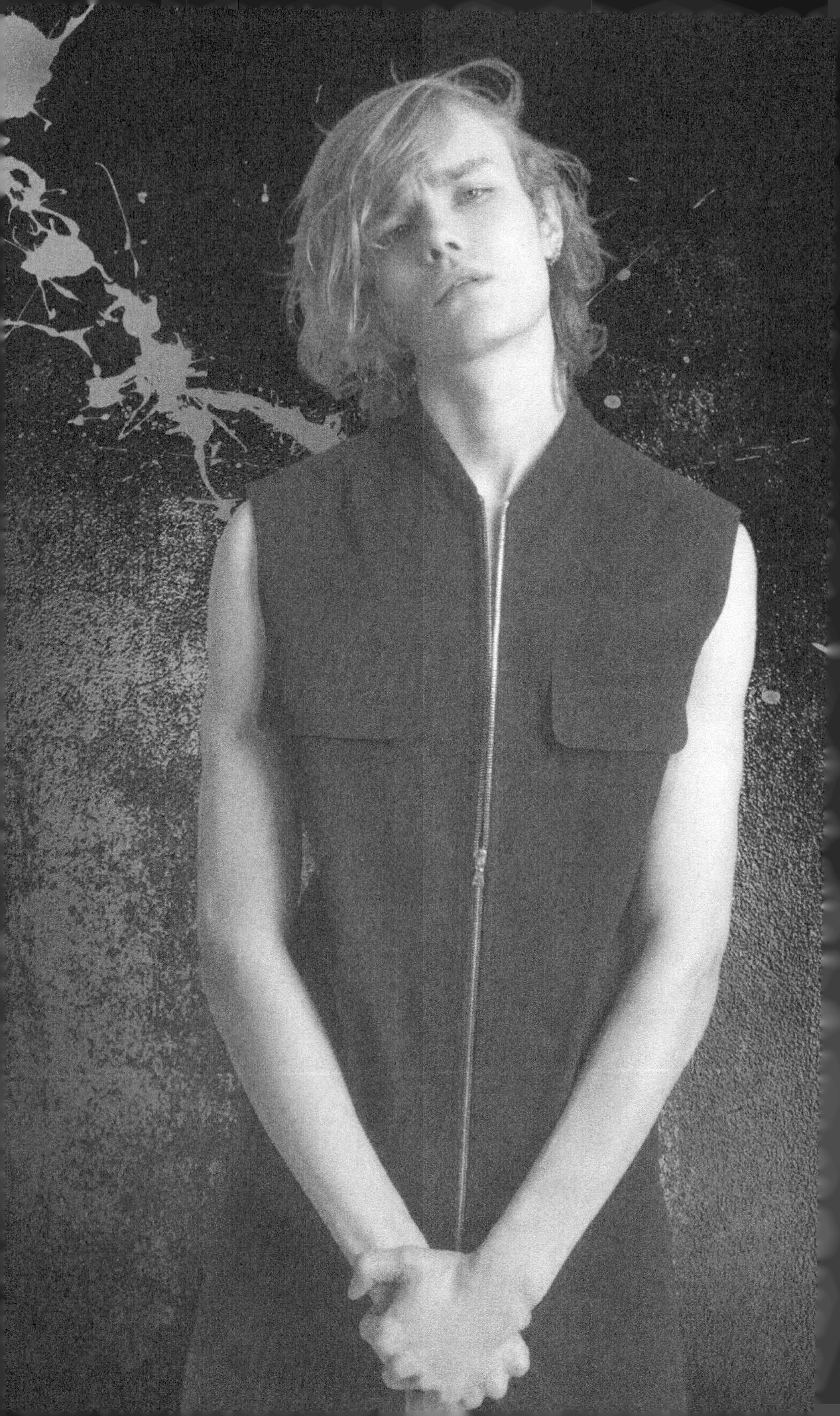

2
OAKLEY

I've known I was different since I was a kid. When those around me played house, there was always a mom, a dad, and a baby. I didn't want to play the dad and live with a mom. I wanted another dad to live with.

Most of the time, the kids I played with didn't care. We were kids. Why *would* we care? Even when you met the occasional asshole kid who had asshole parents and they wanted to tease and bully me because I wanted a dad/dad house instead of a dad/mom house, most of the other kids just brushed him off and excluded him in our play.

When I was nine, I met my best friends. We met on the first day of fourth grade where we were seated together, we became inseparable after that. There were and always have been six of us —Brek, Levis, Haze, Briar, Honey Bee, and me.

Back then, Honey Bee's name was Jessica. It wasn't until the following year when we were in a play, and she was the honeybee and our teacher kept calling her Honey Bee that we picked it up. I suppose her name is still Jessica, but I'm not sure the last time that actually came out of my mouth though. I wonder if she would even answer to it?

The moment I realized I *liked* boys, I was thirteen and a girl asked me to go to the school dance with her. I was mortified that she'd asked me. Horrified that I was going to have to answer her. And terrified of the realization that I'd just come to.

I'm not sure I actually answered her at all. Instead, I ran home and hid under my bed with tears in my eyes thinking that my life had just fallen apart.

I hid there for hours. Even when my parents were on the phone frantically trying to find me, I couldn't come out. I didn't speak as I tried my best not to sob.

My older brother found me. He walked into my room, straight to my bed, got to his knees and crouched to see under it, as if he'd known where to find me the entire time. Dylan is four years older than me. We couldn't be any more different if we tried. He was big and muscled up from playing football and I was lean and lanky from... not playing sports, I suppose.

His hair is dark and short, mine light and curling to the base of my neck. My eyes are a strange brown color while his are a bright blue.

"What're you doing, Oakley?" he asked quietly. "What happened? Whose ass do I need to beat?"

Most of the time, that made me smile. But this time, all it did was make fresh tears leak from my eyes. Dylan's smile faded. He reached under the bed and pulled me out as if I were the cat and not a ninety-pound kid.

His eyes darted to the door where we could still hear my mother on the phone looking for me. Dylan scooped me up and we stepped into my closet where we used to have brothers-only meetings as kids. But this time, he hugged me tightly in the dark space as I cried.

I'm not sure I even said what was wrong that day. He kept me safe from the world while I contemplated how it suddenly felt as if my life fell apart. When he left me, he wrapped me in a blanket and shut the closet door again.

Years later, I'd find the irony in that.

The frantic noise of my parents searching for me stopped. I didn't know what Dylan told them, but no one forced me out of the closet, tried to tell me everything was fine, or asked me what was wrong. They left me alone and I was really thankful for that.

I stayed home from school the next day and when Dylan came home, he once again joined me for a brothers-only meeting. This time, he sat next to me, his hand gripping mine.

"It's okay, you know," he said quietly.

I wasn't sure what he was talking about, nor was I convinced that he was correct, anyway.

"It's not the end of the world, Oakley."

"What's not?" I asked.

"Liking guys."

My shoulders stiffened. "How did you know that?"

He laughed. "Don't be ridiculous. I've always known."

Maybe that should have been a comfort. It wasn't.

"Get big and strong, Oakley. Be bigger than the bullies you'll face," he said.

I didn't get big and strong. However, I did go to the gym with him and his team for the remainder of the year. His team was very supportive of me being there. I wasn't sure if Dylan told them or not; they never said. They also never treated me differently than they always had—which was just their buddy's freshman brother.

Dylan graduated that year and the following, his team still dragged me to the gym with them. Because by the time his friends had moved on, I'd become a fixed part of their team. Not their football team, but still part of their team in some way.

Still, I didn't get big and strong. It only took me two years to come to the conclusion that my body type just didn't do that. However, I did gain muscle. I learned how to wrestle with them and win. I gained coordination and skill, though I was never sure what that skill was exactly.

Throughout my entire high school career, I didn't come out to anyone except my besties. That happened when I was fifteen and we were in the treehouse. It felt natural to finally tell them since we were all experiencing that awkward phase of growing up and feeling puberty in very uncomfortable and embarrassing ways.

I was afraid to tell them, even though I felt foolish for feeling afraid after. Every part of me knew that they'd still be my best friends. But the fear around being gay was really strong in high school and that pressure settled into fear.

Right before graduation, Haze came out as gay to us but swore us to secrecy. His family life wasn't pleasant and while he was never the target, he knew he would be if they knew. We knew about his home life. Especially when we were kids, he told us about how his oldest two brothers and father hurt his third brother, Oren.

We took his secret and did everything we could to keep it safe, which also made me feel better. We were protecting each other.

LOREN

College should have been the safe place for us, but Haze still lived at home. So we used college as a countdown. A means to get him out of there.

But then this past summer, shit hit the fan. Oren was outed, causing the abuse and harassment to escalate. Even when Oren moved out, the nastiness of the rest of their family got loud and was everywhere.

Needless to say, Haze didn't feel safe at home. His anxiety and fear that they'd find out he's gay too and turn on him made him lose a lot of weight and sleep. He was terrified.

Then his father died. We did the only thing we could think of—get out of Anaheim. Without his father there to force him to stay, we made arrangements to leave. The guilt of leaving Oren when he didn't protect him growing up weighed heavily on Haze and maybe it was selfish of us, but we didn't let him hang around. We talked him into moving and letting Oren take care of himself.

Which he had managed. He was out of that house and living with his boyfriend.

It went from bad to worse when one of their older brothers set off bombs outside the house Oren was staying in. Haze was freaking out. Especially since he'd been on the phone with Oren when the bombs went off. He could hear Oren scream and then the alarm drowned out everything else.

It was *hours* before we heard back from Oren and that truly wrecked Haze. The guilt that he'd grown up with significantly increased.

Thankfully, Oren pushed him to keep his plan to move to Arizona with us. He's been really quiet since we got here, but this was a good idea all around.

We're here. We're in this huge house with seven bedrooms and like eighty bathrooms. There's a pool out back and even a fucking tennis court. The house is ginormous.

I know what the world thinks—how do college kids afford this? Honestly, we couldn't if we were actually paying what it's worth. My grandma's friend's cousin's blah, blah, blah offered it to us when she heard about our situation. (My grandmother is a gossip, but she means well.)

So here we are, living in a rich neighborhood just off of Eastern State University's campus. It's a quiet community where we were both welcomed and ignored as soon as we showed up. No one cared that five guys and a girl were sharing a house and what that looked like. No one cared that there were a couple queer kids in the neighborhood.

The only concern was whether we'd have parties. Sure, we could do that now, but… we have zero interest in that kind of lifestyle.

The biggest thing for all of us is that we don't have to hide anymore. High school can be a very unwelcoming place. Coming out then was far too intimidating. We should have been comfortable once we entered the adult world.

But not with Haze's father and brothers. All we wanted to do was protect him. That meant keeping our heads down until we could get him out of there. College graduation had been the first goal we set. Moving the fuck away sooner was the best choice we made.

We have a few cars between us, but most of what we need is within walking distance, so we rarely have to drive. Which is fortunate since it means we can save money and enjoy a coffee from the café down the road a few times a week.

None of us come from money. In an ironic twist, Haze's father had a will and he and his two oldest brothers were each given a third of his assets. Haze's first reaction was to refuse it on principle. It's disgusting that his father literally refused to acknowledge Oren, even in death.

In the end, he took it because it helped us in our new life. He also offered half to Oren, but he refused. Pretty sure he's not hurting for money since he's living with a pro hockey coach. We're really proud of Haze though. That had been the right thing to do.

We're also proud of him for moving toward repairing his relationship with Oren.

I step outside and sit on the porch. There's an enormous house across from ours that sits empty. It has three turrets and a wraparound porch. Nosy kids that we are, we've been over there to peek into the windows. The place is stunning.

All around us are mostly vacant houses. These are winter homes for those who live in the north and don't want to go to Florida like the rest of the old folks do during the winter. In the next couple months, they'll fill up.

Except the one across the street. According to Grandma, it's been up for sale for a year.

Honey Bee says it's haunted. That's why no one wants it. I'm not entirely sure I believe in ghosts, but since she's just trying to make us laugh, I don't comment. Though... I'd be lying if I said I wasn't curious.

Why *hasn't* it sold? Is it just overpriced? As far as I can tell, this neighborhood is highly sought after.

"Hey," Brek says as he steps outside. The door closes quietly behind him and he takes a seat next to me on the steps. "Why do you always sit here instead of in one of the dozen chairs on the porch?"

I glance behind us at said chairs and shrug. "Guess I'm still not used to having chairs," I answer.

Brek snorts. We stare at the house across the road for a while. "You really think it's got ghosts?" Brek asks.

My gaze falls on all the windows, looking for a shadow, slight movement, a breeze behind a closed window. I see nothing. "If I had to guess, I think it's just overpriced," I say. That honestly makes the most sense.

"And no one has broken down the owners?" he asks, shaking his head. "From what others say, it's almost weird that it hasn't sold yet. There's talk, Oak."

"What 'others' are you referring to?"

He grins. "The neighbor down there. She's a Nosy Nelly and a Gossiping... Jane? Isn't there a name that goes with that?" I shake my head, laughing. "Anyway, she says so. But also kids at school when I tell them where I live."

"Why do you volunteer that information?" I ask, frowning. "I don't want some creep to show up."

Brek rolls his eyes. "I don't tell them where *exactly*. Just that we live in the Rolling Green Estates. It's almost eerie how many times someone new asks about the house."

It makes me consider the house again. Maybe it *is* haunted.

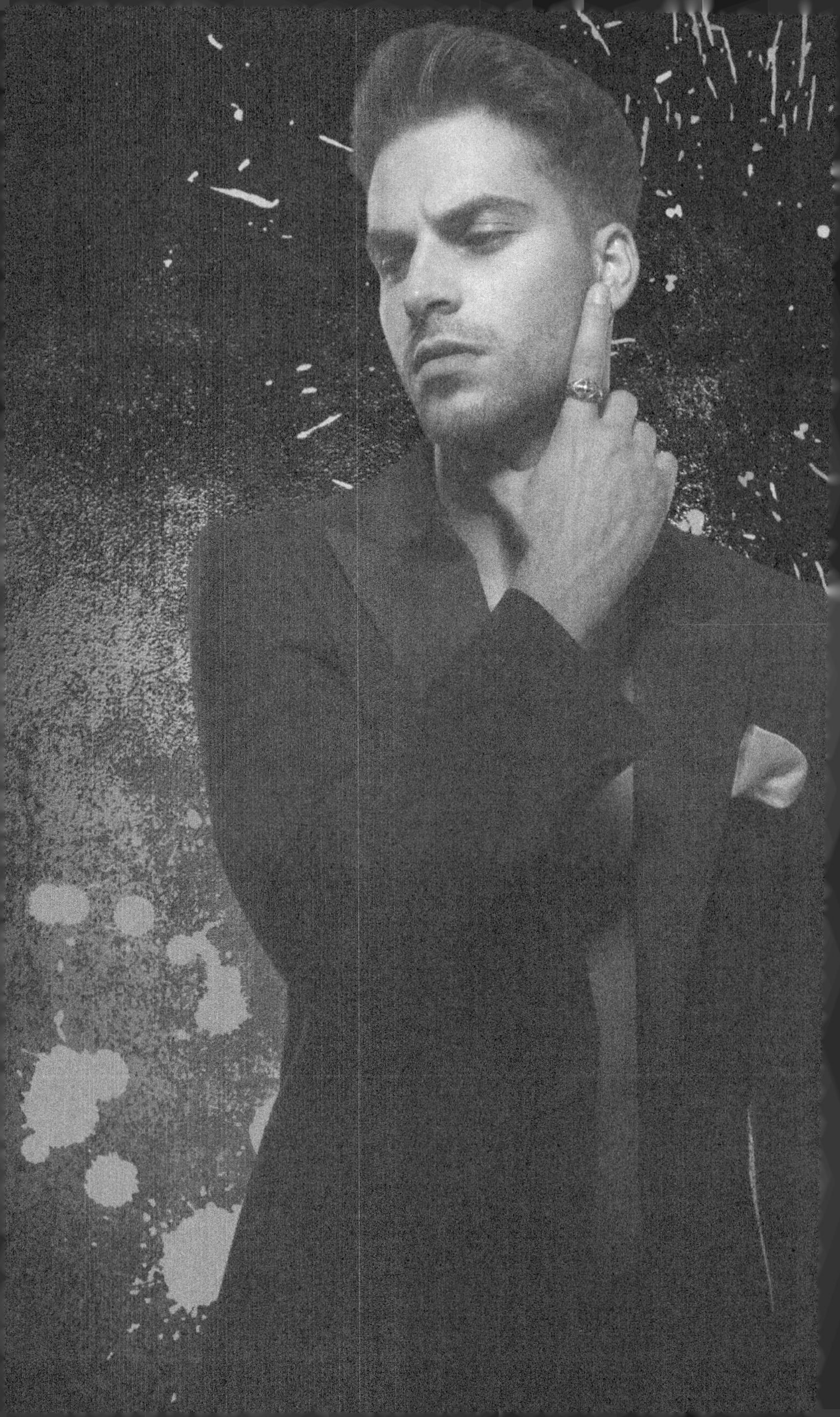

3
LOREN

WE HAVE HOUSES EVERYWHERE. When I was younger, Voss and I would randomly point to a place on the globe and see if Van Doren Estates had property there. Almost always, there was something within fifty miles. It was rare when there wasn't.

Rainforest and deserts… those made sense. I didn't ask when that was the case. Who wanted or even *could* survive in those environments? But then again, there were more times than not when we were surprised to find something close to one of the remote, inhospitable places.

When we asked Dad, he said that they might not be suitable for the long term, but almost anything is perfect for a few days.

Sometimes, I live by that thought.

Imry and I sit in a café close to the campus Daniel is hunting on. From what Imry says, he frequents this particular shop because there are always Eastern State students here.

We've been here for a while, attempting to blend in with the population. Imry has a young face, so I think he does easily enough. I don't always have that kind of luck. Technically speaking, I'm just over two years younger than the triplets. I am the baby of the family. Even my uncles don't have kids.

Our father is fourteen years older than his next oldest sibling. Then there are three more boys after that in quick succession. It's really amusing since Myro is only three years younger than our dad's youngest brother.

That's part of the reason I'm still the youngest in our immediate family. All my uncles are in their early- to mid-thirties. To my knowledge, no one even has a girlfriend. Or boyfriend. Or hell, even a partner. Maybe we're just a family of men who only want fuck buddies.

Except for Avory and Ellory, but I don't really count them in this party since they can't get pregnant and change the fact that I'm the youngest Van Doren. I kind of like that I'm the youngest.

That's not to say that we don't have a large extended family. Granddad Van Doren has five sisters and two brothers, so we know that there are extended family members. Many even work for VDT—Van Doren Technologies.

As I muse on being the youngest and holding that title for as long as I can, my gaze continues to scan our surroundings. I glance down at what I'm wearing and decide that at least as far as aesthetics, I blend in. I usually keep my sunglasses on, even indoors, because it hides the unhinged look that apparently makes people uneasy.

"Eat," Imry says.

I glance at him and then at my plate. I've taken a single bite out of my bagel. Not because it's not good, but... I've been focused on waiting for Daniel to step inside.

We're still in the early stages of tracking his movement again. Because he moved to a college city and hangs out in the places where the student body congregates, we know that it's only a matter of time before he'll choose his victims.

There's only a single suspect, but Daniel has taken notes from our previous encounter and is being more... covert in choosing his victims. Almost as if he knows he's being watched.

I take another bite of my bagel as I scan the café. There's a lot of noise, but it's mostly from the machines whirring behind the counter. Chatter is quiet. The shuffling of feet and scraping of chairs is quiet. Dulled. As if the patrons haven't woken up yet.

Another bite and the door opens. I pause, mid chew, but it's not Daniel. I'm finished with the first half of my bagel by the time Daniel steps inside.

He's dressed in a combination of looking like a college kid and a rich kid. His clothes are designer knockoffs, but to an untrained eye, they look like more expensive fabrics and cuts. His hair is neatly combed to the side, and I can see a scar I gave him just below his right ear when he turns.

I wait for him to spot me, but he doesn't. Pity. I want to see him piss his pants.

The thing is, I don't think he's a good-looking man. Granted, I don't claim to be an expert in judging what makes a man attractive, but I feel like I'm fairly confident that even on a conventional standard, he's not all that impressive to look at.

He's kind of dumpy. I'm not even sure what that means, but I stand by that judgment. His hair is far too neat, his eyes are too close together. His smile is slimy. He's not tall or short, so he just kind of blends in.

Maybe he's got a big dick. Is that what guys are into?

I glance at Imry and wonder if he likes big dick. Is there a tell?

"Why are you looking at me like that?" Imry asks.

"Just wondering if there's a tell for whether a man likes big dicks or not," I answer.

He raises a brow. "What?"

I shrug. "He's not impressive. I was trying to understand how he always finds multiple victims."

Imry laughs quietly and I turn my attention back to Daniel. He's at the counter now, ordering.

"From what I've uncovered, he preys on the vulnerable. Those who are closeted or those who feel insecure about their appearance or their body or something else. He's probably pretty charming and knows how to flirt."

Frowning, I study him at the counter. He's talking to the man that's preparing the coffee and sure enough, he has his attention. Daniel has caught his interest.

"That's his next victim, isn't it?" I ask.

"I don't think so. He's got too much confidence."

"Then why bother?"

"Two reasons. To prove that he could," he says as he nods in Daniel's direction. I track his movement as he crosses the café with his cup and chooses a table to sit at. Like us, he's scanning the area. "And two, that person can say 'yeah, he's been here. He was super nice.'"

"He's calculating," I muse. Honestly, I don't worry too much about the details when I'm handed a target's information. I don't need to know. Someone has already done the clearance and secured a means to collect payment after the fact. My only concern is where my target is and how to take him out.

"Very. He knows when someone is out of his league and he knows when he can manipulate someone to their breaking point and leave him with complete control. He also knows when to walk away when one of his victims isn't bending the way he wants them to."

Given this information, I watch those around the café, paying particular attention to new patrons walking in. *Will this guy be his next victim?*

He seems to be watching two different men as he sips his coffee, not giving any attention to anyone new as they come in. I'm almost enjoying internally debating which one he's going to choose. Breaking them down and attempting to identify the qualities Imry says Daniel looks for.

I turn my attention to the door, but turn back to Daniel when a woman walks in. They aren't his target. Although I'm kind of curious to know whether he could seduce a woman too.

I think about the women I've dated and then nearly laugh. Okay, I don't actually date anyone. I show them just enough attention and interest until they agree to fuck. Then I'm done. I'm upfront about what I'm interested in them for, at least. There's no manipulation or anything. That's really more energy than I'm willing to expend for an orgasm. There are far simpler ways.

But *would* they have bought Daniel's act? Which leads me to the next question—what is this man like when he's not acting? What's driven him to this point? Is it just the thrill of succeeding?

My attention lazily moves to the door when I hear the bell again, but this time, I'm riveted. He looks soft and sweet, wearing a long-sleeved shirt and jeans. His hair is blond, haphazardly held back with an elastic, with loose strands framing his face.

His eye color almost matches his hair color. At this distance, that's exactly what it looks like. He has a very loud backpack. It's blue with bright green lettering. I swear, you could see it from space.

But other than his bright backpack, he's quiet. His presence is muted.

He steps up to the line and doesn't look around much, for which I'm both thankful and frustrated. I want to see into his eyes. You can tell a lot about a person by his eyes. The little glimpse I caught was just *quiet*.

"Looks like he's found his next victim," Imry murmurs.

It's a struggle, but I tear my attention from the man in line to look at Daniel again. Imry's right. He's definitely found his target. However, I'm absolutely livid that it seems his target is this long-haired beauty.

"No," I say, my hands gripping my chair. I'm not sure whether it's to keep myself there or so I don't slam them on the table.

Imry looks at me and while I'd really love to meet his eyes right now, I can't look away from Daniel as he stares at this guy. *My* guy.

My brother chuckles, but I barely hear it. Daniel has definitely chosen his next target. I can almost see his calculations for how he's going to introduce himself. How he's going to dig his claws in.

Hairs stand up all over my body. I swear, I'm ready to attack.

Daniel takes the last sip of his drink and when he gets up, I'm tracking him like he has a homing beacon on him. My anger rises as he gets closer to my guy. They meet at the prep counter where my guy is adding sugar to his coffee.

I see the moment Daniel speaks to him, how my guy looks at him with wide, surprised eyes. A blushing, return smile. He brushes strands of his hair behind his ear and meets Daniel's gaze again.

Fucking hell, he's exactly the kind of sweet man that this fucker would prey on.

Imry's hand grips my arm, pushing me back into my chair. I hadn't realized I was getting to my feet until he stopped me. "No," Imry insists. "Stay here."

"I can't," I say but he doesn't let me go.

"You need to. We're in public."

"But—" Words fail me as I try to explain why I can't let him get near that man. *My* man! He's mine.

I'll examine this later, but right now, I need to keep Daniel away from him. "Im, I realize you're going to have an issue with this, but I'm not letting him leave here with that guy. I don't care if we are in public."

"Don't make me tie you to this chair, Loren," he says warily.

"Imry—"

"You *will* let him leave here. Our job right now is to track his movements. Besides, all he's doing is talking to someone."

While I want to scowl at my brother, I can't take my eyes away from Daniel and my guy. Everything inside me is rolling. I need to get my hands on him. I need to get him away from Daniel.

"I don't really care about the job right now."

"What's gotten into you?" Imry questions. When I don't answer, he grips my hair and forces my eyes to his. "I mean it, Loren. What's the problem here?"

How do I make him understand when the only thing I know is that man belongs to me? I'm not a fucking dog. I don't just bond like that. But the way my chest feels tight and my possessive anger feels like a living thing right now truly feels like I have an animal living inside me.

"Loren," he says with a frown. "Do you need to go home? Myro can finish—"

"I'm not leaving," I snap, my eyes shifting to make sure they haven't left the building yet. Both fortunately and unfortunately, they're sitting at a table together talking. My guy is smiling shyly. Nodding at something Daniel says.

I see what Imry meant, Daniel must be charming. I would never have guessed that. I would have thought that there still needed to be some attraction there. All I see is a snake.

I watch, gritting my teeth, as they exchange phone numbers. However, when they get up to leave together, that's as much as I can take. Pulling myself from Imry's hold, I jerk to my feet and follow them out the door.

"Fucking Christ, Loren," Imry mutters just as I'm pushing open the door. They're only a dozen feet ahead and while I'm mindful to keep my distance, I follow them down the road toward campus. I've only followed them a dozen feet when Imry catches up. "I'm going to put you on a leash," he hisses.

I don't answer. He can put me on a leash all he wants. I'll be dragging his ass behind me.

We pause when they stop at a corner. I'm fuming when Daniel leans in to kiss my guy on the cheek before taking a right and continuing down the road.

Imry has to forcefully push me to follow. I'd rather be following my man and making sure he knows he's mine. That needs to happen.

LOREN

"Loren, if you don't fucking get your head in the game, I'm going to call Dad," Imry threatens.

I glare at him just as he pulls me into a door. We're inside a bookshop, the quiet bell overhead announcing our arrival.

"What's gotten into you?" he hisses.

Staring out the window, I strain to try to see him through the crowd. The cars. The buildings. Obviously, I can't.

Taking a breath, I shake my head. "I need to know who that guy is," I insist.

"Yes, I always identify the victims too," he says. "It's easier to keep them safe and track Alabaster's movements. But that doesn't answer my question. What's gotten into you?"

"He's mine," I answer, feeling a little wild. "I will *not* let Daniel touch him."

Imry's eyes widen as he stares at me. Then he's laughing. "Fuck, Loren. There's not a day that goes by when you don't surprise me."

I have no idea what he's talking about.

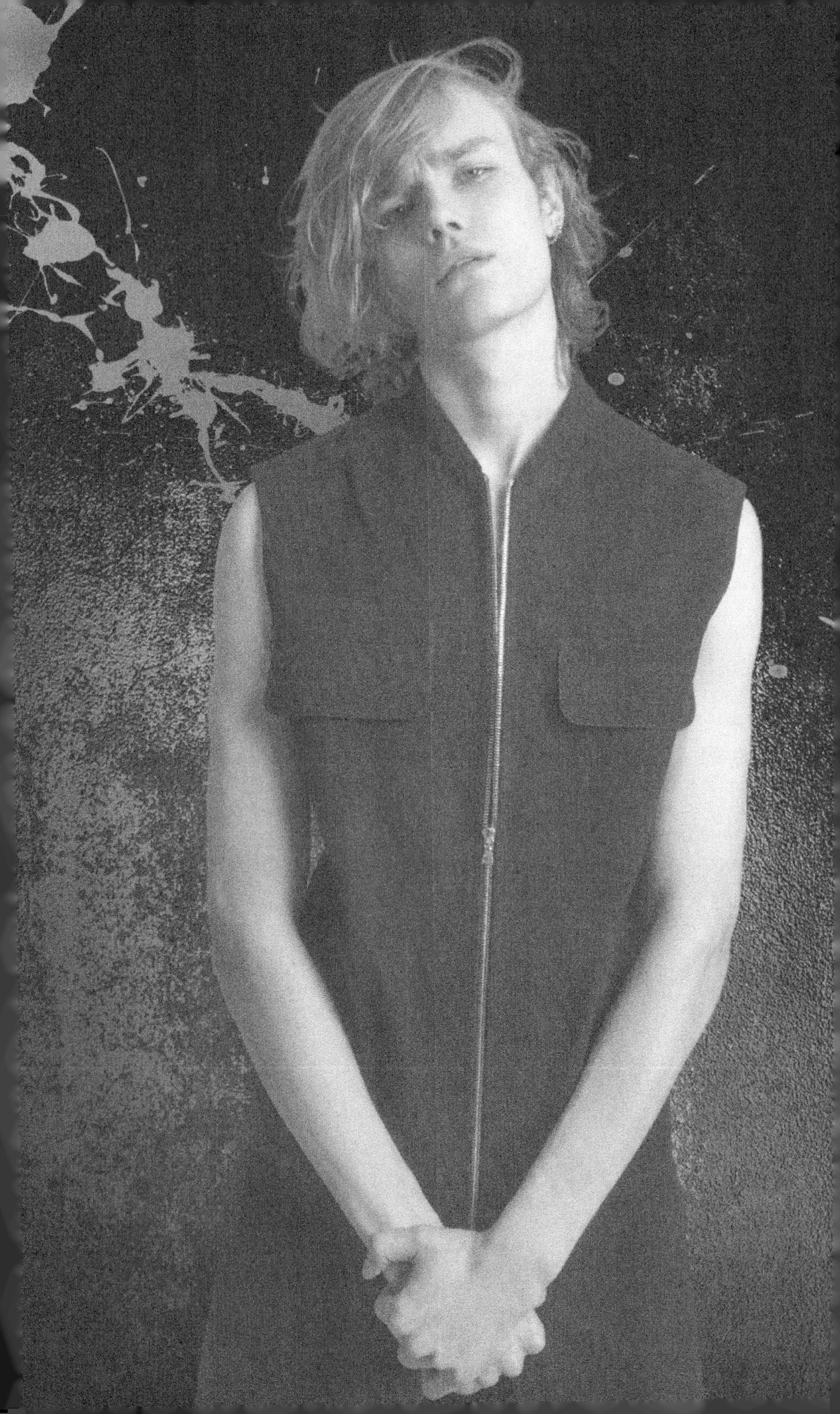

4
OAKLEY

I PULL out one of my boho hair ties and stretch it between my fingers. This one has a little bead on it. Nothing super flashy, and it's likely no one else will see it, but I like the extra little decoration in it. I also appreciate that they're seamless, so they don't pull out my hair.

As I gather my hair at the crown of my head and wrap the elastic around it, I pause to reconsider. I've only recently started putting my hair up, even though my hair isn't that cooperative. It's apparently really fine, so almost right away, the shorter strands around my face fall out.

Which I like. Honey Bee says I hide behind my hair, using it as a protective screen. While I've never thought about it, now that I've started putting it up, I think she's right. I feel really exposed and vulnerable, which seems silly since it's just hair. It's not even that long. My curls make it fall to the point it's just barely touching my shoulders.

I suppose because it's always so windswept, it's constantly getting in my face. It's not like I don't brush it back, but since it rarely stays put, I guess I kind of agree with her deduction.

Especially because I seriously *do* feel more visible now that it's up.

I'm not sure I'm the biggest fan of this feeling.

Up until this point, I didn't think I had confidence issues. My reasons for remaining in the closet weren't as a means to hide *completely*. Just hide from people like Haze's family. His family alone was fucking everywhere. His father had some nasty reach and handholds, and it just never felt safe.

Even when we went to college at home. The guys I saw then were also closeted, so it was a mutual effort to keep who we were and what we were doing under wraps. Again, not because I was scared or embarrassed, but because we were still in Anaheim.

These few months of being in Arizona on our own and in a new school have been incredible. I don't think any of us realized just how heavy the burden of stress was on our shoulders. All of us carried it. Mostly for Haze and his safety, but now that it's gone, I know I felt it for myself, too.

Just the other morning, Levis commented on how relaxed he feels now. As if he left a truly nerve-wracking situation behind. Mind you, Levis is a fucking brown belt in aikido. He trains with a wakizashi—a real blade that can slice through bundled bamboo with one pass when there's skill behind it and it's properly sharpened, which he does frequently.

For Levis to say that he'd felt the tension leave him when we moved here says how very heavy the weight we all carried was. Honestly, we're not all that far away from where we'd been. Less than half a day's drive.

Maybe it's knowing that Haze's father is dead, so he can't reach us anymore. His brother that planted the car bombs is in jail. The last brother left home and has basically fallen off the grid. Those who Jessup Prosser had had in his back pocket within the East End Police Department have also felt the repercussions and there's still a big investigation going on.

But we're not a part of that. We're now a world away, and there's the entire state of Nevada that separates us from California and it feels like we're finally... just... free. Protecting Haze and giving him a safe place with us had taken up a lot of our thoughts and now that we don't need to concentrate on that so much, I feel forty pounds lighter.

That's basically the weight that Haze has on me. Ha.

Taking a breath, I decide to leave the elastic. I don't need to hide anymore.

Flipping the light off, I head downstairs and grab my backpack. It's honestly far too bright, but my brother bought it for me when I started college and I love it. Everybody sees me coming. They know who I am without having to know who I am. *Bright backpack with hair in his face all the time.*

The thought makes me grin as I step outside to wait for Brek. As I usually do, I stare at the empty house, examining the windows for ghosts or movement. I don't really believe in ghosts—though I change my mind depending on how dark it is outside as I stare at the house in question. But honestly, when you're finally free of this world, why would you want to hang around?

"Ready?" Brek asks as he stops at my side.

I nod and turn for the sidewalk as I glance at him. Shaking my head in amusement, I scan the neighborhood as we pass.

Brek is one of those guys you'd love to hate. He's basically a real-life Clark Kent. His body is quite toned, smooth—though I think he does that part himself—has a really pretty tanned complexion, and he has an overall masculine look to him. It's made somewhat softer by his careless hairstyle that's just a mess of strands on his head, always unstyled. I'm confident he doesn't own a comb. He's clean shaven but not baby faced. Like there's always this hint of stubble. Then there's the black-rimmed glasses.

He's like a nerd and a jock rolled into one. Especially considering he's wearing a button-down shirt, sleeves rolled to just below his elbow, but left unbuttoned to show off his physique. That he unfairly does nothing to work for.

Beside him, I feel wholly unimpressive. Especially since graduating high school and no longer working out with the football team. A few of the players earned scholarships to the college we went to and there were days they dragged me with them my freshman year but, you know, we grew up. Life happened and it just stopped.

The muscle mass I had, which was never that great, had long since disappeared. Now I'm just really thin and lanky. Not a bad look. As far as I'm concerned, all body types are beautiful. It's the personality behind them that can be ugly.

"No Honey Bee this morning?" I ask as I glance back at the house just before we round the corner out of the neighborhood.

Brek rolls his eyes. "She's on a date."

"It's eight in the morning," I point out.

He gives me an amused look that says I'm rather naïve. Yeah, okay. She's hooking up. Whatever.

"I think we should all just live together for the rest of our lives," Brek says. "I like normalcy and comfort. It lends a lot of peace to our lives, and we don't have the stress of meeting people or trying to impress them."

It's not the first time he's said something along these lines. I'm not surprised at all. Brek has always been a creature of habit. He thrives on routine and *hates* any change in it. A day or two here and there he can roll with, but not regularly. The only reason he did so well with our move to Arizona is because we all went together. There was familiarity in that.

He hates meeting people and for most of our childhood, he refused to make friends outside of us. He claims he doesn't need any.

I'm pretty convinced that he's never dated. I can't even remember a time when he's shown interest in anyone—male or female. As I examine him, I'm convinced he's probably never even hooked up.

Huh.

"What?" Brek asks.

I shake my head. "Nothing."

He frowns. "You don't agree?"

"With what?"

Brek sighs. "I swear, none of you listen to me."

I laugh. "I was listening, I just got distracted."

"Because I'm hot? You've been staring at me since I spoke." He smirks, teasing.

And yet, that's the most I've ever heard this man even come close to flirting with anyone. Just the way he teases us from time to time. Not that I can say anything. My flirting is even more horrifying than a bobcat's scream in the woods.

"Why do you wear your shirt open like that?" I ask.

Brek looks down and I can immediately see that I've made him self-conscious.

"It's not bad," I insist, gripping his wrist to stop him from covering up. "Sorry. I didn't mean it like that. I'm seriously just curious. You trying to attract someone who wants to drool over your abs?"

Once more, he looks down, but this time, his eyebrows are puckered. "No. It's hot." He looks at me and the hoodie I'm wearing. "How the hell are you wearing a hoodie?"

I laugh. "I've had this for like a decade. There's nothing left to it."

Brek grips the sleeve and rubs it between his fingers. "Yeah, fine, but still far too much material. It's already like seventy-five degrees, Oak."

"Is that really the only reason?"

For the third time, Brek looks down at his chest. "Is this bad? Be honest."

Sighing, I link my arm through his and shake my head. "Sometimes, I think you're rather innocent and we need to protect that about you."

He rolls his eyes and shoves me off him. "I'm not looking for someone to drool on my stomach. That's gross. But if you think—"

"I don't think you look bad, Brek. I clearly need to rethink questions before I spew them. It was merely a thought."

Brek studies me silently. "I have a lot of questions about to why you're thinking about me and my abs, but since this is where we split, I'll save them for later."

"I'm counting down the minutes," I deadpan.

He grins and waves me off, heading for the crosswalk as I turn into the café. Brek has an eight-thirty class, so he rarely stops inside since the lines are usually four or five deep at this time, and he'd be late if he waited. But since mine doesn't begin until nine, I always stop in.

Sure, a frivolous way to spend money that I don't really have a way to replace, but I enjoy the coffees and bagels. It's six dollars happily spent three mornings a week. I bring my food and drink otherwise so I can splurge on this. One of my favorite things about this café is that they offer a student discount, so my breakfast is almost a third cheaper than it would otherwise be.

There are three regular baristas behind the counter and they all know my name and my breakfast choice. It's Patrick today and he smiles. "Morning, bro," he says. "Usual?"

I nod.

"Care to mix it up and add a cinnamon shot? It's new and I promise, it's divine in your regular coffee. I had one this morning. Not too strong, but just a hint of goodness."

"Mmm," I say as I glance up at the menu. Maybe I like my routine too much.

"If you don't like it, I'll replace it with your usual," Patrick promises. "But I'm confident you'll love it, Oakley. Trust me."

Sighing, I nod. "Yeah, twist my ankle. I'll try it."

I'm not sure if it actually costs more, but he charges me the same amount he does every morning. When I first started coming here, my price would vary by like eighty cents, depending on which of the three coffees and bagel spreads I ordered. Now, I'm always a flat out $6.15—regardless of what combination I order.

It isn't long before I have my breakfast in hand and move on to the coffee prep station to gather a napkin and knife. Usually, I add my sugar, but before I do, I take a sip. Yep, still needs sugar.

As I'm taking the lid off and settling it on the napkin to reach for the sugar, a man joins me. Without paying much attention, I shift to the right to give him room, but he tosses his coffee cup into the trash.

"Hi," he says, and I glance up to meet his eyes. He's smiling. There's something… charming about it.

"Hi," I reply, giving him what I hope is a polite smile and return to putting sugar in my coffee.

"Can I be forward and tell you that you have really lovely hair?" he says.

I glance back at him, feeling my cheeks flush. In reflex, I reach up to push some of my hair behind my ear. "Thank you."

"Now that I'm close, your eyes are simply stunning," he continues, and it truly feels like he's staring into them admiringly.

Biting my lip, I turn back to my coffee and put the lid back on. "Thanks," I say. No one notices me. Like, ever. Definitely not enough to compliment me. Never more than a means to throw out the possibility of a hookup.

"Can I join you?" he asks as I pick up my breakfast again.

I nod and he follows me to a table. Almost always, I eat here because it's easier to eat my bagel this way when I'm also carrying a coffee.

"Are you new here?" he asks, sliding his chair a little closer.

My nod is accompanied by a shrug. "We've been here for a few months."

"We? Your family?"

"No. My best friends and I transferred to Eastern State over the summer. We rent a house."

"Ah. That's cool. Have you been to the café before? I swear I live here, but I'd know if I'd seen you before. You're quite beautiful."

I turn my eyes to my bagel again and catch my breath. "I'm here pretty regularly," I answer.

"Hmm." He's quiet as I take a bite. Once I've swallowed, he says, "I'm Jason. I'm a graduate student, so I practically camp out in this café to study." He chuckles.

"Oakley," I say. "This is my third-year undergrad."

Which isn't entirely true. I have more than enough credits to graduate on time with a liberal arts degree in the spring, but I've changed my degree course like a dozen times because I simply don't know what I want to do with my life. What the hell do I want to be when I grow up? What could I possibly do with a liberal arts degree?

Not that there's anything wrong with it. Not at all. I'm not judging that. But in a world where a bachelor's degree no longer ensures that you'll get a job nor get a job with decent pay, even with a very specific degree with a concentrated skill set, what would I even do with it?

"That's an awesome name," Jason says.

"I'm not sure I agree, but thanks."

"My name is as common as they come," he says, laughing. "Growing up, there were like twenty-eight Jasons in my graduating class. I was Jason W or Jason 3 since there were three Jasons with the last name that begins with a W. At least you didn't have to be one of those."

"Okay, fair," I say, smiling.

No, I never had that issue. None of my friends did except Honey Bee, because her name is Jessica. There was a year that we had four in our class. Four! Like, why not split them up?! Thankfully, we always just called her Honey Bee.

Jason stays with me until I finish my bagel, then he asks me for my number, so we exchange them. As I walk away, my phone pings in my pocket. It's already a message from Jason.

> JASON
> It was great meeting you this morning. I can't wait to talk to you again, beautiful.

I try not to smile, but I'm not sure I've ever been called beautiful.

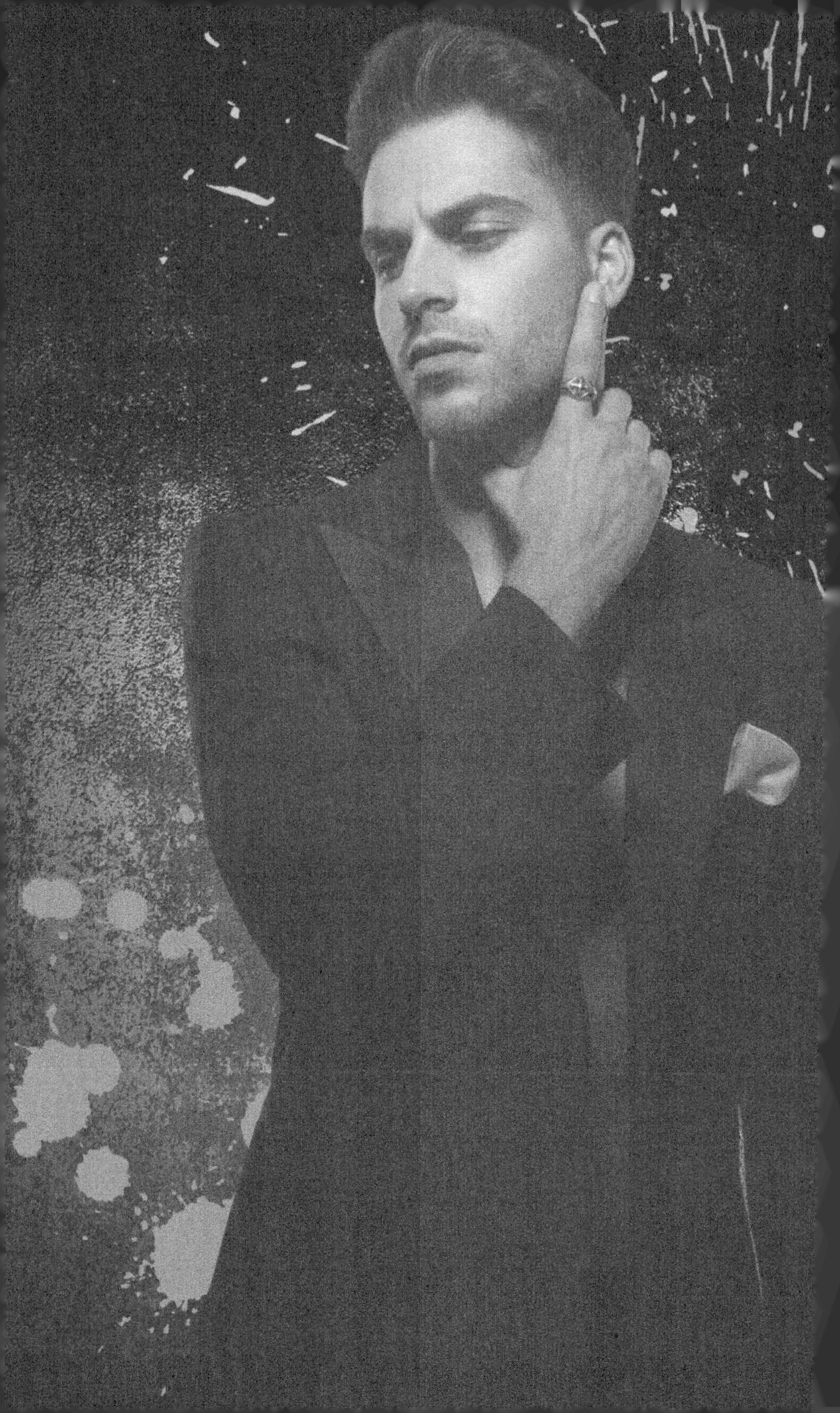

5
LOREN

It takes Imry three hours to identify my guy as Oakley Curzan. I have his date of birth, blood type, and college records in my possession within half a day. The only way I'd be convinced not to follow this guy instead of our target was if Imry found me his information.

Including his address.

We trailed Daniel for the rest of the first day, but once he headed home and Imry made sure the cameras he'd set up were still in place and functional, we headed to Oakley's house.

As luck would have it, there was an empty house for sale right across from the one he was staying in. It took me three minutes to break in and disconnect the alarm. With Voss's help, of course. Thankfully, he rarely asks questions when I need him to hack into a security system for me.

Then again, there's a chance Imry's already told my brothers I've gone off the deep end following a guy that isn't the one I intend to kill. Honestly, I know where Daniel is right now. I should just kill him and be done with it.

Instead, I'm standing in the big window staring at the house Oakley's inside.

Over the next three days, this becomes a pattern. Imry feeds me information regarding Oakley's roommates, which I also memorize. Haze Prosser is a name we're both familiar with since I had his father killed last summer for the belligerent harassment of Noah's friend's friend's friend? Yeah, there was a trail I didn't quite follow. I was honestly so stoked that he'd asked me for help a second time that I didn't even question who I was killing or why.

As it turned out, Jessup needed to be dead. Nasty guy right there. There's no room in the world for people like him.

Levis Li is somewhat fascinating. He spends more time in a dojo than he does studying, yet his grades are impeccable. On paper, he's a real overachiever.

Albrecht Holleran is a rich kid from a very well-off family in Anaheim. He's the sole beneficiary of a very large trust that he'll inherit on his twenty-third birthday. There aren't even any outrageous requirements attached, which I find suspicious. That kind of money isn't usually released to such a young man without any guarantee of maturity and responsibility.

The only girl in the group is Jessica Rivera. Her parents are immigrants from Puerto Rico and own three restaurants. I went to one when I was in California checking out Jessup, and it was really good. I'd eat there many times again. Jessica is studying to become a lawyer, and she's already applied for admission into the local law school. Imry is tracking the progress of the application. Just for fun, he says.

Lastly, there's Briar Keller-Navarro. He's from a family where his parents lived eight hours apart most of the year, but remained married for years. It wasn't until after Briar graduated high school that they divorced, and his father remarried—to a man just barely older than Briar. I'm sure there's an interesting story there. I'm morbidly fascinated by it. Though Briar has been boxing since he was a kid, he has zero interest in going professional. It's just a passion hobby for him.

It's Saturday and Imry is sitting on the floor by the window I'm staring out of. Oakley is outside tossing a football with Jessica and Briar. Jessica is easy enough to identify, but I haven't seen their pictures to know who I'm looking at. Imry has though, so as they've come out of the house, he identifies them for me.

Oakley and his friends all stare at this house often. I noticed it the first morning as I watched them leave, but kept an eye on this house as they walked down the road, I was very curious about why. Once they'd all left and before I followed Oakley—I mean, tracked down Daniel for a day's worth of stalking—I examined the house from the sidewalk just in front of their house.

I didn't see anything exciting. It's just a house. I'm not entirely sure what has them so fascinated. I still don't understand three days later, but they're always watching it. Glancing at it. Studying something about it.

"Why do they do that?" I ask.

Imry looks up from where he's camped at my feet with his tablet. "What?"

"They're always looking this way. I'm sure they don't see me. They're rarely even looking at this window."

He chuckles. "You live in a hole, Loren."

I frown at him.

Still grinning, he says, "If you were paying attention to what people say around you," he chides, "you'd know that the entire community claims this place is haunted."

Okay, first—I do pay attention to what people say around me. As long as it's interesting and relevant. I don't care what Jenny said to Tory about Bobbie's lack of stamina. I don't care whose aunt is flying to Denmark. Gossip is usually what I'm surrounded by and, quite frankly, people need a damn life.

And second—haunted? "You're kidding, right?" I deadpan.

He laughs. "Nope. But I'll have you know that I've been through the house and I haven't heard or seen anything concerning. I've also dug into the history of this house and property. There's a house three doors down, that way"—he points to my right—"that's seen not one but three deaths—one of which was a murder still unsolved to this day, yes I'm looking into it out of curiosity—and is a much more likely environment for a haunting. But this one has been on the market for a year, when it's in a prime location and properties are often sold within a week of listing."

"It being haunted was their first reason that it's not sold?" I ask. That does not give me a lot of faith in this community.

Imry grins. "Those who don't know the market, yes. The *real* reason is that it's not only a million dollars over-priced but that it also has some scary foundation issues. The owners refuse to negotiate." He shrugs.

I look down as if I can see the foundation through the floor. "Are we going to fall into the earth?"

He laughs again. "No. Actually, it's not in the main house. It's in the pool house out back and the foundation problem also compromises the pool itself since it's so close."

"Ah," I say, turning my attention to the window again and watching Oakley.

He has good form when catching and throwing. More so than is strictly natural. While there's not a chance he plays based on his build, but he's several years out of high school... maybe he was a kicker?

Before I can ask, the three across the road are distracted by something or someone coming this way. A car that I'm quite familiar with slows as it nears and pulls into the driveway of the house we're in, followed by a moving truck.

"Im... did this house sell?"

He smirks. "It did."

I'm about to ask why he didn't fucking tell me, when the other two-thirds of my triplet brothers step out. No need to ask now, as I glare at Imry again.

He's still grinning. "I'll have you know that Dad can be very persuasive. Not only did he get the price back to a reasonable listing price but also lowered further for the issues with the foundation."

The front door opens, and the other two brothers step inside with identical grins.

"Hey, baby brother," Avory says.

Imry gets to his feet, and I watch as the three of them share a group hug. It's longer than most other hugs, but I've read that multiple birth babies always have a unique, special, and somewhat ethereal bond. There's this weird telepathy thing and some even have the ability to hear the other's thoughts.

Oh, my favorite curious tidbit is the ability to feel their twin's pain. Like physical. I keep waiting for a day when I receive twin targets. I have some experiments that I plan to conduct before I kill them.

The three break apart and look at me expectantly. "Why are you here?"

"You're fixated and Imry needs more eyes on you," Avory answers as he turns to the door to talk to the movers.

"We're moving in?" I ask. "Don't we already own property in Arizona?"

"Four now," Imry says, "but convincing you to move to one of them was going to be far too exhausting and unsuccessful. This is by far the easier answer."

My gaze drifts out the window. The three passing the football are now joined by the remainder of those who live in the house and they're all staring this way now with surprise and curiosity on their faces.

I know he can't see me, but I stare at Oakley, imagining his eyes connecting with mine. A shiver runs through me.

I've been waiting for Daniel to show up at his house since they spoke at the coffee shop. When he didn't, I expected to see that they'd get together somewhere else. They haven't but how much Oakley's been on his phone, even while home, suggests that they are talking. I hate the way he smiles at his phone. It makes my blood burn.

"I see what you mean," Ellory says, and I glance behind me. He and Imry are watching, both with smirks. "It's unreal."

"Right?" Imry says. "I'm not sure whether to be fascinated about the fact that he's transfixed by a man or that he's showing an interest in someone at all."

"I'm not something you need to investigate," I say, narrowing my eyes.

"Oh, no," Ellory says, still grinning. "I plan to observe you like a science experiment."

Sighing, I turn back to the window. "I should have been an only child."

Both of them snicker. I ignore them and the movement in the house over the next couple of hours. From what I can tell, they only brought the basics—furniture to sit on, beds, clothes, and kitchen shit. It sounds like everyone else is following and will bring the rest of our belongings with them.

"This is entirely unnecessary," I say when the movers leave.

Ellory drops onto the couch with Avory following, swinging his legs over Ellory's lap. They look at me with far more amusement than I think is truly warranted. "I don't know. We've been here for like four hours and you've turned your eyes away from Oakley for maybe ten minutes total."

"Fine," I say. "But why is Dad coming? Myro and Voss are coming too?"

They nod.

"Unnecessary. I'll kill Daniel and…" And what? Because I'm not leaving without Oakley. I'm not even going to pretend to entertain that idea. I'm not even going to lie about it.

Turning back to the window, the six of them have gone inside. I have a feeling kidnapping him and hauling him home with me wouldn't end how I'd like it to. Not that I have a true grasp on how I'd like it to. As much as I've been watching him, I don't have any idea what I want with him.

The only thing I know is that there's no doubt in my mind that he belongs to me. Somehow, that man is just… mine. I'm not even sure what that means, never mind why I feel that way. Or what I am supposed to do about it.

Imry bumps his shoulder into mine. "You know what you should do?"

Warily, I raise a brow. "What?"

"Get rid of Jason and then talk to Oakley."

"And say what?" I ask. "I'm going to need him to come home with me so I can get back to my life?"

"Is that what you want?" Ellory questions.

I scowl at him and stare at Oakley's house without answering. Truth is, I have no idea what I want.

"How about you start with introducing yourself," Imry suggests. "Hi, I'm Loren. Can we hang out?"

"Yeah? Is that how you talk to guys?"

He smirks. "Talking to guys isn't any different from talking to girls. It's always in your intent behind it."

"You have a lot of experience talking to girls, do you?" I ask.

Imry laughs. "No. But I promise, it's not that different."

"You're assuming I want to talk to him."

"You'd rather just stalk him for the rest of your life? He's going to catch on eventually," Avory points out.

"Especially since you fuckers announced our presence here," I counter.

Imry grips my wrist. "Loren." I meet his eyes and pull my hand away, stuffing it in my pocket so he doesn't touch me again. It's not the tense feeling I usually get from being touched, because it's not a problem when it's my brothers or father. But I'd still rather keep my personal space. "It's cool if you like a guy, you know that, right?"

I roll my eyes because I can't help it. "I don't care that he's a guy."

"Ha!" Ellory says, making me turn to look at him and his outburst. "I told you Loren's pansexual."

"I'm not pan," I say without any true conviction.

"He's only been with women," Avory argues.

"How do you even know that?" I ask.

"You don't think we watch our brothers?" Ellory asks.

"Ugh, fuck's sake—"

They laugh. "Not like that," Imry says. "We keep tabs on you to make sure you're not in trouble. Honestly, I thought you knew that."

"I love how you treat me like your dog with a tracker and all," I deadpan, "but you can stop. It's disturbing."

"We mostly watch when you're taking out a target, Loren. Believe it or not, you're not invulnerable. Just because you don't have any sense of self-preservation because you don't experience fear, *we're* afraid for you because we know this about you and we really don't want to lose our brother," Avory explains.

I sigh and rub my eyes. Without meaning to, I glance out the window again. They're inside still.

"So, is this some sexy bi-awakening thing?" Ellory asks. "If you're straight and are suddenly turned on by a man—"

"Stop," I cut him off before he can continue. He grins, linking his fingers with Avory's and leaning his head against Avory's. They give me sappy smiles. "I get that you want to make me a project and believe me, I'm flattered." They laugh, though I'm entirely bemused by this entire thing. "But you didn't all need to come here. I'll figure this out on my own."

"We don't plan to help you figure it out," Imry says. "We're here for support and to keep you out of trouble. Besides, you had to know if you ever picked up and left, we'd follow you. I mean, we're all fucking adults and still choose to live with Daddy. We love being with family. So do you, even if you don't want to admit it."

"I'd be willing to bet you've tried to think of a way to get Oakley to come home with you, haven't you?" Ellory asks.

My shoulders tense. Fuckers.

The three of them grin knowingly. I give them my back and stare out the window. They're right about one thing—Daniel needs to go. Then I can focus on what this weird obsession is and what to do about it.

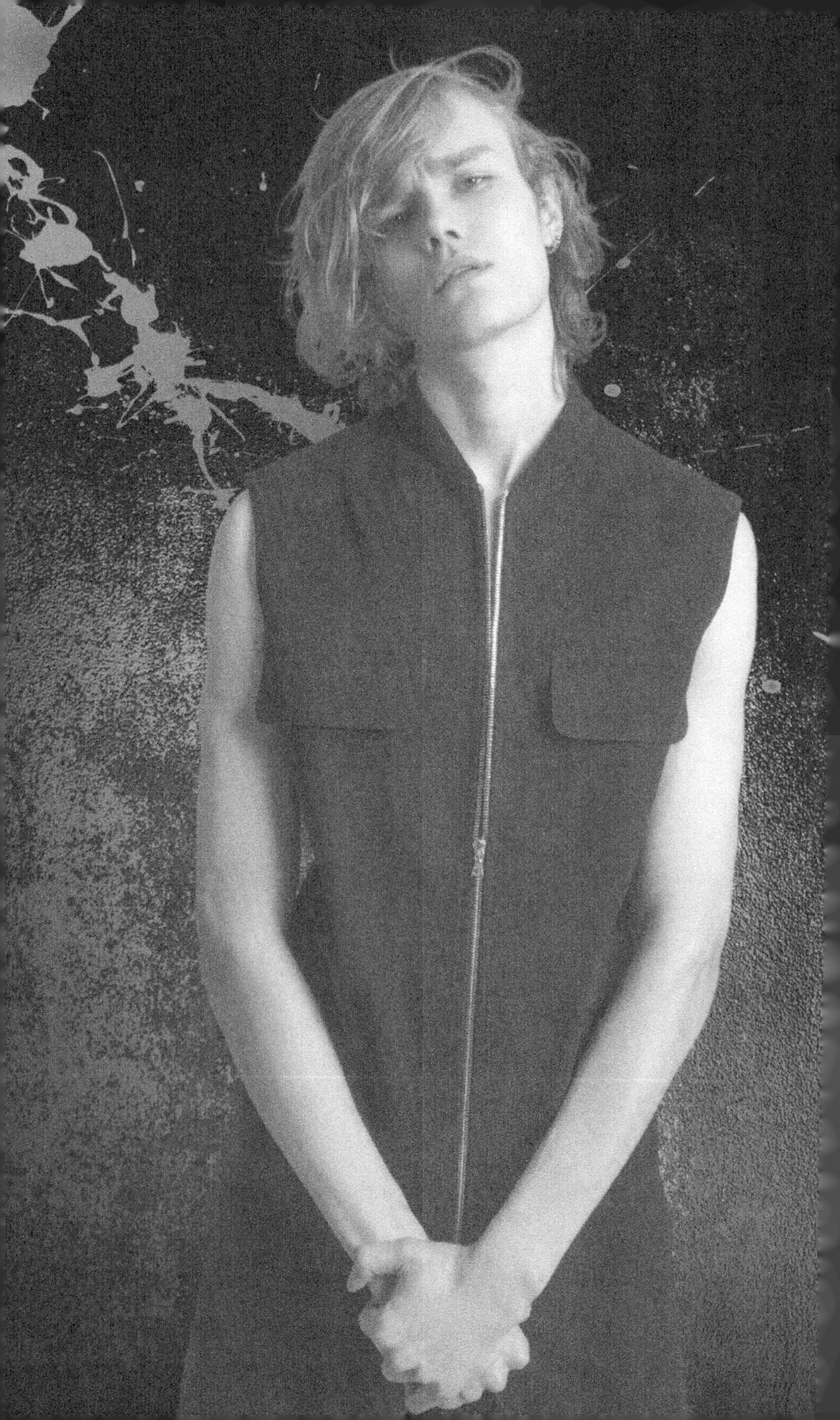

6

OAKLEY

ONE THING I love most about Arizona is the weather. It's hot, but it's not muggy. You can almost always count on a nice day, especially as we move toward winter.

It's Sunday and I'm heading to the coffee shop to meet Jason. The week is always a little too busy for me to commit to plans. I've always made weekdays dedicated to schoolwork, so I can enjoy the weekend. For the record, Friday night is not considered a weekend for me unless I have all my work for next week completed.

Jason tried to convince me just this once to come out with him on Friday, and really didn't like taking no for an answer. The way he kept saying he wanted to spend time with me and get to know me and how he loved how shy I was and my smile—not going to lie, I almost gave in.

Except Honey Bee took my phone and flat-out texted back, 'No. I have homework.' then kept my phone from me until I finished it.

She doesn't truly care about when I get my work done. She doesn't share the same homework schedule I do. But Honey Bee knows I haven't broken this routine for anyone, and she didn't appreciate someone trying to convince me otherwise.

"I'm questioning whether this guy is a good idea if he's trying to change you," she says.

"He's not trying to change me," I argue, rolling my eyes. "He just wants to spend time together."

She's not convinced.

The thing is, I'm not sure she'd truly understand. Honey Bee is beautiful. She gets a lot of attention. She's always complimented, and goes on lots of dates.

I… do not. I have never experienced that kind of attention. I've never had someone truly show an interest in wanting to spend time with me, never mind try to get to know me.

When I leave the house, I stare at the one across the road where two men moved in yesterday. Strangely enough, Briar reported last night that there are actually four men who live there. He'd seen them all sitting outside on the deck. He's convinced that they're brothers.

Maybe we can make friends with the neighbors and learn if the house is haunted. If anyone makes friends with them, it's going to be Honey Bee. We've all bet on how long it'll take one of them to come around and ask out Honey Bee.

My bet is three days. Especially since she's always wearing these adorable little sundresses with a flower in her hair. She looks like a Puerto Rican Barbie and I'm totally here for it. Buying her presents is always a blast because she loves clothes and fashion and will literally make anything we give her a stunning work of art.

When we were in high school, we used to challenge her and hand over the ugliest article of clothing we could find to see if she could make it stunning. Somehow, she always ended up with a date.

Turning my attention back to the sidewalk, I head down the road. I'm feeling a little more self-conscious than usual because I let Honey Bee dress me for my date. She might not like Jason so far, but she will always do her thing and make us look hot when we ask.

Not that I feel hot. I feel... exposed.

Absently, I reach up to my hair to tug it down but abort and stick my hand in my pocket. I'm wearing tan pants that desperately need a belt and a loose shirt that fit better in high school. Putting it on made me realize how much mass I've lost. Maybe I should see if Levis will teach me aikido or something.

Jason is waiting outside with a smile. He hands me a pretty flower and leans in to kiss my cheek, causing my skin to heat.

"Right on time," he says and leads me to his car with his hand on my lower back. He even opens the door for me and waits for me to climb in.

When he joins me, he says, "I was far too excited to finally see you. I've been here for ten minutes."

I smile. "I'm pretty much always just on time. My friends say it's a superpower."

He smiles. "You said you moved here with your friends, right?"

We've talked about them in passing through text, but not in detail. I nod. "Yep. There are six of us."

"Ah. You live together? Do you share rooms?"

"Yes, we live together and no, we don't share rooms," I say, laughing. "Actually, we love living together. This is the first time we've been able to."

"Mmm," he says. "I think living alone is better. You have privacy and the freedom to see whoever you want without judgment."

"My friends aren't like that. We give each other privacy and we have the freedom to see whoever we want without judgment. I'm not sure they'd be good friends otherwise."

"I'm glad your friends are cool. I would have liked to meet them."

Jason wanted to pick me up at home. Honey Bee said he was being pushy about it, but I thought he just wanted to be a gentleman. However, that was one of our rules. This is our house together. We never wanted anyone to feel uncomfortable with a stranger in the house, so we agreed that unless we all invited someone over, then we wouldn't be bringing people home.

I try to explain this to him. "We just don't let anyone come over. Not even to pick us up. It's just a boundary we made."

"Seems a little constricting and controlling. You don't think so?"

I shake my head. "No. Or I wouldn't have agreed to it."

"I can't imagine being around the same people all the time. Day in and day out. Don't you fight?"

"Not at all. What would we fight about?"

Jason shrugs. I'm not sure why, but his fixation on my living situation feels weird. Frowning, I turn my attention out the window and watch as we drive through the city. It isn't long before we're pulling into the fairground parking lot. It's packed, but I'm not surprised. The signs tell me it's the last day of the fair.

He takes my hand as we walk toward the gate. I was sure to bring cash, just in case, and of course, I have my card on my phone. But Jason pays for our tickets, smiling at me as he leads me inside.

LOREN

"I asked you out. My treat," he says.

Something about the way he says it makes my stomach flip. Not necessarily in a good way.

We play a couple games at first, once more Jason pays. Even when I play the game. He's kind of insistent about it. I try not to think much of it when he's always following it up with he wants me to have a good time. He loves to see me smile and wants to spoil me today.

But his tone feels like he's leaving something unsaid. Like there's a second part to that sentence.

"Here you go, sweetheart," the guy behind the booth says, handing me a little narwhal.

I grin and cuddle it to my chest for a minute. "Thank you."

Jason guides me away with his hand on my back. "You must get that a lot."

Glancing at him, I have no idea what he's talking about, but he's frowning. "What?"

"Random guys hitting on you. Flirting."

Looking over my shoulder at the booth we just left, the guy is talking to the customers. He doesn't spare me a glance. "I don't think he was."

"Of course he was. You're beautiful, Oakley."

That no longer sounds like the compliment he makes it out to be.

"I hate that. It's one of my biggest pet peeves."

"What is?"

"When someone flirts with my date, when I'm standing right here. It's so rude." He looks at me. "And you let him."

"Right," I say, dropping my hands to my sides. "Sorry."

He smiles. "Don't be. Honestly, I can't blame them. You really are just precious. It's your smile, I think. And your pretty hair."

Jason steers us away from the games and toward the rides. He's sure to sit close when he can, his arm wrapped around my shoulders or my waist. Almost like he's making sure that everyone around him knows that we're here together.

It makes me feel uncomfortable and I try to put a little distance between us. Jason either doesn't notice and follows or simply refuses to let me. I'm not sure which. He's pretending that the weird vibe he gave me over the game attendant didn't happen. He's acting like he doesn't notice that I'm definitely feeling awkward and embarrassed by his behavior.

For a while, he's nothing but flattering and sweet. So I try to tell myself it was nothing. Earlier was just… maybe insecurity from a past experience. It happens.

I'm starting to relax and have a good time when Jason asks, "That guy's hot, isn't he?"

I glance his way, unsure who he's looking at. "Who?"

"The one who let us on the last ride. He was checking out your ass."

Somehow, I find that really hard to believe. I have no ass to speak of. These pants do not even give the illusion of having one.

"Uh… sure," I say. "I guess I didn't notice."

"How could you not? He was ogling you. Practically drooling."

My shoulders are tensing again as he continues to carry on about this imagined staring. With every word he says, a sour taste gets stronger in my mouth. His hand around mine tightens uncomfortably, to the point where it's almost painful.

"I hate that so much. It's so fucking rude. I literally have your hand in mine and he's checking you out like a piece of meat. And you don't even say anything. You just pretend like you don't notice. Is that how you always are, Oakley?"

I just stare at him. …what??

"I'm going to need you to be more aware of those around you, honey. Don't let people sexualize you, okay?"

…WHAT?! I don't even know what he's talking about.

"I need to use the bathroom," I blurt. It's time to send out a Mayday.

"Sure," he says, smiling. His hand is still painfully tight around mine. "Looks like they're just porta potties. I'll wait outside the door, so no one bothers you."

"That's unnecessary," I insist. "Just stay here."

He frowns. "I'm just trying to protect you."

Right. "Just… stay here. I can pee on my own."

"Of course you can, sweetheart. Want me to hold your phone? Don't want to drop that in there." He laughs as he holds his hand out.

"I'll take my chances. I've yet to lose a phone in a toilet. You can hold this though, thanks." Thrusting the narwhal into his hands, I follow the line down the row of porta potties before he can answer, thankful that the closest open one is a dozen away from the line. Locking myself inside, I pull out my phone and dial Honey Bee.

"Hey, you okay?" she asks.

"I need you to get here *now*," I hiss into the phone. *"Please.* Like, as fast as you can. This guy is just... a huge red flag, and he's creeping me out." I'm feeling slightly panicky at this point.

"Turn on the app, Oak. We're on our way. Stay in the masses, okay?"

I nod. "Hurry."

When I hang up, I turn on the app. When shit started going down with Haze's father and Oren, we decided to be proactive and keep tabs on each other. Especially as Jessup and then Frankie started going off the deep end.

We all installed this tracker app and connected our six phones. While we'd meant it only to make sure Haze was safe when he'd had to go home for the night, I think we all found comfort in being able to see exactly where each other was at all times during that month or so.

Stuffing my phone back in my pocket, I open the door. Jason is right there, walking toward me. He smiles and I suddenly don't find it charming at all. He reaches for me, but I pull my hands away. "I need to wash my hands."

There's no way to avoid the big station where people are gathered around. I take my time using soap and water first and then drying them. Then covering them in hand sanitizer. That buys me an extra minute or so while I swing my hands to dry.

"What would you like to do now?" he asks.

"Can we just walk around?" I ask. "It's been a long time since I've been to a fair and I'd just like to check out the stalls and stuff."

"Of course," he says.

Once again, he must know that he was being a creep because

LOREN

he's now reverted to his previous behavior. Complimentary. Spoiling. But still, his grip on my hand is super tight.

Minutes tick by and my anxiety increases. While I try not to make it obvious that I'm looking for my friends, I stare into the crowd. Jason notices and accuses me of looking for someone. I don't even answer. His hand tightens.

I almost cry when I see Honey Bee stomping her way through the crowd. I recognize that look. Even so, I nearly jump when my petite friend gets between us and forcefully makes Jason release my hand.

"What?" Jason stammers, trying not to lose his grip on me. "What the fuck? Who are you? What're you doing?"

"Let go of him and learn to read some fucking body language," Honey Bee hisses. "Don't make me knee you in the balls."

Jason releases me, and Honey Bee shoves me behind her into our friends' waiting arms. I'm sandwiched between Levis and Brek, with Briar and Haze blocking me from Jason.

"Seriously, I question your ability to read social cues," Honey Bee says. "This date is over. Do not contact Oakley again."

"Oakley?" Jason asks, and I can see him through the small space between Haze and Briar's shoulders. He looks all innocent and confused. "Who is this? What happened—I thought we were having a good time?"

I'd love to say I'm quick with words under pressure and with attention on me. I'm not. So I turn my face away.

"This is kind of a rude ending to a date. After all I've paid—"

Briar thrusts a $50 at his chest. "You're even. Go away."

I'm sure he doesn't move. It's my friends that move. They keep me pressed between them as we make our way through the crowd.

"I'm sorry," I say. "I should have listened to your concerns. He's one giant red flag and not in a sexy book boyfriend way."

Levis wraps an arm around my shoulders. "I think we recently realized that you're not used to hearing someone compliment you because you turned blind to what was right in front of you. I'm sorry we didn't try harder to protect you."

"For the record, you're a fucking catch, Oakley," Haze insists, his hands on my hips as he nuzzles into the back of my hair. "Please, please don't think otherwise. Don't let creeps like that get close because you like their words."

I sigh, feeling smaller than I have in a while.

"We're not trying to lecture you or put you on the spot," Levis says. "I'm sorry we just did that too."

"No," I whisper, shaking my head. "Thank you for coming to rescue me."

"Always," Honey Bee says. "We have each other's backs, no matter what. No matter how long we're friends or where life takes us. We will always come running when someone gives the word."

This is exactly why we're as close as we are.

"Want to stay and enjoy the fair or want to go home and eat ice cream and speculate about the haunted house that's now being lived in?" Brek asks.

I laugh. "Let's stay for a bit. Unless we see Jason around, then I'd rather go home."

They're right. I let compliments make me stupid. There were red

LOREN

flags from the very beginning. I mean, who seriously likes the name Oakley besides my parents?! I'm named after sunglasses!

He was manipulating my emotions from the moment we met, wasn't he? I wrap my arm around my stomach and grip my opposite elbow. Fuck, I feel stupid.

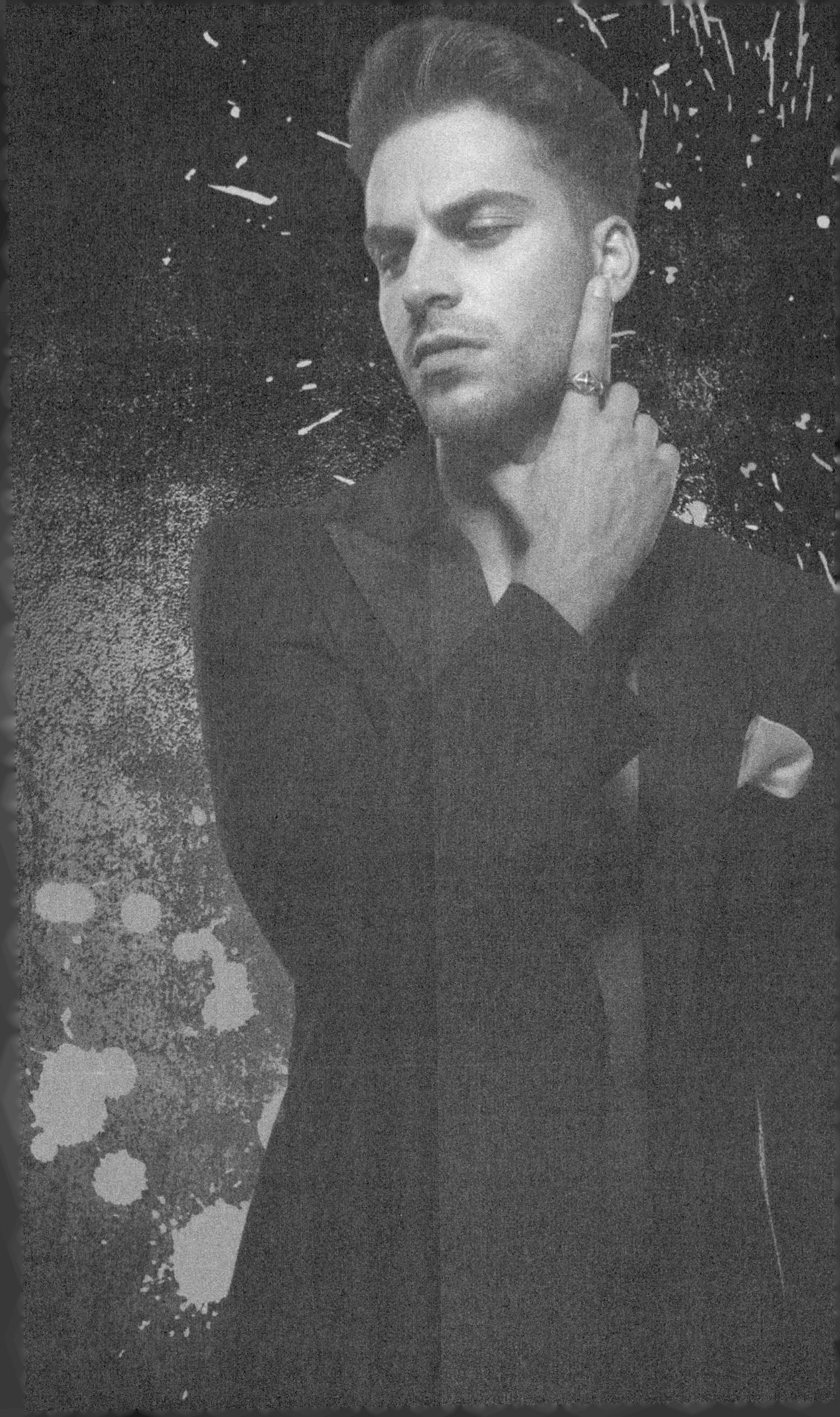

7
LOREN

I FOUND a path that runs behind some of the houses yesterday. While Oakley was at school and Daniel was being tracked by Imry, I wandered the Rolling Green Estates, which is the HOA for half a dozen cul-de-sacs and a few winding neighborhoods between them.

I followed Daniel like a dutiful little killer the day before with Avory and Ellory. I was absolutely furious when he picked up Oakley and while watching them at the fair. The possessive rage that coursed through me had me nearly delirious and ready to tie Daniel to the railroad tracks to listen to him scream and beg.

In fact, that particular death isn't off the table.

It was probably a good thing that two-thirds of the triplets were with me. I was so enraged this slimy fuck was touching Oakley that I was ready to say fuck being invisible and kill him right then and there. Especially when it became obvious Oakley wanted to get away.

There was no way he couldn't read Oakley and see that. None. Those passing by could see it. Daniel wasn't oblivious; he was calculating. If he pretended everything was fine, maybe Oakley might believe it.

Thankfully, Oakley's friends showed up and dragged him away. The bafflement on Daniel's face was entirely fake. And when his friends dragged him off, that expression turned into irritation and anger. I watched as his hands fisted.

Once again, Avory and Ellory kept me rooted to the spot. We followed Daniel out of the fair, my brothers dragging me with them. It was their force alone that kept me there instead of following Oakley. I needed to see him. I needed to be sure he was all right.

Later that night, the memory of that particular emotion in me kept me awake as I tried to work it out. Have I ever felt that way about anyone?

I suppose I could say I have for Avory and Ellory. Mom was always a bitch to them. Always trying to split them up and force them to play with others. To be in separate classes. To play separate sports. At one point, she tried to make them have separate bedrooms.

For as long as I can remember, my brothers and I have always had a group chat. We use it for random things. Voss likes to send memes he finds and since he spends a lot of his time online, sometimes that's all that goes on in the chat.

But we also communicate when we need something. Over the years, we've come up with code words we've never actually discussed, but somehow just innately knew what it meant. The one other time I've felt an overwhelming need to make sure someone was okay was the afternoon we received twin S.O.S. 'stickers' in the chat from Avory and Ellory.

I don't remember what I was doing, but I know that the cold dread that swept through me had me dropping whatever it was and running home. Hell, I hadn't even known for sure where to find them. Home was simply the place that I thought to look first.

Myro was already there, using his big frame to block two-thirds of my triplet brothers, who were sitting at the edge of one of their beds. I could tell by their expressions that they were trying really hard not to be upset. Their jaws were set, eyes filled with hurt and frustration, red as if they'd been crying. Their shoulders were pressed together, and Ellory was breathing heavily.

I may be the youngest, but I'm the only one who has my particular 'affliction,' as our mother called it. Which meant, at that moment, I had absolutely no issues laying my hands on a girl. With all the strength in my sixteen-year-old body, I forcefully shoved our mother out of the room.

She stumbled, crashing her back into the hall wall before tripping and falling. When she looked up at me with shock, horror, and fear, I slammed the door in her face.

I'm pretty sure that moment might have shocked my brothers as well. No one had moved, and when I turned to face them with my hands over my chest, all three brothers stared at me with wide eyes and their mouths open.

I only shrugged; someone needed to do something.

So yeah, the need to protect Oakley was reminiscent of the need to get the aggressor away from my brothers. Those same brothers wouldn't let me go back. Citing that he's with his friends and they'll take care of him. No matter how many times they said as much, I needed to see it for myself.

We followed Daniel home, then they took me home.

I sat in the living room window until our neighbors across the road returned. I stayed there until it got dark, then went outside to examine their windows, looking for Oakley's. He was on the second floor, which meant it wasn't easy seeing in his room. I could see the light on and movement. I only knew it was his room because he stopped in front of the window.

He was looking down, so I imagined there was a desk there or something. Especially considering the length of time he paused. With the cloak of darkness, I examined the corners of the house, the doors, the windows—checking it over to see what kind of security system they had.

There was one, but it didn't appear to be functional once I used the program Voss created to hack... I mean monitor security systems. Not even the video doorbells were on. Seems a little irresponsible, but the neighborhood seemed peaceful enough, so it might be their sense of security that's lulled them into not using it.

Definitely irresponsible, but it also meant I could access their house easier.

Yesterday, in the daylight, I moved around the neighborhood to explore what there was to find. Thus, the path. And today, I wait for everyone in Oakley's house to leave before meandering across the road and heading for the path, following it until I'm out of sight of the surrounding houses.

Just as casually, I approach the back of the house and the sliding door. Honestly, sliding doors are tacky. The owner should replace it with a double door or something more fitting with the neighborhood, like those big glass panel doors that folded open like an accordion and combined the outdoor and indoor space into one living area.

These sliding door locks are a joke, really. When there's no bar assuring the slider remains closed, all it takes is a bobby pin and some jiggling for the lock to come undone. The door slides open silently, and the blast of cool air from inside brushes my skin.

LOREN

I remain still for a minute, listening. I don't think they have pets or guests, but I take several minutes to account for any unexplained and unexpected noises from the inside of an empty house. There are none, so I step inside and slide the door closed behind me.

The room I walk into is a living area. It looks like the typical décor in this kind of neighborhood; not like the college students that live here. Easy enough to explain, it must have come furnished.

There are little personalized touches, though. Blankets that are obviously worn and well used. School books on the table. A pair of shoes, two hoodies, and a T-shirt. The furniture is covered with blankets and sheets, as if to protect them from the wear and tear of use. Or dog fur.

Perhaps the most telling thing is that there isn't just one large television but two, right next to each other. Plus there are several game consoles beneath them on the long shelf that houses the electronics.

The rest of the first floor has rooms you'd expect. There is an enormous kitchen with the expected signs of habitation and use —crumbs, liquid rings and drips on the counter, a few dishes in the sink and a dirty pan on the stove.

Hanging on the fridge is a large whiteboard 3-month calendar. I take a minute to study it. It doesn't take me long to determine that Oakley's color is green. His entire schedule is right here.

As my gaze wanders the little blocks, I absently wonder why they don't just do this via a shared electronic calendar. Do they take pictures of this and refer to it? What if there's a change?

After taking a picture of the calendar, I step into the formal dining room to find it's been converted into a study room and the table has been taken over by paper and notebooks. There are four desks in the room too, two of which have laptops on them.

Stuffing my hands in my pockets to keep from touching anything, I continue through. Today is simply recon. I just want to get the lay of the land and confirm that I found Oakley's room last night.

There's a large entryway I meander through that leads to a short hall and two bedrooms that share a bathroom. One room is clearly a guest room. The other is occupied. I haven't taken much note of the others who live here, so I'm not entirely sure which resident this room belongs to.

This brings me to the stairs. The second floor consists of four bedrooms. The largest, which is likely the primary bedroom suite, is occupied by their female companion. She likes flowers, and her room is impressively neat.

The other three rooms are personalized, but again I'm unsure who occupies which except for Oakley's. I find his easily enough —at the far end of the hall, opposite the stairs and next to Jessica Rivera's bedroom suite.

The doors are all left ajar. I take note of exactly where Oakley's bedroom door is so that I can return it to that same exact distance before pushing it open to step inside.

My eyes land immediately on the bed. It's large, pressed against the wall, and stacked high with a plethora of blankets. The headboard and wall that it's pressed against are lined with more than a dozen pillows.

He has a desk under the window, as I suspected he would. There's also a big, rounded cushy chair under a reading light. There's art on his walls that seems to directly contrast with his young-twenties décor, so I guess they were already hanging when they moved in.

LOREN

On the wall between two more doors is a dresser. Behind one door is the bathroom, and the other is a closet. I stand in front of the desk for a minute and watch out the window, examining where I need to be to see through it unobstructed.

The bedroom isn't messy, though it's not strictly clean either. There's a pile of clothing hanging off the side of the chair. The items on his desk are just as haphazardly strewn around as those in the dining room are. His bed is clearly unmade, though neat enough, and the laundry basket in the bathroom is overflowing.

As much as I'd love to keep snooping, I need to leave soon. I've studied their schedules extensively and I know there's almost always someone coming and going. The most I can ever give myself is an hour. Besides, today's goal was just getting the lay of the land.

Leaving Oakley's bedroom, I make sure to return the door exactly where it had been when I arrived. Just to be thorough, I head to the third floor and peek into the remaining room upstairs. It's one of those large open attic spaces that's been converted into a comfortable and spacious bedroom suite.

Silently taking the stairs down, I listen for sounds, making note of two important things as I go. One, there is only one staircase. Two, there isn't a single creak. I also take note of places to hide if I need to.

What I appreciate is that there are four doors to the outside on the first floor. When I step out the back sliding door again, I note that there are a couple of egress windows from the basement level I didn't explore. As I'm walking back to my house across the street examining their windows as I go, I take note that there are definitely rooms I missed on the first floor. Too anxious to find Oakley's bedroom, I guess.

When I step into the kitchen through the side door, I find my father and two eldest brothers sipping coffee around the counter.

Ah. The rest of the clan is here. Three sets of eyes turn to me where I stopped halfway into the house. Maybe I should have entered through the front door instead.

"Where've you been, Loren?" Myro questions.

"Recon," I say, leaving it vague.

"Considering you didn't take your car and all three triplets are here, I'm guessing your recon was close?" Voss says.

Sighing and rolling my eyes, I step further into the house and shut the door. Thankfully, there aren't any tacky sliding doors in this house. I don't even answer. Why bother? They know exactly where I was. If for no other reason, I know the triplets track me and everyone else. Hell, I think they all track each other.

I don't track anyone. I could pretend that it's because it's an invasion of privacy, but since I just broke into a house for no other reason than to learn something about someone who doesn't know me, clearly that's not something that bothers me.

"You didn't need to come," I promise, pushing my hands into my pockets.

"You were always going to be the brother that wandered off," Voss teases, amused. "And we were always going to follow you."

"Because I can't blend in," I deadpan.

"No," Myro says. "Well, maybe partially. But no. We're one of those weird families that likes to stay close. We're going to end up with like four generations under a single roof—just wait."

His chuckle says he's joking and yet, I don't think any of us doubt his words. We probably will turn out that way. I glance around and note that probably not in this particular house. It's a good size, but it's far too small for four generations.

LOREN

Besides, I'm not sure how I feel about kids. They're fine in passing, I suppose, but how will I feel about them living under the same roof? Always here. Loud. Messy. Stinky and dirty. Crying late at night. Baby things everywhere.

There are horror memes about stepping on Legos barefoot at night. I'm not entirely sure I'm interested in that life.

"You've just freaked him out," Voss says with a smirk as Dad chuckles.

Pressing my lips together, I turn for the hall and the stairs to my room. Unsurprisingly, I chose a bedroom in the front of the house where I can see Oakley's house. Therefore, I can watch when he comes home.

I can also see if someone is there that shouldn't be.

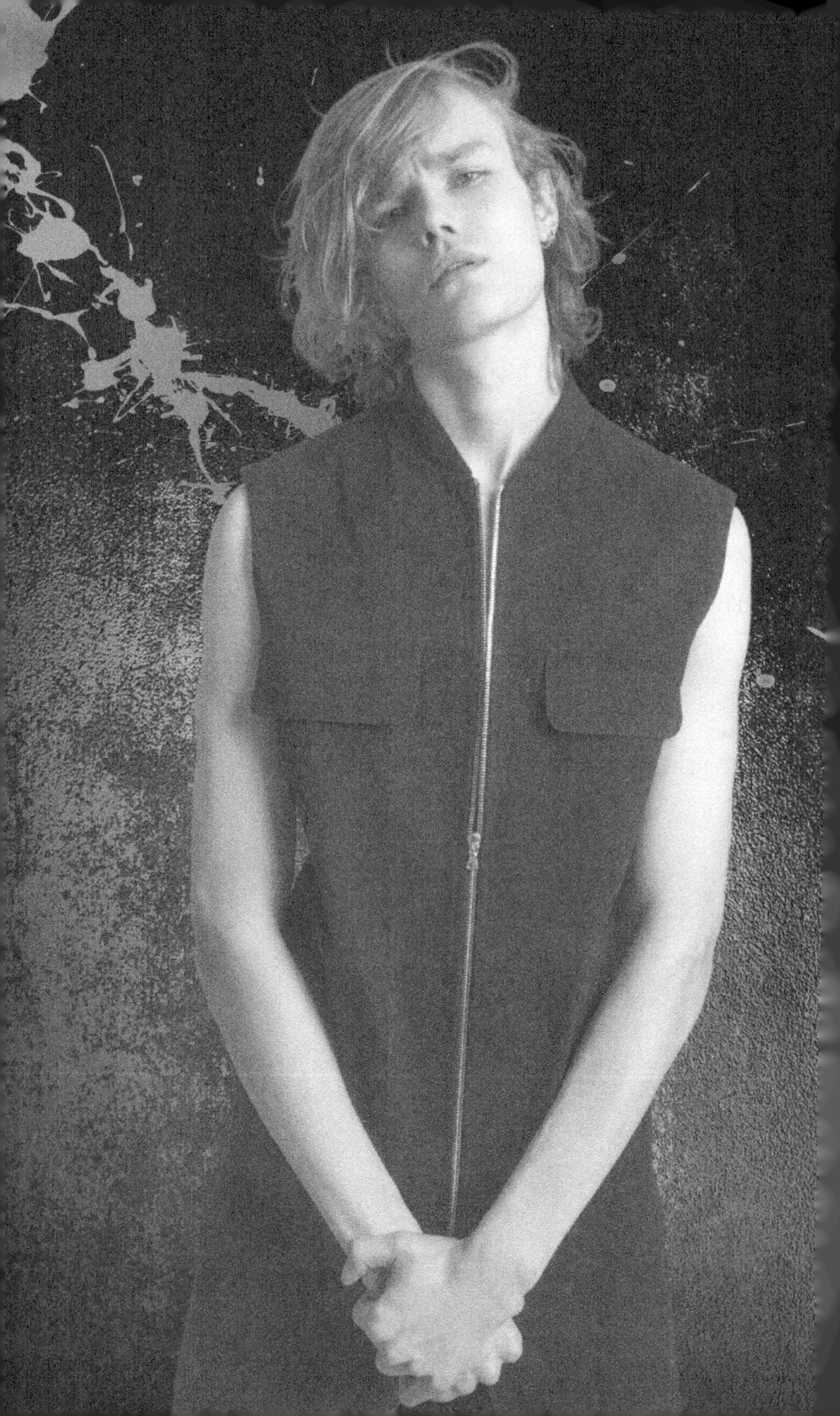

8
OAKLEY

I'M thankful it's Friday. I plan to stay home all weekend. Maybe I won't even leave my bed!

As we get close to the café, my shoulders tense. There are other ways to walk to campus, but this is the most direct route. Especially the buildings that my classes are in. I'm not entirely surprised that I see Jason here every time I stop in for coffee, but the way he watches me makes me uncomfortable.

He even came up to me on Monday and tried to pretend like the day before hadn't happened. Thankfully, I had Levis with me and as soon as he saw Jason, he stepped between us, forcing Jason to back up.

I haven't been in the café since. It's bothersome that I've let this man run me out of the place I enjoy, but for my peace of mind and safety, I think it's for the best.

Considering I've seen Jason in many more places than just the coffee shop since then, I'm getting concerned. So far, I haven't seen him near my house, so there's a chance that it's just been coincidental. I'm not entirely sure I believe that it's just happenstance, though.

I've tried to tell myself he was probably always around before. The first time we met, he even said he frequented the café. There's definitely a possibility that he's always been in my path and I didn't notice before. Now I am aware because he turned into a creep.

He's just everywhere. Always watching me. If I saw him in passing, I might think less of it. But he's always watching. It's to the point where I'm definitely getting uncomfortable. Chills raise the little hairs all over my body when I spot him as I step out of the building my class was just in.

Immediately, I pull out my phone and call Levis. He's still on campus because his class lets out at the same time.

"Hey," he answers.

I turn my back on Jason, which is probably unwise. But we're surrounded by people, so that should mean I'm safe enough, right?

"You still here?"

"Yep. Where are you?"

"Outside Howard Hall," I answer, and glance back. Jason is still there. "He's here."

"Go back inside. I'll be right there."

Levis hangs up and I kind of want to call him back, so I'm not alone. I'm not *actually* alone. There are hundreds of students moving around, both coming and going from Howard. It's course change for the next fifteen minutes, so this crowd will remain thick for at least ten more minutes.

I step back inside and watch out the window. The crowd's density shifts now and then and I can see him staring this way. Hopefully, he can't actually see me right now. With the glare of the sun and the crowd, hopefully I've simply disappeared.

LOREN

While I wait, I try to tell myself that it's a coincidence. There's no way he knows my schedule. I texted him about my classes, sure, but it was more like 'I'm taking a lit class' and not 'my lit class on Fridays at 3pm in Howard Hall' type of conversation.

Does that mean he's been following me? Or does he have some other means to track me down? My heart jumps when the crowd shifts again and I see him heading this way.

"No, no, no, no," I murmur.

This won't be the first time he's tried to talk to me. Far from it. I've blocked his number and his online profiles—which are weirdly only a few months old—but he keeps making more and using apps to change his number so he can call me. My phone ringing is starting to give me anxiety when it's from an unknown number.

He wouldn't actually hurt me, though. Right? He's just going to continue to harass me and attempt to convince me I misunderstood everything. He wasn't being possessive or jealous. That he's used both those words without any input from me says he knows exactly what turned me off.

A hand on my elbow makes me jump. Only because I see Levis when I turn my head do I manage to keep in my scream. He's not looking at me, though. Levis is staring out the window with a very intense expression. He reminds me of one of those martial arts movies where the guy is ready to kill someone and the look he gives in warning screams—*I will skin you alive.*

The thing is, I bet he could make good on any promise. He's that proficient in his art and weapon-handling. I love to watch him move through his warm up routines before starting in on the real thing. If I were to have a crush on any of my friends, it would be Levis.

Jason steps inside and scans the area. His eyes land on me, but then Levis is blocking me from view. I don't have a chance to look around him before I see that Jason's already stepped back outside.

"Let's go," Levis says, and pulls me down the hall. There are multiple exits in every building, of course, so he takes me to the side. "We're calling the police."

I don't argue. However, we don't go to the local police. We go to campus security. I give them Jason's name and description and we report about Jason seemingly following me. Levis also tells them there are multiple witnesses to the fact that Jason's been following me.

Thankfully, campus security tends to take these threats a little more seriously than the police department, from what I understand. I had a friend who told me last year she went to the police because an ex was stalking her, and they tried to write it off that their paths crossing was just a coincidence since they attended the same school and were enrolled in classes near each other.

It got ugly with this guy threatening her often if she didn't agree to go out with him again. He even hit her once when she refused. She didn't go back to the police but told campus security instead. Through them, she pressed charges and he was fined for assault.

It's difficult to convince yourself that the law is on your side when you hear and see stories about them blowing off a threat as unimportant or unbelievable. Time and time again. The thing that really bothers me is that in so many cases, those same disregarded concerns result in violence or death.

Then there's the horror show we learned about from Haze when he was sixteen. How his father had buddies in the police

LOREN

department who forced his *adult* brother back home against his will.

Haze was freaking out over it. Not just for Oren's sake, but also for his own. He'd planned to leave home as soon as he graduated high school. But there was no guarantee that he'd be able to once he witnessed the reach and power his father had.

There are crooked people everywhere. When you get tangled in their web, it's really hard to get out. I can't let myself get caught in Jason's grasp. I don't want to be a victim.

I try not to let his constant presence affect me. There's nothing worse than living in fear. I don't want to live like that. I *refuse* to live like that. That doesn't stop the internal question of 'how long before he stops watching and begins acting?'

Then there's the follow up—why me? Why did he have to choose me? What did I do to catch karma's attention and have them send me Jason? Throughout high school, I lived in fear of being found out that I was gay, it was made only worse by the shit that Haze was going through. Though they weren't a danger to me, but I felt their behavior as a threat. Haze hid his sexuality for fear of his family's abuse. Even knowing that wasn't directed at me and always remembering my brother's words when I admitted that I'm gay—I needed to get big and strong to protect myself—I've always had a shadow of fear and uncertainty hanging over me.

Arizona is supposed to be a clean slate. We chose this specific area because it's known to be queer friendly. Eastern State University has been rated highly as a safe place. It's why we chose it since the other top contenders were still in California and we needed to get out of the state!

Levis wraps his arm around my waist and tugs me close. "It's fine," he says. "Promise."

I take a deep breath. It's hot out but as we move toward November, it's beginning to get cooler. Not a lot, but the average high is definitely creeping lower.

Nodding, I make a concentrated effort to not look at all the faces around me. I don't want to see if Jason's still around. Hopefully he lost us when we went out a different door. Or maybe he found us and saw that we went into campus security.

I'm not sure if he's a student here or not. Thinking back, his stories were kind of contradicting. Sometimes he explained his presence on campus by claiming that he had business there, whether it was taking a single class or because he was a vendor. Other times, he just worked close to campus. And another time he said he was a grad student.

There were so many things he told me that I should have realized the truth for what it was. Jason lies. He's bad news. He's not a good guy.

Almost as soon as I stepped into his car, the energy about him was different from the man I was getting to know via text. Then his behavior got progressively more concerning over the course of our date. Thinking back, I should have been concerned with so many things he texted me too.

My friends are right, though. I don't get a lot of compliments. I've never had a boyfriend, so I'm kind of starved for affection. More than anything, I long for someone to want me. To love me. I want a love story. A real one. Not a romance book with morally gray love interests and all that, but a real-life epic romance where he's just… obsessed with me. I want to be someone's priority. To be the person they can't stop thinking about and receive random texts to tell me so.

The thing is, I'm woefully behind on all that. I don't know how to flirt or talk to people. I'm stupidly shy and introverted. It's fortunate that I was basically handed my friends in fourth grade or I'd probably still be that loner kid that no one knows. Just a body taking up space.

So yeah, I was easily seduced by the idea that finally, someone wanted me. Someone noticed me. They were saying nice things that my heart longed to hear.

As we turn onto our road, Levis' phone rings. He answers and I know that it's his girlfriend right away. It's in his tone and the way he has this small, flirty, sexy smile on his lips. As if she can see it. His arm remains locked around me, protecting me. Maybe comforting me. But now I share his attention with her.

I'm not actually jealous. But listening to them talk only emphasizes how I don't have that. Maybe I won't ever have it.

Levis almost always has a girlfriend. He's always been wanted. We used to laugh over the trail of girls that followed him around. Levis has always had the opportunity to have his pick of the girls surrounding him.

The thing is, he's a good boyfriend. He's literally everything I want in a man. Right down to sending his girl flowers for no reason. Texting her that he's thinking of her. He's so gentlemanly and sweet, that I think we all swoon over him sometimes.

I blame Levis for showing me the kind of man I want. He's made my standards incredibly high. It's my loneliness that overshadowed my intuition telling me that Jason *wasn't* that guy.

Their conversation is just long enough to hear that Levis will pick her up in a few hours and they'll go out on a surprise date Levis has planned.

Swoon!

"Are you going to wear a suit?" I ask when he hangs up.

Levis smirks. "No. But I'll look nice."

"You always look nice," I say, rolling my eyes and glancing at him. He's wearing black pants—not jeans or khakis. I'm not sure what defines the word 'slacks' but I'd call them slacks. His shirt is collared with three buttons, all undone. It's tucked in with a dark brown leather belt wrapped around his trim waist.

It's not only that he's dressed nicely. Everything fits *just right*. Snug, showing a hint of what's underneath. The only place that is more telling than the package just perfectly hinting are his short sleeves that stretch over his thick biceps.

He grins, his arm tightening around me as we reach our house. The new neighbors are outside in the yard. One of them has the hose and is spraying the others. We watch as we get closer. Their cursing and laughter as they run around and try to tackle the one with the hose has me smiling. Levis chuckles.

"They look like a cool family," Levis comments.

"They definitely look like they get along," I agree. Most of us have siblings with various degrees of closeness. I'm close to my brother, and we stay in touch by texting or calling often.

Levis has a younger sister. I think they speak often because that's what's expected of them. Haze has three older brothers, none of which he's close with, though he's recently been trying to repair the relationship with Oren. At first we kind of thought he was doing it out of guilt, though we've tried to assure him that he has no reason to feel guilty. But I think he genuinely wants to have his brother in his life.

Just the one, though. Fuck the other two.

Briar is the middle of three kids that couldn't be more different from each other. They're not close and only ever talk if it has to do with planning something for some family member and only ever see each other at family gatherings.

LOREN

Honey Bee is the second youngest of five. Her relationships are rocky. I'm not even sure what to say outside of that.

And Brek is an only child.

If there was a family that would play like the ones across the road, it would probably be me and Dylan. Seeing them have fun makes my chest tight and I decide maybe I should call my brother. It's been about a week since we spoke. I hate that the older we get and the busier life gets that we talk less and see each other even less frequently.

But I smile as the neighbors' laughter follows us inside.

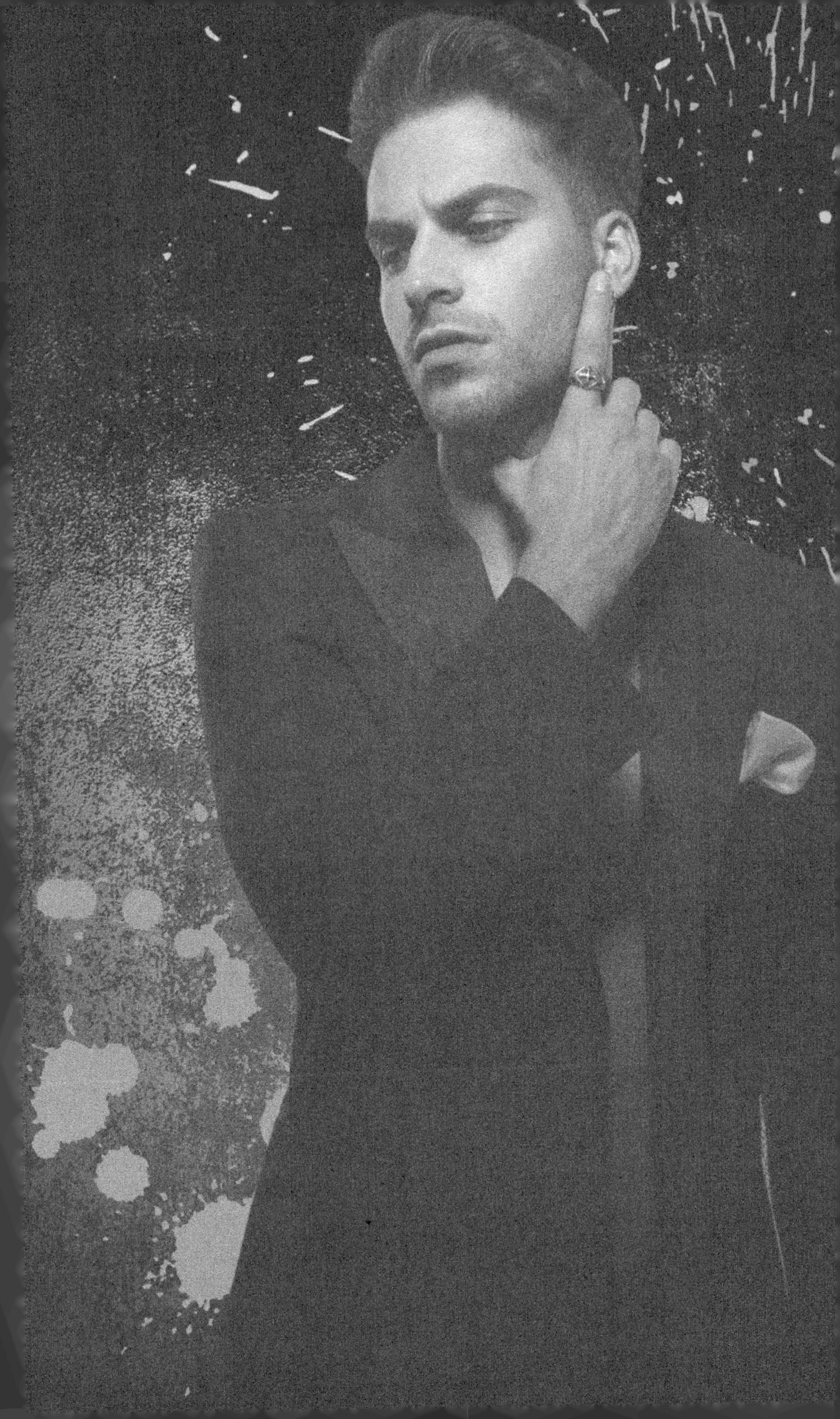

9
LOREN

THE DAY I kill Daniel is the day I see him hanging around outside Oakley's house, even after they told him to leave. The absolute *fury* I felt from him being near my man was overwhelming.

It started as a quiet day sitting in my room, not doing anything. I wasn't even looking out the window. Mostly because I've been trying to convince myself that once I end Daniel, we can leave. I don't *need* Oakley. I don't even know him. What the fuck is wrong with me that I feel such weird possession over a man I've never spoken to?

So I try to convince myself by any means necessary that this is just a job. I'm here in this house because Oakley is his target and Daniel is showing concerning behaviors. I'm biding my time before I have the opportunity to kill my target.

That's it. This is personal because it's a job I should have taken care of already. I shouldn't be revisiting it because I *should* have killed him over a year ago when Noah told me about him. Sometimes, I will take on a project sans contract just because. For example, I will always do it if Noah asks me to.

The memory of which makes me smile. I should call Noah.

Just as I'm picking up my phone, Imry steps into my room. He frowns at me and then glances at my window. Immediately, my body tenses. "What?" I ask.

"He's here."

I don't ask who as I basically launch myself from the bed. I'm in my window within three seconds. The way my blood boils at seeing Daniel banging on their front door has me ready to explode. I can hear the banging now. It's faint, but I hear it. Each impact of his fist reverberates through me and I'm absolutely fucking furious.

There's a struggle inside me as I watch. I don't want to look away in case I miss something important. Like if he makes it inside. Or somehow pulls Oakley through the door. Something that's going to make me lose my mind.

Yet, I *need* to get down there. I need to pull that fucker away and lock him in my trunk until I bring him somewhere that no one will hear his screams. Like the desert. There's lots of desert in Arizona.

Eventually, I break away and careen out my door to the stairs. My head is filled with a single thought—Daniel is going to die today. I'm going to murder that fucking piece of shit for going near what's mine.

Or... because I'm finishing a job I should have already. Yes, that's the reason.

As soon as I throw open the front door with Imry and Myro on my heels, I stop dead. Two police cruisers pull up to Oakley's house and there's a small showdown during which they get out and pull their guns while standing behind their open car doors.

LOREN

Daniel spins around with his hands up, trying to look innocent. I actually hear him call that this is a misunderstanding and that his boyfriend will clear it all up.

I growl. I actually physically growl.

"Dumbass," Imry says. "Like Oakley is going to corroborate his story. They're likely the ones to have called the police."

"You mean in addition to me calling the police," Dad says as he joins us in the door.

We watch as they take Daniel into custody, shoving him into the back of one of the squad cars. Only once he's locked away does the front door open. Several minutes go by while they speak to the police officers. My gaze is ping ponging between Oakley and Daniel—who is scowling out the cruiser window.

Myro pulls me back inside just as the cops turn around. I now watch from inside as Dad crosses the grass toward an officer coming in our direction. They meet on the sidewalk and talk. I try to determine what they're saying, but even with the window cracked, I don't hear much. Just their voices, too low and indistinct to distinguish their words.

After the police leave, I wait all of three minutes before heading to the basement to gather my gear.

The car Myro and I share for murders is in the attached garage, closed off from the rest of the world. It's a generic gray SUV, with nothing to make it stand out. As soon as I stuff my gear into the back and slam it closed, Myro is there. He grips my wrist, preventing me from rounding the car to the driver's side.

"You can't grab him from the police station," he drawls.

"I don't plan to." Actually, I do.

He frowns. "This is the first time in your entire life I've caught you in a lie," he says.

I hear the trunk open behind me and then close again after there's more dumped in. My entire body is jittery. I can't let this man get away. He needs to die.

"In the back," he says.

"I don't need you—"

"Honestly, don't give a fuck what you want right now, Loren," he insists, opening the back door and waiting for me to climb in. Imry is already behind the wheel.

I'm so frustrated, I'm shaking.

"Get in," Myro says.

"I'm going to kill him," I promise.

"I know."

"You're not going to tell me how to do it."

"No, I'm not," he agrees.

I stare at him, irritated and fuming, until finally I drop into the backseat. Myro waits until I'm tucked inside before shutting the door and getting in the passenger seat. I don't need to check my door to know that they've put on the child locks, including the windows.

"If you don't let me out when I want to—"

"Relax, Loren," Imry says, glancing at me in the rearview mirror as the garage door opens. "We're on your side. Daniel Rollins-Alabaster will die today at your hands, however you want to kill him. We're not going to stop you. We have no intention of standing in your way."

"Then why are you here?"

"So you don't get caught."

LOREN

"You outright lied to me, and it was entirely obvious," Myro adds. "On any given day, you're highly volatile when you're as emotional as a wet rag. You're acting on emotion right now. I imagine in your mind, you're justified in killing this man."

"It is justified," I say.

"Why?" Imry asks.

"Because he's harassing Oakley!" They saw that! What kind of question is this?!

"I promise you, the law will not agree that it warrants him being murdered," Myro counters. "Considering Oakley doesn't even know you exist, Loren, there is zero reason right now that would justify your rage in anyone else's mind."

I huff. It comes out just shy of another inhuman growl. I really don't give two fucks what anyone else thinks. Harassing my Oakley is reason enough for him to die. I'd kill anyone bothering him. That's what you do when you... uh... love someone?

I'm sidetracked by this thought as the car moves down the street. Just an hour ago, I was convincing myself that Oakley was nothing. He's just a guy caught in my target's web. I'm looking out for him for this reason alone.

That's why I've followed him to school this last week. And the coffee shop. The store. Library...

Lowering my eyelids, I sit back and fold my hands over my stomach. *I can't love. I don't have the capacity to feel emotions of this kind. He's nothing. He's no one. This doesn't exist for me.*

I go over the cornerstones of my diagnosis as I sit in the backseat and check off all that apply to remind myself that Oakley is nothing to me. Lack of empathy and remorse—yes. Clearly. Arrogant and feeling superior—I mean... sure. Manipulative and deceitful—I absolutely can be and have been when it suits my needs. Anyone without the name Van Doren, except Noah, only ever gets that side of me.

Poor impulse control—I suppose sitting in this car because I planned to pick up an asshole right from the police's parking lot is evidence enough of this. Criminal behavior—see previous remark. Impulsive and reckless—again, see previous remark.

Callous and unemotional—I don't know that I'm often callous, but yes, I am most certainly unemotional. The one I disagree with is poor relationships.

Well, to be more accurate, poor relationships outside of my family and Noah are completely true. I don't have any. The women I fuck are just that—the use of a body. I've only ever pretended to be 'normal' long enough to get what I want.

However, I do not have a poor relationship with anyone in my family. A conversation with Noah reminds me I do have loyalty. It might not be something that's truly driven by emotion or feelings or anything, but it's something deeper than that. These are the people who have always supported me in my most authentic version of myself. My brothers are here because they don't want me to get caught. They're always here, no matter what.

I've killed a man for Noah without question, simply because he asked me to. Well, not in so many words, but I told him I'd take care of him, and I did. Daniel started for this same reason too.

He is still my target for this reason.

Everything means Oakley is simply nothing. He's happenstance. Someone I apparently found pretty. That's it. He's pretty. And I like to fuck pretty girls. Does it matter that he's not a girl?

The car stops and the engine turns off. I blink out of my thoughts and sit forward between the seats. We're parked on a side street, watching the front of the precinct.

LOREN

"You calmed down now?" Imry asks.

I don't answer. I'm feeling slightly confused because I feel no differently concerning all the characterizations of my sociopathy. Yet, I'm reacting as if Oakley is Noah or one of my brothers, even having never met this man.

I can recognize this in myself. But acknowledging it doesn't change how I feel, though. It doesn't change the pit of rage in my chest or the way my blood pulses in my ears with the need to react.

"No," I admit, frustrated.

"We'll bring you somewhere where you can let it out however you want," Myro offers. "Just hold on."

"What happened to keeping it passionless?" I ask.

"You're not going to be able to do that, are you?" Myro asks as he shifts in his seat to look at me. I don't answer. "I'd be rather assured that you have a safe place to do what you need to do than try to convince you to let me kill him instead."

"No," I say, fists clenching.

"I'm not going to. That's my point. Instead, I'm going to make sure you're not caught. Okay?"

He means well. He loves me the way I am, and this is how he shows his loyalty.

I nod. It's jerky because I can't put off the urge to just walk inside and pull this stupid fucker out of there by his hair. He's scum. Surely they'll understand that.

It's hours. Fucking *hours* before he's let out. I both hate and am relieved that he just walks out of the precinct. Fortunately, he's walking this way. When he crosses the street, I'm ready to barrel out of the car and slam him into the side of the brick building next door. I reach for the door just as he passes, but the fucking thing won't open.

I slam my fist into it and turn my outrage to face Imry.

He doesn't say anything. Just starts the car and drives around the block. We spend the next ten minutes following this fucker. If he notices, he doesn't care. It takes far too long before we pull over and both of my brothers get out. There's a scuffle that doesn't last long and then he's in the trunk.

We drive on without a word. My entire body is jittery, knowing he's right here. I can pull down the seat and reach him. He's not moving, though. Not making any sound.

"You better not have killed him," I say.

"Just put him to sleep for a few hours," Myro promises. "Long enough to get us deep into the desert."

I'm even more impatient when we have to stop to fill up the gas tank so we can get back out of the desert. Still, I sit quietly. Patience is not something I'm good at, so I spend the time going over the fact that my rage is unjustified and makes exactly zero sense. I can tell myself that it's because Noah asked me to help, and I let this asshole go.

But even I know it has nothing to do with Noah at this point. It has everything to do with Oakley and the knowledge that he's fucking mine. I don't even care if he doesn't know it.

When we finally stop, it's dark. Only the moon lights the world around us. Daniel started to move around, thump, and yell over the last ten minutes. I use his voice to stoke the flames inside me.

We pull over and my brothers still don't let me out while they prep the area, which consists of putting down an enormous tarp and attaching a grader to the back of the SUV. Once they're satisfied, Myro hauls Daniel out as Imry opens my door and hands me my favorite knife.

There's nothing exciting about the knife; it's basically a stainless steel kitchen knife. Still, I love the familiar weight in my hand as I stalk toward Daniel. He's tied up, but Myro undoes the ropes as I approach.

Daniel stares at me, his eyes darting to the knife. "Who are you? Why are you doing this?"

"You deserve to die," Myro says conversationally.

"Why? What have I done?"

"Playing stupid isn't going to work in your favor," Myro retorts. "Your most recent transgression goes by the name of Oakley."

Daniel's eyes are still on me when Myro releases him and he falls forward onto his hands and knees. Looking up at me, he shakes his head. "He didn't tell me he has a boyfriend. You should be mad at him and not me for dating him. I didn't know."

"He doesn't have a boyfriend," Myro says as I grip Daniel's hair and haul him backward. He screams, but the sound is cut off by the angle in which I have his neck.

"He has a guardian angel," Imry says, amused, as I drive my knife to the handle into his stomach.

He dies slowly over the next hour as I carve into his body, making sure he feels every single tear of his skin. Only when he's lost consciousness, either from blood loss or pain, do I finally kill him.

Myro rolls his body off the tarp and we strip our clothes right there. Myro washes the blood from my skin as Imry rolls up the tarp and stuffs it back into the trunk. We're dressed in sweats as we climb back in the car. Behind us, the grader wipes away our tracks until we're thirty miles away and my brothers haul it back inside.

The car gets dumped into one of the warehouse buildings for our cleaning crew, but the tarp we shove into the incinerator ourselves. Then we head home, though I only feel slightly better about the situation. Daniel is dead, but I'm still not sure what to do about Oakley.

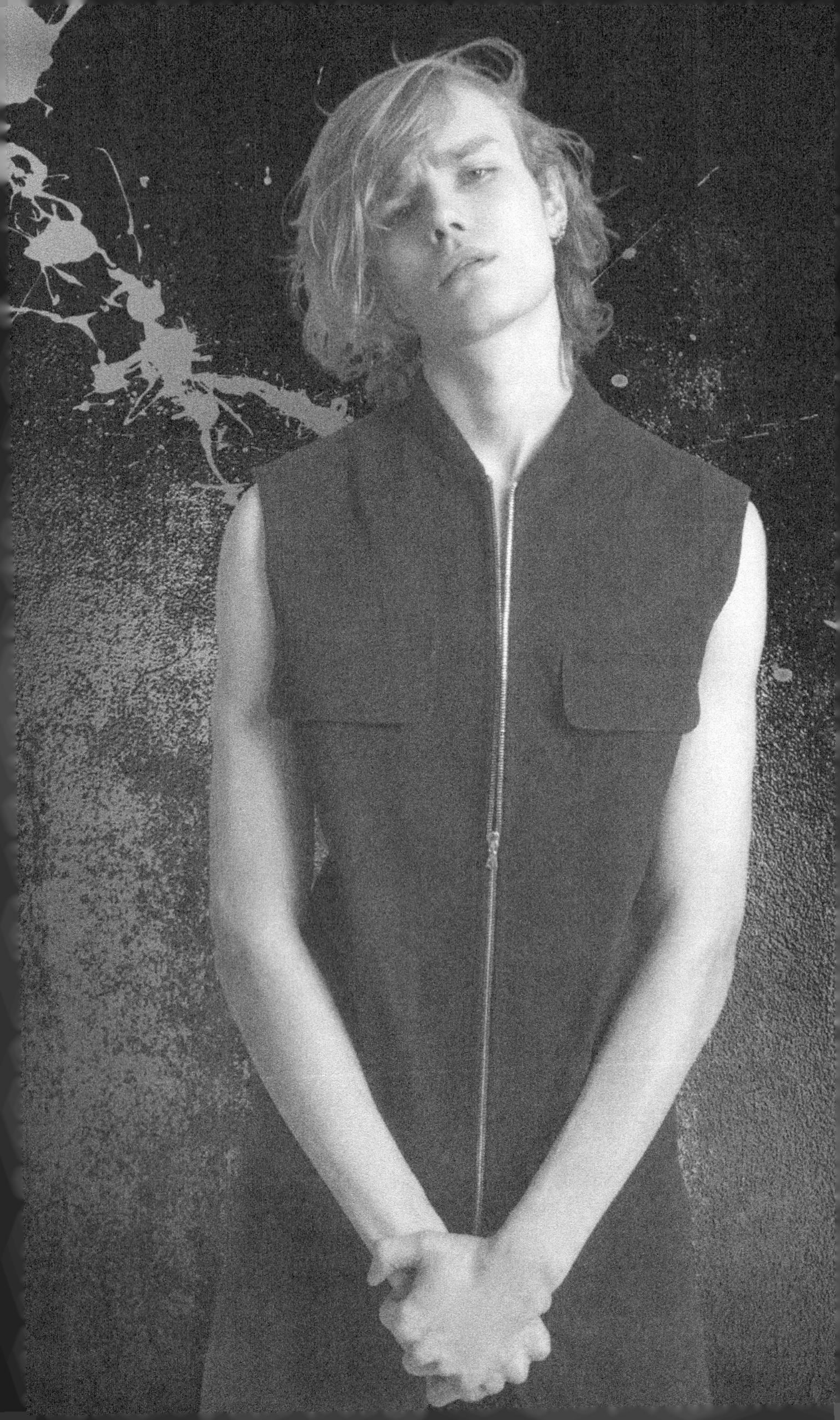

10

OAKLEY

Two weeks go by and I don't see Jason again. I try not to feel too secure in this; people like Jason don't just disappear without a warning. Then again, my restraining order went through, so maybe that's it. Maybe he's taking it seriously.

He has to be, right? That's why he's not around.

Life feels peaceful again. I feel like everything is just... good. School is good—I enjoy my classes. I'm no closer to determining what I actually want to do with my future, but not looking over my shoulder between classes means I can concentrate on them again.

We moved to Arizona for a clean slate and once more, I feel like it's in front of me. I can build my life around this new start.

I sit in the side yard with Honey Bee and Briar as we covertly watch the new neighbors across the street. They always seem to be outside, though I'm struggling to determine how many actually live there. I swear I've seen like five men. They're all definitely adults and we're confident that they're all related. Cousins at the very least, but I'd be shocked if they weren't brothers.

I'm also confident that one man is a parental figure—uncle or father or something. He's not old and there are days when I'm sure he's the hottest one there, which is truly saying something because I don't think I've ever seen such a gorgeous group of men.

I've determined they hang out in their front yard because they have something going on in the back. I've seen construction company vehicles coming and going, though I've yet to see or hear actual construction, which leads me to believe they're getting quotes.

We've been discussing the backyard every time we see one of these trucks outside their house. When we first heard the rumors that the house was haunted, we peeked into windows to see what was inside, but there was nothing. The house was an empty shell.

However, we never went out back. I'm regretting it now since we're all stupidly curious. From what we've seen on satellite views—yes, we were creeps and looked—it's just a luxurious backyard. Nothing to be surprised about given the house itself.

There are three guys out front right now. One of them reminds me of Brek in how he dresses. He's wearing an open knit vest that's open. Jeans, low on his hips and rolled at his ankles with a white belt. He has well-worn brogues or Oxfords on, probably no socks.

Around one wrist is a silver watch, and the other has a handful of leather, bead, and braided bracelets. His hair is kind of floppy, unstyled. I've seen him run his hand through it half a dozen times in ten minutes. He has black-rimmed glasses that are very reminiscent of Brek's too.

His physique isn't quite like Brek's, though, but not far off. He's not toned like Briar or Levis who work at their muscles. He's thin like me, but more defined than I am.

LOREN

Then there's who is unmistakably the oldest of the younger guys. There's just something mature about him, more than anything else. His hair is dark like the other guy's. Actually, all their hair is dark. There's something very similar in the shapes of their faces. I'd be willing to bet their eyes are all similar too.

There are also a set of twins that are very nice to look at. They tend to laugh a lot and wrestle in the grass.

The father often sits on the front deck watching the kids as if they're young. I wonder if he imagines them that way. Remembering them as kids playing in the yard.

"Okay," Honey Bee interrupts, leaning forward a foot or so. It's not like closing that little bit of extra distance is going to make our neighbors clearer. "I think they're in the witness protection program."

Briar laughs. "Why do you think that?"

"Well, they're all related. I think we can at least agree on that."

Me and Briar nod.

"And I think we all agree that they're very much adults. Not even a teenager in sight. Right?"

"Yeah," I agree, having just been thinking about that.

"Now, I know this generation's been living with their family longer because it's far too fucking expensive to live, but I feel that at least half of them are at least late twenties. And that they're *all* living under one roof? It's not even a cheap little suburban house. That thing was stupidly expensive, so it's likely not a financial situation that keeps them together."

"You're not suggesting something taboo, are you?" I ask, raising a brow.

She laughs. "I mean, to each their own, but no."

"Except perhaps the twins," Briar says, tilting his head to the side. "They wrestle an awful lot."

Honey Bee rolls her eyes. "What's the excuse parents use to excuse every boy behavior—boys will be boys?"

Briar smirks. "I'm not saying I care, I'm just saying. Maybe it's something I've seen that I can't quite put my finger on."

The three of us undoubtedly turn our attention to the wrestling twins. I don't witness anything that could be considered… well, as Briar alluded to—taboo. Wrestling has always looked rather gay to me. You can't show me a single image or video and convince me otherwise. Haze and I always used to joke that it's the straight man's way of copping a feel and not having to defend what he's doing.

Like them slapping each other's asses in sports. Honestly, what kind of encouragement or praise is that? 'Nice job' with an ass slap. I've seen porn with that exact thing and not even a sports script in sight.

"I don't know. I think they're a little too… rowdy to be in protection," I say. "Wouldn't you try to stay out of public sight?"

"Like that's going to help you blend in," she disagrees, shaking her head. "No. Appearing like a normal family is much better camouflage."

"I'll give you that," Briar says, "but they're very obviously adults. I'm still trying to figure out why they all live together. Have you seen any of them with a girlfriend?"

"Or boyfriend," Honey Bee adds.

Briar shrugs. "Gender isn't the point."

"No," I say, "but to be fair, if that's the case, we all probably look like Honey Bee's lovers."

Briar snorts and Honey Bee grins. It wouldn't be the first time we'd heard that accusation. One of the most common snide remarks in high school was that we shared Honey Bee. And in case we weren't smart enough to figure out what they were alluding to, some would even tack on—*you know, sexually.*

At first we tried to defend our friendship, but that was exhausting. Instead, we began to just agree. Their look of stupidity when we didn't argue was usually pretty comical.

"My girlfriend thinks so too," Briar says, shrugging.

"I'm impressed she's still hanging around then," Honey Bee teases, turning her attention to Briar.

He shrugs again. "Probably not for much longer. She's trying not to be jealous, but she can't help herself. Especially once I told her we don't allow other people into our space. Not even serious girlfriends."

"Is it serious?" I ask.

Briar grins. "No. I mean, she has potential. I might have given you a different answer a month ago, *before* I began seeing her jealousy. But if she can't accept that my friends are my own and they're not going anywhere, and I don't have to share them with her, blah, blah, blah—then she's just not it for me."

Honey Bee gripped his knee. "Sorry, honey."

Briar is the only one of us that has been all about having a family and kids and whatever since we were young. He's always been a family man wanting that perfect love story. There were times he and I would talk about it extensively. Just kind of share our dreams together since they were similar.

Growing up, we had a bet that Briar would be married and have his first kid by the end of his first year of college. Believe me, he tried. Three girlfriends later, we realized our friendship was seriously a sticking point that served as an obstacle for his dreams.

I'd have been heartbroken if he'd decided that he needed distance from us. I think we all got a little teary and giddy when he quoted the girl band saying that their lover needs to get with their friends or bye bye bye. We even shared some seriously mushy group hugs too.

"Yeah." Briar takes a sip of his lemonade. "I'll find my girl at some point. Maybe not in college, but she's out there."

"Way to keep your head up," Honey Bee says.

Briar snorts. "Thanks for the encouragement."

We turn our attention back to the guys across the street and our game of trying to guess why they suddenly moved in. If they were college kids like us and rooming together to save money, I think none of us would question it. That's pretty common. Maybe not all that common in richy rich neighborhoods like Rolling Green Estates, but it's entirely possible that they have connections like we do.

But the longer they're there, the less convinced we are of this. I'm not entirely convinced they even work. They don't appear to have a regular schedule that takes them from the house.

Maybe they all work remotely…?

"I'm going to look at my homework," I say as I get to my feet and stretch. "Report back on the hotness if something is revealed."

"Done," Briar promises.

I head upstairs and spread out my books on my desk. There's a paper I've been working on for the past week. While I'm vaguely interested in the topic, papers are a little challenging for me. I'm never sure how to organize my thoughts, never mind format it in such a way to make sense.

It doesn't matter how many times I read the resources available on how to write a paper, they only get marginally better. I write out my thoughts and bullet points, then let my friends tell me what kind of order to put it in. Then Honey Bee has a last read through to make sure it makes sense. There have been days when she's rearranged my entire paper. She never changes a word of it, just makes the order work with the words I've written.

I'm in the writing stage now, having all my bullet points put into a reasonable outline that made sense to my friends. It flows decently this way, though there's always something that gives me pause as I try to tie everything together with transitions that make sense.

"Dude," Briar says as he shoves my door open. His sudden appearance makes me jump. I'm about to tease him that I could have been jerking off, but the look on his face stops me short. "You need to see this."

I follow him downstairs, unsure what to expect. It's definitely *not* a news story about a homicide. At first, I'm still not sure what's so interesting about it except that it's relatively close. Eighty miles from here.

It isn't until Jason's face pops up on the screen that my jaw drops and chills run through my body.

"Oh, my god," I whisper, feeling slightly guilty that I was so happy he'd finally disappeared from my life. I was *giddy* that the cops had managed to keep him away when, in reality, he hadn't been following me because he'd been murdered!

"Wait, what did they call him?" I ask as I fall onto the edge of the couch, eyes riveted on the screen.

I don't need to wait for an answer since his name is right below his picture. Based on what he's wearing, it's a mugshot from the day he was here two weeks ago. My stomach churns.

But what catches my attention more than what he's wearing is the name. Daniel Rollins-Alabaster. "That's not the name he told me," I whisper.

"They've already mentioned that," Honey Bee says as she scooches closer to me and wraps her arms around my shoulders. "They mentioned you without actually naming you. Said that he was arrested for harassment that led to a restraining order earlier the day he was killed."

My eyes go wide. "He was… that day?"

"Well, that night," Haze says. "They're saying if they had to guess, he was killed directly following being released from custody. They're asking for anyone who has information to step forward."

"They're also calling the brutal murder a crime of passion," Briar says. "Someone wanted him to feel the pain."

I shudder.

"But they did say that he had been giving false names to those he's interacted with," Honey Bee adds. "After his body was found and identified, they searched his apartment and found half a dozen fake identifications—including Jason Adams, the name he gave you."

My stomach churns and I press my hand to it. "What does this mean?"

She shakes her head as the news changes stories. "Don't know. Except that he wasn't who he said he was and although we already knew this, he was likely a bad man."

LOREN

"Whatever he was up to, you were his next victim," Levis says. "I'm not sorry he's dead."

I'm not entirely sure how I feel. Very clearly, the little pieces of the truth that we know point in the direction that this wasn't a good man. Not even just a man with a possessive streak. He was up to something.

It's sickening that nearly the first words to me out of his mouth were a lie—his name. Tears prickle my eyes because maybe everything was a lie. Everything he's ever said. Including all the nice things.

I'm not beautiful.

Everything he said was a means to manipulate me into... what? Dating him? But why?

Once again, I wasn't actually wanted. Even worse, my insecurities and desperate longing made me stupid enough to fall for his lies. Anyone who calls me beautiful is full of shit.

If I've learned anything from this, it's that. Compliments are red flags. Especially when they're said to me.

The knock on our front door pulls me from my thoughts and we all spin around to stare at it. Levis answers and I'm slightly shocked to see the police there, inquiring if they can come in to ask us some questions about Jason—uh... Daniel.

I get to my feet, feeling slightly numb. As they step inside, I see our neighbors outside watching. Only this time, I see a man I've never seen before. There's something about the way he's looking over here that makes me shiver.

Then the door is closed and I'm looking at two policemen.

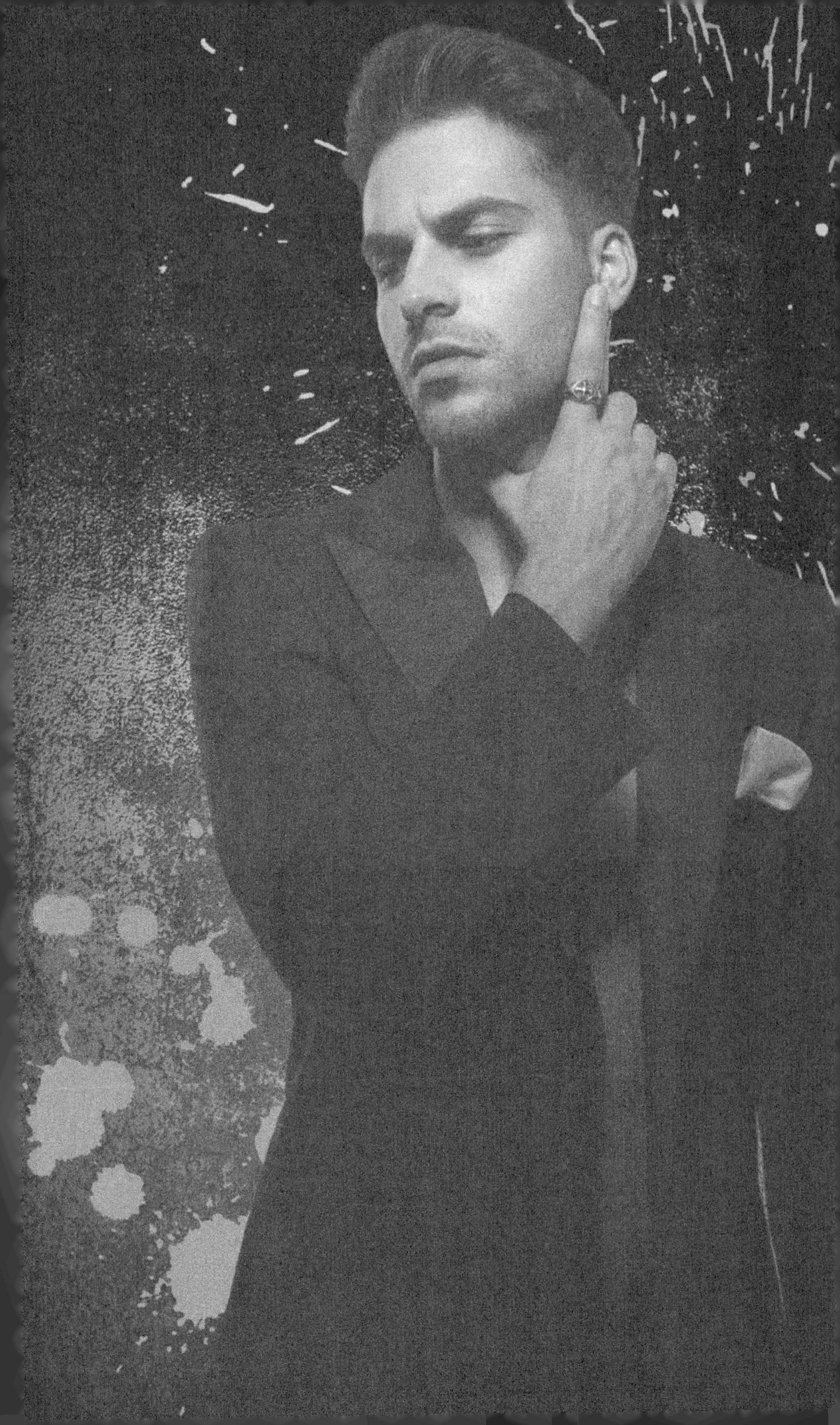

11
LOREN

I can't quite see into the café where Oakley's disappeared. Three or four days a week, he stops in on the way to school. Before he knew Daniel was dead, he'd stopped going inside. I'm not entirely surprised, since that's where they met.

The news updates on Daniel's murder have been less and less. The more of his truth that they uncover, the less the public outcry is for his murder to be solved. I'd wanted to anonymously provide all the information we had on him, but Myro refused to allow it. He didn't want any tie between our family and Daniel.

It's not that I don't understand the danger in that, but I want the world to know I murdered him justly. You know, leaving out the fact that I was doing it because he became a danger to Oakley, and I was obsessed from afar.

My sense of right and wrong might be skewed, but I'm confident the world wouldn't be upset if they learned the full truth behind the man who was Daniel Rollins-Alabaster.

I sip my travel coffee cup that has water in it. Coffee is disgusting. Call it blasphemy if you want, but ew! However, as I sit on the bench across the street watching both doors to the café, I need to blend in as much as possible. Sitting on the bench at the bus stop seems like a fair enough reason to be hanging around.

Oakley's seen me now. While I wasn't exactly trying to be unseen entirely, I was trying to keep off their radar a bit. It makes studying Oakley easier if he and his roommates don't know I'm here. I blew it the night the police found Daniel and they showed up at Oakley's house for questioning. He'd seen me. Our eyes had locked, even from the distance that separated us.

It's become more difficult to convince myself that I need to leave, even though I know I do. What am I going to do with this guy? It's just ridiculous.

Oakley steps out the front door of the café, but I stay seated until he moves further down the road to the corner and crosses the street as he continues to the school. Once he's across, I get up and follow, remaining on the opposite side of the street.

He's easy to keep in sight because of his ridiculously bright backpack. It seems so out of place with him. He doesn't wear bright colors. Not even his shoes or the ties in his hair. Yet his backpack could be seen from an airplane at 30,000 feet!

I follow him to campus and plant myself on the bench across the grass outside the building he has class in. I'm aware there are many other exits, but since I've been following him, I've noted that Oakley uses the front doors most often.

This is the moment I try to convince myself to leave. Daniel is dead. He's safe. I have no business being here. None at all. I can leave.

I. Can. Leave.

My ass remains firmly planted on this bench as I take another sip of water. Rubbing my hand over my face, I sigh in frustration at myself. This doesn't happen often but... I need help.

Pulling my phone out of my pocket, I dial Noah. It's almost nine, so I'm confident he's awake. Whether he has hockey this morning, I'm not sure. We were roommates for a year in college. He's the only person outside of my family that wasn't immediately put off by me. I'm sure I still made him uneasy, but he didn't react like I had the plague. He wasn't immediately afraid or kept his distance.

We became friends.

I was disappointed when he got drafted to the NHL. Well, disappointed for me. It's what he wanted to do, so I was happy for my friend. That's how normal people feel, right? Happy for their friends? Considering he's likely my only friend, I make it a point to be happy for him.

"Hey," he answers.

"Hi," I say, glancing at the building in front of me. There are still stragglers rushing inside, nearly late for the start of class. "Are you busy?"

"Nope. What's up?"

"Hockey's good?" I ask.

He chuckles. "Hockey's good. Lix is good. I'm good. Are you?"

I chew the inside of my lip. "I need some help," I say. "Maybe some advice, actually."

"Okay. I'll see what I can do."

"There's this guy," I start and pause. What exactly am I supposed to say to explain this? With a frustrated sigh, I back up and tell Noah about Daniel and how I found Oakley and then how I killed Daniel. I confess... a lot. Definitely enough to get me in trouble. "Now I know I need to leave, but I can't. My job's done and I should go home, but… I'm here."

I look up at the building again. I'm not sure which classroom he's in. Not that I couldn't easily figure it out. But so far, I've been able to convince myself that I don't need to be that creepy. I got rid of one stalker and replaced him with myself.

"Where is 'here'?"

Pressing my lips together, I try to find anything that's the truth without being the truth. In the end, I just tell him. "Outside the building he's attending class in."

"Loren," he says, laughing. "You're going to get in trouble."

I sigh. "I know. Tell me I need to stop this. I'm being ridiculous, right?"

"Sounds to me like you've fallen in love at first sight," he tells me instead, and I can hear the smile in his voice. "It's very romantic."

I recall a conversation we had last year about being judged on things that we can't change about ourselves. He asked me if I wanted to be with someone and I'd said maybe. We talked about if there was someone in the world who would love me as I am even though my own mother couldn't.

I've thought about it a lot—whether someone would want to be with me knowing that I don't like to be touched often. That I can be cold and unsettling. My emotional range is very small. Not because I'm immature, but because of how I'm built. How I was born.

Will they still want me when I tell them I'm a sociopath? Or will they run the other way?

"You okay?" Noah asks when I don't answer.

"I'm not sure you remember that I'm not able to love," I answer.

He chuckles. "I think you are *refusing* to remember that I told you love means something different for everyone. For you, I've always called the manifestation of your love loyalty. But maybe it's broader than that. I think you're capable of more than you're allowing yourself to believe."

"Yes, I've expanded from loyalty to obsession," I deadpan. Noah bursts out laughing. I can't help the smile that makes my lips curl, even though I try not to.

"I'm going to ask you this again, Loren. Do you *want* to be with someone? With this guy?"

My gaze flickers back to the building. A shiver runs through my body but the truth is... I don't know what I want. I *want* to possess him. To own him. Keep him close and safe and... mine. I'm not sure that's the same as wanting to be with someone.

"I don't know," I admit, feeling frustrated all over again. I let my head fall back and close my eyes. "Maybe."

"Are you lonely?"

I frown. "What?"

He chuckles. "You once told me you might want to be with someone one day because you could get lonely and bored, and you do bad things when you're bored."

I do bad things even when I'm not bored. The good and bad of it is usually dictated by those who have a distorted view of the world and human life. *Not* all life is precious and valuable. *Not* all people deserve to live and die 'as God intended.'

Rapists, traffickers, abusers... their lives are not as valuable as their victims. And that's coming from someone who doesn't often agree with what others perceive as right and wrong.

"This isn't the same thing," I say. "I'm not lonely. I'm not looking for a girlfriend." Then pause and reconsider. "Or a boyfriend, apparently."

Noah chuckles.

"I'm not even bored."

"But you saw him and instantly fell in love with him," Noah retorts. I can tell he's enjoying this, and I kind of appreciate his teasing.

"No. I became instantly obsessed with him."

He sighs. "Loren, we've already established more than once—including in this conversation—that love means different things. I've defined it by loyalty. But love can have more definitions. Obsession can be one of them. There are some parallels between your obsession and my love for Lix."

"Oh, yeah?" I ask, skeptically.

"Absolutely. I think about him constantly. Especially when we're not together. Sometimes it's truly inconvenient, like when I'm on the ice and some random Lix thought intrudes on my concentration. If you look up the definition of 'obsessed,' I promise you, it sounds quite familiar to what I just described. And I'm going to go out on a limb here and say that it's close to what you're experiencing with your neighbor now, isn't it?"

It shouldn't make me feel better. I've never put much stock in being viewed as 'normal.' In fact, I have absolutely zero desire to be like everyone else. Who would want that—to be one of many? I'd rather be one of the few, *superior* to what the world views as *normal*.

So I let Noah's explanation settle me a little. He's not wrong. How he thinks about Lix sounds a lot like how I think about Oakley.

"Two more questions," I continue. "Do you think he's going to be put off by my antisocial disorder?"

"Considering you haven't spoken to him at all and therefore we have absolutely zero to speculate on, I can't really give you my opinion on that. But if he's a good person, if he's the person for you, then I don't think he'll be put off by it. Just... don't mistake his fear or unease for disliking you. Okay?"

I nod. "Yeah. Okay."

"Your second question?"

People begin walking out of the building in front of me. A glance at my watch says it's time for classes to dismiss, so I watch the students stream out of the doors. It's not long before Oakley is in sight, and I watch him from a distance.

"What should I do?" I ask.

"I know you can answer that question without my help." He prompts, "What should you do, Loren?"

"You're going to tell me to talk to him, aren't you?" I ask.

He chuckles. "Yes."

I get up once I nearly lose sight of Oakley. By the time I blend into the crowd and spot his highlighter aesthetic backpack, he's been joined by Levis Li.

"How do I talk to a guy?" I ask.

"I'm offended that you consider me something else," he teases.

I'm sidetracked by his words for a minute. "Sorry. I mean, how do I talk to a guy I'm... maybe interested in? I just realized how weird this is."

Noah laughs. "It's not weird. Liking a guy is completely normal. Just as normal as liking a girl."

"I'm not sure that's true when you've only ever been attracted to women in the past. For me, this is weird."

"No, it's just new," he insists. "And I'll say it again, it's not any different."

"I think you're forgetting who you're talking to," I say. "My version of talking to anyone outside of my family and you is with a—" I cut myself off just before saying 'a knife at their throats before I assist them in bleeding out.' I'm quite literally surrounded by people that would be alarmed with that. "It's not, uh, pretty. Generally speaking, my only goal when talking to a woman is how to get them in bed."

"Such a slut," he mutters. I can hear his amusement, so I just shrug, not denying it. I also don't bring up that I haven't slutted since spotting Oakley. Maybe it's my turn to move into my second virginity. "Okay, then try this. Talk to him like you talked to me the first time."

Generally speaking, I remember most things that happen in my life. Do I remember the day I met Noah Kain? Shy, pretty, reserved, maybe even a little mousy. I followed him to hockey one afternoon and the man on the ice was so different from the frightened and exhausted teenager I shared a room with. I'd wanted to know the man on the ice. The person Noah was innately. Not the mask he wears in the world.

"Yeah, okay."

Oakley steps inside a building for his next class, and I continue walking. There's no bench right outside this one, so I tend to try to time my meandering around campus right for this period.

"I have to head to weight training," Noah says. "I'll call you after and we can continue this conversation. Okay?"

"Yep. Thanks."

LOREN

"Sure. I'm looking forward to meeting your man."

I roll my eyes. "He's not my man." Ohhh... If there was ever a lie I spoke out loud...

Noah laughs. "Sure, Loren. Keep telling yourself that."

We hang up and I turn around to head back toward the building Oakley went into. Usually, I spend my time circling. Examining the building and those around it. Seeing what there is to see and learn.

When I turn around, I come face to face with Levis, and have to stop abruptly so I don't run into him. He's standing there with his arms crossed over his chest, staring at me with a very unimpressed expression.

"Is it a coincidence that I see you everywhere?" he asks.

"Yes," I say. "I suppose that happens when we're neighbors and frequent the same places."

The key to telling half-truths is the *half-truths*. There needs to be some truth in what you say and if you can keep it vague enough so that it's all, technically speaking, a truth, then there's no lie to detect. As with now. What I said was an absolute truth. It just didn't answer what he was asking without asking.

"Where are you headed, Van Doren?" he asks.

Maybe I should be surprised that he knows who I am. Well, relatively speaking, I suppose. He didn't say my first name. From what I've learned about him via my observation and research, I'm not really surprised at all. In fact, I'm very sure he knows exactly which Van Doren I am.

I suppose this means we're not going to pretend to be clueless concerning identities right now and I can address him by name, too. "I'm getting exercise so nowhere in particular. Where are you headed, Li?"

I don't miss the way he tries to fight the amused smile as he stares at me.

"Nowhere in particular since I don't have class until one. I have a feeling you know that, though."

Does he think I'm following him? Have I been caught and yet misunderstood? Should I tell him I *do* know that he has a class at one and where it's located? That would only further confirm what he suspects, even though it's not the truth. Just a happenstance, a coincidence.

When I don't answer, Levis drops his hands into his pockets. "Let's walk this way. You're Loren, right?"

I glance back at the building Oakley's in before turning and falling into stride beside Levis. "Yes. You're Levis, right?"

He chuckles. "Are you going to turn every question back on me?"

"There's a possibility that I will."

"Good to know. What're you doing here, Loren? Don't ask me what I'm doing here because we both know that you know the answer to that question."

I decide on another half-truth. "It's a beautiful campus to walk around. Safe. Peaceful. Many paths to choose from and avoid muscle memory when I walk around."

"So you're not a student here." It's not a question.

"I've talked to enrollment," I say, shrugging. "But I don't know what course of study I'm interested in, and it seems like a waste of time and money to enroll just for the sake of enrolling." That *is* entirely true. I just left out the fact I was trying to find a way to enroll in Oakley's classes next semester.

LOREN

He snorts. "Yeah, I get that. My friend faces the same issue—not knowing what he's truly interested in."

"How does he choose his classes?"

Levis shakes his head. "Based on interest, I guess. He keeps hoping that he'll stumble upon something that truly ignites some passion so he can find his direction."

I nod. Though I'm not sure which of his friends he's talking about, I understand that sentiment. I graduated with a medical biology degree two years ago and fuck knows whether I'm ever going to use it.

"I don't suppose that's a very cost-effective way to attend college."

He laughs. "His family has some money and they've encouraged him to follow his dreams, even if it takes him a while to realize them."

Okay, he's either talking about Oakley or Albrecht. Both of their families have some money. I appreciate this conversation narrowing down.

Now... how can I steer it to talking about Oakley...?

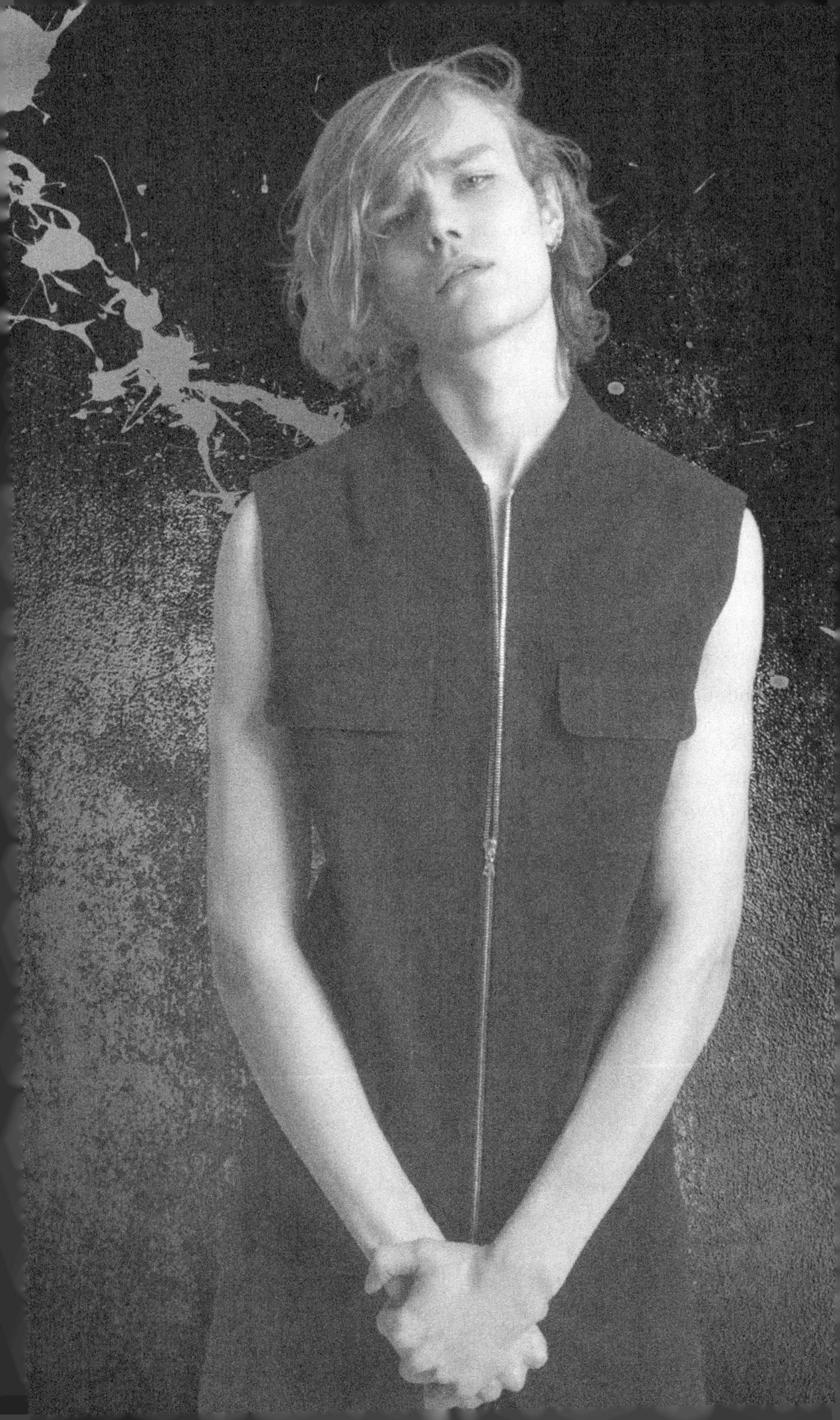

12

OAKLEY

REGISTRATION for next semester's courses is still two months away, but I still look at the catalog periodically. Honestly, I think I should just take the liberal arts degree and stop spending money until I know what I want to do.

I haven't done this because most people never return to school after they leave. Then again, school no longer guarantees you anything—not a job, not better pay, not better treatment. That isn't the world we live in any longer. Now, we're subject to the same treatment and expectations that those just leaving high school and entering the job market are. The only difference is they're not laden with debt.

Fortunately, I won't have the debt to contend with, since my grandmother pays for my tuition outside of grants and scholarships. I'm one of the lucky ones. Most of the people I know, including those I live with, don't have that same luck.

Still, I'd like to live the rest of my life doing something I enjoy. If I have to work for the next fifty or more years, I don't want to spend that time being miserable. The thing is, I have no idea what I want to do with my life. I've taken a class in probably every field of study at this point and... nothing feels right. Nothing makes me excited.

I pocket my phone as I step into the store on my way home. It's my night to cook dinner. We each take a night a week and then the seventh is a free for all, which means we either order out or amass the leftovers to clean out the fridge.

Sometimes, we plan ahead and grocery shop together. That had been our plan when moving out here. It's only actually happened like three times. Most of the time, we shop on our way home on our night to cook. The only thing we really buy together is the bulk items that we order online—like toilet tissue and paper towels, dish soap, and laundry detergent. Things like that.

The abrupt change in the air temperature when I step inside makes me shiver. Picking up a basket, I start wandering through the aisles since I have no idea what I want to cook tonight. I'm not the best cook, so I usually grab burgers or something I can throw in the oven. I didn't have to cook growing up, so I never learned more than the basics.

After wandering for a while, I decide to try something new. Dangerous, I know. There's a chance that no one is going to eat tonight. But spaghetti doesn't appear that difficult. Pasta and sauce. I grab a large bag of frozen meatballs—the kind we all really like. And just so we're eating a well-rounded meal, I scour the freezer section for some frozen vegetables. I settle on buttered corn because I think that's one we all like.

As an afterthought, I toss a couple loaves of garlic bread into my basket before heading up to the self-checkout. Once I've paid and loaded everything into a bag, I hike it on my shoulders and turn.

LOREN

Not for the first time today, I see my neighbor from across the road. My heart immediately jumps into my throat. He's stunning, but there's something cold in his eyes. He rarely has any expression at all—just blank-faced. And when he's wearing his sunglasses, I can't help feeling like someone just walked over my grave when I look at him.

He looks in my direction when he feels me watching him and fuck, the way my insides twist. I can't tell if it's with fear or arousal. He's seriously just... breathtaking.

Honey Bee came home the other day nearly beside herself when she identified the guys across the road as *the* Van Dorens. The primary family—whatever that means. The older man is Jalon Van Doren, president of the Van Doren empire.

And with him are all six of his children—Myro, Voss, the triplets, Imry, Avory, and Ellory, and Loren.

The man I keep seeing is Loren Van Doren.

I've been telling myself it's a coincidence because what else can it be? I see him everywhere. At home makes the most sense since they moved in across the street. Which, by the way, has made our hypotheses about why six grown ass men live with their father still completely wild now that we know who they are.

Seeing him at the store all the time seems reasonable too since it's the closest to our neighborhood. Even seeing him at school isn't completely unusual; if he's a student there. It's just... serendipity. Right?

With my bag slung over my shoulder, I head outside, back into the heat. I shiver again but not from the cold air. The sudden change always makes me shiver.

The walk home is quiet. Sometimes, I glance over my shoulder out of habit. Still waiting for Jason to appear. I mean Daniel. There's a part of me that wants the case to continue to be publicized. I want to know all the details. The last I heard, they uncovered more than a dozen identities in his apartment, but more shocking than that, there were people coming forward *from other states* with even more identities he's used in the past.

One man even claimed that Daniel/Jason had been an abusive boyfriend for six months before he just vanished one day. That made me sick. As horrible as it might make me, all I could think was that could have been me. That's what Daniel/Jason wanted with me.

Nope. No. I shove it out of my mind. He's dead. Wrong or right, he's dead and I don't need to worry about him.

As my house comes into view, I glance at the Van Doren house and, as always, wonder if it's haunted. Now I wonder if Daniel/Jason is haunting someone. Hopefully, he's being tortured for eternity; though to believe in hell would mean I believe in something and I'm not sure I do.

The kitchen faces the front and side of the house. I always thought that was weird. Don't kitchen's normally face somewhere that you'd like to look? People spend a lot of time in the kitchen and who wants to stare at the street while you cook or do the dishes?

People who want to know what their neighbors are doing, I guess.

The house is quiet as I unload my wares and put them away for later. Maybe I'll research spaghetti and see how I can make it super impressive. Just for fun.

It's still early, so I head into the side yard with a glass of iced tea and take a seat with my phone while I search for recipes. It isn't long before our neighbors start to come outside. They spend a lot of time outside. In fact, since they moved in, I've noticed a lot of our neighbors spend more time outside.

LOREN

Admiring the Van Dorens probably. I mean, I guess we do that too.

I'm scrolling through the search results when Loren walks up the road with a bag in his hand. His head is turned this way, looking at my house like we do his. Maybe there are rumors that our house is haunted too.

He doesn't go inside but sits on the front deck watching his brothers. They're building something but I'm not sure what it is. I try not to imagine that Loren's looking this way. He's not. Why would he be? He's one of the hottest men I've ever seen, so I can't imagine why he's staring over here. There's nothing for him in our house.

The Van Dorens are a very interesting family. Jalon's face is everywhere. He's constantly making speeches and donating to some organization or another and attending conferences or rallies and stuff. He's a very public figure.

You'd imagine his sons would be too, but they're rarely in the news or tabloids. I'm not entirely sure how they're kept out of the public eye, but it's rather impressive that they are. There's so little known about them beyond speculation I find them even more interesting now they're so close.

What we do know is that they all work for Van Doren Technologies. We know that the oldest and youngest sons—Myro and Loren—work in contracts. Reading and interpreting contracts, advising, consulting. That kind of thing. The triplets work in the law offices. And the last son works in technology. He's also a fucking genius. There was a huge article on him in TECH STEW magazine a couple years ago. I don't read that magazine normally, but I'm like everyone else in the world—when something legit comes out about one of the Van Dorens, I take a peek.

The only other thing we know about the younger generation of Van Dorens is that the triplets are gay, and Van Doren Technologies makes very substantial donations and loudly supports all kinds of LGBTQ rights. I even went to one of the Pride Parades they sponsored in L.A. two years ago.

The side door opens and I shift to see Levis step outside. He smiles and takes a seat beside me. "Neighbor watching?" he asks.

I shrug. "Trying to determine what they're building while also scrolling for recipes."

"I saw spaghetti fixings," Levis says.

"Yep. Wondering if I can elevate it a bit. Earn some extra cooking points."

He laughs.

I find and tag a recipe, then move on to the next before my gaze drifts over my phone and I'm looking across the street again. My stomach flips when it still feels like Loren is looking at me. He wouldn't be, though. He's just looking in this direction. He's probably watching his brothers. It's not like I can see his eyes from here to know for sure.

"He's interesting," Levis comments.

I glance at him, trying to determine what he's talking about. He's watching the Van Dorens like I am. "Who?"

"Loren," he answers and my heart flutters at his name. "I ran into him the other day on campus, and we talked for a while."

"You did?"

Levis nods. For a reason I can't explain, I get a weird sense of jealousy at that. "Yep. He's been hanging around school a lot and after your stalker situation, I've been a little concerned."

"About me?"

He smiles. "You, yes. But I guess I'm just more aware of our surroundings and who's there. Part of me expects to see him often since he lives across the street, but he's not a student at Eastern State, which I suspected and he freely told me. So yeah, I was a little concerned."

"Why is he there, then?" I ask.

"He says he's been talking to enrollment, but he doesn't have any real sense of what he wants to study. So he can't justify wasting time and money on classes he's not interested in unless they're working toward something he wants to do."

I huff. "Yeah, I get that."

"I know. I told him you had the same issue. But unlike him, you keep dipping your toes into something new every semester, hoping that you'll finally find what speaks to you."

My breath catches. "You were talking to him about me?"

I'm not sure if it's my tone or my words that makes Levis look at me. I flush and can't even think of a reason I asked that question.

"Yeah. But I didn't say your name, I don't think. Though I doubt he doesn't know who you are. He knew who I was."

"But you're you and you're hot," I say. When he grins, my cheeks burn, and I scrunch my face. "Not what I meant."

"So I'm not hot," he denies.

"No, you are!" I shake my head. "Stop fishing for compliments."

Levis laughs.

"I just mean…" I don't know what I mean so I don't finish. "Never mind."

"He's interesting," Levis repeats. "I also think there's something not quite… uh… how do I say this?" He stares across the street, maybe looking at Loren as he contemplates the words he wants to say. "I don't know, exactly. There's something almost threatening about him, but I can't pinpoint why I feel that way."

I shiver and look at Loren again. Still, it feels like he's looking in this direction. "Is he watching us?" I ask.

"See? This is why I approached him the other day. I get this weird feeling that he's *intentionally* crossing paths with us. And yes, it appears he's watching us too. But I don't really have any legs to stand on since we've been staring at them since they moved in."

That's entirely true. At first it was curiosity about whether they're living in a haunted house. Then it was speculation on why five adult sons are living together with their father. Now, I'm not sure what we're using as a reason to watch our hot neighbors.

"Be careful, okay?" Levis says. "I don't feel threatened personally by Loren or any of them and I don't get the creepy vibe that Jason Daniel Theodore Patrick Whatever gave." I snort at him randomly listing names we've heard he's used. "But there's something about him that makes me a bit wary."

I shake my head. "He's never come near me," I say. "He's always kept his distance. I doubt he'll change that."

Why would he? If he were going to be interested in anyone, it's Honey Bee. The only gay Van Dorens are the triplets. That's why Jalon is active in supporting the community. He's said as much; I've heard the words out of his mouth on live television.

So there's no way that gorgeous man is actually looking at me. He's not showing up intentionally in my path *for me*. It's entirely a coincidence.

LOREN

Besides, I recently learned what it means to have someone's attention and I'm not sure I'm entirely into trying that again. I'd like to have a boyfriend. I'd give anything to have someone to love me. But getting to that point is a little terrifying when people like Daniel/Jason are the ones who are interested in me.

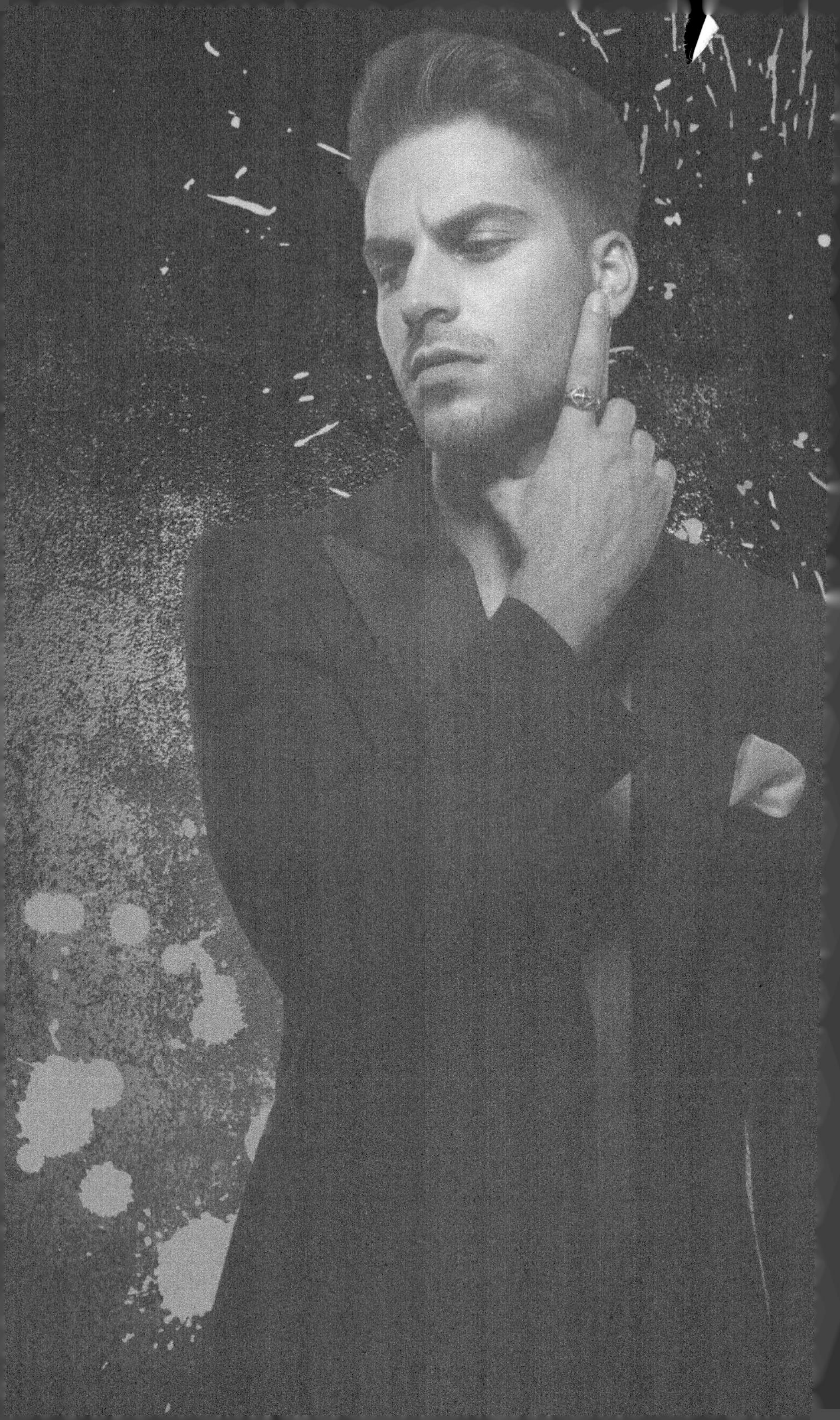

13
LOREN

We're turning up our driveway when Jessica Rivera is suddenly there. I'm not entirely sure where she came from since I didn't see her outside. She just popped up out of nowhere and she's not looking happy.

"I don't know what your game is, Van Doren, but stop following us around. We've dealt with a stalker already—don't think I won't call the police," she threatens.

I'll admit, I'm impressed with her venom.

"Hmm." Myro hums. There's a slight smirk on his face as he watches her. Amused? Fascinated like I am?

"You do realize we live here, right?" I say, gesturing blandly to the house. "And you realize that considering the places we have in common, we're likely going to cross paths, right?"

"Don't think I don't see through you," she hisses. "You can play up your innocence all you want, but I can fucking see you always showing up right *after* one of us arrives."

Okay, so she hasn't quite put it together yet. That's fortunate. I glance over her head at our house. Sure enough, I can see Dad standing in the dining room window. Imry is in the open door now, hands in pockets and leaning against the frame as he watches.

Turning my attention back to Jessica, I shrug. "You can call the police if you'd like. I'll be happy to talk to them."

I wouldn't be happy to talk to them. I don't actually have a reason for being on campus other than Oakley.

"Just stay away," she says. "Whatever you want, we're not interested."

Her dark eyes flicker up to Myro before she walks around us to cross the street. Myro and I turn to watch her stomp toward her house. I'm amused, and a little fascinated as her long hair fans out behind her. It's quite a pretty color, nearly the same tone as her eyes.

"She's got some fire," Myro notes.

Levis is outside, watching her approach the house. They exchange words, though she doesn't break her stride as she disappears inside. He stares at the door before turning his attention to us. I'm not surprised when he heads our way.

"Have you spoken to any of them before?" Myro asks.

I nod. "Him. We've spoken a few times now."

"And?"

I'm not sure what he's asking, so I shrug.

Our conversation ends as Levis approaches. His smile is amused, but I can read the wariness in his expression today. I'd put him at ease over the few times we've run into each other. Whatever she said to him has made his discomfort return.

He meets my eyes, giving me a small incline of his head in

greeting before turning to my brother. "I'm Levis," he introduces. "You are?"

Myro grins because we all know that Levis knows who he is. "Myro. Nice to meet you."

Levis nods, his gaze back on mine. "So, Loren... want to tell me why you're really hanging around?"

"You mean besides the fact that I live here?" I ask.

"Yes."

"I'm not sure I have a reason outside of that. Seems a rather silly waste of money to stay in a hotel room when I have a perfectly good bedroom right here."

My half-truths aren't quite cutting it today. Levis nods as he considers me.

"I don't really know what you want me to say. I live here. Shop at the closest store. Buy coffee at the closest café on the way to school. Explore the school and talk to the office as I determine what I want to do with my life." I shrug. "All things we've talked about."

He nods again in that vague way of his. "Are you following us?"

"No." There's no 'us' in who I'm following. However, I think my answer becomes less believable when my eyes flit to his house.

"How about you try that answer again," Levis says. His tone has gotten less friendly now.

"I'm not following you. Or your girl," I insist, shrugging. "I don't really care if you believe me. Nothing you say is going to change the fact that we're going to be in the same place often. You can find peace in that, or you can constantly look over your shoulder with suspicion. It's your choice how you want to live. One of those options is going to get exhausting."

"Indeed," Myro says.

Levis looks at him, and while Myro has his attention for the next few seconds, I study Levis. Lying to him would be easy enough. I *could* make myself a little more invisible as I stalk my man. But I'm not going to. I'm working myself up to speaking to him. If I can just find something to talk to him about.

I understand and agree when Noah tells me that talking to a guy is much like talking to a girl. Except, in my experience, I have *never* spoken socially to a girl for more than a hookup. I'm not sure I want sex from Oakley at all. And thus, I'm not sure what to talk to him about.

But I want him to be used to my presence. It's a *conscious* decision to be visible. What I need to do is maybe put a little more effort into looking like I have a purpose than I do.

"I don't believe you," he says after a minute.

I shrug.

"If I had to take a guess based on the places and times I've seen you the most, you're tailing Oakley. Why?"

It's on the tip of my tongue to ask 'which one is Oakley?' but there's no way I could pull that off. So I don't try. Instead, I glance at his house again as I consider my options. Admit it? Admit I'm fucking obsessed with this man I have never spoken to? That I'm entirely out of my element and am unsure what to do about it? What do I speak to him about, exactly? Oakley's friend would be a great person to ask.

I meet Levis' eyes again. My lips part, but there are no words. Glancing up at Myro, I hope he sees that I'm not entirely sure what I'm supposed to say here.

Myro chuckles. He gently grips my shoulder in support, but doesn't offer anything else.

Sighing, I shake my head. "I don't have a reason that isn't going to sound a bit..."

"Psychotic?"

"That's close, but you're a little off."

Levis' eyes narrow.

"Love at first sight," I say abruptly and then immediately want to take the words back. They sound better than obsessed upon first sight, but I feel like that's a little misleading. Channeling my conversation with Noah is not going to work in my favor right now.

Levis' eyes now widen a little. "Oakley?" he asks.

"Why are you surprised? He's mesmerizing." I can hear the offense in my voice at his surprise that it's Oakley I'm following. The way I bristle makes me say weird shit, though. That's not a cool thing to learn about myself right now.

He shakes his head. Then laughs. "Not—no. Sorry. Not how I meant it. Oakley's one of the best people I know. I'm not surprised exactly, just..."

"You're surprised," Myro says.

Levis laughs again. "Strange turn of events. Why didn't you just say something the other day when I confronted you?"

I frown and cross my arms. "I hate this conversation," I mutter, earning myself laughter from both of them this time, and don't offer anything else.

"Look. He was just being stalked by some creep who ended up murdered, so we're a little overprotective of each other right now, especially Oakley. You're not doing anything to hide the fact that you're following him, which I'm going to decide to appreciate, but you're also not approaching this right, either. Why haven't you talked to him?"

"About what?" I ask, a little desperately. "What the hell do I talk to a guy about?"

Levis tilts his head, and my outburst makes Myro laugh under his breath. *Again.*

This time, it's Levis who isn't quite sure what to say. I'm expecting him to say, 'the same thing you'd talk to a girl about,' so I'm relieved when he doesn't respond with that. I get it. It's essentially the same thing. But for me, it's really, truly not.

"Oakley likes flowers and origami. He'd love to get into crafts, but they're very overwhelming to him—he doesn't know where to begin. He has a small collection of rocks that he adds to when something feels significant and a rock catches his eye. Oakley is very loyal to his friends. He's shy and... soft. He loves romance, loves love. More than anything, he wants to be wanted."

I nod, listening raptly now. Finally!

"So help me, Loren, I will kill you if you hurt him."

I'm so surprised by the venom in his voice that I take a step backward and reconsider him.

"I have mastered a lot of fucking ways to kill a man," he continues, more conversationally than his threat, "and believe me when I tell you that the threat of jail time is not enough to prevent me from protecting my friends."

I grin. "I understand that."

Levis nods. It's minute and his stare remains locked with mine. Intense. "I think you do. He's not going to warm up to anyone easily, especially not now, so you have your work cut out for you. You better sweep him off his feet."

LOREN

"I'm not sure I'm good at romance," I say. "I'm…"

"Not quite psychotic," Levis fills in, his eyelids hooding. "It makes a lot of sense in hindsight."

That's apparently the end of our conversation as he turns back toward his house and walks away. I'm slightly dumbfounded. The entire discussion was a bit surprising.

"I like him," Myro says.

I frown at my brother as Levis disappears behind his front door. "He would have had me figured out on his own within the next week."

"Which part?" Myro asks, gripping my wrist and pulling me toward our house. Dad is still in the window and now all three triplets are in the door.

"All of it," I say. "I think he knows I'm diagnosed and he'll have it named correctly the next time we speak. He already suspected I was following Oakley the day we first ran into each other."

We're close enough to the triplets that they've heard this part of the conversation. They're not happy.

"That's not how you stalk," Imry says.

"I think he wanted to be caught," Myro adds.

"I think I did too. Maybe not by Jessica but I'm not upset about Levis figuring it out," I admit.

"Curious that you now have a girl aversion," Avory teases, grinning.

"I don't have a girl aversion," I say, rolling my eyes. "She's just a little… intense."

They all find that amusing. I'm not sure I agree.

"So? How's the Asian hunk?" Avory asks. "Is his voice as sexy as his abs?"

I frown and glance over my shoulder, as if looking at the house will make Levis appear again. "He was wearing a shirt," I point out. "How am I supposed to know what his abs look like?"

"How do *you* know what his abs look like?" Myro asks.

The triplets shrug. I've always been rather impressed with the level of innocence they can portray in their faces when they want to.

"Admit it—that house is filled with hot men," Ellory says. "You can't *not* see that."

"That doesn't answer how you've seen his abs," Myro says, shutting the front door behind us.

"You better not be staring into their windows," Dad chastises as we walk into the dining room. He's frowning at the triplets.

"No," Ellory says. "He practices aikido behind their house. But I think the sexiest thing he does is thrust that damn sword like he's tearing someone apart." He fans himself.

Avory nods and I'm sure they're somehow sharing a fantasy right now. I glance at Imry, wondering if he's sharing it too. But he's shaking his head at the two-thirds triplets.

"But really—is his voice super sexy?" Avory asks.

"Uh… sure," I say, glancing at Myro. I'm not sure what constitutes a sexy voice.

Myro shrugs. "The girl threatening Loren is the sexy part to me. Can't help you there."

They sigh dramatically.

"That was a long conversation," Imry points out.

"Yes, well... we're friends," I say, shrugging. "We've talked several times over the last couple weeks."

Myro grips my shoulder once more and I know he's about to rat me out.

"Our baby brother has not been stealthy in his stalking, which I think he's been doing on purpose. From what I've gleaned, Levis called him out a week ago."

"Two weeks," I correct.

"Two weeks ago, but he somehow convinced Levis that his presence was coincidental, as it would be when living under the circumstances we do—neighbors, etc. However, since Jessica also noticed, threatened Loren with the police, and then stomped away, Levis no longer believed that *all* his coincidental appearances were quite so accidental."

"And..." Imry prompts.

Myro grins. "And baby brother has made a big stride in admitting the truth to someone, including himself."

"He told Levis that he's stalking Oakley?" Avory asks, bewildered.

"Yes. Also may have said—"

"Don't," I warn. "Given my options for what I could say, I chose the less crazy explanation."

"Which was what?" Avory asks.

"You have to tell us," Ellory says.

"No," I insist.

"Let's just say that he didn't lie at all. Not even a lie that he hides well. And instead of being pissed, Levis gave him some tips on what to talk to Oakley about."

The triplets look at me with surprise. I sigh, glaring at the four of them. Fuckers. "I'm going upstairs," I announce, and leave the room without a word.

Dad's hand lands on my arm on my way by, and I pause. He smiles. A small, reassuring, encouraging smile I've seen many times in my life. Mostly all those times right after he told off my mother for trying to force me to 'be like everyone else.' Dad never wanted me to pretend to be anything other than I am.

I'm not sure exactly why I receive that smile this time, but the tension in my shoulders relaxes a little. He gives me a slight nod and releases me.

I often wonder what kind of hell life would have been like if we'd had two parents like our mother. Where would we be today? I'm confident I'd be in jail. I have an outlet for my violent tendencies. But if I didn't?

This weird situation I find myself in right now would likely look very different.

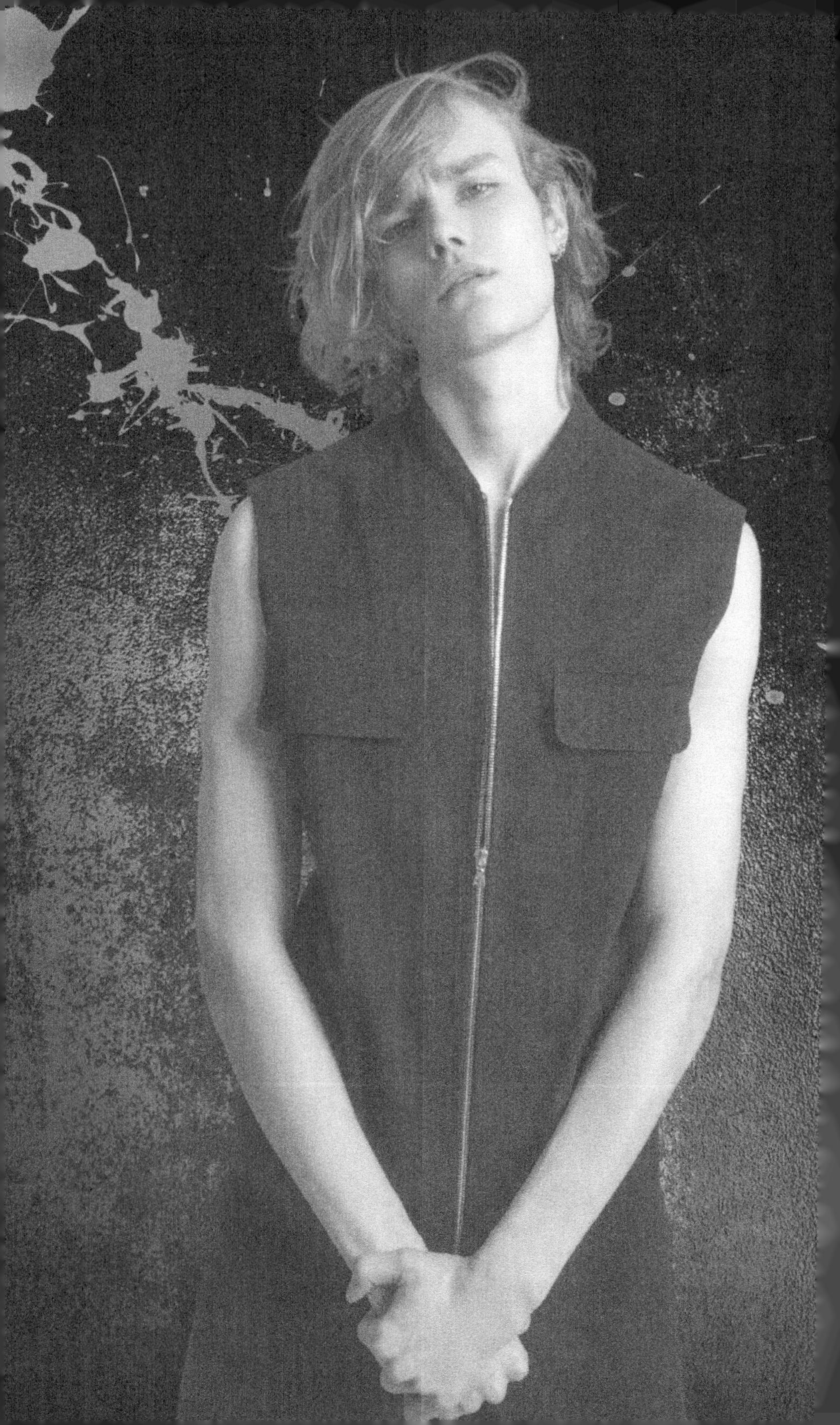

14
OAKLEY

We don't spend a lot of time watching hockey. Mostly, we watch the Carolina Blue Hawks' games because that's where Haze's brother's boyfriend coaches. It's in quiet support of his brother. I know just enough about hockey not to look like a complete idiot. But only because Haze has been forced to watch it his entire life. We would watch games when he attended in case he ever made it onto the big screen over the rink. That meant we couldn't *not* learn something about the sport.

I'm not sure I'm actually interested in hockey. I mean, they wear tight pants, so that's nice. And if you've ever seen them stretch before a game, you know that I've thought many dirty things about these men.

It is a rather impressive game. Their skill on skates is extraordinary enough alone. But they're constantly trying to fight, take each other's heads off and crush each other like pancakes against the boards—all while chasing this little black puck and getting it into a net blocked by a beast of a person in thick pads.

I don't have to be interested in hockey to find it fascinatingly violent.

On my left, Levis' attention is split between his phone and the television. I think he's just hanging out with us because he doesn't have anything going on right now. He likes hockey better when we go in person. But right now he'd much rather be talking to his girlfriend.

I try not to let it bother me. It *doesn't* bother me. I'm just jealous that I don't know how to find that. Well, not a girlfriend—no thanks—but a relationship. Someone to text with all the time. Someone who wants my attention. I want to be on the other end with a guy like Levis who is smiling at his phone as he texts me.

Instead, I attract the creeps like Daniel/Jason. What did I ever do to piss off karma? Where is the fairness in this?!

A sound like a *pop thunk* makes the three of us look toward the front window. Haze leans forward to get a clear view across the road just as Briar comes down the stairs and opens the front door to look.

"What're they doing?" Levis asks.

"I think... that's a bow and arrow," he answers.

"In the front yard?" Haze asks. "They're going to kill someone."

"No. Along the side of the house. I'm guessing they have a target I can't see," Briar says.

I scoot forward on the couch so I can look out the window too. The amount of time we spend watching the Van Dorens is probably criminal. But they're fascinating. And gorgeous. In our defense, we're not the only ones who watch them all the time.

"I'm tired of watching them from here," Briar declares as he pushes the door open wider. "I'm going to see if they're friendly."

LOREN

Haze gets up to follow him out. I'm content to remain where I'm at, but when Levis gets to his feet, he grabs my hand and pulls me along. "Time to socialize, Oak," he says.

I scowl at him. I'm awkward and weird when I try to talk to other people! It's just embarrassing.

It's Saturday, so I'm not surprised to see everyone outside. All seven Van Dorens in their various degrees of sexy as hell in different stages of undress. Goddamn. I may drool.

"Hi," Briar says a few feet ahead of us, stopping on the sidewalk outside their house. "I'm Briar." He glances behind him and gestures. "Haze, Levis, and Oakley. In case you didn't see us walk out the front door, we live across the street."

I'm decent at recognizing them at this point. Except the triplets. If any multiple births look alike, it's these three. Even their hair seems to fall just the same as the other two. I wonder if they do it on purpose.

I pay attention when Myro introduces the triplets. Ellory is wearing a black tank, Avory is wearing a white tee, and Imry isn't wearing a shirt at all. I watch them just long enough to repeat that in my head. Ellory black, Avory white, Imry skin. Okay, committed to memory. They're not allowed to ever change.

When I look up, my heart catches in my throat. Loren's sitting on the deck with their father, his eyes locked on mine. Why's he watching me? I'm suddenly self-conscious. Do I have something in my teeth? Is my hair a mess?

Actually, my hair is always a mess. That's not new. But he's so put together, maybe he hates my mess. Is my presence making him angry?

"Did I see you have a bow?" Briar asks and I turn my attention away from Loren.

"Yeah!" Imry says. "You know how to shoot?"

"Nope but I've been dying to learn for ages."

"Come here," Voss invites, offering Briar the bow in his hands. "Are you right- or left-handed?"

"Right."

Voss nods and hands him the bow. I watch as he shifts Briar with his hands on Briar's hips, tapping his feet apart with his own. Voss's explanation is quiet as he teaches Briar how to hold the bow, explaining how to stretch and aim.

They go through the motions, Voss buddy shadowing him as if he were another skin. Briar nods occasionally and asks questions. I'm a little baffled about how he can stand there with a hot guy pressed against him and concentrate. Does he feel Voss's dick?

I shift and try to slyly decide if they're pressed that close. It's hard to tell from this angle, but hell, that's all I'd be thinking about. Just slightly pressing my ass back. Maybe a little rub.

Okay, obviously I'm a little horny right now. It's been a while. Since before Daniel/Jason. Still, I can't stop the warmth in my belly as I watch how close Voss stands as he teaches Briar. And damn, Briar is stupidly unaffected.

Straight men, I swear!

The first *pop thunk* makes me jump. I'd been so engrossed about imagining chemistry between them, I'd missed the moment it went from teaching to shooting.

"Nice," Voss praises. "Try another."

This time, he's not standing behind Briar, but to his side. He shifts Briar's arms a little, still quietly coaching him, and then backs away. Briar lets it go and this time, it hits the rings. The outside rings, but still the rings.

Briar looks at us with a beaming grin.

"You're a quick student," Voss says. "Go ahead and shoot some more."

I shift beside Levis to get a closer look at the target. It's at the other end of the house and I recognize it as what they'd been building the other day.

Prickles on my neck make me realize that I'm still being watched. I glance at Loren again and sure enough, his eyes are locked on me. Is he trying to make me uncomfortable? Am I uncomfortable?

Chewing the inside of my lip, I press my arm to Levis's. He drapes his arm around my shoulders, his attention still on Briar. He's smiling, nodding along to Briar's progress. Honestly, I'm big impressed by how close he is to the center already.

"Have you shot a bow before?" Voss asks, eyes narrowed.

Briar laughs. "Not in real life. I have in video games. VR."

"I'm a little jealous that you're so good at it so quickly."

"Trust me, there's not much I'm good at this fast, so I'm going to take this win where I can."

"We've got some pizzas being delivered," Imry interjects. "I can add on a few more if you'd like to hang out a while."

Briar nods, looking in our direction. "Yeah, sounds cool."

Haze is crouched on the ground on Levis's other side, watching Briar shoot. He shrugs his agreement. Levis and I do the same.

"Anyone else want to try?" Voss asks when Briar hands him the bow and heads down to retrieve the arrows.

I most certainly do not. That's far too much distraction with a man pressed against me. Considering I'm slightly heated just watching two straight men shoot, I'm certainly not in the mood to be touched by a hot stranger right now.

Haze decides he'd like to try, though. I watch as Voss repeats the process that he performed with Briar. Haze isn't quite so good right off. He goes through the quiver of arrows twice and only hits the target twice. He spends a good ten minutes with Imry searching the tree line for the arrows that didn't even hit the target.

After lunch, Haze gives it another try, and only has to hunt missed one arrow. Maybe he was hungry.

Then Levis decides he wants to try. He hasn't shot since he was a kid, so he welcomes Voss's guidance. He's an even better shot than Briar. For the next half an hour, we watch Briar and Levis try to outdo the other.

The entire time, Loren watches me. I'm not sure he looked away at all. My stomach continues to twist and flutter. My heart races.

By the time Briar and Levis call it a draw, the Van Dorens have pulled out cornhole boards. I'm not very athletic or coordinated when it comes to physical activity. I could likely pull the bowstring, though. Then again, it's been a long time since I tried to do anything that required any kind of strength.

While they occupy themselves with cornhole, I wander to the bow and pick it up. It's not wooden, but one of those new ones with lots of physics involved as strings go over levers and whatever.

I turn when a shadow falls next to mine and my breath catches to find Loren there. Watching me. I set down the bow, unsure if I should have been touching it.

LOREN

Loren picks it up and hands it back to me. "Do you know how to shoot?" he asks.

Holy hell, his voice! I've never heard something so... like the night. Dark, quiet, hypnotic, maybe a little dangerous.

I shake my head. "I'm not sure if I can even pull the string back," I say.

"You can," he promises, nodding.

I'm not so confident, but his encouragement is enough to make me try. Even if I make a fool of myself. How embarrassing will it be if I can't?

I lift my left arm holding the bow and grip the string with my two fingers. There's immediate resistance, but it gets more difficult as I pull back. Holding it in place makes my arms shake.

I'm holding my breath as I try to control the snap back as I slacken the string. Jesus, I'm out of shape.

"Want to shoot?" he asks, and my eyes meet his.

I can't look away. I'm not sure if it's the beauty of his eyes or his voice, or maybe just the way he looks at me. Swallowing, I shake my head.

"If you're not comfortable with me teaching you, I can get Voss," Loren offers.

"Why wouldn't I be comfortable with you teaching me?" I ask.

He shrugs. "I make most people uneasy."

The way my heart clenches at those words. Loren says them as if he's only commenting on the color of the sky or the weather. Not like it bothers him. Maybe it doesn't. Or maybe he's been living with that for a very long time and has grown numb to it.

"You can teach me," I say before I realize what I'm saying. "I'm not uneasy."

Loren's head tilts to the side a little. When his lips curl just a bit, my stomach flutters for real. I bet he's breathtaking when he smiles.

I watch him, feeling slightly lightheaded, as he moves around me. He's bigger than me, which I don't think is particularly hard. I feel his heat everywhere when he steps close. His hands are gentle on my wrist as he brings up my arm, shadowing my grip with his.

My heart races, and his breath brushes over my neck, raising chills along my body. I glance down, praying to the fucking universe that I'm not obviously hard right now. I think the tight underwear I'm wearing are working for me.

"I can adjust the tension if it's too much," Loren offers, his voice low in my ear.

I shiver at the way his voice moves through my body. He steps backward, his grip on me loosening. Twisting around, I look at him over my shoulder, letting the string go slack again. My muscles cry in protest. My arm feels like a noodle.

"Do I make you uncomfortable being so close?" he asks.

I shake my head.

"Are you sure, Oakley?"

Fucking hell, the way he says my name!

"I'm sure," I say. No, let's be honest. It comes out in a whisper.

Loren steps closer, pressing a little more fully into my back. It doesn't last long, which is fortunate because I'm on the verge of groaning. My palms are sweaty when he reaches for my hands again. If I shoot an arrow, it's likely going to go through a window.

"Let your muscles learn the correct hold," he murmurs.

My muscles are trembling. Swallowing my tongue, I nod and try to concentrate on what I'm doing. Standing still. Perfectly still. Just how he has me.

His hand on the bow lets go and rests on my hip. Yep, that makes my dick jump in excitement. I risk a glance down and note that the hint of a bulge is definitely present.

"Not so stiff," he says. "If you're rigid, then the shot will be too stiff. You need to be strong but fluid. Like the bend of the bow."

"That's kind of poetic," I say quietly.

He chuckles, the sound grips my balls, and I swallow my moan. Yep, I'm far too horny for this.

Letting my arm fall, I slacken the string and set the bow down against the side of the house where I'd initially found it. "My arms are limp noodles," I say as an excuse. "I definitely don't have the muscle tone for this."

His eyes drop to my arms and then down my body. I try like hell not to shift self-consciously, well aware that my dick is truly trying to chub right now.

"Your muscle tone is perfect," he says.

My cheeks heat. "Not for a bow."

"I disagree," he insists.

I glance at the bow. Part of me wants to prove him wrong. To show him I absolutely *don't* have the strength. Stupid self-deprecation has me picking up the bow and an arrow and returning to where I'd been standing.

Loren stands at my back. Without words, he guides me, but his hands fall away once he's sure I'm in the right position. I don't take long to aim because my arms are already shaking. Taking a breath and letting it out slowly, I stare at the target along the shaft of the arrow.

When my breath fully releases, I let the arrow go.

Thunk.

Lowering the bow, I stare. It's dead center. Not possible. I look at the bow as if it betrayed me. That's just not possible. It's not!

Looking at Loren over my shoulder, I nearly swoon. He's smiling at me. Smug. Magnificent. I was right—a smile makes him breathtaking. He's definitely taken my breath from my lungs and I can't inhale for the life of me.

I'm not even sure I want to.

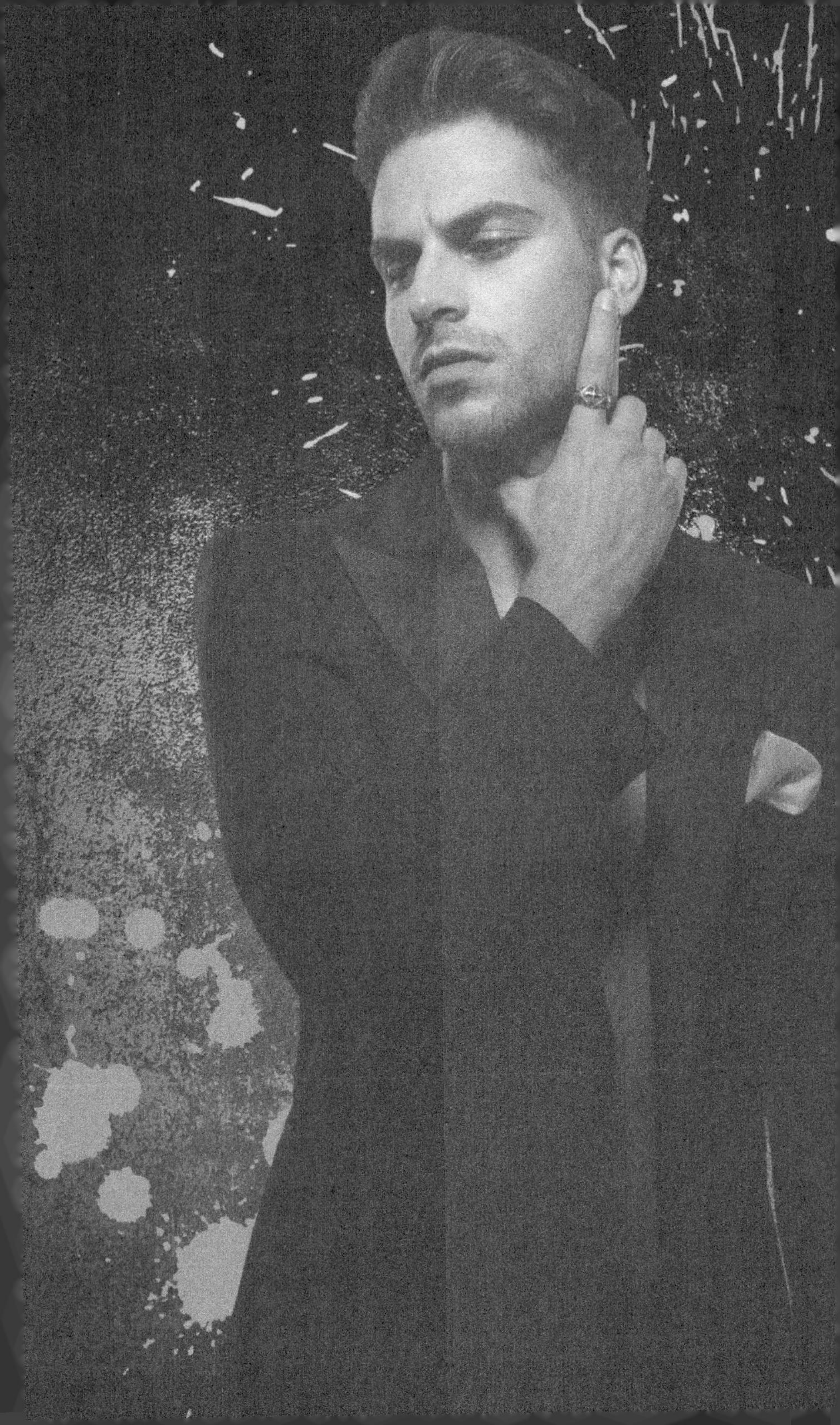

15
LOREN

THE DIFFERENCE between right and wrong isn't taught in school. Yet, we *are* taught throughout our lives that we always want to be in the right. Whether that's in our actions, intent, or verbally. Sometimes that lesson backfires and people use being right as a means to gloat. A competition instead of something wholesome.

Experts in antisocial disorders say that sociopaths will often defend their wrongdoing at the expense of others. I'm sure that it's common, but I don't find it necessary. What I find truly interesting is that psychopathy is said to be a genetic disease, while sociopathy is mostly an environmental affliction. The irony is that I have a very healthy and strong relationship with my family.

Except my mother. Can one person create a sociopath? I've always wanted to ask someone.

For me, the line between right and wrong isn't always clear cut. It's gray. To me, something that is wrong to another person is clearly defined as right. There are only certain circumstances when I know the world thinks what I'm doing is wrong and I actually understand their reasoning.

For instance, breaking into Oakley's house again? Yes, I know that's not something I should be doing. Yet, I easily unlock the back sliding door and let myself in after they've all left this morning. I only have an hour, but this time, my mission is specific.

Once Levis gave me some tips on Oakley and after having him in my yard while our households played together, I'm ready to come undone with frustration. Until I actually had my hands on him, my skin on his, this has all been rather... two dimensional. My goal has been to make him mine, though I never understood what that meant.

Touching him added a very different element I hadn't been expecting. Feeling his heartbeat, hearing his breaths, the tremble of his arms, his ass pressing back against me as I guided him in holding a bow... it was all very surprising. Up to that point, I was confident that this had no physical element to it at all.

I can admit when I'm wrong.

After assuring myself that there's no one inside, I move to the front of the house where the stairs are. This is the only part I take my time on, just to make absolutely certain there aren't any creaks or squeaks on the path to the stairs. I check the floors all around each outside exit and then each and every stair all the way to the second landing.

I'm thankful that the owners kept this house well maintained. Once again, I take careful note of exactly how far open Oakley's door is before creeping inside. I leave the door open as it had been so I can hear the rest of the house. I have an hour at best. In reality, I should get out in forty minutes.

The room hasn't changed since I was last here. Beginning at the bed, I run my fingers over the blankets. They're soft. There's a lot of them. I wonder if he sleeps under them all or on top. The pillows are mostly covered in solid color cases except one that's

LOREN

in a Care Bear case. There's a radish pillow and a carrot. Some weird rounded stuffed animal with oddly small wings and horns. And a square pillow reads 'never let anyone dull your sparkle.'

Beside the bed is a nightstand, with one drawer on top and a door on the bottom. I slide open the drawer and peek inside. There's a few hair ties, three bottles of lube. I pick one up that reads 'slick as silk.' Another in the drawer says 'glide.' There's also a new box of condoms.

There's a pad of paper and a pencil, two remotes—though I'm not sure what they're for since I don't see a television anywhere. Cough drops, tissues, hand sanitizer, ibuprofen, and an e-reader.

Picking up the e-reader, I shift it in the light to see where his fingerprints have been most frequent. When I don't see any, I wager a guess that it's not passcode protected. Turning it on, I smile because it's not. I spend a few minutes scrolling through the books he has, taking notes so I can download a couple to read. It's helpful that there's a little banner over the ones he's finished.

Putting it back where I found it, I close the drawer and crouch down to open the door next. I'm greeted by a large silicone dick standing up. There's a towel covering the bottom of the shelf and other toys are lined up like soldiers. I grin as I examine the contents of the cabinet. He doesn't have a huge collection, but there are a handful of different options. I'm guessing this one in the front might be a favorite, since it's easily accessible.

Closing the door, I stand again and move to his dresser. In the top drawer is what you'd expect to find. Socks and underwear. Since nothing is folded, I pull out various pieces. There's a little bit of everything. Boxer briefs, briefs, jocks, some short shorts that look like his ass cheeks might hang out.

As I'm pulling them out, I wonder what he's wearing right now. Which of these sexy little things does Oakley have on? When I pull out a thong, I raise my eyebrow. I didn't know they made these for men. It's clearly for a man though, since there's extra fabric in the front for dick bulge.

Curious. Is it inappropriate to ask what kind of underwear he's wearing right now? Probably.

Putting everything back as close as possible to how it was when I opened the drawer, I go through the next three and find the usual suspects—tee-shirts, shorts, pants of various materials, a few long-sleeved shirts. In the closet, I find hoodies. There's a single suit and a helmet. I frown at the helmet, unsure what he uses it for. In all of my stalking, I haven't seen a motorcycle.

The desk has things a desk would, notebooks, paper, writing utensils. There's a tablet sitting on top. This one I find passcode protected. It only takes me two tries to guess the code and let myself in. There are a few games on here and the student portal app—which I open, pleased to find that he has the username and password remembered.

There are also a few streaming apps that I poke through. I'm not sure which of these programs he watches since they're logged in under his friends' names. My guess would be that they all share the logins.

I spend some time looking through his pictures. Most of them are old, likely downloaded from social media as they've been posted by friends and family. I'm not surprised to find a bunch of him as a kid with his friends.

I go through his browsing history and then his email before shutting it all down again and replacing it where I found it.

Stepping into his bathroom and flicking on the light, I find his dirty laundry has recently been emptied. There's only one pair of shorts in the bottom of the basket. A damp towel hangs over the shower curtain rod. Within the shower, I take his body wash and inhale. A shiver of appreciation moves through me as I replace it.

Opening the drawers in the vanity, I find one filled with nothing but hair ties. I grin as I pick one up to examine it. It's brown and tan, three braided strands attached with beads.

The door downstairs closing makes me snap my head up and look into Oakley's bedroom. Shutting the drawer in the vanity, I quickly turn off the light in the bathroom and plunge myself into darkness as I listen.

It's easy to recognize their voices at this point. I've spent enough time with Levis to know his easily. They've been hanging out in our yard recently too, which I appreciate because it gets me closer to Oakley, even if I still haven't managed to have a real conversation yet.

That's why I'm here right now. Well, that's what I'm telling myself. I need to get more comfortable. I need to familiarize myself with him. Learn everything I can learn before actually talking to him.

This shouldn't be so hard!

Jessica's voice is obviously the easiest to identify, and I'm confident that the second voice is Briar's. Their voices get closer.

"Yep, I'm heading out in ten. Rutger is meeting me at the field," Jessica says.

Briar snorts. "I'm still unimpressed with that name."

"You're named after a plant," she counters. "A thorny patch!"

He laughs.

Their doors close, one and then the other. I remain where I am for just a second longer before moving back into Oakley's room. Quiet.

Assured that they're going to be in their rooms for a few minutes since they shut their doors, I head into the hall and down the stairs. I'm not sure who this builder is, but they need an award for building such a solid structure that there isn't any noise.

I make it outside easily enough, shutting the sliding door behind me. The key to moving around in the daylight in places you're not supposed to be is acting like you are supposed to be there. No creeping around or slinking in the bushes. I walk from the back door to the side of the house, keeping out of sight of both of their windows while also keeping my gait casual.

Instead of going home, I head down the street toward the café. My fingers continue to twist around the hair tie I still have in my hand, making me smile. There's a single strand of hair on it, but I don't pull it off. Nope. I slide the elastic onto my wrist and wear it like a bracelet, including his DNA in the hair strand.

I'm aware I've crossed a line. I just don't care. There aren't any excuses that I could offer. I want to know Oakley and I'm not quite confident enough to speak to him yet. I'll get there. Soon.

But first, I need to find a way to observe him without others around. I don't want questions. Or for people to get bothered or uncomfortable with my staring. I'm not entirely sure how to make this happen, though.

EXCEPT I KNOW exactly how to make it happen. I'm watching through my bedroom window as, one by one, their lights go off. The last one is out just before one in the morning, but I give it another hour, watching for movement.

Then I sneak back over. The air is cool as I cross the street. Keeping close to the house, I make my way around out back. They don't have motion lights; their lights stay on all the time. It would probably be safer for them if they were motion-activated. Hell, it would be safer for them if they used their damn alarm.

Letting myself in for the second time today, I listen for movement. Levis sleeps on the first floor close to the front door and the stairs. He's honestly the biggest threat in the house. Still, I take my chances.

There are dim lights all over the place. Little night lights in outlets, dully illuminating the walking path. I'm careful not to make a sound as I creep my way through the first floor and then up the stairs.

I should have checked whether Oakley's door squeaked. I feel like I would have noticed that the two times I've moved his door. All the bedroom doors on the second floor are closed. What if Oakley locks his door at night? Do people do that? I haven't in the past. I'm not sure my brothers have either. Not even Avory and Ellory and sometimes, they really should!

With my hand on the knob, I slowly turn it, waiting for it to give. There's noise from behind the door. A fan? I didn't see a fan. The slightest click I feel more than hear lets me know the door is unlatched. Glancing behind me to assure no one else is disturbed, I push the door open just enough for me to slip inside.

Silence. Except for the fan sound, which I quickly realize is coming from his phone. He likes white noise to sleep. That's good information to know.

Shutting the door, I move close to his bed, keeping myself from the moonlight reaching through his drawn curtains.

Oakley's cast in darkness. His hair curls at the ends, messy around his head. He looks so soft and peaceful. Tucked within the enormous amount of blankets, he's under a couple with a foot hanging out and the blankets drawn up to his chin.

It's impossible to determine whether he wears clothes to bed or if he's naked. I'm slightly surprised when my cock decides we like the idea of him being naked under the blankets.

I stand over him for several minutes, just watching. Admiring. Committing everything about him to memory. He's perfect. I've never seen someone so pure. So sweet. Beautiful.

Sitting in his chair, I continue to stare at him as the night wears on, thinking about my conversation with Noah about him. My conversation with Levis about him. Putting everything I've observed and collected into neat little rows as a picture of Oakley forms in my mind.

It's time to talk to him.

Okay, not right now. Even I know that it wouldn't end well if I wake him up now to talk to him. But soon. I think I might be ready.

I need to make sure he knows he's mine, but I'm not going to get to that point unless I actually speak to him. Infuriating, I know. There should be simpler ways than this.

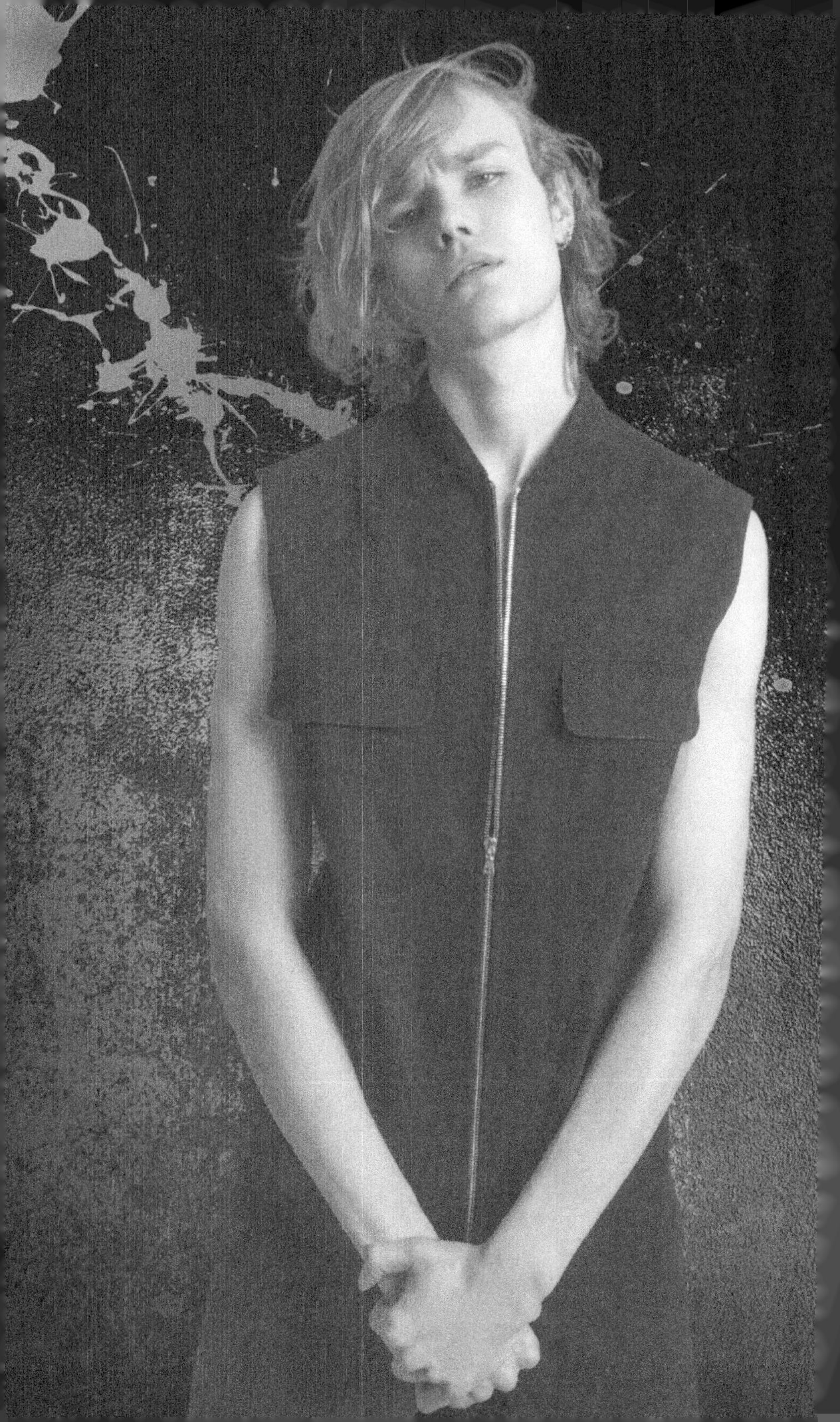

16

OAKLEY

I've been dreaming about Loren for the past six nights. The feel of his hands over mine. How his hot breath brushed over my skin. The exact tenor of his voice close to my ear. His body heat seeping into me as he stood close.

And his smile. Goddamn, that smile. I've never seen someone so transformed when they smile. He's gorgeous without it; but man, when he smiles, it's just so damn radiant. Breathtaking. I seriously forget how to breathe.

Since the first time hanging out with the Van Dorens, we've been there several times. Honey Bee was a little skeptical and hesitant at first. She wouldn't say why, but after some time, she seemed to have warmed up.

More specifically, she seems to have warmed up to Myro. I've never seen someone flirt so smoothly! It's almost mesmerizing. Honey Bee truly tried to remain indifferent, but I think we all could see her restraints crumbling as she falls for him a little more every time we're together.

Meanwhile, Loren is... distant. He watches me as if he can't look away. When I separate myself from everyone, he'll make his way to me. Our exchanges are quiet and brief. I swear, I think we're both shy. I'm not sure *why* he stares, so I'm not entirely sure how to handle the situation.

Around me, everyone in the room seems to surge to their feet as a single unit. I look around, slightly perplexed. When did I even get to school?! This is becoming a problem. I've now missed whatever's happened in this class twice this week because I can't stop thinking about Loren. Which is ridiculous. We've barely said anything to each other. I can't keep obsessing about this infatuation.

As I follow my classmates out, I log into my student portal to see what I missed this period and make note to spend extra time studying tonight. Thankfully, all the professors are really good about having their lectures uploaded. Not the entire lecture, like we don't get their verbal transcript, but we have their digital presentations. That's something.

Sighing, I stuff my phone into my pocket just as I step outside and practically collide with Loren. My breath catches as I stare. His smile is small. That super sexy hint of a smile.

"Loren!" I say, breathless.

His smile ticks up a little. "Can I take you to lunch?" he asks.

Holy fuck. He's here. To see me! I nod, unable to find words. I think I've swallowed my tongue.

Loren gestures to the walkway and I finally step out of the path of the door where people are trying to move around me.

"I, uh… have class in forty minutes," I say.

He nods. "We can eat at the café in the student center," he offers.

"Okay."

A beat passes. "What is your class about?"

"The one I just left?" I ask lamely.

Loren nods, his gaze flickering to mine.

"That class is about ancient cultures. It's really fascinating most of the time."

"What did you learn today?" Loren asks.

I flush and duck my head. "Honestly, I don't know. I've been sidetracked."

The way he smiles, I swear he knows I lost the entire fifty-five minutes because I was thinking about him and his hand on my hip!

"What about ancient cultures do you like?"

"Everything. In some ways, they were far more advanced than we are. Maybe not in technology, but in the way they treat people. I also find it amusing that we think society today is extraordinarily violent when, in reality, *every* culture is violent. We discover thousand-year-old murders and sacrificial burials all the time. Every era is riddled with war. Violence isn't new. It's part of human nature."

Loren tilts his head and I think I've just spewed far too much. Before I can quickly put my foot in my mouth further, Loren says, "I've never thought about it that way. Given what we know about the cultures before modern day, I can definitely see that pattern."

Excited, I continue, "And it makes complete sense about why we evolved this way. We aren't a world of brand-new cultures randomly popping up. We build on those that came before us! Taking what we're familiar with and adding to it the parts that we feel are better. Take Paganism and Christianity, for example. In an effort to not only wipe out Paganism—but also as a means to more easily convert Pagans—Christians built their churches and temples and places of worship on holy Pagan sites. They absorbed Pagan traditions and holidays like Yule into Christmas, Ostara into Easter, Samhain into... well, I suppose Halloween isn't really a Christian holiday."

Loren's watching me with a smile. That same sexy one that makes my insides flutter.

"Yes. All true."

I take a breath, trying to let it go so I don't get too wild over this.

"Sounds like you enjoy that class," Loren says.

"I do. I love learning about the past. Especially the ancient past. I'm not sure humans ever truly learn from their mistakes since we're always just repeating ourselves—wars over religion, wars over territory, wars over politics." I shake my head. "But it's fascinating all the same."

We arrive at the café and we order. We're quiet as we wait for our food. Loren takes the tray when it's offered, and I follow him outside, where we sit at a small table. He hands me my paper bowl of loaded fries and takes his sandwich.

"What's your next class?" he asks.

I laugh. "Astronomy."

Loren pauses in bringing his sandwich to his mouth. "Yeah?"

Nodding, I pop a fry into mine. "Yep. It's actually going toward my math and science requirement and should boost my GPA because of all the physics involved, so it's cool. If I'd have been able to take this course instead of basic physics, I'd have had a much better grade."

"I'm not seeing the connection between ancient cultures and astronomy," Loren says.

I shake my head. "There isn't one. Unless we're talking about ancient astronomers. I'm also taking Invented Languages, which explores languages made by writers for popular shows and books. And Digital Mapping."

Loren watches me with amusement. "How do they fit together?"

Grinning, I shrug. "Like I said, they don't. The thing is, I don't know what I want to do with my life. I have all my core courses finished and now I'm just exploring whatever I can find, hoping that something will finally just feel right. I want to be excited about work but... I just haven't found *it* yet."

Loren hums as he chews. He's still watching me. Always watching me. But I don't mind. His eyes are so pretty.

"I have a medical biology degree," he says. "But it's kind of useless. The degree is designed as a stepping stone to a graduate degree in medicine—any part of medicine. Not just a doctor, but a pharmacist, physical therapy." He waves his hand. "I never had any interest in a career in medicine, but I'm fascinated by the human body and how it works, thus a useless degree."

"I've read that you work for your dad in contracts," I say.

Loren pauses with his sandwich raised. A smile curls his lips. "Did you look me up?"

My cheeks burn. "Yes. When we figured out who moved in across the road, we looked you up."

He's definitely pleased with this, even as I want to crawl under the table. He chews his bite and nods. "Yes," he confirms after he swallows. "I read contracts quite thoroughly and make sure they're executed as detailed and that the payment agreement, whatever it may be, is issued. It's not steady work. Sometimes it takes me hours to complete and other times weeks, depending on the nature of the contract."

"So... why are you here?" I ask.

"To eat lunch with you," he answers.

My stomach flutters. "Okay, but why are you usually here? I see you around a lot."

Loren nods and sits back in his chair. "Did you know there are thirty-eight miles of trails on campus?"

I shake my head. "I didn't know that."

He nods again. "I'm bored when I don't have a contract, so I wander around a lot. The trails here are beautiful." He pauses, studying me for a minute. "You're here."

The way he makes me catch my breath! I flush, bowing my head to try to hide my smile.

"I've been thinking about enrolling in classes but, like you, I don't know what I want to do. I have a degree that I don't use. Do I really need another one? Seems like a waste of time and money for me when I'll just be passing the time in class."

"I know that feeling. My grandmother pays for any of my tuition not covered by scholarships and grants. She doesn't mind. I only have one brother and he's already in his career—happily, so that's goals right there. I keep offering to drop out until I figure out my life, but she insists that as long as I'm furthering my education and enjoying myself, then I should stay. But yeah, I feel like I'm wasting time and money."

Loren shakes his head. "Your grandmother is right. You're furthering your education, and you clearly love your classes. Which means it's not a waste of either."

"Yeah. I don't argue much because I know once I leave college and get a job, I'll never end up going back. Most people don't, even when they say they will. My biggest fear is getting a job I hate but being stuck in it."

"Maybe you don't want to work at all," he says, grinning.

I love his smile. Every time I see it, everything inside me turns to fire. "And do what with my life?"

He shrugs. "You could be a kept man."

I laugh, shaking my head. "Ha! I don't know if I'd even enjoy that. I'd probably get bored. Besides, who would want to support someone completely?"

"You could get a hobby. A dozen hobbies—crafts and hiking and taking pictures," he says, and I find myself smiling. I could totally see that. "With the right person, I'd definitely support them without complaint."

It's difficult trying to convince myself that there's no hint in his words. Is it because I want there to be? It's not like we know each other well. This is the very first time we've had any real conversation.

I'm lonely. I want to be wanted. But that's gotten me into trouble very recently.

Brushing my hair back, I eat my fries for a few more minutes. They're basically cold and soggy now, since I've spent so much time focusing on Loren. It's hard not to. He's just... dreamy. And he wants my attention.

"If being a kept man is my calling in life, I really am wasting my time and Grandmother's money," I tease.

Loren shakes his head. "No. For the same reasons as before. Some people would love to be a professional student. Maybe *that's* your destiny."

"Then I'm going to need a sugar daddy," I say, laughing.

"I'm sure that can be arranged," he practically purrs. I shiver at his tone. It's not suggestive, is it?

My watch vibrates on my wrist, and I look down. A notification reminds me I have class in ten minutes. Which sucks because I'd much rather stay here.

"I have to get to class," I say.

Loren takes my fries, his wrapper, and the tray to return it inside. He comes back and falls into step beside me. "Do you have a class after the next one?"

"No. This is the last today."

"Can I see you after class?"

My heart jumps and I'm pretty sure I'm going to choke on it. It takes me a few seconds just to get myself under control. The most I manage is a nod and a squeaky 'yes.' He smiles, pleased, and I find my way into the classroom.

I manage to pay attention a bit, but only because I'm fascinated with space. My heart is racing by the time class is over. Part of me thinks Loren will have forgotten me. That he'll have found something better to do. Or maybe I just imagined the entire thing.

But when I step outside, he's right there. Hands in his pockets, waiting. As soon as my eyes meet his, he smiles. Small, sexy, swoony. My insides turn to jelly as I approach on wobbly legs.

"Want to take a walk?" Loren asks.

I nod.

"Is your bag heavy? I can carry it for you."

It's really hard not to smile as I shake my head. "It's not heavy. Just my tablet and a notebook inside."

Loren nods. For a minute, we're quiet as we move around students rushing to class or sports or something. When he leads me down a trail I'd have never seen before, the noise surrounding us instantly falls a few decibels. It's peaceful. And soon, it's beautiful too.

The path is paved and surrounded by foliage. There are birds singing and the trickle of water somewhere nearby.

"I didn't know this was here," I say.

"There are signs, but if you aren't looking for them, I don't think you'd notice them. All the trails could be defined better," Loren says.

We spend hours walking the trails. At some point, Loren takes my backpack, but I'm only barely aware of it. It's almost dark by the time we head home and he walks me to my door. I feel like I'm floating.

"Can I have your number?" Loren asks.

I nod and there's a charged moment when we enter our numbers into the other's phone. With them pocketed again, Loren hands me my backpack.

"I'll see you tomorrow," he says. It's not a question. There's no room for miscommunication in that.

Biting my lip, I nod again. I should tell him I had a good night. A great time with him all day. I can't wait to see him again. To talk to him more. But I think if I open my mouth, I may vomit.

Our eyes remain locked as the minute stretches. Then he leans in and presses his mouth to the corner of mine. "Good night, Oakley," he whispers.

"Goodnight."

Just so I don't pass out from forgetting how to breathe, I push open the front door and step inside. Everyone is there and they all turn to look at me expectantly. While I try to wipe the smile from my face, it's fucking impossible. I'm grinning like a lunatic.

"Good night?" Levis asks at the same time Honey Bee says, "Where have you been?"

I shake my head. Saying the words out loud feels like a jinx. I'm not ready for what's barely begun to end, so I don't put it into the universe.

"The best night," I admit. "The best day!"

"You look happy," Briar says. "You meet someone without a boat filled with red flags?"

"I think everyone has *some* red flags but yeah, not like Daniel/Jason." Probably. How do I know when all I can think about is the way he makes me feel?

But the biggest difference is he wasn't constantly distracting me with compliments. After spending hours with Loren, I can honestly say that it's like a night and day experience. Daniel/Jason was manipulative from the moment we met. It's easy to look back now and know that everything he said was calculated.

I'm pretty sure Loren was genuine today. I guess I don't know that for sure, but I feel different. I feel happy.

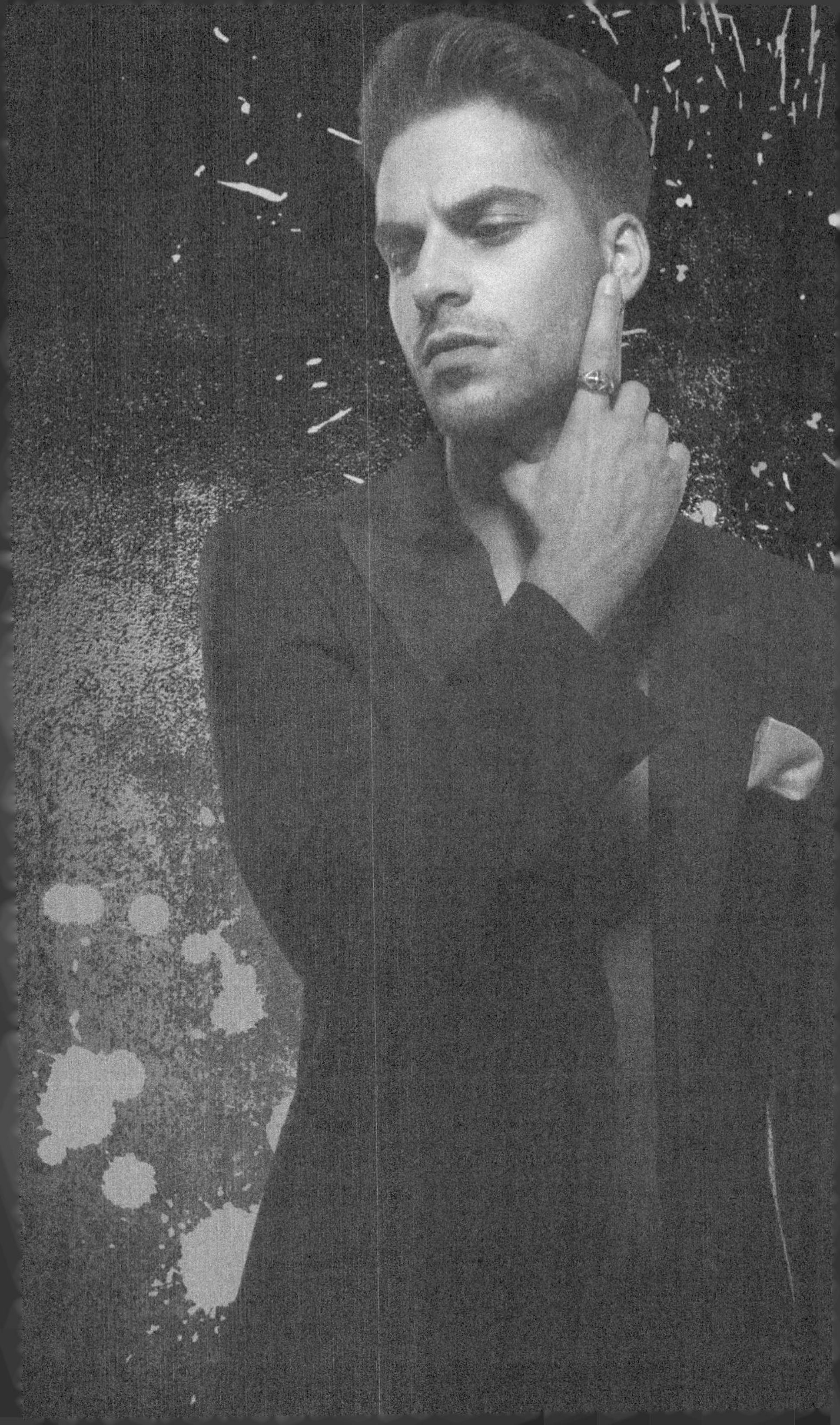

17
LOREN

I'VE SPENT QUITE a bit of time with Oakley over the last few days. I enjoy his voice and the way he blushes. When we hang out in the larger group, he's quiet. Almost meek. But when we're alone, he's vibrant and passionate about so many things.

Levis is right. He loves sweet things and romantic gestures. However, I'm in way over my head when it comes to thinking of them. I only know that he does because of some of the conversations we've had.

I'm wandering around my room contemplating what to do that might be romantic when I remember my conversation with Noah about love languages. Pulling out my phone, I dial his number and then look at the time. I probably should do those things in reverse.

"Hey!" Noah greets. "What's up, Loren?"

"Love languages," I say. "Also, hello. Are you well?"

He laughs. "Yeah, I'm good. What about love languages?"

"How do I tell what someone's is? Is romance a love language?"

He hums. "Kind of. I think it's the acts of service in romance. Letting them know you're thinking of them with little gestures. You know?"

"I don't. I need help. Oakley likes romance. I don't know how to do that."

"I take it you've finally talked to him?"

I try not to smile. Honestly, I do. But I feel like I smile a lot lately. "Yes. Often. We go on long walks and talk."

"That's romantic," he says.

"It is?"

Noah laughs. "Yes. So, some common romantic gestures are small, thoughtful gifts. Emphasis on thoughtful. Like, what's something Oakley likes?"

"Rocks," I answer. "He likes space and flowers and ancient history. Books, movies. Pretty landscapes. Compliments but not like… thrown in your face."

"You've listed a whole lot of things that you can do right there, Loren. Give him a flower."

"What kind of flower?"

I can hear Noah's smile when he answers. "Does he have a favorite? Different flowers have meaning. Some colors of flowers have their own meanings too."

This sounds awfully complicated.

"What are other romantic things?"

"You're overthinking, Loren. I have an idea. I think you've probably figured out by now the kinds of things that will make him smile, right?"

"Yes." I love his smile.

"Use that as a starting point. What can you do that will make him smile? Don't go overboard. True romance isn't a trip to Paris. It's the intent behind it. As cliché as it sounds, it's the thought that counts."

"Okay, fine. Romance is putting a smile on Oakley's face."

"Exactly," Noah says.

"Good. I can try that. How's hockey?"

"L.A. has had better years," he admits, laughing.

"But the team is good to you?"

"Yeah, Loren. They're good to me. I've made some new friends and they're really great."

"And Elixon? He's still treating you well?"

"Very much. I promise, everything in my life is perfect right now, Loren. The newest development with Oakley aside, you're doing well?"

"Yes," I answer. I try to think of anything at all to tell him that might be interesting and not along the lines of killing people, but I seem to have consumed most of my life with Oakley right now. "I have nothing going on, I guess. Just Oakley."

"That's cool, Loren. Want to tell me about him?"

"Um…" What do I say? I love the way he sleeps. Yes, I still sneak in at night because I love to watch him sleep. To know that it's peaceful and he's unbothered by bad dreams. Sometimes he smiles in his sleep, and I imagine that he's dreaming about me.

No. That's probably not how I should begin a conversation.

"Oakley is very enthusiastic about his studies," I say and smile as I think about walking him to school this morning and he recapped what he learned yesterday about the ancient Kush people. "He has so many passions that I think he has a difficult time settling on one. He thinks he's just not interested enough in anything, but I think his true challenge is finding something that he's *more* passionate about than everything else."

"What else?"

"He's very loyal." Noah and I have talked about loyalty in the past, so I know he knows what it means to me. "He's had the same group of friends since he was nine. They live together now and go to school together. They've recently started hanging around with my family and it's very different from my relationship with my brothers, but you can see their bonds. How loyal they are to each other."

"Perfect. What else?"

"He has really long hair. Well, not as long as Jessica's, but it's grown just past his shoulders so the ends curl. He tries to keep it tied back, but the sides fall out right away. He always looks so windswept, but I think it's just his energy. It's bound up tight, kept quiet, until he's comfortable to talk. His passion is like his hair—wild and untamed and beautiful."

"That's really sweet."

"Is it?"

"Yeah. I think you have romance in you, but maybe you don't know how to identify it."

I think about this as I look out my window. Oakley's home. I walked him home an hour ago.

"I might want to kiss him," I admit.

"Might?"

Sighing, I admit, "I'm not sure I'm good at romantic kissing."

Noah chuckles. "You're cute, Loren. You know that?"

LOREN

"I'm glad you think so. You going to help me or tease me?"

"I'm not sure how you want me to help you. That kind of experimentation is usually had in college. If you'd asked me to help you learn how to romantic kiss then, I might have."

"Why can't you teach me now?"

"I'm not kissing you now, Loren," he says, laughing.

"Ah. This is a practical application."

He cackles further. "Yes. I'm not sure I can even tell you what to do."

"I've kissed him but, like… just barely touching his lips. More on his cheek. I've done that a few times."

"He's receptive, I'm assuming."

"Yes?" I think about it for a minute. "Yes," I say more firmly. "He smiles and blushes when I do; so, yeah. I'm at least 95% sure he's receptive."

"You could take out the guesswork and just ask," Noah says.

"That doesn't sound romantic at all," I retort.

"Okay, how about this: lips to lips. Not a lot of pressure. Read his body language. If he's stiff and doesn't loosen up, he's probably uncomfortable and you should stop. If he kind of leans into you, wraps his arms around you, that kind of thing—he's into it and you can keep kissing."

"No tongue."

Noah finds this highly amusing. I can hear his laughter when he answers. "Read the situation, Loren."

I huff in frustration.

"Does this mean you've overcome your touch aversion?" Noah asks.

My head tilts to the side and I find myself looking out the window again. "No. I haven't really touched him. The desire to is there, though."

"This might be awkward, but I think it's important for this conversation. Do you desire to touch him romantically or sexually?"

I frown. "Maybe both."

"You're filled with maybes."

"This is all very new for me. I've never wanted to be around someone this long, never mind talking to them. Or touch them. Sex has always been transactional and I'm definitely not interested in anything transactional with Oakley. However, I do want to have sex with him, which presents a lot of new challenges I'm not sure I'm ready for."

Noah chuckles. "Not that I have much experience here, but it's not that different in principle. There's a hole. You stick it in. But I'm going to preface that with a warning that you need to prep, regardless of whose hole is taking what."

I'm not entirely sure how I feel about this, and talking about it makes me a little jittery.

"Yeah, thanks. Back to kissing. We can come back to sex talk another time." Noah laughs. "So no tongue. That equates to romance."

"I mean, you can kiss with your tongue romantically. Loren, sweetheart, honey, have you thought about letting him guide the situation?"

"He recently had a stalker," I say. "It's made him a little... cautious. I'm not good at reading people on a normal day, even when I try, so this is quite a bit out of my comfort zone. I've never wanted to read someone so fucking bad."

"Back up. He had a stalker?"

"Yes, Daniel."

"Ah, right. Proceed."

"That's it, though. Levis said it made him very uneasy and distrusting and he was already shy and introverted, so there's a good chance that he's just going to wait on me. So I need to know what to do."

"I'm going to guess that these random names you're throwing out here are his friends?"

"Yes, sorry. His friends I mentioned. Did I mention them?"

He laughs again. "You did."

"Think I can buy out your contract this year so you can be here to coach me?" I ask. Only slightly teasing.

Noah cackles. "Yeah, I'm not doing that, but I'm flattered you think I have that much to teach you. I promise you, you're overthinking this. It sounds to me like he likes you, Loren. I know this is going to be difficult, but you need to read the situation in the moment and act based on how you're both feeling. Okay?"

"Killing people is easier than this," I mutter under my breath and stare out the window again. The sun has set, so the street is lit with lamps, creating little umbrellas of light.

"I'm going to pretend that you said something entirely different from what I think I just heard."

"I didn't say anything, so that's a good idea," I say.

He huffs. "Sleep on it. I swear to you, it's not as hard as it feels right now."

Sighing heavily, I agree and let him go. It's not nearly late enough to break into their house and watch Oakley sleep, so I sit in the window and watch the lights. It takes a very long time for them to finally turn down.

It's earlier than normal and I'll probably have to walk around for a while before I slip into their house if I don't want to catch anyone awake, but I head downstairs and stop in my tracks. Dad's sitting in the chair in the hall, his hands steepled as he looks at me.

Expectantly.

I'm not sure what to say. It's not like I can pretend I'm not sneaking out right now. Actually, I'm *not* sneaking. I planned to just walk out the front door.

Yet, I stay rooted where I am on the second to last step.

"Where are you going, Loren?" Dad asks.

To be clear, I don't lie to my family often. Certainly not about important things. I'm not sure I've ever lied to Dad. Even though it's on the tip of my tongue to claim I'm going for a walk, the lie is too heavy, so I drop onto the step with a flourish and scowl.

"To watch Oakley sleep."

"Is that really how you want your relationship with him to end?"

Everything inside me bristles. "No. It's not ending."

"You think he's going to wake up with a wide smile to see you sitting in the shadows of his room in the dead of night? When he screams and his friends rush in, you think they're going to let it go?" Dad asks.

LOREN

It's not like I haven't thought about this. Honestly, if Oakley wasn't such a heavy sleeper, I wouldn't have gotten away with this at all.

"No," I admit.

He nods. We're silently watching each other for a long time. Eventually, Dad stands. "There's an appropriate way to proceed and a very inappropriate path to follow, son. Choose the right one, Loren."

His hand lands on my shoulder as he climbs the stairs beside me.

I want to point out that right and wrong mean different things to me, except his warning is now ringing loudly in my ears. I've made progress with Oakley. While this is all very new to me and I'm not entirely sure exactly what I'm feeling, I *don't* want it to end.

Getting to my feet, I cross the hall to the front door and open it. Our front door is practically directly across the street from theirs. If their door was open, I could see straight through to the back sliding doors I break in through.

The air is cool as its fingers brush my cheeks. I *need* to see him right now. I need to know he's okay. That he's not having nightmares. I want to see that he's sleeping peacefully.

Instead, I shut the door and turn around, climbing back up the stairs to my room. It's late. Almost midnight, but I have to do something or I'm *going* to give in and watch him sleep.

I dial his number and close my eyes.

"Loren?" he answers, his voice sleepy. "Are you okay?"

"Are you having nightmares?" I ask.

There's a pause. "No. Why? Are you?"

Kind of. My nightmare right now is that he's not sleeping peacefully and I'm here. Not that I could do anything if I were there, and he didn't know I was there.

"No. Can I take you to dinner tomorrow?"

I hear his smile when he answers. "Yes. You can."

Sighing, I nod. "Will you do me a favor, Oakley?"

"What's that?"

"Call me if you have a nightmare."

Another pause. "Okay."

"Promise?"

"Yeah, Loren. I promise."

"I'm sorry I woke you. I hope you sleep well."

"You too, Loren. Goodnight."

"Goodnight."

He hangs up and I fall back on my bed, closing my eyes. This is going to be a long fucking night.

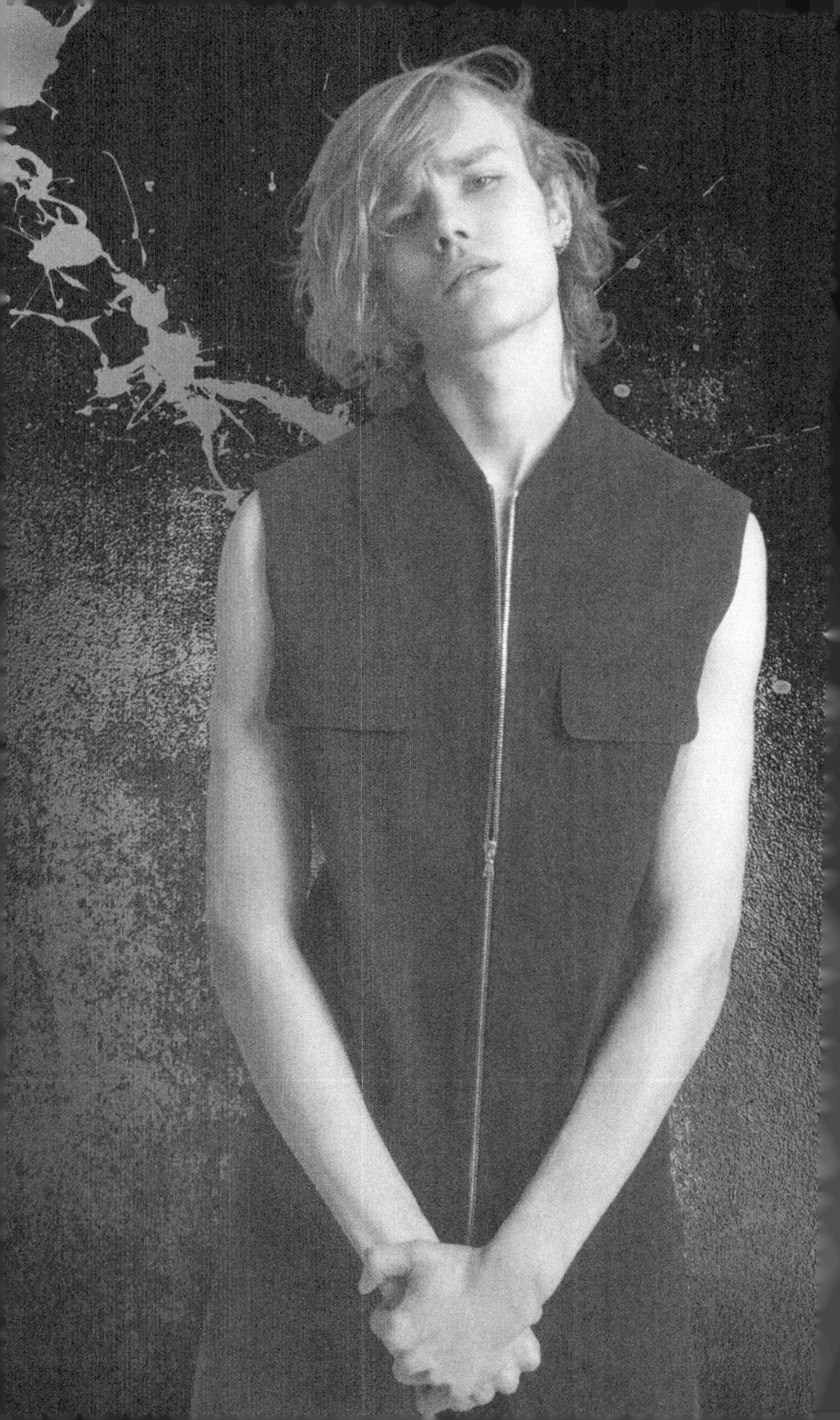

18

OAKLEY

On Tuesday, Loren gave me an origami puffy heart when he met me outside to walk to school. On Wednesday when he met me for lunch, he had the most beautiful purple and white flower I'd ever seen. Thursday evening, when he walked me to my door, he kissed me for real.

When I say my heart nearly stopped, I cannot emphasize that enough. He was super cute. Incredibly unsure. But when I stepped into him, his arms came around me and he gained a lot more confidence.

There was no tongue involved. Just our lips moving together. His arms wrapped around me and mine around him. Then he hugged me after, keeping me tucked in his arms for a few minutes as we held each other.

It was honestly the best day of my life.

This morning, he brought me a small rock the size of my palm with two penguins kissing on it, surrounded by hearts. He said his brothers painted it for him. I've been smiling like a fool all day as I carry it around.

It's too soon to be in love, right?

I keep reminding myself about how I definitely jumped in blindly with Daniel/Jason. I remind myself about all the red flags he waved and I'd ignored. But I don't see any of those red flags. He knows about my roommates and hasn't had anything bad to say. He's met them. I'm even sure he and Levis are friends. I've seen them hanging out when I get out of class and Loren is waiting for me.

There aren't any moments of jealousy or manipulation. He's not said something that makes me uncomfortable and then covered it with a generic compliment. In fact, his compliments aren't generic at all.

I'm not dreaming this up, right?

"Hey," Brek greets when he meets me in the hall. Today is the first day Loren isn't going to be around until this evening. He has a job. A contract. I'm not entirely sure why that means he won't be around, but I don't question it.

"Hi," I say. "Classes over, or you have one more? I forget what day it is."

He snorts. "One more. You gonna hang around?"

I shake my head. "I have to stop at the museum for class. They just opened a new exhibit on the Kush dynasty and now we have a paper due in a week."

"Fun."

I shrug. He doesn't share my love of history. Which is fine.

"What's that?"

He's looking at my hand, so I open my grip to show him the rock on my palm. I'm still grinning. I can't help myself.

"Where'd you get that?"

LOREN

"Someone," I hedge.

There's no way they haven't figured out that I've been spending time with Loren. But considering the way Brek scowls at me, I'm not about to say so.

"It's cute," I say, closing my hand and bringing it to my chest.

Brek shrugs. "Yep."

"Does it offend you in some way?"

He looks at me warily. "No."

"Then why the sudden attitude?"

"I just don't want you to get in over your head again. You don't think he's a little…"

I'm right that they've figured out that I'm hanging around with Loren. I'm not sure if we're 'seeing' each other since we haven't really said as much, but in my head, we are.

"A little what? Courteous? Kind? Thoughtful?"

Brek looks at me and I can tell he has a whole lot to say about this. He's not going to, though. "No. Is he all that?"

"Very much."

"He stares a lot. And Honey Bee was sure he was following us around. You're not concerned about that?"

I shrug. "He wants to spend time with me. He likes our conversations. Loren's interested in what I say, and remembers what's important to me."

Brek flinches like that was a direct jab at him. It wasn't. We have our own likes and that's completely fine. He looks away.

"So do I," he mutters.

"I didn't say you didn't, but you're trying to make me distrust Loren based on the fact he's around the same places we are? That's really what you're going with?"

"He doesn't even go to school here," he says, almost poutily.

"No. He doesn't. He walks the thirty-eight miles worth of trails, talks to the admissions office while he decides whether or not he wants another degree, and he's here to see me. Yes, he's said as much. That's one of the reasons he comes to campus. Do you think if he was being shady, he'd freely admit as much, Brek?"

"Don't get mad at me. I'm wary of people hanging around where they don't need to be."

"Because I have bad taste in men, right?"

"No! I'm not trying to fight, Oakley. I'm just worried. I miss you. You're hardly ever around anymore."

"But I'm the one you're giving a hard time to even though Honey Bee, Levis, and Briar are all seeing someone."

"They're still home all the time," he insists. "This is the most I've seen you in like, two weeks."

"Maybe it's time for you to get a girlfriend too. We're adults now and it's time that we expand our relationships, including you," I say. "I'm going to the museum. I'll see you later."

I half expect him to say something sarcastic like, 'will I?' or 'do you even still live there?' but he doesn't answer as I stomp off.

As I'm storming down the road, not paying attention to anything around me, there's a little voice in my head saying I'm being very defensive for some reason and maybe I need to think about it. Okay, I admit that at first, Loren always popping up felt *a little* unsettling. Him always watching me felt *somewhat* unnerving.

But he was nervous to talk to me. Just as I'm nervous to talk to everyone. Like me, he relaxes and opens up when it's just the two of us. We talk freely, comfortably. It's not hard to understand that maybe he's not as easy-going as everyone else.

I round a building and slam into a body.

"Woah," he says, his hands gripping me. I recognize his voice right away and pick up my head to look at one of the Van Doren triplets. Since he's not in a black tank, white tee, or shirtless, I'm not at all sure which one this is. "You okay?"

I huff. "Yes. Sorry."

"You look agitated."

Taking a deep breath, I hold it until my lungs force me to let it out. "I was arguing with Brek. It's fine."

"You shouldn't stay mad at your friends," he says, dropping his hands. There's a smile on his face as he looks at me. "They're almost always looking out for you."

"Yeah, well, when they're upset that I'm seeing someone for no reason except that I'm not home anymore, I think that's jealousy more than an altruistic reason."

"Is he upset that you're seeing my brother?"

I chew the inside of my lip. "I don't know exactly what his issue is. After making a bad decision on a guy because he says nice things to me and I'm not used to hearing nice things... Suddenly, all I make is bad decisions."

Only after the words are out of my mouth do I realize what I said. I flinch and glance up at him. "Sorry, that was far more ranting than you needed to hear."

He chuckles. "It's okay. Sounds to me like maybe he's worried about you."

"Do I have something to worry about?" I press in frustration.

Triplet brother tilts his head. There's a smile on his face, but it's almost absent. Reflective. Thoughtful. "No. *You* don't."

It's the way he emphasized you that has me staring at him. "Does Brek?" I ask.

His smile is vague now. "I think you need to trust your gut, Oakley. If something bothers you, listen to it. But if you're only feeling unsure now because of outside input, I think everything is fine."

That's a little... unsettling. "Right." He didn't answer the question. But he did say that I'm safe. I have nothing to worry about.

Maybe Loren doesn't like Brek?

"Okay, well..."

He grins. "I'm Imry. Ellory and Avory are almost *always* together. So if you see one of us alone, it's most likely me. Just so you know."

"How do you tell the other two apart?" I ask. "And when you're all together?"

Imry smiles. "You don't. I'm not even sure my brothers have it figured out."

"Have your parents?"

"Mom never did either except..." he pauses, then shakes his head. "Dad knows. I can't recall a single time when he's named us wrongly."

I almost ask about their mom because I've never seen her. No one mentions her. Loren and I talk about family sometimes and I've never once heard him so much as reference her. It's like the boys all randomly popped into existence.

"That's cool. You could at least get different haircuts."

Imry laughs. "Life is more entertaining this way. But I *did* just tell you how to figure us out to some degree. Keep it in mind."

He winks and steps around me. "I'm glad you and my brother are getting close, Oakley. He's not a people person and I can count on one hand how many people he likes outside of his family. You're something special."

My heart flutters as I smile after him. I feel better. The anger I felt toward Brek fades as I continue down the street. Now that I'm not feeling frustrated towards Brek, I can definitely see how he is just worried.

He's not even wrong. I *know* I fucked up and gained myself a crazy fucker. He turned out to be even crazier, with multiple identities and a history of domestic violence and restraining orders. Then he pissed off someone enough to be brutally murdered in the middle of the desert!

I get it. If that had happened to any of my friends, I'd feel the same way. I'd probably question everything they do for fear that they'd repeat the same mistake.

My phone pings and I reach into my pocket to pull it out.

> **BREK**
> I'm sorry. I don't want to fight. I just miss you.

> **ME**
> I'm sorry I was so defensive. I shouldn't have felt attacked.

> **BREK**
> See you at home later?

> **ME**
> Yes. definitely.

Much better. I should have apologized first, but he just came to the conclusion before I did. Seconds before, but still he got there first. I hate fighting with them. We rarely fight. Rarely take offense at something another says. We've been friends for so long, it's natural to maneuver around each other. Like extended limbs.

Closing out of my text conversation with Brek, I open mine with Loren. Last night we were talking about constellations and the stories behind them. It looks like a normal, mundane conversation, but the way he asked questions and then naturally threw in some really sweet things that just *fit* with our discussion makes me smile.

I feel the weight of the rock he gave me in my pocket, the image of the little penguins kissing danced before my eyes as I read.

> **LOREN**
>
> Constellations always look like the stars are reaching out to each other. Holding hands.
>
> Would you let me hold your hand? What would our constellation shape be? I like the idea of my story being written in the stars and passed down through lifetimes.

The way his questions shift, bounce around, and come back to the topic all in a single text make me think that he's literally just writing exactly what he's thinking. He's letting me in. Giving me a glimpse at the parts of him that are deeper than the world sees.

I glance up and come to a stop. How the hell did I get here?

No, more importantly—where is *here?*

Spinning in a slow circle, I determine I'm in an alleyway, but neither end looks like it dumps out onto the main road. There's a wall on either end, so the path must turn. The buildings aren't ridiculously tall, but they're made of stone and metal and glass, reaching up a dozen stories.

Okay, no big deal. I close my text conversations and open the maps app. While I wait for it to load, I listen. Straining my ears for the sounds of traffic, trying to ignore the way my heart races.

This is fine. I'm not in Chicago or NYC or... even a big city. Tucson isn't a huge city, right? We're on the outer limits. This is a college town. I'm safe. Perfectly safe.

But my maps won't load. The little dot is surrounded by gray.

"It's fine," I mutter and choose the direction I came from to walk. The alley is clean. There aren't signs of anything other than someone had moved in recently and there's a load of empty boxes flattened just outside a door.

I move quickly and round the corner, my pulse increasing when I don't see the road. How did I not see this? How was I so engrossed in my text messages that I got myself lost in fucking alleys?!

College town. This is a college town. I'm perfectly safe.

Taking a breath, I keep walking, peeking down different alleys and choosing the ones that look cleanest. Who knew the city had this kind of labyrinth in it?

Finally, I see the main street. I'm so relieved that I nearly cry. Stuffing my phone in my pocket, I nearly jog toward it. I'm about a dozen feet from reaching the sidewalk where I see people walking casually and a steady stream of cars on the street when a door suddenly opens.

A man steps out and I come to a stop. He's not looking at me, but toward the street. His hood is pulled up.

Oh, god, please keep walking.

I'm not heard. When the man turns my way, I see a long knife in his hand, and pretend I don't see blood on it.

My eyes widen and I turn to run the other way, dropping my bag right there so it doesn't hinder my progress. I'm not sure I've run so fast in my life and yet, it's not enough. His hand digs into the back of my shirt and I scream. But the sound is cut off when something wraps around my neck.

Reflex has my hands reaching for it, trying to tug it away because I can't breathe. Gasping for breath as the world around me darkens and blinks out of focus.

I try to scream. To kick. To dig at what feels like a rope around my neck. Tears fall and I lose the energy to keep struggling.

I can't breathe.

I can't... breathe...

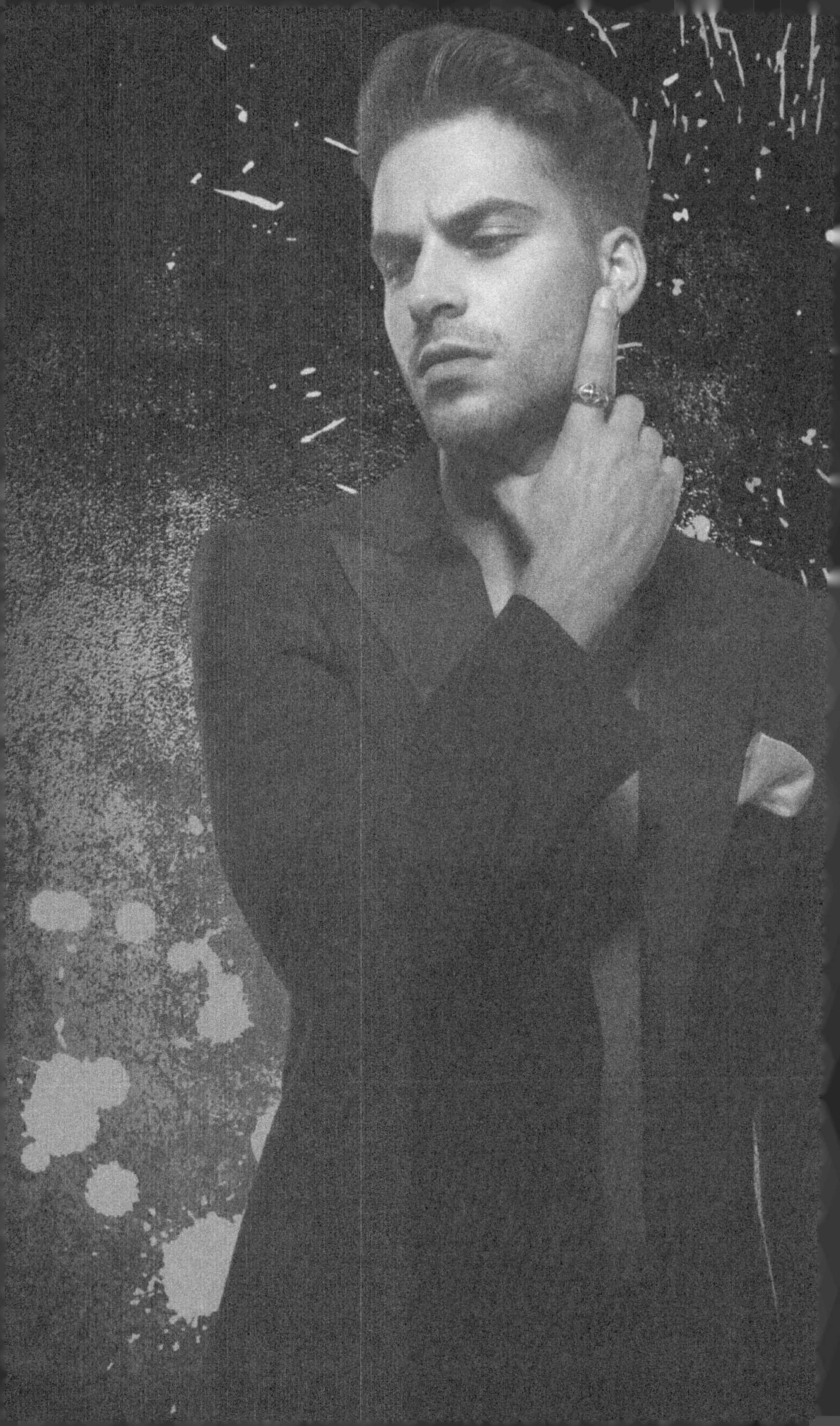

19
LOREN

I ENJOY KILLING PEOPLE. Myro and I talk about it a lot because he worries about my humanity. I have no remorse, regardless of who I kill. There are no mercy killings; no mercy at all. Honestly, I enjoy hearing them beg and knowing that I hold the fate of their lives in my hands.

It makes me really happy when they call me a psychopath and I can correct them with an accurate diagnosis. The looks on their faces usually stay with me while I'm cleaning up, leaving me with a smile.

Killing isn't personal for me. Myro used to conduct some experiments by giving me details about the target to see if I responded differently for different circumstances—murderers, assailants, rapists, traffickers, drug smugglers, etc. The short answer is no. Sometimes, if I found something particularly offensive, I drew it out, but usually by watching them bleed out from a single laceration. The time that comes to mind most readily is the one that drowned a litter of puppies because they thought they were too ugly and no one would want them.

It wasn't because he'd been abusing his son for fifteen years. Not because he'd run over his son's leg and told the hospital he fell out of a tree. Or because his wife mysteriously died when the kid was three.

None of that bothered me. Just drowning puppies.

Yeah… I don't know how my mind works. Logically, *I know* I should have been bothered by the bulk of his file. I suppose the fact that it doesn't, means the part of me lacking empathy is strong.

Watching their lives drain away while I kill them. Cataloging their fear and how it progresses throughout my time with them. Anger, bargaining, desperation, acceptance. A lot like grief, but all with a heavy backdrop of fear.

I won't say it's exhilarating. It's *fun*, sure, but I don't get a burst of endorphins or anything. Everyone has their hobbies. Mine just takes lives as if they're ants.

There has only been one life that has been personal—Daniel. Even that wouldn't have been if it hadn't been for Oakley. When Noah told me about him, it wasn't personal. Had this man been harassing Noah, I think it would have been very different. But he was abusive to Noah's boyfriend's brother. There was enough removal of close ties to me that the reason was irrelevant.

Noah wouldn't call for a spider's death. So if he was calling to ask me for help with a person, clearly they weren't good people. I recruited Imry to help me—after listening to Myro warn me about telling people what I do.

I don't *tell* people. I didn't even tell Noah. Assuring someone that I will protect them isn't admitting to murder. Making them understand that if they ever need something that they should tell me, isn't confessing that I'm a cold-blooded killer.

Noah is a smart man. He simply read between the lines. To be fair, he didn't *ask*. He simply told me a story that upset him and dropped a name. I kept him updated on progress that I felt was important—like the fact the name he gave me wasn't real. That was important to have in case this man showed up in the boyfriend's brother's life again under a new pseudonym online or something.

Arguably, I can claim to have done a good deed!

And since we're making arguments, I can also say that about taking out Daniel. Imry found no less than thirteen victims in Daniel's past. He wasn't even counting Oakley since Oakley got himself out before it got to that point. But we're talking assault victims, abuse victims, and there were even some sexual violence victims in there.

If you ask his victims, I did a good thing. If you ask most of the world, I did a good thing. The only people who would disagree are those who feel that *every* life is sacred and all that bullshit. Those same people who believe that they should be able to dictate how one lives, what rights they have to their own bodies, who they're allowed to love, etc.

Hypocrisy at its finest.

I bet if I killed those people, no one would complain.

Today is the first day I'm scoping out a target since Oakley came into my life—Daniel aside. I'm slightly stressed. Not because I feel like Oakley isn't safe, but because I like to be present every moment that he's awake. I want his every minute. I want to make him smile and laugh and watch him blush.

I'm not sure if Myro is trying to temper my obsession or if this contract is out of his depth. Unlike me, Myro struggles with some contracts. His empathy is strong, so the list of transgressions needs to be brutal or hit on something that he finds particularly awful.

While I don't always understand which of his triggers flip the switch and allow him to murder someone, I've examined the list of wrongdoing that this contract gives, and I don't see anything particularly upsetting. There are no drowned puppies. Or skinned kitties. No plucked birds.

Hmm. I'm seeing a pattern here. I don't like animal abuse. That's good to know.

I *think* Myro's biggest issues are concerning the particularly abhorrent abuse and assault of women and children. Then again, there have been a couple that had neither and he didn't lose sleep over it, so he's just a puzzle I haven't worked out yet.

After the brief conversation with my father the other night, I've stopped watching Oakley sleep. It means I get less sleep, if you can believe that, because I hate not knowing if he's sleeping peacefully. Imry says asking him to set up a video feed facing his bed at night is pushing some boundaries that I shouldn't cross in our relationship yet.

At least he said 'yet.' Hopefully that means at some point, it'll be appropriate to ask. I feel like it's a small ask, anyway. I just need to know he's sleeping okay, and nothing is bothering him while he sleeps.

Grudgingly, I agreed to take a look at this contract so I walked Oakley to school, kissed him outside his classroom, and gifted him a little rock that I had my brother paint for me last night and told him I had to deal with a contract today so I'd see him this evening.

Walking away knowing that I won't see him in an hour, but closer to six hours was surprisingly difficult. I had half a mind to call Noah and explain this weird dislike and reluctance to leaving him for a long period. Is this what love feels like? Has my sociopathy evolved to include such things with specific people involved?

Love or not, it's only the promise of the possibility of watching someone's life fade before my eyes that convinces me I can leave Oakley for a little while. Just a while. Then I can kiss him later and I'm pretty sure it'll be the very best day of my life so far.

AFTER A DAY of scoping out this guy's routine, I've had enough. It's not like I've been entirely able to concentrate on this task because I know Oakley's out of school and has been for a bit. This particular target is dull as fuck too. I've been trying to remind myself that Daniel is dead. He no longer has an obsessive stalker creep.

Except me.

I smirk because I'm not even sorry.

Turning my car around, I head back toward home. There's a lot of traffic for some reason, so I'm moving downtown slowly. Oakley told me this morning he'd be at the museum for a few hours after school for a project. His class has been out for an hour, so I decide to head there.

When I'm stopped in the middle of the road, scanning the crowd, my gaze spots something in a dark alley. Something bright. Like a highlighter.

My gut clenches as I stare at it. I try to reason with myself that it's not what I think it is. Oakley's backpack has no place in a dark alley.

When traffic begins to move again, I pull off the road and park in a convenience store parking lot around the corner. There are always a few knives in my car. Not my favorite one, but there are several options. I strap one to my calf, then lower my pant leg and slip a folding hunting knife in my pocket before getting out.

They're unnecessary. I miss Oakley, so I'm simply seeing things. That's it.

When I get out of the car and lock it, I dial Oakley's phone. It rings and rings and rings before going to voicemail. I try again.

It's fine. It makes perfect sense that it's on silent mode because he's in the museum only a few blocks further down the road. I can practically see it from here. This isn't his backpack!

But as I turn into the alley, my gut clenches. There's no way I can mistake it. I've been staring at it for a month as I tailed him.

Glancing over my shoulder, I reach into my pocket for the knife and flick it open. Then stop over the backpack. It's unopened. Dropped haphazardly on the ground. Picking it up, I sling it over my back and then study the surrounding ground.

The alley is remarkably clean. A strange kind of clean.

I remain still for a minute, straining to hear anything other than the road noise behind me. Which is oddly dulled even a few dozen feet away. But I can't hear anything.

Logically, taking into account the direction the backpack is facing and that it was clearly abandoned quickly, I move further into the alley and remind myself that this doesn't mean anything. Maybe his backpack was stolen, and someone realized he doesn't carry much in it. But I can clearly feel his tablet. Surely that wouldn't still be in there.

And this damn thing is highlighter colored, it sticks out like a neon light. If it was stolen, it would have been thrown into a dumpster. Not tossed into an alley.

The further I move, the less I hear. It's stupidly quiet. Very inconvenient. I'm trying very hard not to be pissed that I wasn't with him today. Fuck the stupid contract. What if Oakley needed me and I was wasting my time taking out someone else's garbage?

I pause when I hear scraping. It takes me a minute to locate the direction of the sound and I have to change my trajectory. I come upon a phone. When I click on the screen, I'm greeted with a picture of the six people who live across the road and a notification of a missed call from me.

Pocketing it, I move a little quicker. An unsettling feeling that I'm not entirely familiar with creeps up my spine. My hands shake. The knife I have gripped tightly in my hand feels slick while my body feels cold. A dark pit forms in my stomach, making it difficult to swallow. There's darkness licking at the edges of my vision as I hyperfixate on the sound ahead.

When I round the corner, the world shrinks to a single pinpoint. The furious grip on my knife becomes crushing. The opposite hand clenches so tightly, my nails dig into my palm. My nostrils flare, and everything inside me fills with fire as I surge forward.

Oakley's limp body is being pulled by a rope around his neck. The man doesn't know I'm there until I'm practically on top of him. He spins, swinging a long knife at me wildly. Stopping it is easy as I slam my wrist into his, causing his knife to fly from his grip.

He's already dropped the rope as he turns to face me. Perhaps he sees that I'm completely out of my mind right now because his eyes widen and he turns to run. Too bad for him, one of us is being driven by a blind rage and unfortunately for this fucker, it's not him.

I see very little of the next several minutes as I drive my knife into his gut and tear it up. When he tries to scream, I slam the tip of my blade through his trachea and out the back of his neck. I keep him on his feet as I continue to filet this fucker until he's been dead for a while.

It takes several more minutes to get myself under control enough to drop my knife and get to Oakley. There's blood everywhere. I'm covered. Oakley's covered. The man is... unrecognizable.

Dropping to my knees, I gently pull the rope from Oakley's neck. He's breathing, but barely. My hands tremble as I look around me, unsure of what to do now. I need to get Oakley away from here. I need to get him... somewhere. But he's covered in blood, and I don't know if any of it's his.

Wiping my hands on my pants, which does very little to clean them off, I pull my phone out and call my brother. The phone struggles to connect in the alley, but eventually, the call goes through and Myro answers.

"I need your help," I blurt.

"What happened? What did you do?"

"I won't be taking any more contracts," I say. "Hurry. I don't know if he's going to live and I'm going to lose my mind if he dies, Myro."

"Where are you?"

I'm entirely unfamiliar with my own tears, so it takes a minute for me to figure out that's what's happening right now when my eyesight gets strangely distorted and blurry, like I'm underwater. While I know I need to look around for any kind of indicator about where I am, my eyes remain glued to Oakley's face.

"You have to find me," I insist. "I don't care how."

He curses. "Don't move. Can anyone see you?"

"I don't know. There are windows. I think."

LOREN

Nope, can't even look up long enough to confirm that.

"Listen to me, Loren. Are you listening?"

"Kind of. Like fifty percent."

He snorts. "Put your first two fingers on Oakley's neck. Right under his chin, but to the side. If his chin is twelve o'clock, press them at one-thirty."

I switch my phone to the other hand and do as Myro says.

"You'll have to press into his skin. Not so hard as to hurt him, but you need to find his pulse."

It takes several attempts. To be fair, I know how to find a pulse under normal circumstances. Those being any other time when Oakley doesn't have claw marks and a nasty bruise around rope burn on his neck. Eventually I find it. It's faint, but there's a chance that's just me because my hand's shaking.

"He's alive," I whisper. "Hurry up, Myro."

"I'm on my way. Tell me what else you see. What are his injuries?"

I listen to my brother as best I can, taking inventory of Oakley and relaying what I see. This is how he finds me when he pulls a car into the alley with Voss in tow.

Voss immediately vomits. He doesn't do well with blood. There's likely a lot of it.

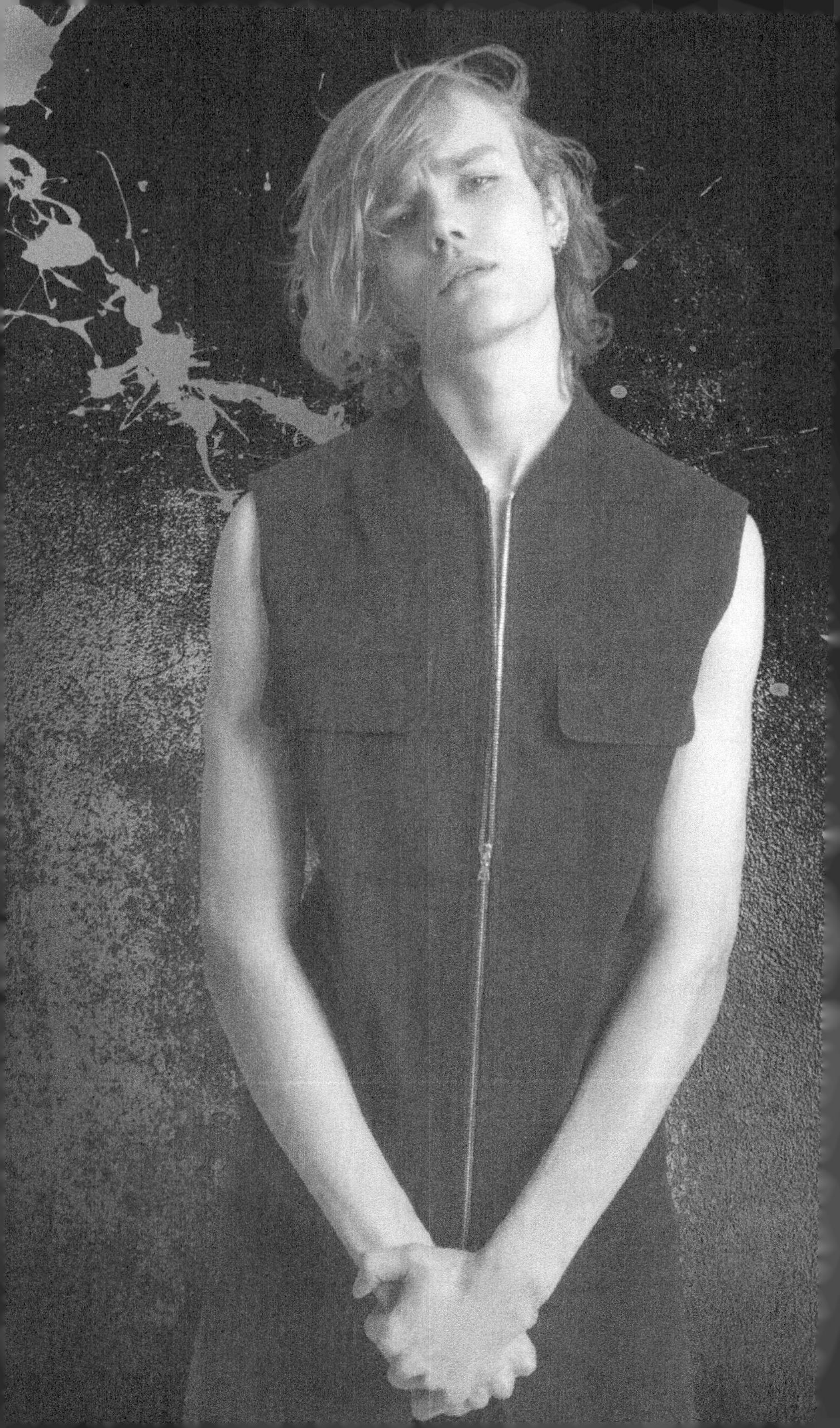

20
OAKLEY

I RECOGNIZE Loren's voice easily enough. I've heard it a lot, both while awake and in my dreams. It's difficult to tell if I'm dreaming right now or not. My body and neck ache. My head hurts like I ran into a wall. There's this dull throbbing that I can't quite place.

The second voice is a little more difficult to identify. I *think* it's Myro, but that's more from process of elimination than it is confidence. It's not any of my friends. There's not a tone they could speak in that I'd not recognize. It's not Loren's father, Jalon. While I haven't heard him talk a lot, I think the fact that this voice is far more familiar than his confirms that it's not Jalon.

It's not one of the triplets. I'm not sure why I'm convinced of that, but I am. I'm also pretty confident it's not Voss, either. There's something almost melodic about Voss' voice and this one doesn't have that tone.

Myro, then.

"I'm not leaving," Loren says. I'd say that it sounds stubborn and maybe a little petulant, but there's a hard edge to it, too.

"Dad needs—"

"Then Dad can come here. I'm not leaving."

"He's perfectly safe now, Loren."

"You tried to convince me of that earlier today and he was nearly killed," Loren hissed. "No."

"He's in our house. In your room."

"No."

He chuckles. "Let us know when he wakes up, okay?"

"Maybe."

He chuckles again. I don't hear footsteps, but the quiet click of the door tells me that the second voice, most likely Myro, has left.

The room is silent. I don't hear anything, even breathing. I think it's the silence that puts me to sleep again. When I'm next coherent, there's a light pressure on my wrist. I'm not entirely sure what it is, but at least three-quarters of my concentration is trying to figure it out. The rest is taking an inventory of how much I ache.

I haven't felt this achy since I used to train with my brother's football team. That was… far too long ago.

When I open my eyes, Loren is sitting there and my breath catches. He's watching me. Like all those times he's just stared. It's just as intense, but there's something else there too. Concern?

"Hi," I whisper.

His lips quirk up. "Hi," he answers and the pressure on my wrist tightens slightly. He's not just holding my wrist but feeling my pulse. "Are you in pain? Do you need a drink?"

Definitely concern. Worry. Loren Van Doren is worried about me.

I shake my head, but I think I need both. "What happened?" Bits and pieces touch my memory. There's a strange phantom sensation of pain around my neck and not being able to breathe.

Loren tilts his head slightly as he studies me. He doesn't answer, but I think he's trying to determine what he wants to say.

"The truth, okay?" I ask.

He sighs. "I need you to tell me what you need," he counters. "Even on my best days, I don't understand people. Most of the time, it's because I've never cared to try, which is really coming back to bite me right now when I need to know what you need."

"I want to know what happened?"

Loren nods. "I'll tell you, and I understand your need to know, but that's not what I'm talking about. I need you to tell me *all* your needs—physical, emotional, mental, sexual—everything."

My cheeks heat slightly and I nod.

"I will tell you, but you tell me first. What do you need, Oakley?"

Taking a breath, I take inventory of, well, everything. I'm scared. The little glimpses of something that feels like a nightmare are getting stronger. More pronounced. I shiver. Fear and anxiety make me tense.

"I need a hug," I whisper. "I, umm, want to be held."

When I peek at him, he looks slightly surprised. Apparently, he wasn't expecting that.

"Just so I'm clear, is this a physical need or an emotional need?" he asks as he gets to his feet. He's wearing something different than what he'd had on this morning. Now he's in gym shorts and a long-sleeved shirt.

"Both, probably."

He climbs on the bed and pulls me to his chest. I press my face into his neck and take a deep breath, inhaling everything that is Loren Van Doren. He smells like body wash, laundry detergent, and something that is distinctly him.

His arms are tight around me, holding me as if he's scared too.

"Will you tell me what happened now?" I ask.

There's no indication that he heard me. His grip on me doesn't change. His heartbeat remains steady. His breathing is consistent.

"I saw your backpack in an alley and went to investigate," Loren starts, his voice quiet.

That seems to be a trigger because it all comes rushing back to me. The man that burst out of the door, turning on me with a knife. Dropping my backpack and running. The rope around my neck. Not being able to breathe. I don't remember passing out, but I must have.

Tears sting my eyes. I could have died.

"I found your phone. Then I found you."

"The man who…"

"He's dead."

My breath catches. "How?" I whisper.

Loren doesn't answer. His grip tightens around me. Minutes pass. I can hear them as if there's a clock in the room ticking.

"Let's start somewhere else," he says. I'm not entirely sure what that means, but I don't have to ask before he continues, "When I was younger, I was diagnosed with an antisocial personality disorder. There's some confusion about whether a child can be diagnosed as such, but I promise you, I had it then just as much as I do now. Back then, it was just an umbrella. When I was seventeen, I was finally given the much more accurate label."

I'm not sure what an antisocial personality disorder is. "I'm following, but not."

He huffs quiet laughter. Almost absent. Just a whisper of humor. I smile, further burying my nose in his neck.

"I'm a sociopath," he says quietly.

It takes a tremendous amount of effort not to stiffen entirely. "I... Uh, what—"

"I have... quirks, tendencies that can be offputting to most people. But the thing you need to truly understand is what I told you a few minutes ago. I don't know how to read people. Part of that is self-inflicted. It doesn't come naturally to me, but the self-inflicted part is that I never tried to learn. I didn't care. Obviously, I'm now a little frustrated with past me because I can't decipher what you need unless you tell me."

"Okay," I say. "I'll tell you."

"Are you afraid of me now, Oakley?"

His voice is quiet and I think it's to be gentler. But coming from a sociopath who may or may not have just killed a man to save me, I'm not sure it's comforting.

"I won't hurt you," he promises, arms somehow tightening once more. It's almost painful how tightly he's holding. "I'll never hurt you, Oakley. I'll never let anyone else hurt you either."

"Did you kill that man?" I whisper.

"Yes. He was going to kill you and I lost my shit when I saw him dragging you like that. I'm not sorry."

I shouldn't smile. But fuck, the grin that covers my face is almost manic. I take another deep inhale, my fingers digging into his back. "Tell me more, please."

He nods. I feel his lips press to my head and I grin again.

"The most important thing you should know right now is that I'm very different from everyone else around you. I don't feel empathy. I don't experience remorse. I can have violent tendencies, but they're in a controlled environment, so to speak. My idea of right and wrong is likely different from yours. I tend to be reckless and disregard my personal safety or that of others. I don't always control my impulses. But where I differ from the black and white definition of a sociopath is that I definitely attempt to find reason and logic *before* I act, but again, my right and wrong isn't the same as everyone else's so my reasoning might be wrong to some people. Another place where I differ is that I *am* able to form close bonds and relationships. My brothers and father, my friend Noah, you—they're the most important people in my life and I'll do anything to protect them."

Warmth floods me and I close my eyes. "Why me?"

"This might not be the answer you want, but I don't know why. I saw you for the first time the day you met Daniel Rollins-Alabaster. I can't explain what overcame me, but I knew as soon as you walked in the door to the café that you were mine. However, I'm shit at communicating and even shittier at talking to people, so I wasn't sure what to do about it. Then Daniel became a threat, so I had to eliminate him, which he already had coming. I still didn't know how to talk to you, so I spent the next month just observing you."

My heart nearly stops and I'm not sure which question to ask first. "Did you kill him too?"

"I did," he admits.

"Oh my god," I whisper.

"He had a very long list of reasons he needed to die," Loren says, shrugging.

I'm not sure how to feel right now.

"He was going to hurt you." There's no defensiveness in his voice, but I recognize that he's trying to explain the reason why he murdered a man. Gruesomely, if the news was anything to go by. "He'd already gotten far too close to you. I don't need to know how to understand people to have read your body language that he was already making you uncomfortable."

"You were following me," I say.

"Yes."

I laugh because it's so matter of fact and unapologetic. This can't be real right now.

"Jessica figured it out. Actually, Levis did first. Levis truly figured it out, while Jessica thought I was following all of you. Instead of being mad at me, Levis told me some things you liked and gave me a few ideas of what to talk to you about."

Now I'm just smiling like a fucking idiot. This man has just admitted to killing two people and to stalking me, but I feel ridiculously giddy.

"I didn't know that," I admit.

"Yes, you did. You saw me everywhere. In hindsight, I definitely wanted you to see me because I wanted you to be comfortable with my presence while I worked up the courage to talk to you."

This is such a surreal conversation right now. Loren is the epitome of confidence, while I am the poster boy for insecurity. And *he* didn't know how to talk to *me*.

I lean back so I can look at him. Still smiling, mind you, because apparently murdering people to keep me safe is now a thing I'm totally into. Never mind it's the biggest red flag in existence.

"You could have just said hi," I tease.

"Yes. well." Loren shrugs. His hand raises and his fingers gently touch my neck. "There's a few more things I need you to know right now."

"Okay," I say.

"I have an aversion to touch…" I immediately try to pull away, but his arms tighten and he grins. "Not right this second, but I just need you to understand that if I need to put some distance between us physically, it has nothing to do with you at all. I enjoy being close to you. I like you in my arms. But this is very new to me, and I anticipate there's going to be times when I'm going to need some space. Please, don't take it personally."

I nod. Even though he just emphasized like three times that it doesn't have anything to do with me, I innately try to pull away a little. Am I making him uncomfortable now? How will I know when he doesn't want to be touched?

"Look at me," he instructs, and I raise my eyes to his. "I'm not going to ever lie to you. I will tell you if I don't want to be touched. So believe me right now when I tell you that I don't want you to move away."

I take a breath and nod again. "Okay," I say on an exhale.

His lips touch mine and it's like a shot to my muscles. I immediately go limp, allowing him to bring my body back flush to his again.

"I like this," he promises against my lips. "Even when I need space, it's not ever going to be because I don't like touching you. For me, touch aversion can be tactile or sensation or for personal space. I'm not always clear as to why or what might trigger it. It could be something as stupid as it's a Tuesday and the birds singing irritates me."

I laugh. His smile is small, but pleased.

"I'm going to emphasize again that this is very new to me. I'm probably going to be the least easy person to be with."

My heart races at his words. "You want to be with me?" I whisper.

His grin says he thinks I'm cute right now. "I wanted you the moment I saw you, Oakley. When I tell you that Imry had to forcefully keep me in my seat, I mean it. He'll tell you. Because I make it a habit to understand myself as much as I can—and I have exactly zero experience with relationships outside of my siblings and one friend—I didn't know what I felt. I thought it was just… possession? Quite quickly I realized it was definitely an obsession. But I was still under the impression that it was…" Loren bites his lip and then shakes his head a little. "I'm inclined to say ownership, but that's not it. I wanted your smile. Your laughter. Your time. I didn't think it was—romantic?—or physical or anything. Just… possessive. I'm not sure that makes sense outside of my own head."

"It's different now?" I ask.

His smile makes my insides flip. "It's all the things now. It has been since the moment I touched you when we were playing with the bow. But there's one other thing that you need to know right now, which I think might be the most difficult to accept."

"What?" Honestly, I'm not sure what he could add to this list of things I've just learned.

"There's a lot of ways to say this, but I think the easiest way for you to understand is to say that I don't have the same emotional range as most people. I'm black and white with a lack of emotional depth."

"You already said you have a lack of empathy," I point out.

"Yes, but more than that, one of the classic symptoms of antisocial personality disorders is the lack of the ability to create bonds. The experts say that we aren't able to love."

His expression is… blank. For the first time, the clear expression registers what it actually is. Loren's lack of emotion. Not because he's a jerk or whatever. But because he simply doesn't feel it.

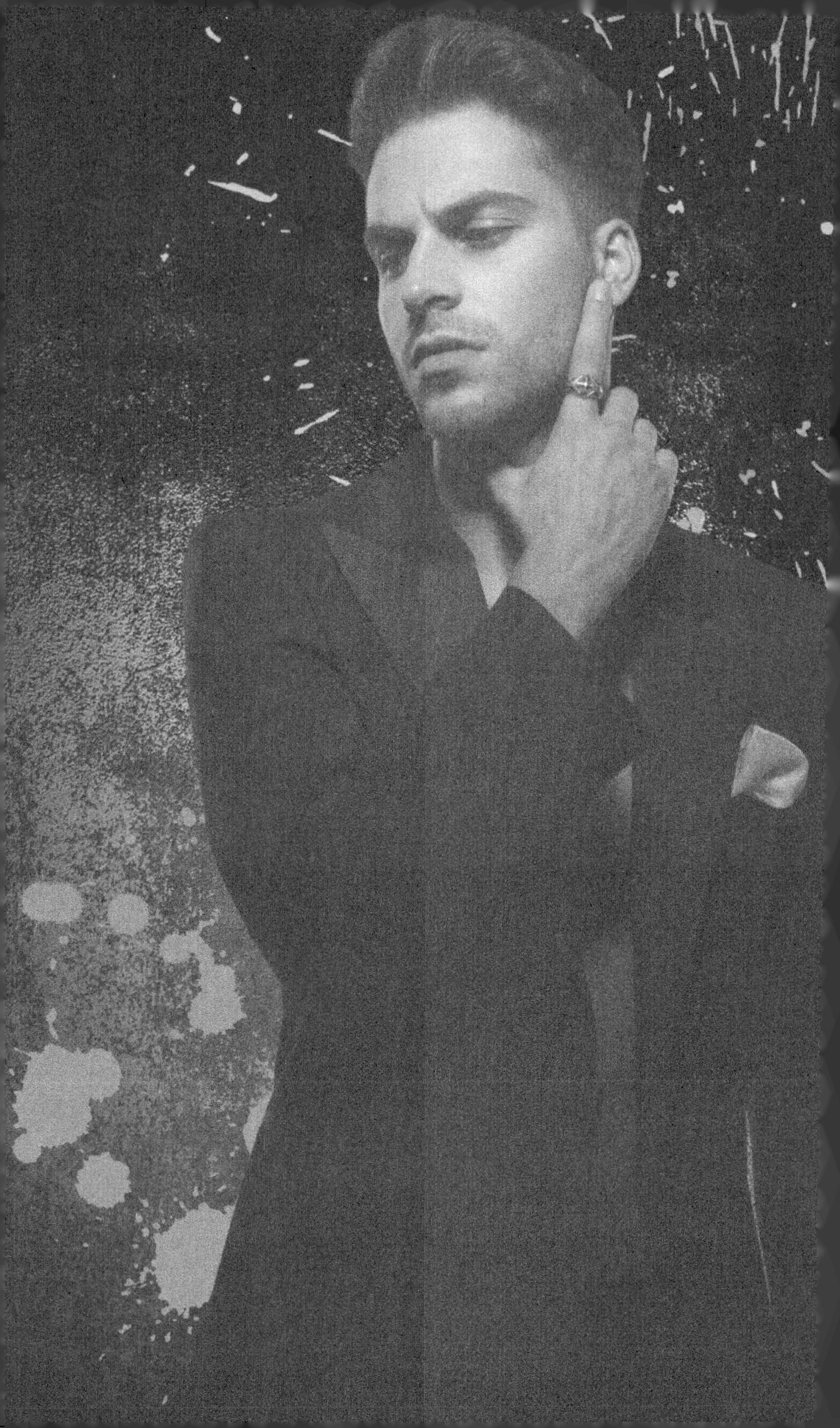

21

LOREN

Looking at Oakley right now is like looking into the mirror if it showed the exact opposite reaction. I *need* him to accept this, but there's no true fear or dread or worry that he's not going to. It just means I need to find a way to make him understand.

"Noah and I talked about love a lot over the last year, and he thinks I do have the capacity to love. It's just defined differently by me. He says love isn't a one-size-fits-all kind of emotion. There are a lot of different kinds of love."

"The ancient Greek had anywhere from six to nine different types of love," Oakley interjects, smiling. "Different scholars claim different things."

His enthusiasm over history never ceases to make me smile. "Noah thinks my love just looks differently than most people's. Some of the things you like—romance, for example—aren't going to come naturally to me. But if I put a different definition to what romance means, I can usually find something that puts a smile on your face. I want to keep you smiling. I want to hear about your life. I want to be the person who makes you happy. I want to see you all the time and I want you to feel that way, too. Noah thinks this is love for me."

"You're saying that Noah thinks you love me now?" he asks, eyes wide.

"I also appreciate that you're very expressive, even when I don't always know exactly what you're expressing," I continue, grinning and ignoring his question, running my finger along his jaw. "Noah thinks I experienced love at first sight, which seemed like the least crazy thing I could say to Levis the other day or week or whatever. So I also volunteered that as an explanation as to why I was following you. Although, full disclaimer, if he hasn't already figured out that I'm a sociopath, he's going to at some point. He's very observant."

Oakley smiles. "He is. Also, he seems to like you, so even if he has figured it out, he isn't holding it against you."

"Good. But what I need to know is if you can love me knowing that I might not be able to return that sentiment in a way you're familiar with."

"If I say I can't?"

There's no good answer right here, so I feel like maybe this is a trap. "There's a chance that I'm still never going to leave," I say. "But I won't ever harm you either."

His answering smile is soft. Oakley stares at me, his eyes flitting between mine and all over my face. I want to ask what he sees. What he's thinking. But I let him work it out for himself. In reality, there's no 'chance' about it. I will always be in his shadow. As soon as I saw this man, a part of me was rewritten to include Oakley in my makeup. He's a part of me and quite frankly, I will not live without him.

"Okay," he says finally.

"That's not very specific on what you're agreeing to."

Oakley's smile widens. "The way I see it, everyone is different. As your friend Noah says, love is different for everyone. Not to get philosophical, but all relationships are different too. I've never had one, so it's not like I have anything to compare one to; so the way I see it, we can just build something together that's right for both of us. Right?"

"Mmm," I respond. "Are you naturally shy?"

My question surprises him and his eyes widen a little before he laughs. "Yes."

"I'm not necessarily shy, but I'm not social. I'm the aggressor when I know what I want and how to get it—I don't mean that violently." I pull him closer, bringing his hips to mine. His cheeks pinken. "I've never done anything with a guy, and we've already established that I've never had a relationship, *and* I suck at reading people in general, so initiating anything on my part is likely going to be rare. I needed coaching to know how and when I could kiss you."

Oakley likes everything I said, but especially the last admission. His smile is so big and wide. It's a light all on its own. "You asked for advice about me?"

"More than once."

"So... if I want to touch you, should I ask?" he says, wrapping his arms around my neck and bringing his mouth to mine. His lips hover, not quite touching. He's so close that I can no longer see him clearly.

"Not necessarily. But again, don't get upset if I need space."

"Do you need space right now?"

I shake my head.

"Can I touch you right now?"

"I'm not sure how much more you can be touching me," I comment, raising a brow.

I'm not generally naïve. For the record. I'm going to chalk this moment of dumbassery up to being distracted that Oakley's so close, he's alive, and he seems to accept me and still wants to be with me.

"You're awfully cute," he says, grinning. "Can I touch your skin, Loren?" His top hand moves from behind my head over my shoulder, between us down my chest and stomach to the hem of my shirt.

"Oh. Yeah. You can touch me."

He laughs quietly, his hand sliding under my shirt to rest on my stomach. His hand is warm. Hot. I can feel the heat seeping into me and igniting my blood.

"I just realized what you said. You've never been with a guy?" he asks suddenly, pulling his face back to look at me clearly.

I blink at the sudden change in his body language and tone. No longer quiet and teasing, heated. Now surprised and... disbelieving?

"No. Does that bother you?"

Once again, I can't read the expression on his face. But I'm really trying. "No," he whispers. "I just... I've never been someone's first before. First anything."

"How about you're not my first then? You're my last. My only. Does that make it better?"

Okay, I *think* he liked that. His eyes look a little glassy now. Oakley nods and then his mouth is on mine.

LOREN

His kisses are never aggressive. To this point, they've only ever been soft and exploratory. I thought we were getting comfortable with each other during our last kisses.

Maybe it was me slowing us down.

I've been slightly hard since I climbed into bed with him. It couldn't be helped. Not when being this close, especially when he's wearing so little. As soon as we got him back here, I took off his dirty clothes and Myro washed his wounds because I was shaking too bad to do so. Then I tucked him into my bed and covered him up.

I dig my fingers into his hair, tangling the long strands around them. He moans into my mouth and the sound goes straight to my core. His hand on my stomach moves further up my torso, touching me. Exploring. Dipping along my ribs and around my back.

His tongue dips into my mouth. It's easy to lose myself in him. Letting him be the one to move this wherever he wants it to go. I'd give him my kidney right now if he asked. Fuck, I'd let him take it without asking.

"Is this okay?" he asks, breaking his mouth from mine.

"You don't need to ask," I tell him. "I'm sure you can feel that it's okay."

He smiles, kissing me again. The way his mouth moves against mine, leading my tongue into the dance he choreographed, has me chasing his lips when he pulls away again. "Will you take your clothes off, Loren?"

I nod but don't move, trying to get his mouth to mine again.

Oakley grins. "Now?"

Grunting, I pull away and quickly shove my clothes off. My gaze doesn't leave Oakley. While I undress, he pushes the blankets off him and my eyes trail down his body, looking for any injuries we missed.

There aren't any that I can see. Some bruises but I knew they were there.

His fingers in the elastic of my underwear make me pause again. He tugs them gently. "These too?"

I push them away and then still, watching him stare at my dick. I'm not self-conscious. I'm probably pretty average. Glancing down, I decide that I am average. Maybe a little bigger? What's average again?

When Oakley licks his lips, I decide that I don't even care.

"Can I touch you?" he whispers.

I huff. Reaching for his hand, I place it over my dick. Oakley grins, his eyes flickering to mine. "You really don't need to keep asking, Oakley. I'm perfectly capable of telling you if I don't want to do something."

"Yes, well, I'm very aware that you haven't touched another guy and haven't had one touching you. I imagine it could be a little… intimidating? Confusing?" His eyebrows knit together.

"Why?" I ask.

His eyes flicker to mine again. "Uh… I think a sexual awakening tends to do all those things initially."

"I hope I didn't mislead you. I'm plenty sexually awakened."

Oakley laughs, his hand wrapping around my dick. It jumps in his hold. Jesus, I like his hand around me.

"I love that you're you," he says and gives a gentle tug on my cock to pull me nearer.

I'm not entirely sure what that means, but I lower myself to hover over him. Oakley spreads his legs on either side of mine. He's still in his underwear—boxer briefs—they're snug and I can see how hard he is right now too.

The desire to touch him is strong, but I kind of just want to let him touch me right now.

"Thanks," I say, pulling my thoughts back to what he said.

"I want to keep checking." Oakley scooches down onto his back so he's laying under me. Fucking hell, have I ever seen someone sexier? It makes my breath catch. Like I literally forget how to take a proper breath looking at him right now. "For my own peace of mind. And I think it'll prompt you to make sure you're comfortable too. All right?"

"Oakley, you could ask for my kidney and I would say yes right now."

He laughs. "Kiss me, Loren."

As if I were on strings, I drop to him, bringing my mouth to his. Still, I let him orchestrate this as I lose myself in the way he's touching me. Alternating between jerking my dick and learning its shape. The weight of my balls. Pressing against my taint until I'm practically growling into his mouth.

Oakley shoves me onto my back and climbs on top of me. The way I nearly come when he becomes more assertive has my head spinning. Then he's moving down, dragging his tongue along my skin. There's a vague thought that I hope I got all the blood off me.

"This okay?" he asks.

"Yep."

His tongue flickers over my cockhead and my hips jerk. He grins. "This okay?"

"Oakley, I swear—"

His grin widens. I don't get to finish my empty threat before he takes my dick into his mouth. My hand immediately goes to his hair, gathering it in my fist. I need to see his face. I need to watch him swallow me and hollow his cheeks as he sucks gently.

His pretty eyes meet mine and I'm so fucking close to filling his mouth. The way he's looking at me! Like he enjoys this.

I stare. There's no convincing myself to look anywhere else. My mouth is open as I try to suck in air. A lungful eludes me.

And then he's buried his nose in my pelvis, bringing me to the back of his throat, and sucking like I'm a lollipop. My eyes roll. My hips jerk. I try to pull him off, try to warn him, but I think I only manage some incoherent sounds before I've lost it down his throat.

In the seconds that it takes me to empty, my entire body tingles with pleasure. I'm so fucking hot right now, I break out in a sweat.

Then Oakley's moving back up my body, kissing along my torso. I grip his hair with both my hands and bring his mouth to mine.

It's a miscalculation. Even though I'm very aware that I just came down his throat, my brain misfires because the taste of my release on his tongue surprises me. I'm momentarily disturbed until his body comes down on mine and I can feel how wet his underwear is.

I pull my mouth from his. "Did you—"

Oakley's cheeks heat and he nods. "You're hot on a regular day, but the sounds you make when I'm sucking your dick are definitely sensory overload."

It's been a while since I got off. Like, the week before seeing Oakley. I've been preoccupied. Now I don't think I'm going to remain *off* for any real length of time. I bring his mouth to mine again, kissing him hard.

He groans into me, his body already moving against mine as he climbs on top. Oakley wiggles out of his underwear and then wraps our not quite hard dicks in his fist. My hips jerk into his hand and a brand-new heat wave surges through me.

I'm never going to get tired of the way he touches me. Ever!

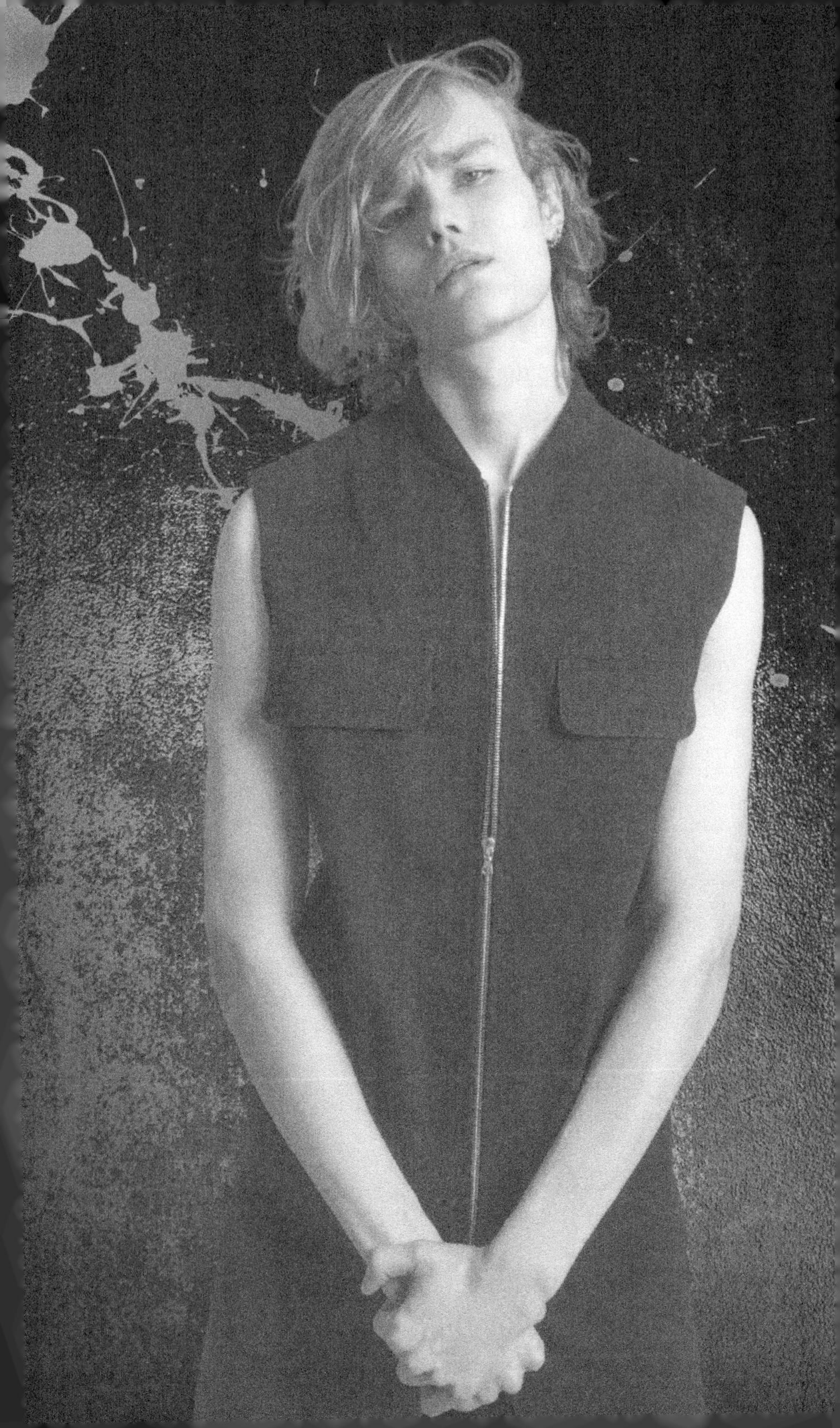

22
OAKLEY

FOR THE NEXT WEEK, I spend nearly every waking moment with Loren. I spend every night with him too. Since my friends and I have the rule that we don't bring people over, I stay at his house. Most of the time, I wake alone. But by the time I get out of the shower, he's back in his bedroom with breakfast.

There's almost always something on the tray with the food. A flower. Hearts made of various materials. Sometimes something silly, like a squishy penis or a little dragon claw. Yesterday, there was a necklace of pretty stones, and I may have smiled the *entire* day and touched it continuously.

This morning, I wake up to Loren still in bed with me. Maybe because it's Saturday. There's only been one time that he's pushed away from me. I admit I immediately got a pit in my stomach that made me feel nauseous. For someone who claims to not be able to read me, he knew right away. Loren pulled me closer, but just out of reach of touching him, made me look at him, and said the sweetest fucking shit to me.

The thing is, I trust he won't lie to me. I also believe that he *thinks* he doesn't know romance or love. So all the things he said were the truth as he saw it. Beautiful, sweet, romantic, loving. He's the most attentive man I've ever fucking met.

However, he's a complete fucking submissive in bed. I'm not complaining. In fact, I've found that I totally love it.

Loren said that he's unsure about what to do with a guy. But now that I'm confident he knows what's about to go down before it does and he still naturally lets me take the lead, I think it's more along the lines of this is just who he is.

I don't think he was wrong, though. It took him a bit to find his confidence to truly touch me. There's a part of me that wonders if it had to do with his aversion to touch or if he was unsure how to, or if he was afraid to overstep. We talk about sex stuff a lot. I burn like I'm on fire when I bring it up, but I really want to make sure I'm not pushing him or pressuring him.

We haven't had sex, but I made it clear that I much prefer to bottom. He appears indifferent to position, even when I asked how he'd feel bottoming.

My eyes open and I'm staring at the wall while sprawled across Loren's chest. One arm is secure around my upper back, as the other's s fingers are moving smoothly through my hair. He loves my hair. His hands are almost always in it. It's super fucking cute when he tries to get it into a hair elastic. I assure him it's unruly on a good day for me and I've yet to master it. He says we'll practice together.

"What are you thinking about?" Loren asks, his voice quiet. There's no sleepy tenor to it, so I think he's been awake for a while.

"You," I answer, turning my head to kiss his chest. We're naked. I love being naked with him. The feel of his skin on mine. There's nothing separating our heartbeats.

"You're thinking about sex again, aren't you?"

I laugh, turning my heating cheeks into his chest. In the quiet moments, I always bring up sex. But even if he sounds aloof to the fact that he's definitely found himself in a very different kind of sexual relationship, I don't want him to freak out. So I talk about all the gay things I can think of, just so he knows what's on the table. Or what's not, though we haven't really come across anything that he's opposed to.

Shifting so my body is completely on top of him, my legs fall over his hips. I cross my arms over my chest and look at him with my chin resting over them. His fingers drop to my neck and softly touch the place where my wounds are healing. It's been a treat trying to explain them away. There's seriously zero doubt about what's happened.

My friends have been fucking furious. All I've managed to convince them of is that Loren didn't have anything to do with them there, and he's the reason I'm still alive.

"They're healing," I say.

He frowns. So he's not focused on my wounds, I wiggle my dick over his. Immediately, his eyes flare with heat and I grin.

"You are thinking about sex, aren't you? Vixen."

I laugh. "So… want to do something new?"

"Anything you want."

"No, no. We've been over this."

His smile tells me he's humoring me when he asks, "What do you have in mind?"

"I want to ride your cock," I say.

Loren's breath catches. Every subtle movement in his body is complete reflex. The way his dick jumps. The slight rolling of his hips. And the soft touch of his hand on my back digging in a bit more.

"Are you ready for that?" he asks.

I laugh and sit up. "Are *you*? And I want the truth."

"Don't relationships have milestones they're supposed to reach?" he asks. "Some order of things? A timeline?"

"Is this your way of saying you're not ready? You can just say it. I won't be upset."

His eyelids hood. "No. I'm cognizant of the fact that maybe we're moving quickly, and I know I can be overwhelming, and I really don't want you to decide you need space because I might lose my mind if you do that. Sex is a big step, right?"

"You're not overwhelming, Loren," I say. It really irritates me that people have made him feel that way. Shifting, I slide up his body so my face is hovering over his. "I'm never overwhelmed by you. I'm not frustrated or uneasy or scared or put off or anything else that you've said in the last week. Stop trying to warn me about the way other people have made you feel about yourself."

"That's the part you wanted to address right now?" he asks, amused.

"Yes. As much as I talk about sex because I want you to be comfortable in this new territory for you, you seem to want to preempt *you*. One of these things is already unnecessary."

"The sex talk part, right?" he suggests, raising a brow.

I bite his lip, making him laugh. "I'm serious."

Loren sighs. "I am too. Even though I make people feel that way, *I* don't feel any particular way about how they feel. I don't feel bad that I make people uncomfortable, Oakley. But I don't want

LOREN

you to feel that way. Just as you don't want me to feel uncomfortable about sex with a guy. We're working toward the same thing, but in two different areas."

Maybe it doesn't make sense, but his explanation makes my chest warm. "Yes, it's a big step," I say, getting back to what he felt was most important in what he initially said. "Everything we're doing feels quick, yes, but... you said you knew when you saw me that I'm yours, right?"

He hums in agreement.

"Then can't you accept I *know* that everything we're doing now is right? I feel good being with you. I trust you. It's sick that I even love that you've killed two men who were going to hurt me. I don't care that you're not just like everyone else. I'm slightly intimidated by being your introduction into gay shit, but that's the *only* thing that concerns me, hence my constant sex talk."

Loren doesn't respond. His eyes are locked on mine, intensely staring because he has no other mode. I'm startled into laughter when he says, "Ride my dick, Oakley."

Still laughing, I move up his body so I can reach into his side table drawer for lube and a condom. The condoms are new, I'm not sure when he even got them. They just appeared one day, so I know he's also been thinking about sex.

His hands move over my back and down to my thighs as I feel around blindly in his drawer. I know where my stuff is without looking. Then again, his mouth on my skin is distracting. Especially when his hands move up to my ass cheeks, then gently pull them apart, and his finger presses softly against my hole.

Yep, he's totally been thinking about this.

Finally, I lay my hand on what I need and pull back. His hands remain touching my ass, so I shimmy around and pull his hand back to give him a dollop of lube on his fingers.

There aren't many times I've ever seen this man with questions in his eyes. It's so endearing when I do. I nod and bring his hand around me.

He rarely touches my ass, but I think, based on everything I've learned about him since we started talking, he's been working himself up to it. There's no hesitation when his fingers move along my crack or when the pad of his middle finger presses against my hole.

He's gentle. Always so damn gentle. I lean forward, pressing my forehead into his headboard so he has access to me. His mouth finds my skin and he's kissing me. Licking me. Sucking me gently. His finger breaks through my tight ring, and I release a breath, relaxing my body.

Loren pulls me further up. The next thing I know, he has my cock in his mouth as he nearly expertly fingers my ass. It's calculated, like so much about him. When he pushes in deeper, he sucks me a little harder. When he adds another finger, he distracts me from the burn with my cock at the back of his throat.

I'm fucking panting, my hips rocking all on their own as he works me over. I'm going to be finished before we even get started if he keeps going.

The strength I find to pull my dick from his mouth should be commemorated in stone. I push his hand away. With trembling fingers, I roll the condom onto his cock and get it dripping with lube. I'm so ready. So here for this. I need to feel him inside me.

Shifting my body, I hover over him. "Okay?" I ask, breathlessly.

LOREN

For once, he doesn't seem to be in the mood to question me or assure me I don't need to ask. He nods, watching me with his intense stare.

Holding the head of his dick in place, I press my body down. He's done a really fucking good job stretching me, so his cockhead slides in. Then I'm bearing down on his perfect dick.

"Oakley," he groans, his hands coming up to frame my face. His grip is tight but always so gentle.

Loren's hips rock as I take his dick to the root. For a second, I pause to catch my breath. Planting my hands on his chest and getting my feet under me, I start to ride.

I've never been one to babble when I fuck, but words seem to tumble from my mouth.

"Loren," I groan. "Your dick is so good. You're made for an ass."

He snorts. His gaze hasn't moved from my face. Neither have his hands.

"You like this? Like me on your cock?"

Loren nods.

"Feels good, right?"

"So good," he says, voice low, raw.

"You're so sexy. So good. Are you good?"

The side of his mouth lifts in a half smile. "I've never been called good," he teases.

"I suppose you haven't. You're... bad. Oh! Naughty. You're a naughty, naughty boy." I giggle. "Like that better?"

He's still grinning, finding me amusing. "Yes. Better."

I ride him until I run out of energy. Then I bring my legs back under me and collapse. "Fuck me, Loren. Make us come."

His hands drop, moving under my legs and spreading them apart. I feel him shift, digging his heels into the bed. I have just enough time to wrap my arms around him before he's fucking into me.

"Oh my god," I groan, gripping him tightly. My head spins, but once more, words just tumble out. Probably slurred. Most likely incoherent. "So good. Do you know how much I love that you protect me like you do? I've never had someone care about me like that. Enough to kill someone. You've killed people for me."

"I'll do it again," he grunts.

The way he's thrusting into me has my head spinning.

"You're born to fuck me like this, you know that?" He snorts again, but it's lost in a grunt. "You do it perfectly. God, you're so good at this. I'm going to come on your dick. Is that okay?"

He groans. "Yes."

"Keep fucking me, Loren. Keep—Fuck, I love that you're a villain. You're my villain. Harder. Please, I need to come."

His hands grip my thighs, fingers digging in. Somehow, he manages to fuck me harder. My head spins wildly. "Come with me. Come, Loren. Fuck, fuck, fuck. Come. Please."

I know when he does. I've memorized the way his breath hitches and the deep tenor of his groan when he comes. My mouth latches on to his collarbone, but his dick keeps driving in. With every thrust, I see stars. Meteors. My teeth sink into his skin.

He groans, his cock burying deep as I feel it pulse inside me and finally, my orgasm rushes out. I'm blinded, crying out, the sound muffled by how hard I'm biting him. I can feel my orgasm in my toes. The way his dick pulses makes my ass clench.

Then we drop. I'm an overdone noodle, panting like a dog. Hell, I'm even licking the spot where I bit him like a dog, lapping up the traces of blood I released.

"Sorry," I mutter.

"For what?" he asks. I love how breathless he sounds.

"You sound super sexy right now."

He huffs. One hand moves into my hair, gripping it tightly. His other moves down to my ass. I feel his finger touch my hole, right where his dick is still lodged inside me.

"You like the feel of that?" I ask.

Loren nods, humming his agreement.

"Me too." I tuck my face into his neck. "Maybe we can stay like this for another minute."

He nods again, his finger continuing to feel the way my hole stretches over his cock.

"I bit you," I admit. "I think I drew blood. That's what I was apologizing for."

"Bite me anywhere you want. Whenever you want," he says. He sounds so relaxed. Happy. I smile.

There's a knock at the door and I turn my head.

"Yeah?" Loren calls and the door opens. My eyes widen.

Myro steps inside and then backs out quickly. "Fucking Christ, Loren. It's okay not to share everything with me."

"You opened the door," Loren retorts, clearly amused.

"Downstairs, bro. When you're finished."

"I wouldn't have answered you if we weren't finished," he says. "I probably wouldn't have heard you. Oakley has some mad dirty talking skills, and I was enthralled. Trust me when I tell you, you didn't exist three minutes ago."

"Jesus," I mutter, face burning.

Myro sighs in exasperation. "Downstairs."

"I think I have to go downstairs," Loren tells me when the door clicks shut.

"That was seriously not something that you needed to share with him," I say, lifting my face to peek at him.

Loren's grinning. "One of my favorite things to do is watch my brothers squirm. But I won't share our sex life if it makes you uncomfortable. I'm sorry I didn't ask first. Though you should know, had he been upstairs a minute ago, he'd have heard you through the door. You're not quiet."

I bury my face in his chest. "You're mean."

His arms wrap around me and he kisses my head. We lay quietly for several minutes. "Are you mad?"

"No. I'm a little embarrassed."

"Don't be. You're quite good. I'm going to swear off sex with anyone else for a repeat of that."

"Fucking hell," I mutter. He's still grinning, and I can feel it when he presses his lips to my head. "For the record, you better be swearing off sex with anyone else, even if I'm bad in bed."

"I already did the moment I saw you, Oakley."

Despite the heat in my cheeks, I smile.

We get out of bed and I make him shower alone, otherwise there's a chance we might not get out of the bedroom this morning. He's dressed when I step into the closet with a towel wrapped around my waist, and Loren immediately backs me against the wall.

The way he keeps a foot between us while still crowding in and towering over me, I think he doesn't want to be touched right now. So I don't. The warmth in his eyes is just… consuming.

"I'm probably going to be downstairs for a while. You can stay if you want."

"I'll go home for a bit."

"Promise me you won't go somewhere without me. Don't leave the house."

Loren's been obsessive since the guy tried to kill me in an alley. I'm not even sad about it. In fact, it's difficult trying not to smile. "Promise."

He nods but doesn't back away. "When I need some space, this is still good," he says before pressing his lips to my forehead quickly. "I like you close, even if I don't want to be touched."

I nod.

"I'll call you when I'm done with whatever Dad wants."

He likely knows what his father wants, but I nod again. Once he's gone, I search for my clothes. I find my socks and pants, but the shirt and underwear are elusive, so I go commando and borrow one of Loren's shirts.

Dressed, I open his door and practically trip over myself when I find Voss standing there, leaning against the window across the hall. For the first time, it occurs to me that maybe they don't like me with their brother. Maybe they don't like me at all.

When Voss smiles, it doesn't look particularly hostile. Still, I'm fucking nervous and shift my weight back and forth.

"He's told you, hasn't he?" Voss says.

I don't have to pretend to be confused right now. I have no idea what he's talking about.

"That he's a killer," Voss clarifies.

Swallowing, I nod. "He killed Daniel and the guy who was going to kill me to protect me," I say defensively.

Voss studies me. It's both similar and very unlike the way Loren stares. "Yes," he agrees at last. "He trusts you with that information. He's killed those men to keep you safe, and you need to keep him safe by never repeating it."

"I won't."

"To anyone, Oakley. Including your friends. No one can know that he's killed those men. I need you to understand the severity of this."

I huff. "You don't think I know?" I snap, irritated.

"I think you trust your friends and therefore you wouldn't see any reason not to trust them with this. But Loren didn't trust you, believing you'd tell them. He trusts you to keep this to yourself. I can count on one hand how many people he trusts. Please don't break that trust."

"There's more people in this house than can be counted on one hand," I retort.

"The triplets count as one," he says, grinning.

I laugh, even though I think he's threatening me.

"He's not a very trusting person," Voss continues, his voice quieter now. "I could get into a lot of evidence to explain this to you, but I have a feeling you already know all that. You're smart and I know Loren's already been telling you the things about himself that he finds…"

"Off-putting to others?" I ask.

He nods, smiling. "Yes. He's more aware than he thinks he is. He'll go to the ends of the earth to protect you, Oakley. The only thing I want from you is to know that you'll do the same for him."

"You don't need to threaten me to keep me quiet," I promise.

Voss looks amused. "I'm not at all threatening you. To do that would put Loren in a very uncomfortable position, and I wouldn't do that to my brother. I'm making sure that you—"

"I have no intention of sharing it with anyone. Ever. I'll take it to my grave. Not least of all, he's saved my life. More than once, probably. But that aside, I really like him. He's a good guy, even though he doesn't like to be called a good guy."

He snorts. "He really doesn't."

"I'll protect him. I promise."

Voss nods, his smile much more open now. "Good. I hope we get to see you more often than when you're sneaking out of his room or into it."

I flush. "Uh, yeah."

Two things occur to me as I step outside the Van Doren house. One, Voss is very protective of his brother. I really love that. And two, I don't think Loren's killed just two men. Voss asked if I knew he was a killer. Not whether I knew he killed two men for me. His course of conversation changed once I stated what I knew.

Loren is a killer and I don't think Daniel and the guy who accosted me in the alley were his first kills.

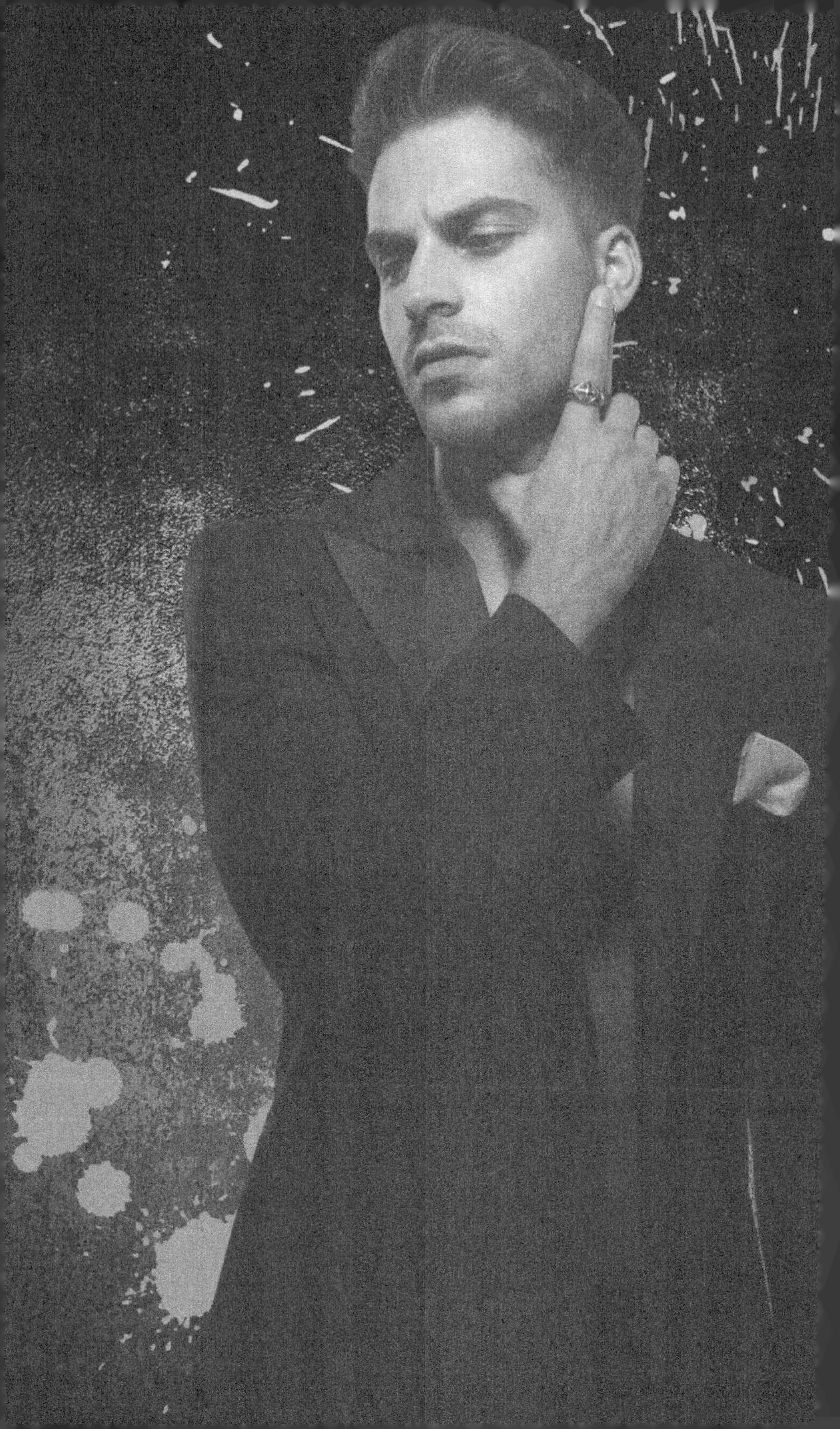

23
LOREN

At our normal house, we separate work from living. There isn't just a room that's dedicated to work—it's an entire, unconnected building. There isn't even a covered roof connecting the spaces.

It's weird that we aren't leaving the house.

There's a downstairs suite in the daylight basement that we've converted into a suitable space. The large closet now houses lots of computer equipment that needs to stay cool, so it's been outfitted with a specialized venting system. The bathroom we obviously left alone. And the bedroom is now our conference room, complete with a large monitor on the wall. There's also a kitchenette and an apartment sized fridge.

The triplets, Myro, and Dad are already there, sitting around the table. Imry is casually swinging his chair from side to side, though his gaze locks on mine as I walk in. I take the seat closest to the door, dropping into it next to Avory and Ellory.

I can already tell from the way they're grinning at me that coming here was a mistake.

"Gay sex is the best, huh?" Ellory asks.

I raise a brow and then glare at Myro. He shrugs.

"You answered," Myro defends.

"I didn't say 'enter.' I said 'yeah?' You chose to interpret that to mean you could walk in."

"He's right," Imry agrees. "I know that we've chosen to stay with Dad, but we are all definitely adults. Probably shouldn't just walk in."

"I knocked," Myro says with a heavy sigh.

"And I answered. I didn't say you should come in. What you saw is all on you. Though you should have kept that to yourself."

He chuckles. "I didn't repeat it. I just said you were occupied right now. They interpreted that on their own, and you just confirmed it." He gestures to Avory and Ellory.

I look at them again. They're still grinning at me as if they expect an answer.

Ellory leans forward. "You can totally admit it's better, bro."

"How do you even know it's better?" Imry asks. "How many girls have you been with?"

"None," Ellory and Avory say together.

I glance at Dad. He's sitting back in his chair, amused. I'm not sure if it's because he has all boys, or if it's because he remembers being a teenager, but he's never tried to curb our conversations. When Mom used to, Dad made sure we understood that home was a safe place, and we were allowed to ask questions and have whatever discussions we wanted.

"Then you can't compare," Imry says.

"But Loren can," Avory teases, and once more they're looking at me expectantly.

"I'm not talking about this. Where's Voss?"

"He's coming. He was making breakfast when I found him earlier," Myro answers.

I sit back in my chair, ignoring Avory and Ellory as best I can. Meeting Dad's eyes, he chuckles. "How is Oakley?" he asks.

"He's fine."

"He's not experiencing any lasting trauma—medically or mentally?"

I consider the last week. He's gotten more talkative than he had been. More confident. The longer we spend together, the more I see who he truly is.

I'm entirely enamored of him.

"He doesn't like the wounds on his neck," I admit. "He's afraid they'll scar."

"They likely won't," Myro says, and I glance in his direction. "The rope burn and bruising will fade easily enough. The gouges may take a little longer, but I think they'll also fade. We have some scar cream if you'd like to give it to him."

I nod. "Yes. He'd like that. Thanks."

Voss walks into the room, shutting the door behind him. He's carrying a large travel mug and has a gourmet meal on his plate when he sits down. He's also got the attention of the full room on him.

He shrugs. "This is a really early meeting."

"It's nine," Dad deadpans.

Voss takes a bite of his eggs Benedict and shrugs, slapping Imry's hand away when he reaches for a piece of bacon.

Myro shakes his head, sighing. His focus turns to me. "When do you think you'll be ready to resume the contract, Loren?"

I shake my head. "I told you—I'm done."

The room is silent as they stare at me. Not that I blame them. Everyone knows I love to kill people. I do so in a controlled environment so I don't get myself in trouble.

"You're done completely," Myro says. It's not a question. "You're retiring from contract exterminations. No more murder."

Well, when he puts it like that…

"I'm not leaving Oakley alone," I insist.

"Where is he now?" Imry asks.

"Next door. He's promised not to leave without me."

"How long do you think you can keep that up?" Myro asks.

"Indefinitely."

"What happens when he graduates and gets a job?" Imry asks.

"Maybe I'll work with him."

"Loren—" Myro starts.

"He somehow managed to attract two crazy fuckers intent on hurting him," I say. "He walked right into the grasp of a damn serial killer! I'm *not* leaving him alone."

Two days ago, they told me Voss identified the man I killed in the alley that had intended to murder Oakley. He'd been killing for over a decade. There were a whole lot of bodies tied to a single M.O., but no suspects to speak of. Oakley had somehow managed to wander straight into his fucking nest.

LOREN

"If I'd killed Daniel last summer, Oakley would have been spared his attention. But how was I to know we had a serial killer here? Don't we look that shit up?"

"Easy," Dad says, and I take a breath to regulate my irritation. "If you'd have exterminated Daniel last summer, you'd not have met Oakley."

I'm about to argue when he continues.

"Daniel relocating here is the reason you came to Tucson. Tracking him is the reason you were in the café. Being in the café is how you found Oakley. Some things need to happen in a certain order for other events to take place. If I'd have divorced your mother when I first started seeing the signs of her troublesome opinions, I wouldn't have my youngest four sons. However, sometimes in hindsight, we realize that some situations should have been resolved sooner rather than later. I should have taken you kids out of her presence a lot sooner than I did. Just as you feel you should have gotten rid of Daniel before he truly had a chance to get close to Oakley. But there are times when we have to stand back and recognize that the past is the past and all we can focus on is the future," Dad explains.

"You know we don't blame you for not taking us out sooner, right?" Avory questions.

Dad inclines his head. "I know you don't. But I do. I kept telling myself that after *this* conversation, she'll get her head out of her ass. I wanted to believe she could be a good mother—the mother you deserved. She wasn't and I should have accepted that far sooner than I did."

Ellory gets up and walks around the table, hugging Dad from behind. "We aren't upset," he reiterates. "We knew you were trying to keep us together so we could have a happy childhood. And we had each other. Myro could have left, but he stayed to protect us, too."

"Probably wise. Mom might have been Loren's first kill," Voss says. His tone is indifferent. I'm not sure there's any love lost for our mother. Which I gather is a little sad for both him and Myro because she'd been very different as a mother before I was born, and it was clear I was different.

Voss isn't wrong. I didn't care about the way she treated me. My brothers and Dad have always made it clear there wasn't anything wrong with me, and I didn't need to change, regardless of what Mom said. That was enough reassurance for me.

But the way she treated Avory and Ellory... that's why Voss is right. There's a very high probability that if Dad hadn't taken us when he did, I would have killed Mom. I'd grown up seeing the way she made them feel, and with each new incident, I grew that much angrier.

Dad patted his arms, resting his head along Ellory's. "I'm relieved you don't resent me. You boys have always been my first priority, the beings I love most in this world. All I wanted was to do right by you."

"You did, Dad," Myro says. "It's Mom who didn't."

Dad closes his eyes for a minute. "Okay, we've gotten off topic. I only brought up Mom to illustrate a point." Ellory kisses the side of his head before taking his seat beside Avory again. They lean into each other, shoulder to shoulder, but their attention is on the discussion at hand. "Some events, though uncomfortable, might have been necessary. You have Oakley now, but you wouldn't have if you'd killed Daniel last summer."

"Fine. I can make peace with that," I say. "But you're not going to be able to write off the second guy as easily. If I'd have been there instead of tailing a target, he'd have not wandered into that man's preying grounds."

LOREN

"You're right," Dad agrees, causing my brothers to look at him in surprise. "He wouldn't have run into the serial killer."

It's very unusual when I'm agreed with this easily while I'm being somewhat... obstinate. I frown.

"Or you both would have, and he'd have seen you kill someone with your bare hands," Dad says.

There it is... I tense at the thought.

Dad leans forward and grips my wrist. My skin prickles. I've already had a lot of touch lately, and I think I've reached my threshold for today. "Loren, I'm going to allow you all the time you want to work through your fear of Oakley being hurt while you're somewhere else. For your own mental health, it's necessary. But I need you to pay attention to your own signs, son. Recognize when your thirst for violence becomes too strong. Oakley might be able to romanticize you killing his attackers, but if he sees you kill someone or if you hurt someone he cares about, it's going to be a very different situation. You can't just be attending to Oakley's safety and his needs; you need to pay equal attention to your own."

"Dad—always teaching us lessons," Voss mutters as he sits back in his chair.

The thing is, I know he's right. But the thought of leaving Oakley again and something happening to him when I *should have* been there makes me irrationally pissed. I thought I'd reached a new level of enjoying watching someone die with Daniel. But that man had barely laid a hand on Oakley.

The serial killer, though. He was unrecognizable when I was finished. It took Voss *days* to identify him. For Voss, that's a very long time. He ended up having to use dental records and DNA. He didn't have any fingerprints left. There was no way to reconstruct his face. I annihilated him.

"You know, if you need to attend to a contract, we can make sure Oakley's safe," Avory promises. "We give you a hard time, but that's because you're our brother and it's our job. But we'd never let anything happen to someone you care about."

I know that. The problem is, I thought Oakley was safe. There's no reason he shouldn't have been safe that day. How did he make it through more than twenty years without someone watching over him? He's here for less than a handful of months and he attracts two crazy fuckers.

Three, if I'm included in that.

"Yeah," I agree. "Okay."

"You should look for signs that he needs to speak to someone professionally about what happened to him," Myro says.

I sigh, giving him a wry look. "You're going to have to spell that out, Myro."

He chuckles. "I'll send you a couple links. I've only seen him in passing since you practically sneak him in and out, so I haven't been able to get a good read on whether he's dealing with some lasting mental trauma."

"I think Loren's distracting him well," Avory teases, winking at me.

I roll my eyes.

"You don't need to keep him hidden, baby brother," Imry says, kicking me under the table. "I'm a little offended that the people who aren't related to us that you care about, you keep hidden. As if we'll steal them."

"Who have I kept hidden?"

"Your hockey buddy, for one," Imry says. "And you're trying to keep Oakley hidden too."

I frown. "I'm not hiding either of them. Noah lives in L.A. He travels for like eight months a year. *I* barely see him."

"He has summers off," Voss points out.

Rolling my eyes, I shrug. "I'll see if he wants to come over. Is a sleepover okay, Dad?" I deadpan.

He chuckles. "No girls."

That garners far more laughter than I think it earns. "You know he's gay, right?"

More laughter.

"Yes," Dad says.

"Ah. I see. Funny."

And still more laughter. I'm beginning not to like my brothers.

"Okay, Noah's taken care of. Now back to Oakley. When will you stop hiding him?" Avory asks.

"Aren't you already involved?" I huff. "Leave Oakley alone."

"We are," Avory and Ellory say together.

"But we want to know the person you're so obsessed with. We love you and we want to support you in your relationship," Myro says.

"We'd like to spend time with you and Oakley, preferably not when you're in bed," Imry says, shrugging.

"I didn't invite him in!"

"Take a breath, Loren," Dad soothes, chuckling. "What your brothers are trying to say is that if he's important to you, he's important to us. *When you're ready*, we'd love to have a chance to welcome him into the family. Dinner. Games. Once the pool is rebuilt, we can hang out in the backyard. Okay?"

It's not unreasonable. It's not like they haven't already spent time with Oakley. But before, the rest of Oakley's household was here too. This is different. What they're asking for is different.

I'm not sure I want to share Oakley's attention.

But I'm really… relieved?… that I have their support. Besides, I *want* them to like Oakley. It would be awful if they didn't.

"Dinner," I suggest. That seems like a relatively short event. Then I can take him away and have him to myself. "Okay, yes. We can have dinner."

"Sounds good," Dad says. "You choose the night and let us know."

I nod.

As the youngest, I'm not great at sharing. I've always had my own things. Sharing Oakley's attention is probably really going to suck.

But my family is important to me too. Besides, I don't particularly want to live somewhere without my family. That means Oakley will have to live here with them.

Not that I think he's ready for that conversation yet. I'm not even ready for him to spend time with my family without me.

Little baby steps.

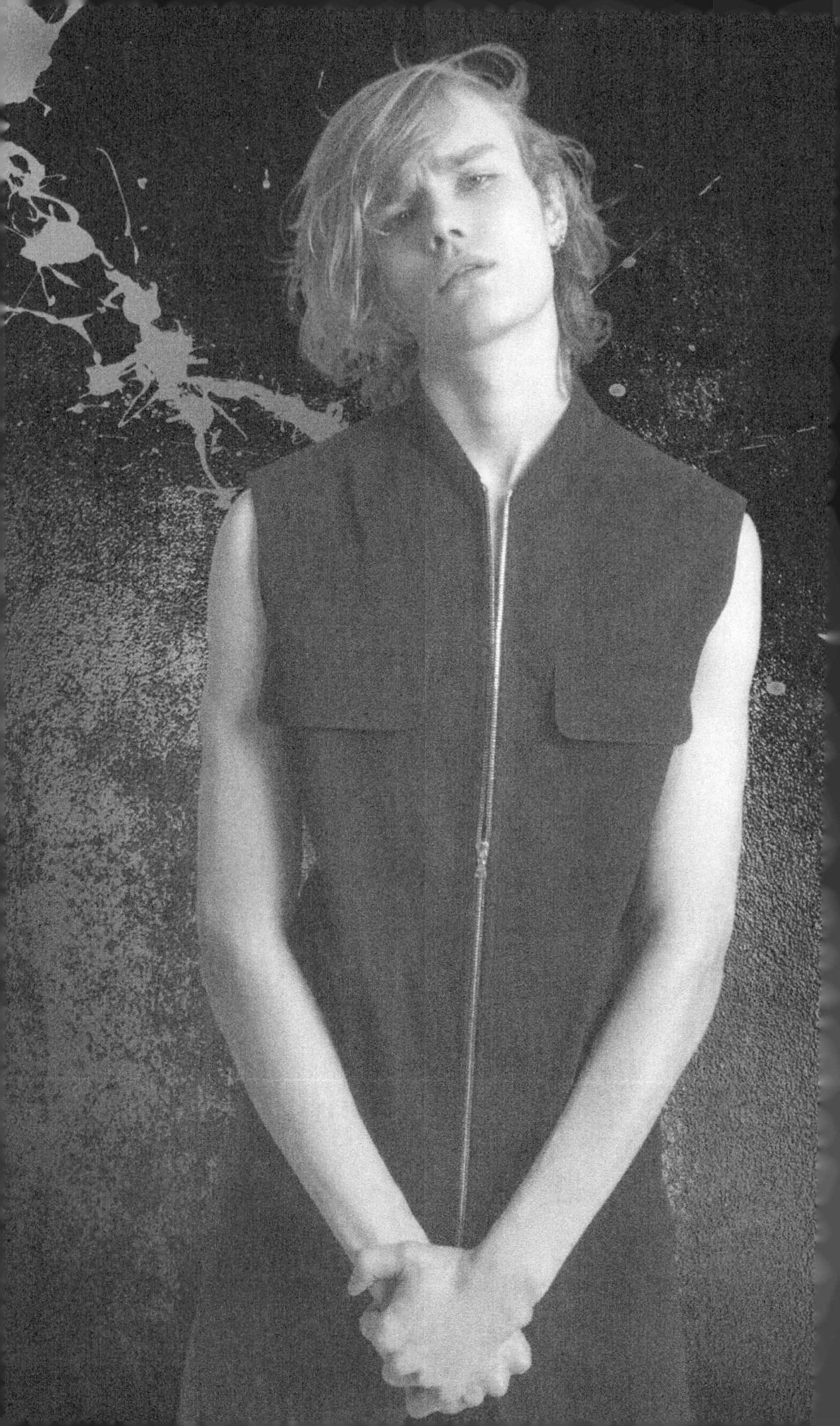

24
OAKLEY

I THOUGHT I'd be able to get to my room and put some underwear on without having to see anyone first, but luck is not on my side. Everyone is sitting in the living room when I walk in and they all turn to look at me.

For a moment, silence passes between us until Briar says, "Just can't wipe that smile off your face, can you?"

I don't even realize I'm smiling, but now that he said so… no, I can't.

Shutting the door behind me, I cross the room and drop into the chair. Then wince because it's been quite a while since I had sex and yep, I can feel it.

"Good night?" Haze asks. His smile is small, reminding me a lot of Loren. Unassuming. Quiet. There's a lot behind the smile, but he keeps it closed off from the world.

"Yes," I admit. "Also, a good morning."

Haze chuckles.

I bring my knees up and wrap my arms around my legs. They're looking at my neck. I can feel their eyes as if their fingers are brushing the wounds.

They're beginning to itch. It's been absolute torture trying not to scratch at them. But I don't want them to scar and live the rest of my life with people staring at my neck.

My friends were… not nearly as ready to accept the explanation I gave them about being attacked and Loren rescuing me. It's the truth; however, they've been waiting for the news to report *something*.

As if they know my thoughts, Briar says, "I haven't seen a report yet."

I sigh, reflexively wrapping my hand around my neck. "I told you—I didn't press charges." There isn't someone alive to press them against.

Obviously, I couldn't tell him that. Even without Voss warning me this morning, I wouldn't have said anything.

"We believe that," Levis says. "We're not convinced you should let it go."

"You don't have to be convinced. You just have to support my decision and trust that it's taken care of," I insist.

"Loren rescued you," Honey Bee muses as if she's trying to get the missing pieces to appear and fall into place.

"I'm not going to talk about this again," I say and get to my feet.

"All right, all right," Briar says, raising his hand. "We'll drop it."

"Looking at the remnants of that… fight… makes us upset," Honey Bee admits. "We're just worried."

"I know and I appreciate it. As it turns out, you had grounds to be worried. But I promise you, I'm good. Everything is fine."

LOREN

The truth is, I haven't told them the full details because that would lead to *a lot* of questions that I simply can't answer. It was almost midnight when my phone rang the day of the attack; Honey Bee was freaking out because no one had seen or heard from me since my argument with Brek.

It took me a long time to assure her I was fine, that I'd had an accident and was healing, but I'd be home the following day. With Myro and Jalon's help, we came up with a story. Since there was simply no way to say anything other than I had been attacked with something around my neck, we had to start there. Then somehow tie Loren in since I was at their house, and leave the attacker anonymous, which wasn't hard because we didn't actually know who he was.

At the time, anyway. While Loren didn't say, I'm sure he now knows who he was.

"One more question," Levis says. I sigh. "This isn't just some kinky shit that got out of hand, is it?"

My eyes widen. Briar spits out his drink and then chokes on it as he tries to catch his breath. Haze laughs, slapping his back. Even Brek manages to crack a smile, though it's not at the question so much as it is Briar sputtering.

"No," I promise, once I'm relatively sure Briar's going to make it. "I'm not really into kinky shit. I'll leave that for you."

He shrugs one shoulder, not confirming or denying that he's interested in kinky shit. Not gonna lie, I'm slightly intrigued now.

"You hanging out for the day or taking off as soon as he's free?" Brek asks.

There's no mistaking the bitterness in his voice, even as he tries to hide it. He's been weird for a while now; ever since I started talking to Loren. While he still refuses to admit to not liking Loren, I'm not sure what to do about it.

"That depends. If you're going to act like an ass and still not give me a legitimate reason why, I'm leaving as soon as he's done doing whatever it is Loren does. Your choice."

I can tell there's a whole lot that he wants to say, but Brek doesn't answer. Honey Bee untucks her legs and scooches across the cushion to cuddle into his side. Brek sighs, wrapping his arm around her shoulders, now avoiding my eyes.

"Any closer to deciding on a major?" Briar asks.

Giving him a thankful smile that he's moved the conversation away from Loren, I shake my head. "Honestly, the classes I like the best, I'm not sure how to make a career out of them. I love ancient cultures, but where is the practical application in that?"

Every single one of my friends is graduating this spring. All five. Then there's me. Still stupidly undecided. I think I have enough courses for a double major in a number of fields by now because of taking extra classes during semesters and summer courses. But fuck if I know what to do with any of them.

"You can be a researcher," Honey Bee suggests. "Or an archaeologist and discover lost cities and treasures."

I nod absently. The thing is, I'm fascinated with this stuff but… neither of those things sound particularly appealing.

"You want to be a professional student," Levis says, amused.

Sighing, I nod and drop my face into my hands. "Why can't that be a thing?! I could test out new courses and stuff."

"Maybe you need a sugar daddy," Briar teases, not for the first time.

Brek scowls, turning his attention to the window.

"Maybe," I say, shrugging. "Any leads on jobs?" I ask.

"Actually," Levis starts, "I've been talking to Jalon. I might take an internship at Van Doren Technologies for a bit. They have their fingers in probably every single career field imaginable and since they seem friendly enough across the street, I thought I'd see what he thought about it."

"He agreed?" Briar asked.

Levis shrugs. "He's suggesting that I work for the summer in information technology, but if I want the position that I've been talking about, I really need a master's degree. He's not wrong, and I've had it on my mind for a while now."

"That's a lot more school, isn't it?" Brek asks.

Levis shrugs. "A Ph.D. is like five more years after a master's degree. Usually, you can get a masters in just a couple. I'm not ruling out either."

"That doesn't surprise me in the least," Honey Bee says. "You're such an overachiever."

He smirks, shrugging.

"Are you still with the same girl?" I ask.

Levis nods.

"She the one?"

He shrugs. "Could be. She's sweet."

"And hot," Briar says.

Honey Bee nods. "There's like three girls in the world I'd swing that way for, and I think yours is one of them." She fans herself while pretending to drool.

Levis grins. "She's hot," he agrees. "She's also smart and sweet. Our dreams for the future seem to align."

"Then what's the holdup?" Honey Bee asks.

"The fact that we've only been together for four months."

"Oh no, that's fair," Briar says. "Give them time to let their true colors show."

"She seems genuine so far," Levis said, "and hasn't gotten jealous over our living situation or how much time we spend together. She says she's excited to meet Honey Bee and is sure you'll be quick friends." He shrugs.

"Girls have said that before," Honey Bee says.

We all glance at Briar.

He waves us off. "Single for the win right now."

Honey Bee gives him a pouty look. "Sorry, Briar."

Briar shrugs. "I'm learning not to fall so quickly. Less disappointing that way."

"Any new prospects?" I ask.

"A couple. I feel like I need to have an elevator pitch that lists the things they need to be down with before I even talk to them."

"I can totally make one for you," Brek says. "I've been looking for a project that's beyond the required shit my courses have lined up."

Briar laughs. "Knock yourself out, bro. It definitely can't hurt."

"I'm thinking a little pamphlet," Brek says, dropping his head onto the back of the couch thoughtfully. "Oh! I could make it digital and interactive!"

"He's going to be handing them a QR code and having them take questionnaires," Haze says.

"Hey, that's cool. I want my wife and kids already." Briar pouts. "I'm really kind of tired of waiting."

"Such a sap," I mutter.

He meets my eyes and we exchange grins. We both know I want that too. Well, not the wife part.

"Haze?" Honey Bee asks.

He looks up from his phone. "Yes?"

"Any boyfriends we should know about?"

"Plural? No. Two seems like a lot of work."

"I could totally handle two lovers," Brek says wistfully, making us all look at him. A beat passes and he picks his head up. "What? One to ride me and one to sit on my face. I think that sounds really good, no?"

"So you want a threesome," Briar says. "That's different from having two girlfriends, dude."

"Well, yeah, I guess. Okay, yes, definitely. But I don't just want a threesome. I think cuddling with two bodies would be great. This side is cold right now." He raises the arm that Honey Bee isn't under.

"We've tainted his view of the world by always being in a group," Levis says, amused.

"Do you have two girlfriends?" Honey Bee asks.

Brek laughs. "Not even one. I swear, all the girls I meet are only looking to fuck around, and I'm not entirely sure I'm into that right now."

"Aw. Our sweet Brekky is growing up," Briar says, grinning.

Brek rolls his eyes.

"Anyway," I call out. "Back to you, Haze. Boyfriend?"

Haze shakes his head.

"Who're you talking to right now, then?" Honey Bee asks, eyeing his phone. "Hook up?"

He snorts. "No. My professor, actually. I hate this assignment and I want to swap it. He's at least entertaining the idea."

"Are you intentionally being elusive and not answering the question about whether you're seeing someone or...?" Briar asks.

"I'm not being elusive. I'm not seeing anyone."

"Are you interested in someone?" I ask.

Haze shakes his head, shrugging. After a minute, he sighs. "You know, I thought it would be great to just be... out. Without fear or worry about my brothers and father. Oren's far away and I don't have to keep thinking about coming home and finding him curled in the corner of his bed because they're fucking shit to him. Yet... I still feel..."

He trails off.

Levis gets up and squishes into the cushion next to him, wrapping our big guy in a hug. Haze laughs but drops his head on Levis' shoulder.

"I'm fine," Haze insists. "Seriously, I feel a lot fucking better being here. I'm not exactly scared to tell people. I mean, the girls that hit on me know because I make sure they do but, I don't know. Maybe I'm not ready to make an announcement. It feels too big, too much pressure."

"That's cool," Levis says. "You don't have a deadline to meet."

"Yeah, but the more you guys shack up with partners and shit, the more I realize I want that. I can't exactly have it both ways.

It's not like I want to hide a relationship either, but not hiding means being out in the world and again, I'm not sure I'm there. So what's the option right in the middle because I think I need that one?"

"I'm not going to say this to pressure you in any way, Haze," I start. "I know how scared you've been. I've taken on your fear a lot over the years because I was afraid of your family, and I was afraid that they'd take you away from us if they knew I was gay. And I just want you to know that it *is* scary finally telling everyone the truth and making it readily known, embracing that part of myself, but it's also really, really freeing. I feel good. I don't have to constantly chant in my head *that's too gay* as a means of policing how I act or what I wear or how I talk. For the first time in my life, I'm not carrying this weight around on my shoulders."

"You're confusing those feel-good endorphins from freedom of expression with regular sex," Honey Bee teases.

I roll my eyes, as Haze and Briar snort in amusement.

"Joking aside, I'm really, really happy that you've finally been able to freely be who you are," Honey Bee admits. "It's been so fun these last few months seeing you share glimpses of yourself with the rest of the world and not just us. I'm really proud of you."

"Thanks," I say.

"Thanks for that," Haze says. "I really appreciate knowing that you struggled, but you feel it was worth it."

"Definitely. For a lot of reasons, this was the right move for me. Even if we did it for you," I say.

Haze shakes his head.

"We did it for all of us," Levis comments. "Haze's safety was definitely a top priority, but I think it was the best decision we've all made together."

"Together," Honey Bee says, grinning.

"Together," we agree as a group. Even Brek is smiling right now.

Sometimes I wonder how long we can keep this sentimentality before we're pulled apart in different directions. Life happens. We're adults now. We're cultivating relationships. How long before this is nothing but a memory?

The knowledge that these moments are numbered makes my chest ache.

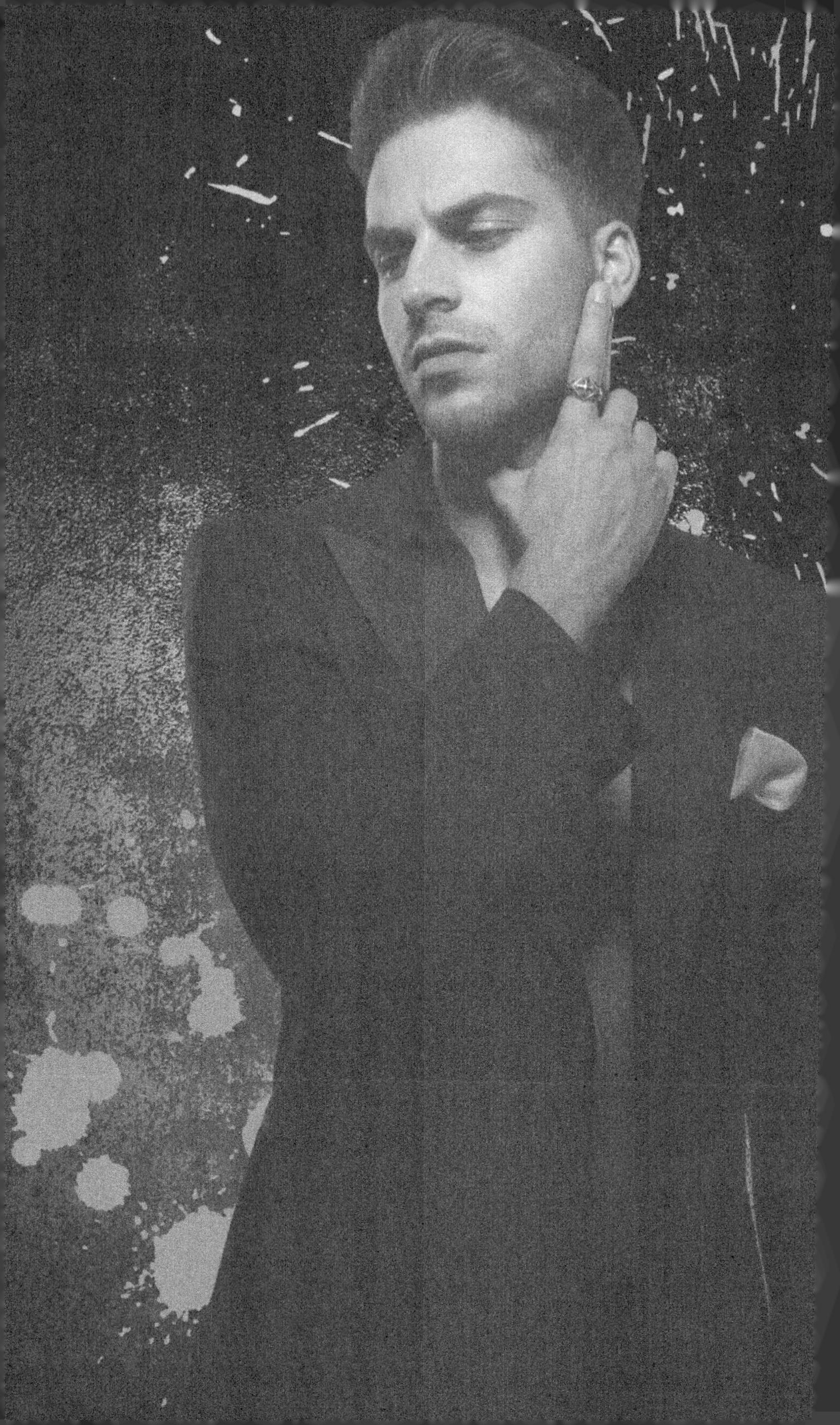

25
LOREN

I'M REGRETTING this as I walk across the road to retrieve Oakley for this date night. Can I call it a date night? I pause and pull out my phone, hitting dial without even looking at the time. Again.

Noah answers.

"I'm sorry, I have no idea if you're busy," I say.

He laughs. "Your timing always seems to be spot on. What's up, Loren Van Doren?"

I smirk and step backward onto the sidewalk as a car drives by. "I need to know if inviting Oakley over for dinner with my family is a date."

"You're getting caught up in technicalities that don't really matter. It's a big step for you to introduce him to your family without thinking about the pressure of whether you're on a date or not," Noah says.

"They've met several times," I tell him. "Oakley's household has been hanging with us in the yard for a while now; at least once a week, but oftentimes more."

"Ah."

"But this feels…" I can't decide how it feels. Am I nervous? Is that what this feeling is? Anxiety maybe. I'm anxious for how this is going to go.

"It feels big," Noah says when I don't finish. "Kind of imposing. The unknown outcome makes you uncomfortable."

I sigh. "Yes. All that."

"Again, I don't think you need to think in terms of whether this is a date or not. Concentrate on making Oakley comfortable. And yourself comfortable too. Okay?"

"Yes. But is meeting the family normally a date thing?"

"Mmm… no, I wouldn't call it a date. It's a progression in the relationship. Usually when you're both feeling serious about a future together."

Ah. Well, that's fine then. We're sharing a future. I've already determined that. Though it occurs to me that perhaps I should make sure Oakley likes that idea too.

"They think I keep you from them too."

Noah laughs. "Who?"

"My family. Want to come over this summer?"

He laughs again. "Sure."

"Good. Now they'll have to find something else to give me a hard time about."

Noah chuckles. "Family functions must be a riot at your house."

"Yes. That's how I'd describe them. You can bring Lix too. In case that wasn't clear."

"Thanks, Loren. Go pick up your boyfriend."

"Bye." But as we hang up, I'm now stuck for another reason and call him back. "Is he my boyfriend?" I ask when Noah answers.

"Honey, you're way, way overthinking right now. And I can't answer that. It's a conversation and decision between you two."

I huff. "Okay, fine."

"Seriously, just enjoy the night, Loren. All your favorite people in the same room."

"Most of them," I clarify. "Bye."

He's chuckling when I hang up. This time I make it across the road. Albrecht is watching me through the window upstairs. I get the feeling he's not my biggest fan. With a smile, I wave and then knock on the door. He glowers at me and disappears.

The door opens. At first, it's Jessica, but Levis pulls her back with an arm around the front of her shoulders. "Down, girl," he says, grinning at me and bringing her back into the house.

"If you're not going to ask him his intentions, then I should," she says.

"I've already done that."

"But not for tonight!" she insists.

Levis gives me an amused look. "What are your intentions with Oakley?"

"I'm going to take him to dinner at my house with my family. Then bring him up to my room and make sure he orgasms at least twice before we go to sleep. He won't be home until tomorrow."

Levis' smile widens, but Jessica's jaw drops.

"He's very literal," Levis tells Jessica. "Now you know."

"Know what?" Oakley asks as he steps off the stairs with Haze behind him.

"That you're having dinner with his family and then he's going to fuck you twice," Jessica informs him.

Oakley's eyes go wide, his cheeks reddening.

"That's not what I said," I disagree, frowning. "You shouldn't interpret what someone says when there's a wide margin for error."

Jessica rolls her eyes.

"No, that's fair," Levis says, his grin still wide. "He said that he'd give Oakley two orgasms before they sleep. Orgasms can be achieved without penetration."

"Ohmygod," Oakley mutters and rushes for the door, shoving Levis out of the way and then pushing me from the steps. "Let's go."

I wrap my arm around his waist and bring him down the front steps as he buries his face into my chest. "Why did you say that?" he gripes. I can feel the heat of his face through my shirt.

Levis laughs as he shuts the door.

"He asked what my intentions were. That's my plan for the night."

"Jesus, Loren," he says but his arms wrap around my waist. For a minute, I stand there and just hug him against me. He smells good.

Bringing my hand into his hair, I find it's only half up. I love the curls, how they twist around my fingers as if they're hanging on. Tethering to me.

"Want to be my boyfriend?" I ask.

LOREN

Oakley laughs, rubbing his face into my chest before standing back. His cheeks are still a pretty shade of red. Now I can see the way his hair falls and frames his face.

"You're beautiful."

His smile softens. "Yes, I want to be your boyfriend. We need to work on the kinds of things you can tell my friends about our activities."

"You don't talk to them about sex?"

"I do, but… not quite the same way, I guess."

"Hmm." I kiss him, and he sighs into me.

"You really want me to be your boyfriend?" he asks quietly.

"It didn't occur to me I should have already asked you. I decided you were mine and didn't exactly tell you about that decision. So… here we are."

Oakley grins. "Not asking my opinion on it, huh?"

"You can definitely tell me your opinion. I always want your opinion."

"But it's not going to change your decision," he clarifies, smirking.

"Unlikely."

He lets his head fall back and laughs. I get a good look at the marks on his neck. My hackles still rise whenever I see them. Dropping my face, I kiss along the bruises. Feeling the rough patches of skin where the gouges are healing.

"I'm sorry I didn't get to you sooner," I whisper.

His arms wrap around my head, keeping my face buried in his neck. "Don't apologize," he whispers. "That incident led to a lot of really great things."

"It did?"

"Yes. Waking up to you. All your admissions. This moment right now. Where would we be if that hadn't happened?"

I huff. "My family says the same thing."

"They're very wise."

"Don't tell them that. They're arrogant enough."

I don't have to look at him to know he's smiling. He sighs and I can feel that he's happy. I love his happiness. And that I put it there.

"Ready?" he asks.

No. I'm not sure that I am.

To be clear, I'm not concerned that they won't like him. I'm quite confident they already do. I suppose it's because I'm not sure why they're so intent on me sharing his time. His focus. I want that for myself.

Pulling back, I kiss his lips again and take his hand, then we walk across the road. Right before I open the door, Oakley says, "You need to tell me which triplet is which when we get inside."

I grin. "If I can tell, I'll let you know."

"You can't tell?"

"Imry is easy. But unless Avory and Ellory are feeling chatty, I can't tell them apart."

"If they're chatty, you can?"

"Most of the time, though don't ask me how. Maybe it's a feeling."

He laughs. "Okay."

Pushing open the door, we're immediately greeted with a wall of delicious aromas. I swear, I wasn't gone that long, but it smells wonderful.

"Wow," Oakley says. "Who's the cook?"

"Dad. But Voss makes killer breakfast."

I find everyone milling about around the island in the kitchen. As soon as we walk in, I point. "That's Imry."

Oakley nods. My voice makes everyone turn and their smiles are all wide.

"Hey," Myro greets. "Want a drink?"

He's already leaning into my side, but it becomes a little heavier right now with everyone's attention on him. Letting go of his hand, I wrap my arm around his waist, letting him tuck himself into me as much as he wants.

"Water, please," Oakley says.

"Sparkling? Still? Flavored?"

Oakley glances at me with a curious look. "Voss is a water snob," I tell him.

"True," Voss admits, shrugging. "You will not be drinking tap here, though I've made sure that our filters are top of the line, so even that would be good."

"Still is fine, thanks," Oakley says.

Myro hands Oakley a water and me a glass of iced tea.

"Do you have any allergies, Oakley?" Dad asks. "Loren didn't think you did, so I ran with that."

"I don't," he says.

"Good to know. You're all welcome to sit. I'll be finished in a minute."

Myro stays in the kitchen to help Dad and we move into the dining room. Thankfully, there's nothing fancy set up. Did I watch a bunch of videos on what to expect when bringing Oakley to dinner? Yes. They were not helpful and probably led to more confusion than anything.

I pull out Oakley's chair and he blushes as he sits.

"Why don't you pull my chair out?" Ellory says, looking at Avory with a frown.

"That's Ellory," I say, pointing at him.

"How do you know that?" Avory asks.

"He's needier than you. He wants to be spoiled. You're content to do the spoiling."

Their eyes flicker to Oakley and they fall silent. Avory pulls Ellory's chair out and they sit. By the way they're looking at me, I think I might have said something they don't like.

Oakley looks between them curiously.

"Have them memorized?" Voss asks, breaking through the weird silence that settled around us.

"Imry is in green. Avory in blue. Ellory in gray," Oakley confirms. "Please don't change your shirts."

The triplets grin.

Dad and Myro come in with large platters. Voss and the triplets leave to help them bring in the rest and before long, the table is filled with food. A lot of food. It feels like a holiday.

"Dig in," Dad says.

LOREN

Thankfully, there's never any waiting for someone to take the first dish. My brothers are perpetually growing boys, so they don't need to be convinced to start eating.

"Do you have large gatherings here?" Oakley asks.

I look around, trying to determine why he asked. "No, not really. Why?"

"This table can seat a dozen," he points out, smiling.

"Ah," Dad says, offering him a bowl of roasted potatoes. My favorite kind. I make sure Oakley takes several. "It filled the space. No other reason."

"We do have four uncles that visit during holidays," Myro adds. "Dad's little brothers."

"Oh! Arath and Noaz," Oakley says, and I think we all pause to look at him. His cheeks redden. "Honey Bee found them online."

Dad chuckles. "Yes. Arath is my next younger brother. Noaz is my youngest. Oxley and Kairo are the middle brothers."

"Uncle Kairo is the true middle child though, despite Uncle Oxley being the chronological middle child," Voss says. "Man, the tantrums that guy can throw!"

Dad laughs. "Indeed."

"Uncle Noaz is only three years older than me," Myro says. "And Uncle Arath is only six years older than me. So we all kind of grew up together as a big family of kids."

"Wow," Oakley says. "I didn't know that."

"You'll meet them for Thanksgiving," I promise.

Oakley looks at me, a soft smile on his face.

"Did you ask him to join us, or are you telling him now?" Dad asks.

My chewing slows and I glance at Oakley.

My brothers chuckle. "Loren rarely asks anything. Feel free to tell him no when you need to," Imry tells Oakley.

Oakley nods.

"If you already have plans, that's completely okay too," Voss says.

He shakes his head. "I don't. But... Haze is probably going to stay here. His family is, uh, split up, I guess."

"We're aware of the issues in Anaheim," Myro says. "Jessup was his father, no?"

Oakley nods.

"He's more than welcome to join us too," Dad says.

Oakley sighs. "Thanks. I'm hoping he and his brother, Oren, are able to connect for Christmas at least. Oren's boyfriend is a hockey coach, so I don't think they have enough time off for Thanksgiving."

"Did you know Loren has a hockey friend?" Avory asks.

Oakley nods. "Noah. Though that doesn't tell me a lot."

"Noah Kain," I say, then look at my brothers. "He's a wingman for L.A. I invited him over this summer so you can stop thinking I hide him."

The triplets grin hugely.

"Do you hide him?" Oakley asks.

"No more than I hide you."

"Loren's not good about sharing his things," Ellory comments. "He was meant to be an only child."

I nod solemnly. "Yet, somehow, I was born last."

LOREN

"Took us some time to create perfection," Dad says, winking at me.

"Ouch," Myro says in mock offense. I grin.

We're quiet for a while before Myro asks, "So, I've been curious about why you call Jessica Honey Bee."

"He really has been. I've heard a lot of theories," Voss adds.

"I like nicknames and we're an odd family that doesn't have any," Myro explains, shrugging.

"Not true," Avory says. "Sometimes you call me Ave and Ellory El or Elly. Imry is Im."

"Okay, but those are just shortened names. I mean like a true nickname outside of the stereotypical babe or baby or generic."

"In grade school, we were all in a class play. Jess was the honeybee and one of many Jessicas in class, so we just started calling her Honey Bee and never stopped," Oakley explains.

"Ah. That's cute," Myro says.

They start talking about Oakley's friends and classes, answering whatever questions he has. After a while, I sit back and watch. Listen. I find myself smiling.

Noah was right. I was totally overthinking this. This moment is almost perfect. All my favorite people save for one are right here. Smiling. Talking. Having a good time. Even Dad is involved in the conversation.

Yep, I can definitely live with this.

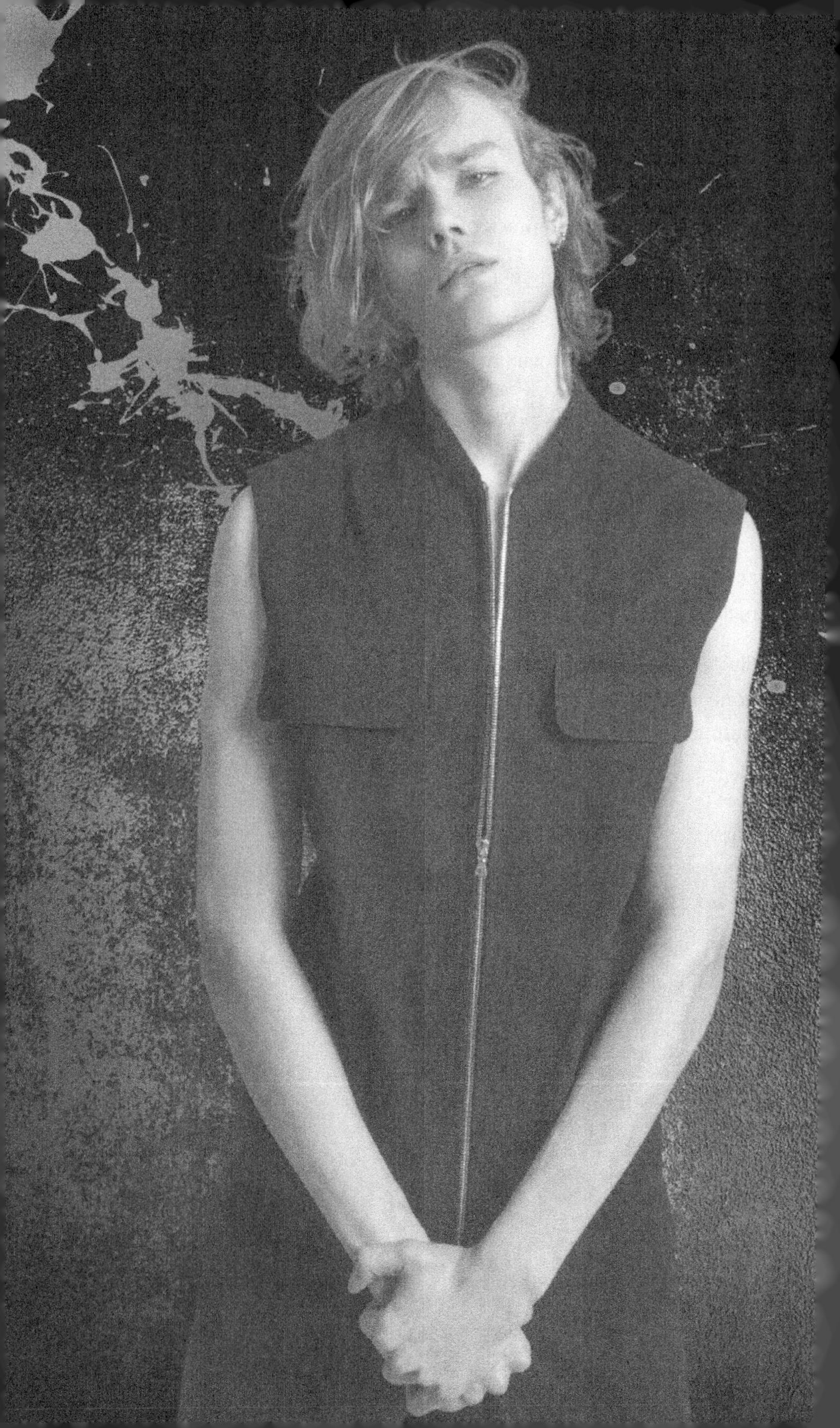

26

OAKLEY

As soon as we're in his room and the door is shut, Loren has me in his arms, his mouth on mine. I grip his hair tightly, kissing him roughly and hungrily. "Get undressed," I mutter between kisses.

He grunts, but we don't let each other go for a minute. When we finally break apart, we're scrambling out of our clothes. Loren rarely dictates anything once we move into sexy time, but before I can pull off my underwear, his hands wrap around my wrists and he pulls them away.

The look in his eyes makes me flush. My heart flutters. He always looks at me like I'm the most beautiful person he's ever seen. But right now, I feel almost divine.

Loren releases my hands and turns me around. The groan that meets my ears makes me shiver. "I've been waiting for you to wear these," he says, voice low and growly.

I glance down. They're nothing special. A jock. I mean, they're super cute, I admit. But I didn't think they were anything ridiculously hot. Peeking at him over my shoulder, I decide that yes, Loren is totally into jockstraps. Wonder if I could get him in one.

"Loren?"

His eyes flicker up to mine and the heat I see there nearly burns me. "Put a condom on. Now."

He moves without thought. When I go to the bed and bend over the edge, I hear him groan again. A muttered curse. Then his hands are on my bare ass cheeks. His fingers follow the elastic around them and then dip between my cheeks, pressing gently against my hole.

"Get me ready."

Loren follows direction well. He's efficient but careful. Always so fucking careful. As if he's afraid to break me. That doesn't stop him from being thorough.

By the time I'm mewling like a damn cat, I reach behind me and yank him forward. "Get inside me, Loren. Fuck me."

His body blankets mine. Right away, he begins pushing inside. Deeply. He's not huge, and I love that because I love to be fucked hard. Big dicks make that uncomfortable. It can be far too painful to be fucked how I like with a big dick.

He's also not small. I feel him in all the good places.

Reaching for his arms, I pull them under me as if they were pillows. "Fuck me," I tell him. "Hard."

Loren does; for a long time. I babble because I can't stop myself. He's not a talker, which is probably a good thing because I talk enough for the both of us. He does answer when prompted, though.

"How does it feel?" I ask, needing to hear his voice.

"Better than breathing," he grunts. "I want to live inside you, Oakley."

"Do you like to fuck hard or slow?"

"I don't care. I just want to be a part of your body."

Seriously, the things that come out of his mouth make me swoon, while also bringing me that much closer to orgasm.

"Tell me how good you feel," I demand. "Fuck me harder." His voice does all the things to me. There's never a time when it's not sexy as fuck, but when he's breathless and filled with lust, I can almost feel how good he feels.

His thrusts escalate. With each deep pound, I grunt. Stars blinking behind my eyes. I'm not sure how he always manages to give me what I demand, but he does. Every time.

"So hot," he pants. "Tight little hole, squeezing me. You like it hard as much as I do—you're perfect."

I sink my teeth into his arm as my load releases in my jock. "Come," I demand around his flesh. His thrusts stop with him deep inside me. I can feel his dick pulsing. I swear, it does so in time with mine.

He's not loud. Not at all. But with his mouth close to my ear, I can hear all the quiet sounds he makes. His moans, grunts, panting. It's so fucking sexy.

His body drops on mine and I pull my teeth from his arm. It's far from the first bite on his body. I've never been a biter before. I'm not sure if this is some kind of animalistic claiming need that's been awoken inside me and I need the world to see that this man is mine or if I'm trying to contain myself from the intensity of the orgasm. Very likely, it's a combination of both.

When he begins to shift, I let go of his arms to reach behind me, grabbing his ass cheeks to keep him rooted inside me. Loren groans, burying his face in my hair.

"You're still hard," I murmur, clenching my ass.

He grunts. I feel his body shiver on top of me.

"Touch me," I instruct.

He pulls one of his hands from under my head and pushes it between my body and the bed until he can cup my cock locked inside my soggy jock. "So sexy," he grunts, his hips wiggling a bit. "I had no idea I'd find these so sexy."

I grin and close my eyes. Loren shifts his other hand so he can bury it in my hair. He almost always has his hands in my hair.

"Stay like this a while longer?" I ask.

He hums, seemingly just as content as I am to have his cock in my ass. I'm actually surprised that he's as hard as he is right now. I'm confident he got off, too.

"Do I make you this hard, Loren?" I ask quietly.

His chuckle tickles my neck. "So hard," he murmurs.

"Is it the jockstrap?"

His hand flexes around my dick. "Yes and no. You make me hard anyway, but I've been waiting to see this on you. It's so sexy."

I grin and then my eyebrows pinch. "You've been waiting to see this on me?" He nods. "This exact one?" He nods again. "How did you know I have it?"

Loren doesn't answer. His lips brush my jaw, making me shiver.

"Tell me," I whisper.

"You know I followed you."

My heart races at his words. I did know that. He's told me.

LOREN

"Did you... break into my house?"

"I did."

My breath catches. "Why?"

Loren sighs. "Because I didn't know how to talk to you. Levis gave me some pointers, but I didn't know where to begin. I didn't know how to approach you. So I continued to follow you and when you were in class, I broke into your house to learn more about you."

I'm not sure if I'm a twisted fucker but my ass rolls, moving on his cock. "Hold still," I whisper. "Okay?"

He nods.

"Keep telling me."

"The first time, I was just getting the lay of the land. Finding your room was easy since I'd already seen you from your window at night."

My heart jumps. He'd been watching me through my window! For some reason, my hips move a little more. His damn dick is still so hard it's like having a flashlight in my ass.

Not that I know what that feels like...

"The second time I opened all your drawers. Touching your shirts. Examining your underwear. You have several that intrigue me." His voice isn't as steady now with my constant rocking. I spread my legs, so he's between them, giving me more leverage to dig my knees into the bed, and keep my fingers digging into his ass cheeks to hold him in place.

Breathless, he continues. "Then I broke into your tablet to see what apps you have. I touched your bedding and counted your pillows. I examined your bed."

"You opened all my drawers?" I ask, squeezing my eyes shut. Oh, god, please tell me he didn't open my toy drawer!

Loren presses a smile into my hair. "Yes. I saw your toy soldiers lined up for service. You have some interesting toys I'm definitely into seeing you use."

My face heats. "Oh, my god."

He chuckles. "But I had to leave there in a hurry when Jessica and Briar got home. I had one of your hair ties in my hand and I kept it. I wore it every day, with your hair still wrapped around it. So I had your DNA on me. Like I was wearing you."

I groan, driving myself onto his cock and grinding my hips. "What else?"

"I watched you sleep," he admits, grunting. My heart nearly stops.

"Why?"

"I wanted to know that you were peaceful. That you weren't having nightmares. I thought if I could be close to you while you were asleep, I might learn what to talk to you about."

"Why did you stop?" I ask. My orgasm is so close. So, so close. Listening to someone tell me how they've been stalking me, invading my privacy, shouldn't turn me on this much. I'm fucking sick.

"My dad said you'd be terrified of me if you woke up to me being there. He said that you'd never trust me then."

It's on my tongue to say he's wrong, but he's not. I would have freaked out.

I can't explain how the things he says makes me feel. Yes, this is maybe the biggest red flag to ever fly. And yet… I feel so fucking wanted. Loren spent weeks trying to get the courage to talk to me. At the moment, I would have been horrified. Mortified that he'd invaded my space. Terrified to find him there. But right now, I just feel... loved.

Closing my eyes, I concentrate on how good he feels inside me. How every rock of my hips brushes against my prostate. I'm practically vibrating. On top of the overwhelming warmth inside me from his words, I make a very reckless decision.

"Take your condom off," I whisper.

Loren doesn't question me. I let him up long enough to discard it. I hear the quiet slap of it hitting the wood floor.

"Back inside me," I whisper. "Come in my ass."

His dick doesn't feel different and yet, I'm convinced it does. His hands return to where they were and I grip his ass again, keeping him right where I want him.

"Tell me more," I whisper. "Squeeze my dick tighter. When I come, you come. Fill my ass, Loren."

He shivers almost violently. His breath is ragged now. His voice is raw. I work myself on his dick, letting his voice and the words he's saying that should be making me run as fast as I can, as far as I can, drive me on.

"I never want to let you out of my sight," he grunts. There's a slight rock in his hips now, as if he can't help himself. "I'm terrified of losing you. Of someone taking you from me when I'm somewhere else and can't be there to protect you. I want to keep you forever."

"Tell me about that," I say. So close. The grip of his hand around my dick has me seeing heaven. He's going to have nail marks in his ass when I'm done.

"I want to keep you," he repeats. I almost can't make out his words. He's close. Voice shaking, scratchy, a low growl penetrated by groans and gasps. "Keep you here where I can make sure you're safe. Where no one will ever hurt you. I will make you smile every day, forever. All you have to do is live, Oakley. Smile for me. Laugh. I'll give you the world." He shivers and I barely hear the last two words: "Love me," he whispers.

My body jerks as I come, burying my face into the blanket. Everything inside me feels like it's on fire as I moan through my orgasm.

Then Loren's coming too. His weight presses me down again as he buries himself as deep as he can. His dick feels like it has its own heartbeat. I swear, I can feel his cum fill my ass.

Irresponsible. The word bounces around in my head. Dangerous. But I don't even care. Risky. I needed to have his DNA, just like he had mine. I want to tie myself to this man in every fucking way I can.

I want to lose myself in his obsession.

Loren takes a deep breath and lets it out slowly. A long, content sigh. He buries his face in my hair, a smile on his lips.

"We'll get tested tomorrow," I whisper. "I'm sorry—I shouldn't have told you to take the condom off."

He hums, but I think he's already asleep.

I can't sleep yet. I'm tired. Fucking exhausted. But everything I've learned about him since the being attacked dances around in my head like the macarena. It's on repeat, waving a bajillion red flags at me, telling me I should be afraid.

But with Loren's body weight on top of me, his hand buried in my hair holding me possessively, his hot breath on my neck as he sleeps peacefully, and his heartbeat a steady drum against my chest, I'm anything but afraid.

LOREN

I love this. This is how I've always wanted to be loved. To be treated. His obsessive love is just... home. I want to get lost in it.

I'll take everything he gives me. I'll go wherever he wants me to be. As long as he's always there to shower his particular brand of love on me.

He's *my* sociopath and I wouldn't change a thing about him. Ever.

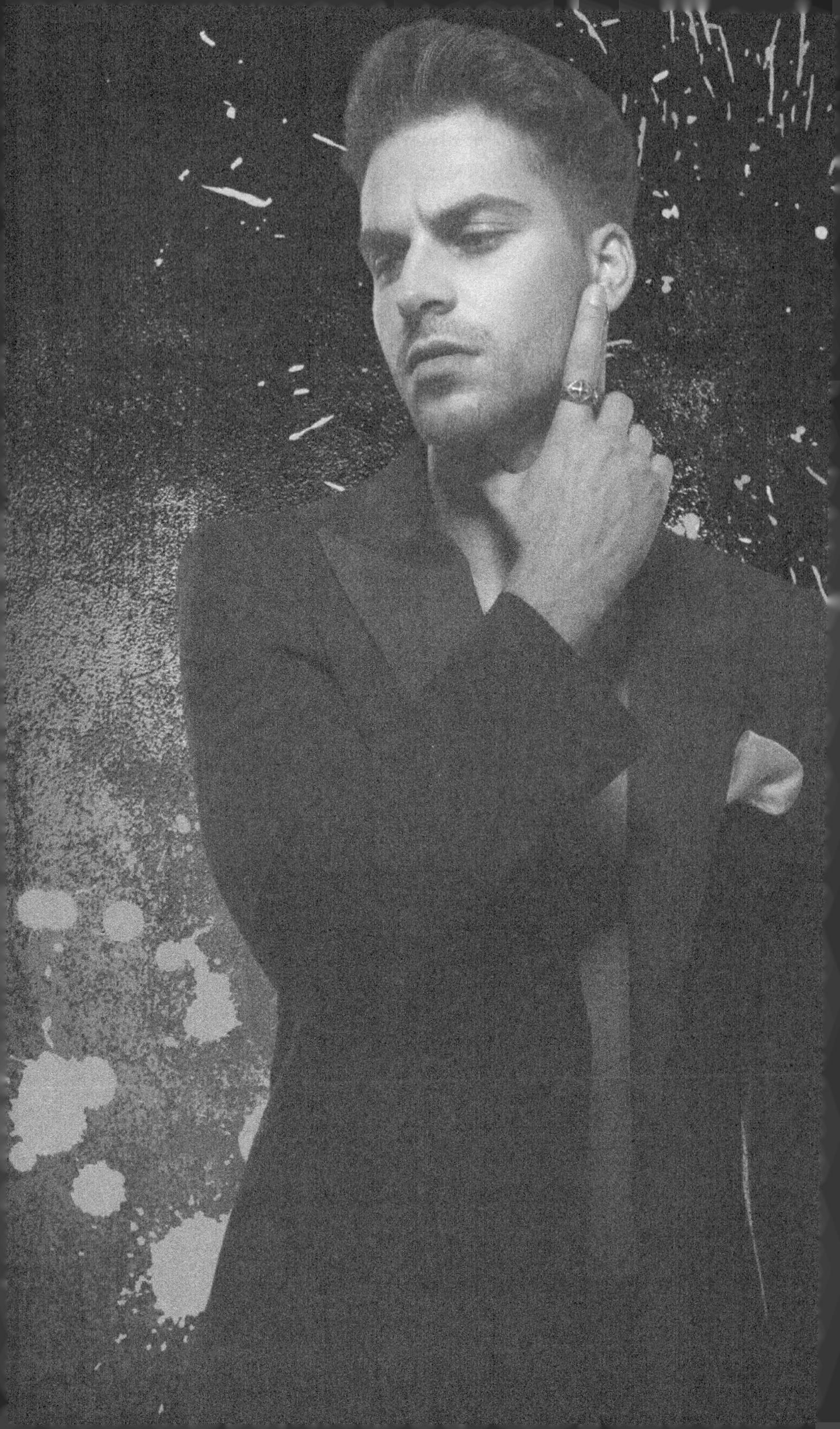

27
LOREN

There's been something different about Oakley for the past few days. Since dinner with my family. He's shy again, but incredibly... soft? I'm sure that's not the word I want, but it's the one that comes to mind.

I wake up this morning with my skin feeling tight and itchy. It's an uncomfortable feeling that makes me agitated if I can't get it to stop. Usually, that means that I need to stop being touched.

It's not as easy as usual since I have Oakley asleep in my arms. I don't *want* to let him go, but I can feel the tension increasing inside me. My muscles are stiffening. My skin feels so tight it's going to crack.

Irritated at myself, I carefully extract myself from Oakley and put a few inches between us. I can still feel his body heat, which still makes me slightly uncomfortable, but it's not so bad. I don't feel like I'm coming out of my skin right now.

As I close my eyes, Oakley moves closer, his fingers wrapping around my arm. Immediately, I stiffen again, my entire body flinching. This isn't a good time to have this particular affliction!

Once again, I move a few inches away and roll on my side. Wrapping the blanket around his hand, I cover it with mine. I've never tried to work around this feeling before. It's bizarrely frustrating and yet I'm a bit fascinated with the puzzle. Is the blanket between our skin enough to turn off the way my skin crawls? Or is it the pressure of having someone else touching me, not just skin-to-skin?

The blanket seems to do okay.

Sighing, I close my eyes. I'm likely not going to sleep again, but I'm also not ready to get out of bed. As I'm drifting in that half sleep state, I think about Oakley's bed. All the blankets and pillows, the way it's pressed against the wall. I wonder if my bed is comfortable enough for him. Maybe he'd like something more like his bed.

I can make that happen. When I let him go home today, I'll go shopping for some more bedding, then get the triplets to help me move my bed against the wall. Actually, I don't think the frame is that heavy, I can probably do it myself.

"Loren?"

Opening my eyes, I find Oakley watching me, his eyebrows knit together.

"Are you okay?"

"Yes. Why?"

"I just... You feel far away."

I hate the uncertainty in his voice. It's incredibly frustrating knowing that I put it there. Sighing, I lean in close and press my lips to his, stifling the shudder of tension that moves through my body at the contact. "Remember what I said? Sometimes I need some space, but it has nothing to do with you. This has been my thing for as long as I can remember."

Oakley inhales deeply and nods. "Okay."

"Go take a shower. I promise, this is a me thing entirely. Rather inconvenient at times."

He tries to smile, but I can see his insecurity shining through his eyes. So different from last night when he rode me like a cowboy, commanding me exactly how he wanted me.

He's confident in sex, but he's insecure in life. And maybe I'm a little opposite. No, that's not it. I'm not insecure in sex. I just like to let him use me to find his pleasure. His happiness is far more important to me than my own and if he can feel good using my body, I'm sure as fuck going to let him.

Besides, I love how needy he sounds when he's telling me what to do. How he wants me to fuck him. To hold him down or steady him on top of me. Whether he wants me to hold still or do all the work. I don't even care what it is. I want it all. I want to feel him coming on my cock.

The way he says my name is intoxicating. How he gets off from the things I say, which is almost always in answer to something he's asked me.

"Go," I whisper. "Shower. I'll be right here."

Oakley takes another breath and nods. I watch as my boyfriend climbs out of bed, naked. As he disappears into the bathroom, I glance at my bedroom door. I know it's locked. Oakley makes sure to lock it every night now. He doesn't want someone to accidently come in when my dick is in his ass again.

He's had a hard time looking into Myro's eyes ever since. Even though we're now weeks beyond that. Wait... has it been that long? I'm not sure it has. It just feels like it's been ages.

That's a good thing, right? That we feel so comfortable together?

I climb out of bed and pull on my underwear before gathering Oakley's clothing from the night before. I arrange them on the bed and then frown. We need a better procedure than this. Going home the next day in the same clothes you wore the night before... isn't that what they call the walk of shame?

Honestly, there's no shame in spending the night with your boyfriend. Or even going home after a good night of fucking. If anything, it should be called an 'I got fucked and you didn't' march.

Smirking, I stand in the door of my closet and decide I have plenty of room. The bathroom door opens and Oakley steps out, a waft of steam clouding around him. He gives me a shy smile but the way his shoulders are slightly hunched, I can tell that he's still feeling insecure.

Look at me recognizing how he feels!!

Crossing the space, I grip his shoulders. Yeah, nope—still feeling like I need some space. However, I don't let him go as I press a kiss to his head. He doesn't touch me in return, though. "Get dressed."

He nods and I let him go. Returning to my closet, I pull on a pair of pants and grab a large bag and my favorite shirt from the hanger. Before he can slip into his tee, I pull my shirt over his head. He laughs and pushes his arms through the sleeves.

"This is my favorite," I tell him. "I wear it all the time."

Oakley smiles, wrapping his arms around himself.

I push the bag into his hands. "Pack some clothes so you don't always have to wear the ones from the night before, okay?"

His cheeks flush and he nods. "Yes."

Once he's dressed, I pull him against me. The blanket separating us probably worked because the surface space that I was touching him through it was small. This is not. I can't hide the way my muscles tense, but I hug him tightly anyway.

"Loren, you don't have to—"

"I want to. But yeah, I need some space this morning. So go hang out with your friends, okay? I'll bring you home this afternoon."

He presses his lips to my shoulder and despite the way my skin crawls, I can feel him smile. "Okay."

"Oh," I say, and pull away. I rummage around in my closet again until I find my leather gloves. Pulling them from the box, I slip the right one on and then offer my hand to Oakley.

He looks at it dubiously. "You weren't wearing this when you..."

I grin. "No. These are brand new. And no, I didn't ruin the last set with blood. Leather is finicky and I got them muddy."

Oakley doesn't look entirely convinced, but he still takes my hand. This is as comfortable as the blanket was, and I decide it's not just touch but pressure. Honestly, I'm impressed I don't feel this way all the time with how much Oakley and I touch. I'll take that as a win.

I walk him across the road and stop at the front door. After a long kiss so he knows that I *want* to touch him, I push the duffle bag into his hands. "Clothes and whatever else. I'll come back in a bit."

He nods. "Okay."

"Don't leave without me."

His smile is both amused and warm. "I won't."

I only head back to my house once he's safely behind the door.

SEVERAL HOURS later I have my bed pushed against the wall, but it looks weird. Maybe this is why my first thought was the triplets. With a sigh of resignation, I open my door and look for my brothers.

Avory and Ellory's door is shut. Unlike Myro, I don't open it when one of them answers with "Yes?"

"I need help," I say and even I can hear the pouting in my voice.

There's no noise beyond the door but a minute later, it opens. Twin faces look at me with wide smiles.

"I'm dying to know what made you actually ask for help," one says.

"And why you came to us instead of Imry," the other adds.

They're only in pants—matching pants so that's going to be an issue.

"You can give me a hard time and I'll ask someone else, or you can help me without comment," I mutter.

"We can do both." That's Avory. I'm at least 65% confident in that.

"In my room." I turn and head back down the hall.

"If you got Oakley stuck in some weird position, we're taking pictures."

That was Ellory. He's on my right. 68% confident.

I don't answer. As soon as we walk in, one comments, "What the hell did you buy?"

Glancing at the bags pouring from my closet, I shrug. I'm not sure they'd understand. They have one blanket between the two of them.

LOREN

"What I really want to know is how you lugged them all upstairs without anyone hearing you."

Avory. Definitely Avory.

"Voss helped me. Without asking questions," I say pointedly.

"What do you need help with?"

I nod in the direction of the bed. "It looks weird there. But I need it to be against the wall."

"Why?"

"Without questions!" I insist.

"This better be kinky," Ellory mutters as he steps further into the room. Yes, confident that is Ellory. Well, still in the sixty/forty confidence range.

"Just tell me where it'll not look so weird."

"The shape of the room and the balance of furniture are working against you. Come on."

I follow beside triplet number three, and we move furniture around until I barely recognize the room. However, it feels much better. Weird that I even notice that shit, honestly.

"Thank you. You can leave now."

"You're really not going to tell us what this is about?"

"Are you going to give me a hard time if I do?" I challenge.

"I'm sure it's going to be adorable," Ellory says. That's definitely Ellory. Probably.

Huffing, I admit, "I'm trying to make my bed more like Oakley's," and gesture to the dozens of blankets and pillows I just bought.

They grin. I can tell that they have a lot to say about it.

"You may leave," I repeat.

"You don't want help with this?"

"I do not. I'm just putting blankets on the bed."

"How about you go help Dad with the greenhouse in the back and we'll set up your bed," Avory suggests. Yep, that's Avory.

This feels like a losing battle. Either I stay here and listen to them harass me, or I leave and let them make my bed. No matter which choice I settle on, they're not leaving. I realize now why I rarely ask them for help.

They meddle.

"I swear to hell, I'm going to skin you alive if you do anything other than make the bed," I hiss.

"At least he isn't swearing to god," Ellory murmurs, pretending not to smile.

"Yep, never again," I say as I head for the door. "I will die on the hill by myself before I ask you for help again."

Their twin laughter follows me as I hurry out of the room. As I'm heading downstairs, I realize what they said about Dad and shift course to head for the backyard. Sure enough, among the rubble that is the backyard with the disassembled pool and pool house, I find Dad in the back corner. Building. With his hands. Alone.

Where are the contractors?

I pick my way through the war zone and stop just beyond his pile of building shit to stare at him. After he's finished measuring or something, he looks up.

"Hey."

"I didn't know you owned anything other than suits," I say.

LOREN

He laughs. "Of course, I do."

"And casual suits."

Dad laughs again and sits back on his haunches. "What's up, Loren?"

"Nothing. Avory and Ellory kicked me out of my room."

He raises a brow. "I'm not sure I want to know."

"Probably not. Even though I invited them in, I don't think I do either."

Dad stands and nods in the direction of a few chairs. Grabbing a couple bottles of Voss' waters, he hands one to me and we sit.

"Why are you building this?" I ask. I'm actually impressed. It has a shape and looks sturdy. I had no idea my dad could do this kind of thing.

"Believe it or not, your uncles and I used to help our father and grandfather build a whole lot of structures. One year when Noaz was ten and you were just a baby, we had a whole barn raising for Grandpa's farm."

Obviously, I have no memory of that.

"Myro might remember. Voss was busy herding the triplets while your mother took care of you, but Myro tried to help us. He was adorable."

I smile. The memories outside of Van Doren Technologies are few and far between. Not that they all felt like business. I remember running around with the triplets in Dad's office and along the corridors, peeking in on his staff.

They used to play hide and seek with us. Once, we had his entire floor playing tag. My favorite lady he had working for him used to play Go Fish with me.

Most of my family memories were either at home, battling our mother's clouded opinion about how her boys should love and live and behave, or at Dad's office. The latter were the happier ones.

Then when I got older and my temper started to truly develop, the fun changed from Go Fish to things on the aggressive side. He's never said so, but I think I'm the reason for the incarnation of the contract killing branch of Van Doren Technologies.

"What's this for? They said it's a greenhouse?"

Dad nods. "Your grandmother used to love when grandpa would bring her fresh flowers and greenery. I've seen you give Oakley flowers and the way he smiles when you do reminds me of Grandma so I thought maybe you'd like to have some flowers on hand for your friend."

"My boyfriend," I correct.

He smiles. It's not a normal smile. There's something… proud in it. Happy. I think. But I'm not sure why he's looking at me that way.

Dad pats my leg. "Your boyfriend. I'm really happy for you, Loren."

I nod, taking a sip of water. The sense of peace that surrounds me right now is new. I hope to keep it for the rest of my life.

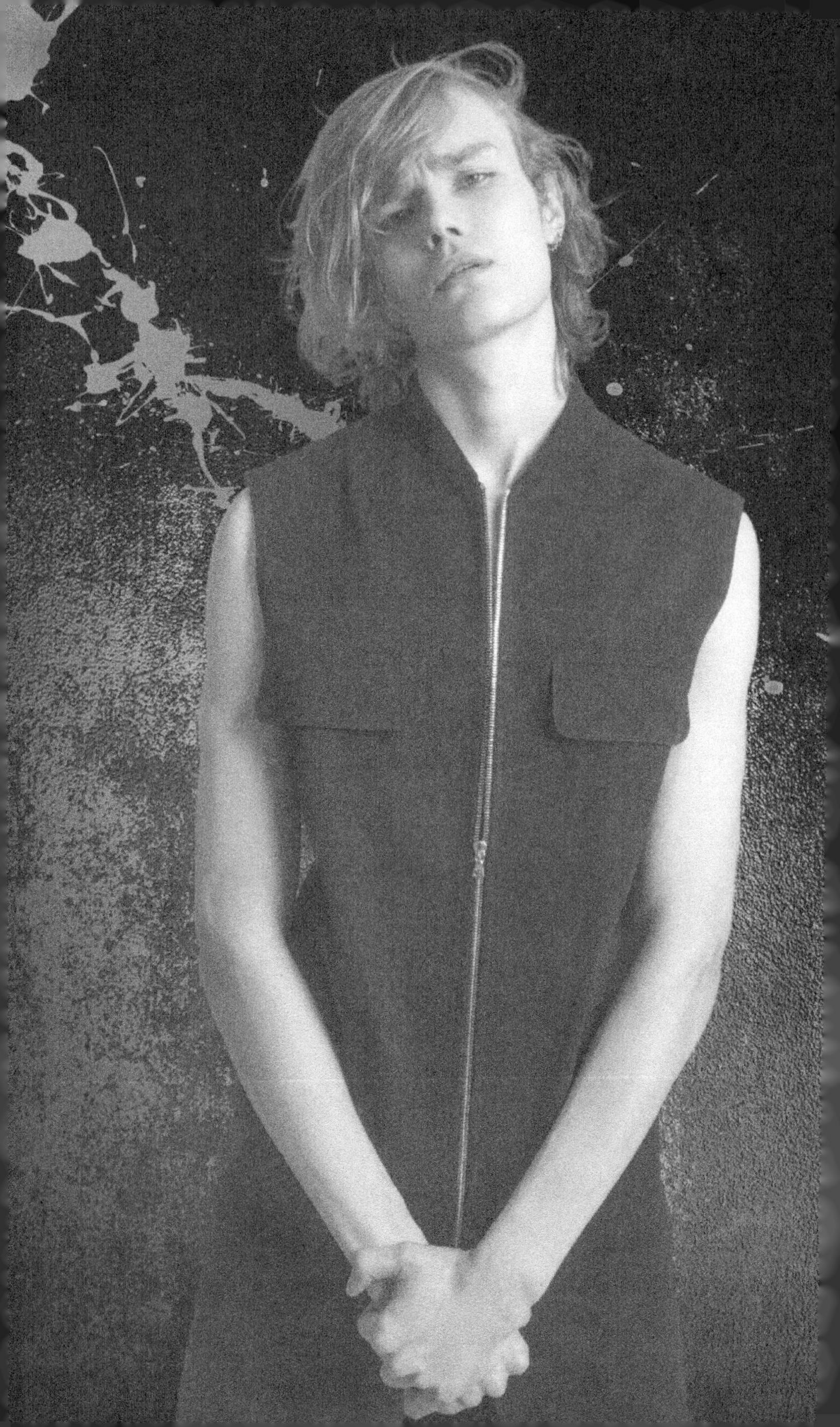

28

OAKLEY

We're getting close to winter break, which means finals. For the life of me, I can't concentrate. I miss Loren, which is ridiculous since I left him like an hour ago.

I'm feeling whiny. If I open my mouth, I know my tone is going to be pathetic. On the verge of throwing a tantrum and I'm not even sure what I want. I want finals to be over. I want to be cuddled. I want, I want, I want.

Sighing, I look up from my textbook and glance outside. Arizona almost always has nice weather. It's hotter than Anaheim because there's no ocean but I don't hate the temperature. It's dry, which I really like because it's much better for my hair.

A knock on my door has me twisting in my chair. My door is open and Briar stands in the door. "Hey," he says.

I smile. "Hey."

"Studying?"

"Pretending to. You?"

He huffs. "Same. Want some company?"

Turning my desk chair, I nod and he comes in, dropping into the comfy one in the corner.

"What subject?" he asks.

"Right now, ancient cultures. I swear I know this, but I keep thinking I'm going to panic and freeze up."

He groans. "Tell me about it. I've taken the online practice test for my first final like eight times and though I've scored high enough to account for error, I'm not convinced it's telling the truth."

"Finals should be illegal. The amount of stress it puts on us is ridiculous."

Briar chuckles. "No Loren today?"

It's difficult not to smile at the mention of Loren. I glance at the door as Brek walks by, but he just meets my eyes and keeps walking.

"Is he being weird lately or is it just me?" I ask, frowning.

"It's not just you, but it's more obvious when you're home."

"Great."

"Albrecht!" Briar calls. "Get in here and gripe about finals with us."

I hear Brek curse as he always does when we use his full name. Something drops and he swears again. Briar chuckles.

A minute later, he's standing in my doorway, giving Briar an irritated look.

Briar grins. "Come on, sweetcakes. Commiserate with us."

Brek scowls but steps into my room. There's a textbook in his hand, though I'm looking at the back of it so I can't see what subject. He takes a seat on the floor, leaning against the bed.

LOREN

"The others still at school?" I ask.

"Levis is with Brianna," Briar says. "I think Honey Bee is working out her frustrations as well."

I roll my eyes.

"No idea where Haze is. I think his last class ended the same time mine did—an hour and a half ago—so... gym? He must do something to keep up that bulk."

"He could be like Brek and naturally toned," I suggest, looking at Brek.

He raises his eyes to mine and gives me a weary smile.

"Okay, seriously. Why are you being so weird lately? And apparently more so when I'm here. What's up with that?" I ask, crossing my arms. "What did I say or do to upset you?"

Brek shakes his head. "Nothing," he mutters.

"Really? In that tone?"

"What do you want me to say? Glad you're finally home? Although can this really be considered your home since you haven't slept here in like a month and most of your clothes are missing?" he snaps.

"You're upset that I'm not here much?" I ask.

"Why did you move in if you're just going to move out with the first boy—"

"Ouch," I say at the same time Briar cuts him off with, "Stop."

My stomach turns sour as I stare at him. He's never purposefully said hurtful things before, so this is really kind of... out of left field.

"That's really rude," Briar said. "No need to be a dick and

definitely no need to spew some bullshit that you know isn't true."

Brek doesn't answer. He's not looking at me, but staring at my door.

"I didn't move in with him," I say, "but yes, I brought some of my clothes because it's silly to take a shower in the morning and put on dirty clothes. But I'm here every day. I see you *here* every day. And for the record, he's the second boy who showed me attention. Not the first. That would be Daniel/Jason, remember?"

He still doesn't answer. When a minute goes by in weird silence, I ask, "Do you not like Loren for some reason? Is that what your problem is?"

"He's... He gives me a bad feeling," Brek mutters.

"Because he's a sociopath," I admit and both guys look at me. Brek's eyes get wide, but Briar just stares as if he's waiting for me to tell him I'm joking. "He's naturally *different* from everyone else because he doesn't compute like the average person. Most of the time, he reads the tone of a conversation based on cues and emotions he doesn't experience. So yeah, maybe he gives you a weird vibe."

Silence fills the room.

"I thought there was a personality thing with him," Briar says after a while. "I thought maybe a mood disorder or something."

I shrug. "It's not a secret so much as it's not something he advertises. Personally, I love that he doesn't pretend to be like everyone else. As someone who's had to pretend to fit in for most of their life, I know how exhausting that is."

Briar nods. "Absolutely."

"You're dating a sociopath?" Brek asks. "Isn't that dangerous?"

LOREN

"So is riding a bus. I'll take my chances."

Briar laughs.

I'm not sure which is more awkward—Brek staring adamantly at the door as he refuses to look at me or the way he's staring at me now, like I'm out of my mind.

"I don't really care if you don't like him," I admit quietly. "Everyone else seems to, so this is a you problem. If you had legitimate concerns as there were with Daniel/Jason, I'd definitely listen; I've learned my lesson and won't ignore *all* my friends when you're telling me there's something wrong. But everyone else likes Loren except you. And you've been acting really weird, so I definitely think there's something up with you, not Loren."

"Honey Bee didn't like him for a while either," Brek says defensively.

"She didn't," I agree. "But that's been cleared up and she likes him just fine."

"Why didn't she like him?"

"I'm not giving you more ammunition for whatever mood you're in, so don't worry about it."

Brek tries to hide his scowl.

"Where *is* Loren?" Briar asks.

I shrug. "At home, probably. He was helping his father with something in the backyard this week. Which, by the way, is a construction site. The house isn't haunted. It didn't sell because there was a huge foundation issue between the pool and pool house that inspections kept showing *and* it was way overpriced on top of that. That's why it sat empty for so long."

"That's an expensive piece of property to let sit empty for so long," Briar says. "Talk about a waste of money."

"I guess when you reach a certain number of commas in your bank account, it's not that big a deal," I suggest, shrugging.

The afternoon remains quiet and somewhat awkward with Brek resolutely not speaking to either of us, though he doesn't get up from the floor. Every time Loren comes up, he scowls and stares into his textbook.

When Haze gets home, Briar heads downstairs to check where he's been, which leaves me and Brek. It's not at all uncomfortable.

He continues to ignore me, so I roll my eyes and face my desk again. Eventually, he gets up. I tell myself to just let it go, but when he reaches the door, I spin around.

"Can't you just be happy for me?" I ask. Brek freezes in the door mid-step. "I'm happy, Brek. I'm really happy. Loren treats me so good and he cares about me. Why does my being happy make you so unhappy?"

His shoulders rise and fall. He's quiet for so long I don't think he's going to respond.

"Maybe he's not the right person for you," he says quietly.

What?! What does that even mean? "Okay, well… shouldn't I get to figure that out on my own? Because maybe he is."

Brek inhales. I don't miss the subtle shaking of his head. "Yeah. Fine." And then he walks out.

Did Loren threaten him? Is he scared of Loren? Is that what this is about?

Or maybe he wants Loren? Hmm. Yeah, I could see that. Except not really. Brek is straight.

LOREN

Turning back to my desk, I pause. But is he straight? I've never even seen him with a girl. Or a guy. I've never seen him show interest in anyone.

Shaking my head, I try to focus on my studies again. Thankfully, I'm saved from that torture for too long when Loren comes to the front door to take me home.

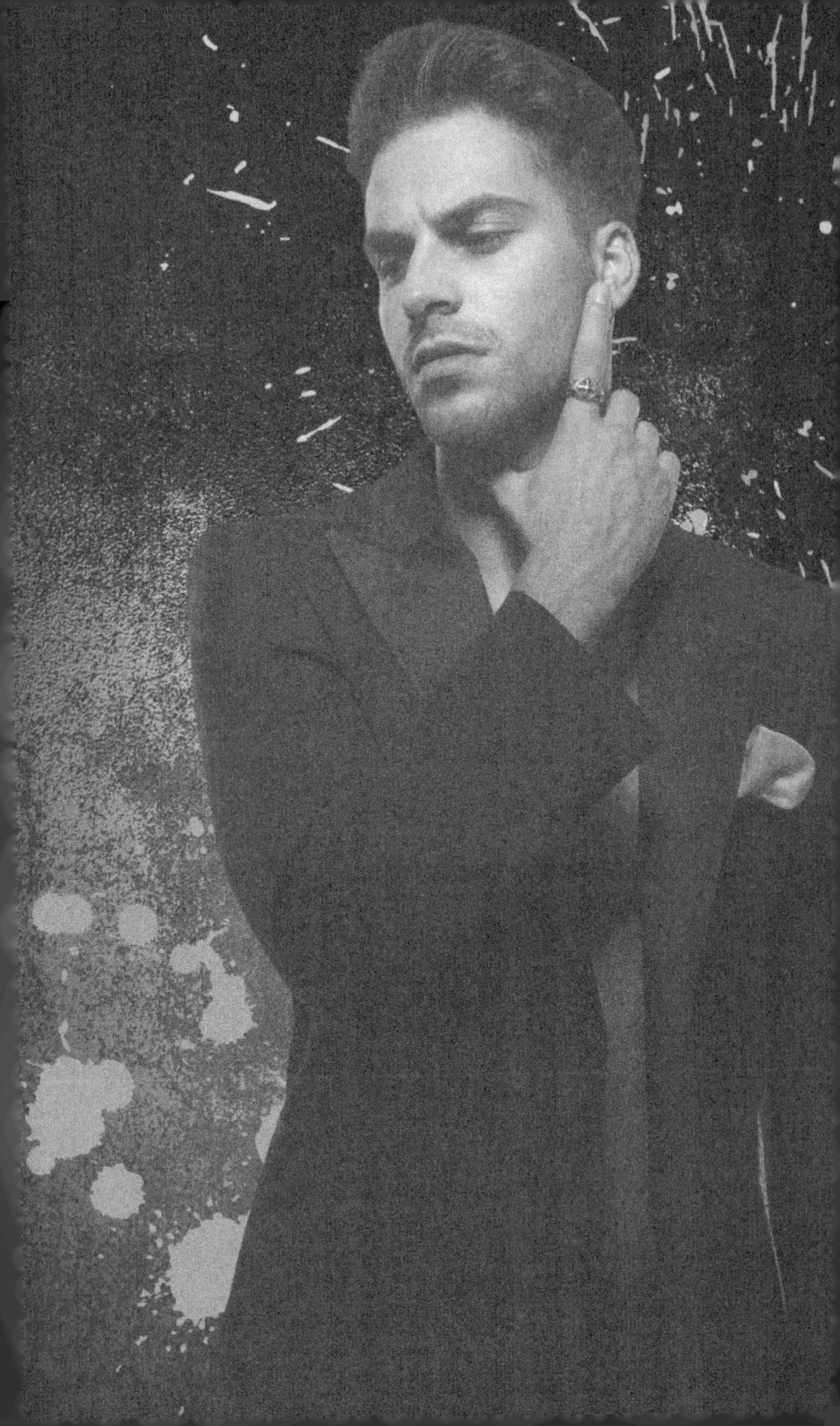

29
LOREN

I'm not sure when the last time I've been to a library was. It's a very strange kind of quiet. There's rustling and whispers. Dark spots and a weird flickering light in the back corner. People move around like phantoms. I swear, I saw one person glide.

The idea that all libraries must be haunted crosses my mind as I take a seat next to Oakley. A million lives live within the pages and every time those pages are opened, a little more life is breathed into the characters. How many times does the book need to be read before the world within breaks free and surrounds us?

Maybe people get sucked into books!

I glance at the books Oakley has open. A couple on space and one about ancient Mesopotamia. What a strange combination they'd create if all three books burst into existence in front of us. Crumbling stone buildings set on the side of mountains on Mars and the moons of Saturn.

Hmm. There's a chance I have a more active imagination than I thought.

I skim over the page one of the astronomy books is open to before looking at Oakley. His hair is wrapped loosely in an elastic, but falling around his face. Loose curls make his eyes stand out, even though they're practically the same color as his hair. It's completely mesmerizing.

He has such long lashes too. Soft lips. A perfect pert nose. Such a smooth jaw line. Elegant neck that leads into a delicate collarbone. My gaze stops on the remnants of the marks on his neck, mostly from his fingernails as he tried to claw the rope away. I've been making sure we apply scar cream every morning and evening. They're fading.

I'd hate for them to always be there. Not because they take away from his beauty but because his eyes constantly snag on them in his reflection. They're a reminder that someone nearly murdered him, and I hate he carries around that fear. If I could kill that fucker again, I would. Over and over and over.

Sliding my chair closer, I look over his shoulder. His lips curl. "You don't have to hang around if you're bored, Loren," he says in a hushed voice. "I'm just studying."

"This place is haunted," I mutter, pressing my lips to his shoulder.

He picks his head up and looks at me. His eyes widened slightly. "What?"

I shrug. "Think about all the stories that are let loose in here every day. There's that flickering light in the back too."

"That's probably electrical. Or a dying bulb."

"Or a ghost," I say.

He stares. Blinks. Then breaks out into a big smile, trying to contain his laughter. "You're so damn cute."

I humph. "I'm fine. Study. I'm just watching."

"And looking out for ghosts," he teases, turning back to his book.

"It's possible."

"Science doesn't agree."

"Science also says there are a lot of unexplained and unidentified things in the world."

He's still grinning.

For a while, I entertain myself with thoughts of things science can't explain. I even track down an anatomy book to remind myself of the many arteries and ways people can die. Humans truly are fragile.

However, it's not long before I'm bored again. I admire Oakley for a while longer before I need to touch him. Sliding my chair against his, I lean into him, wrapping an arm around his waist and dropping the other hand to his thigh.

Oakley smiles but doesn't comment. I watch as he highlights in his notebook and scribbles more notes. He has pretty handwriting. It's kind of loopy and flows like a river.

Moving my hand along his thigh, I curl it under his leg. My thumb brushes his cock, and he inhales.

"Are you trying to distract me?" he murmurs.

I shake my head. "No. Keep studying. I just need to touch you."

He huffs. Since he doesn't tell me not to, I shift my hand so I'm over his dick and rub him through his pants. He hardens in my hand as I do in my pants.

"What underwear are you wearing?" I whisper.

Oakley shivers. "Uh... Ones you like." His cheeks heat and yep, I'm here for this.

Glancing around, there isn't anyone immediately nearby. "Keep studying," I murmur before dropping out of the chair and crawling under the table.

"What are you doing?" he hisses.

I pull his chair close, earning myself a quiet bark of laughter. He allows me to shimmy his ass to the edge of the chair and I bury my face between his legs.

Oakley makes a choking sound. "Jesus," he whispers.

His backpack is on the floor, so I poke my hand inside the small pockets until I find one of those little travel size bottles of lube. I knew where it was, since I put it there. Hooking my fingers in the elastic of his pants, I pull them down to his calves.

"Loren, we're going to get in trouble," he hisses.

"Not if you're quiet," I say.

He snorts.

"Want me to stop?" I ask, rubbing my thumb along the underside of his hard cock in his sexy underwear. I haven't seen these before, but Oakley's right—I like them a lot.

"Fuck," he curses. "No, I don't want you to stop."

Scooching his ass a little closer to me, I find the back of the underwear are open. Just like a jock, but they're not quite the same. Oh! It's a thong.

Fucking hell. I groan and move the bit of fabric out of the way.

I love to press my fingers into his hole. Mostly, I love to watch his face when I do. I can't see that right now, so I watch his dick instead as I toy with him. He's so tight. So small. It's a pretty hole which I find funny because... it's a damn asshole. What could possibly be pretty about it? But it is. Because it's Oakley's.

With a bit of lube rubbed in, I press my finger inside him. His body tenses, jerks slightly, and then relaxes. His dick enjoys this. It also jumps and twitches. There's a growing wet spot at the crown.

When I get my finger in deep, he lets out a ragged breath. Fingering him is fun. Everything with him is fun. I'm not even sure what my favorite part is. I move the front of his underwear out of my way and then add a second finger.

Oakley trying to stifle the sounds he makes is heady. Watching his cock's response to the way I'm slowly fingering him is like a movie. I didn't know dicks could be so expressive. When he really likes something, I'm rewarded with a bead of pre-cum.

When that bead is dripping down his length, I've had enough playing around and bring him into my mouth. Sucking dick is weird. Part of that is mental. Like, I know what this thing is used for. I know where it's been and what it goes through all too well.

It's a strange kind of hard. A soft kind of hard, like you can squeeze it and meet only the resistance of how thick he is. Then there's the way the skin moves over the erectile inside. And don't get me started on how these things can start as the size of a green bean and grow into an eggplant. I'm not even being pun-y.

I've not spent a lot of time contemplating dick in my life. Only once Oakley looked at mine and licked his lips that first time did it ever occur to me to wonder how I might measure up to other dicks he's come in contact with. I've since done some research and I've decided I'm most definitely somewhere around average.

Since then, I've also been thinking about the toys I've seen in his nightstand. Those were not average. They were very big.

Speaking of big, Oakley is bigger than I anticipated him being. I've seen a lot of memes that claim twinks have the biggest dicks because they're the least likely to as far as romanticized images of men are concerned. When I asked Oakley if he considered himself a twink, he giggled for twenty minutes but yes, he does.

Which makes sense that his dick is bigger than average. My jaw is already aching as I suck on him. I don't think he's giant. I've now been self-educated in cock shapes and sizes since getting naked with Oakley.

However, sucking dick is a strange art that I'm not sure I've mastered. Most of the time, I'm just playing with his dick in my mouth because, quite frankly, it's a very strange turn of events for me. I'm not sure how to feel about it.

I give Oakley's cock a suck and he coughs. His hands reach under the table and pull my face away. "Stop," he hisses.

Backing away, I lick my lips and watch as he scrambles to pull up his pants. Then he's sliding the chair back and he ducks his head down. He's looking a little frazzled. "Come with me," he says, swiping the lube from the floor.

He's already practically running, so I have to hurry to catch up. When he pushes the stairwell door open, I think we're going to stop there, but he's racing up the stairs. I stay on his heels and find myself in a small room with a table and a few padded chairs.

Oakley shuts the door, wedges a chair under the handle and turns out the light. There's a transom window that lets in light, and my man is looking a little haggard. He scowls at me, but turns and presses his back against the wall.

"Get on your knees," he whispers.

I drop in front of him, grabbing for his pants as I do. Oakley steadies himself with his hands on the wall as I resume what I was doing with a fresh dollop of lube on my fingers. This time, I suck him with everything in me.

He groans, making these sexy as sin choking sounds. His hands grip my hair as he bends over. Since he seems to need help staying upright, I press my free hand into his chest. His body slides down the wall a bit and the next thing I know, he has my fingers in his mouth.

I look up and fucking shit, the look on his face has my entire body burning. I've never seen someone so wrecked. It's a giddy feeling knowing I did that to him.

However, when he starts sucking my fingers, his teeth biting in, it goes straight to my balls and I groan around his cock. He mumbles around my fingers and I think I might get off just like this. Who knew this could be so sexy?! My head spins when he sucks on them some more, seemingly directly correlating to when I'm sucking him.

I feel it like his mouth is around my sac.

Then his hand tightens in my hair, his hips buck forward making his dick lodge in my throat, and he cries out around my fingers as he comes. The hot release fills my mouth, but I'm choking around his cockhead, so it basically comes back out all over him.

Oakley's shaking when he drops into my arms. His sudden fall causes me to fall backward and we end up in a heap against the legs of the table, laughing.

"We need to go home," he pants. "I have an idea."

"Does it involve your cock because I'm all for this idea."

He grins and shakily gets to his feet, pulling his pants up. "Let's go."

There's no way we don't look like exactly what we'd been doing. I wipe my face on the back of my hand, but when Oakley looks at me once we've gathered his books and we're on our way to check them out, he stops in his tracks and laughs. His face is bright red.

With the bottom of his shirt, he wipes my face. "You look like you've just been given a facial."

"I'm fine with that," I admit, but let him clean me up. I love the way he's smiling at me right now. His blush. His smile is breathless, amused, and soft.

There's something about this moment that takes my breath away.

Oakley bows his head and drops his shirt. "We need to get home."

I take his books once he's checked them out and then we walk the few miles back to my house. He's focused, so he bypasses my brothers when we make our way through the front door and practically runs up the stairs.

"What did you do?" Imry asks.

"I got a facial," I say, shrugging and following my boyfriend to my room. My brothers sputter with laughter downstairs.

"You did *not* just say that," Oakley groans as he shuts the door and locks it behind me. He's always making sure the door is locked. Guess he doesn't want to take the chance on someone walking in while he's on my dick again.

I shrug. "It has multiple meanings."

He huffs and takes the books from me. "Take your clothes off, Loren."

Watching him set the books on the desk I moved in here for him and then propping one open, I strip down until I'm naked. He turns as he takes his clothes off too. "Get on your knees with your back against the desk."

I do and look up at him.

Oakley shivers. "You have no idea how hot it is to see you like this."

"Why?"

He shakes his head. "I don't know. You're just... sexy. Possessive and kind of crazy, but you're on your knees for me."

"I'll do anything to make you happy."

The smile on his face makes his eyes shiny. He moves forward, his not quite hard dick in his hand. "I want you to suck me but not *suck*. Just... keep me in your mouth and... like light pressure? Does that make sense?"

I nod.

He hands me the lube. "Fingers in my ass too. I don't want to get off. I just want to feel you while I study. Okay?"

"Yep."

Oakley stands over me and I take his dick into my mouth again. We spend a minute adjusting because of the height. Then I cover my cock in lube for a comfortable slow jerk before sticking my lubed fingers back in his ass.

I listen to his breathing and keep my mouth firmly locked around his growing cock. I suck, but more like one might on a pacifier. Gentle. Rhythmic.

His breathing is heavy. His legs shake. I work my fingers in deeply and pull them out again. Oakley moans.

"Wait," he says as he pushes away. I let him go and watch as he looks around the room. "Over here."

Picking up his book, he heads for the bed and drops it, pointing to the edge for me. Once more, I take my position and we resume. I press into his body again and he groans.

"God you feel good, Loren," he murmurs. "I love to feel you."

I rub my tongue along the underside of his cock as I softly suckle on his dick. He's hard now. Hard and leaking.

Oakley makes a frustrated sound and stands back again. I can see the irritation in his eyes when I look up at him.

"What do you need?" I ask.

"A comfortable position for this. I know what I want, but I don't know how to make it happen." There's frustrated tears in his eyes.

Getting up, I press my lips to his. "Get on the bed."

Oakley nods and climbs on. I prop his books against the pillows and then join him, arranging one of the pillows under his head. Bringing him onto his side, I curl between his legs, the top one over my shoulder.

For the third time since getting home, I take his dick in my mouth and press two fingers into his ass.

He moans. "Yes," he moans, both in relief and pleasure. "Just like that. Perfect."

I smile and close my eyes, sucking on him and playing with his hole. He seems content enough, so I lose myself in the moment until he says, "Three fingers, Loren. Please."

I fumble for the lube and then do as he wants. He groans, his hips rocking gently against me.

"Good," he mutters breathlessly. "So good. Keep going, okay?"

Nodding, I settle again and let him study while I give him all the muted gratification he wants.

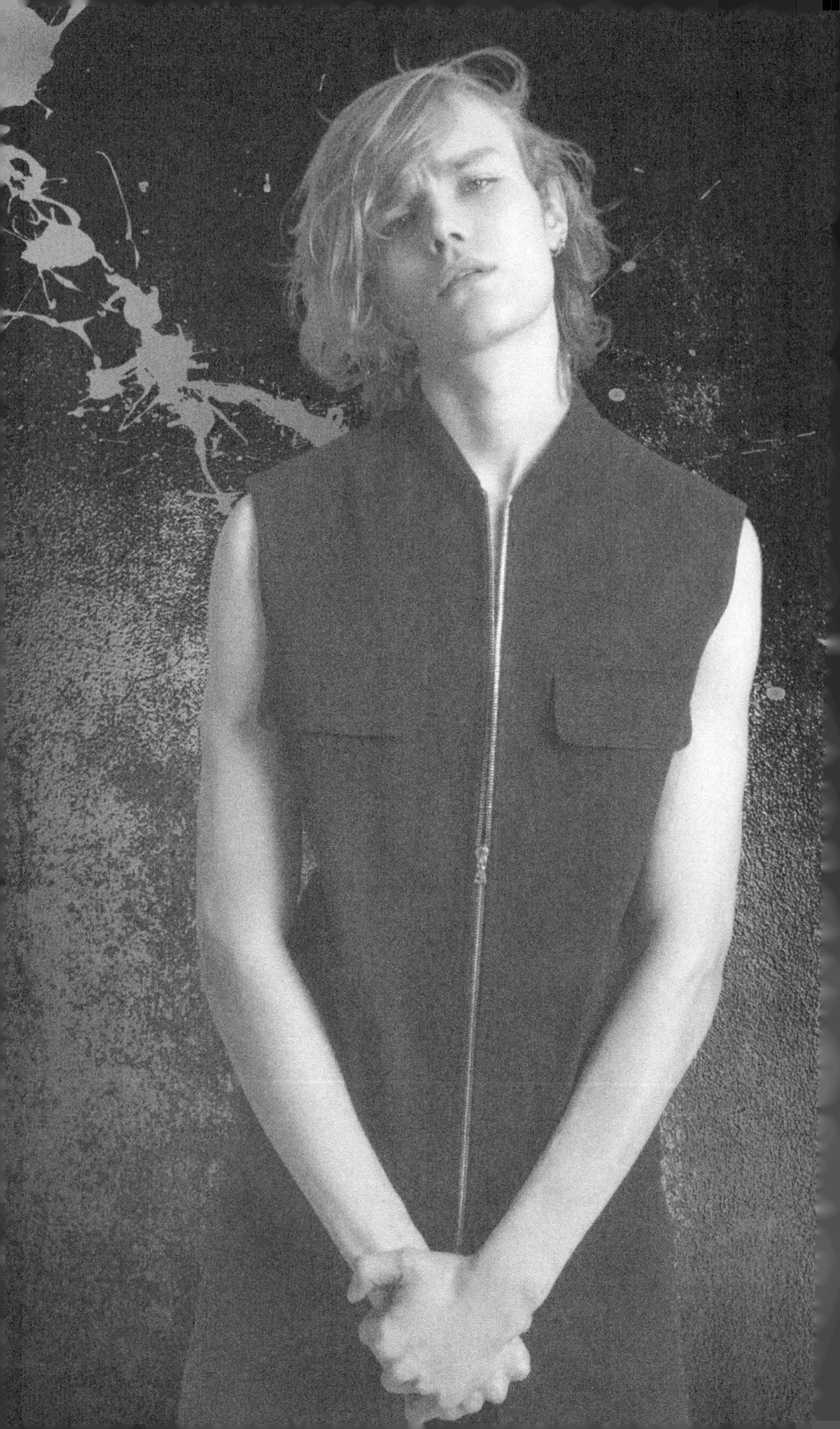

30
OAKLEY

I've unlocked a new kink. I'm sure Loren's jaw is so fucking sore, but he never complains. This afternoon was my last final and I think I did pretty well. For the past week, every time I studied, we curled up on Loren's bed with my dick in his mouth and his fingers in my ass.

It should have been distracting. I should have been completely mindless. But he kept me suspended with just enough endorphins and barely breathless that I was almost super fixated on my work. I couldn't take notes in the first night's position. Which Loren remedied the second night when I got frustrated and he changed our position again, so I had use of my arms in relative comfort.

I've never been cared for by someone like this. Sometimes I think his entire drive in life is to make me happy. To give me whatever I ask for. He's so soft and tender with me, it constantly brings tears to my eyes.

When he asked me what I wanted to do to celebrate my last final of the semester, I told him I wanted to celebrate the same way he's been helping me study.

I'm not sure if it's that I know I have his entire focus like this or something else, but this is now my new favorite thing in the entire world. Don't get me wrong, I *love* when we do other things. Anything else. Doesn't even have to be sexual.

But there's something incredibly intimate and personal about this that makes me feel like I'm bleeding for him.

We've been like this for twenty minutes, I think. He worked up to three fingers, so my ass is nice and stretched. I'm not balls deep in his mouth, but he has me fully locked inside him with a firm, steady, soft suction constantly applied.

He knows what I like. He knows what I need.

I'm not sure if it's the removal of finals stress that's making me emotional right now or something else, but I feel like I'm on the verge of breaking down. Not in a bad way, though. Like, I want to cry but... good cry. The only reason I manage to keep it in right now is because I think it'll upset Loren.

"Deeper," I whisper.

The jolt of pleasure that surges through me when he pushes three fingers deep inside me has me moaning. Somehow, in this position, I remain still and let him do what I tell him to without rocking too much.

My fingers dig into his hair and I close my eyes. I feel his mouth everywhere. With each deep thrust of his fingers—slow and thick—my body heats hotter and hotter. I don't want to come, but I do.

"Loren," I moan, breathless.

I can feel his attention, waiting for me to tell him what I want. What I need. But again, I'm not sure what I need right now. I just need more.

LOREN

The whine in my throat lodges, and I press my hips to his face. Loren takes me, even as he tries not to gag. His fingers drive deeper, but I need more.

"More," I whine. I beg. "Please, Loren."

I'm surprised when he interprets that as another finger and I'm suddenly being stretched wider to accommodate. My champ of a boyfriend also buries my dick deeper into his throat. My eyes roll and I can't keep myself as still any longer.

I jerk, unsure if it's from the new burning in my ass or the way his throat constricts around my dick. For a while, I'm content like this. The new sensations are overwhelming, slightly achy, and fucking good. My skin burns, my mind swims, my eyes tear up. All in good ways.

"Loren," I whisper.

He rolls over so he's flat under me and wraps his free arm around my lower back, keeping me there. Keeping me plunged into his throat as he works my ass with almost his whole hand. Fuck, it feels good.

My hips rock on their own, pulling out of him and surging back down. The pleasure is intense. Consuming. Fuck, I don't want it to stop.

But I'm whining, I need something. I feel like a fucking baby right now because I don't know what that is. So I fuck his mouth harder, but that's not reaching what I need. With a frustrated screech I try to keep quiet, I roll off him and stare at the ceiling.

Loren climbs up my body and hovers over me. I smile because he's so ruffled and beautiful.

"What can I do?" he asks.

My heart breaks because he thinks it's him. I pull him down roughly and he drops. "You know how you tell me your touch aversion is a you thing?" I ask. He grins and nods. "This right now is a me thing. I don't know what I want. I want you, but I just need more. Even though I don't know what that means right now. I love what you're doing but I like, need you to climb inside me or something."

His grin widens.

We settle together, wrapping around each other. I'm sweaty, but so is he. "Do you like doing that?" I ask.

Loren nods.

I run my fingers along his jaw. "Does it hurt after a while? I'm a complete baby and can't suck dick for long without my jaw aching."

He hums, a smile on his sexy lips. "Yes, my jaw aches by the time you're done, but I don't mind at all. I would happily do this all day."

"You're incredible," I whisper.

Loren brushes his lips to mine. "You are too. Tell me how you want me to touch you."

"I like your fingers in my ass," I say, feeling my cheeks heat.

He wiggles us around so he can get my leg over his arm and regain access to my ass. It's not the best angle, but it still feels good. There's something about this position, though. I'm staring into his eyes. Sharing his breath.

"I love you," I whisper, and then my eyes go wide. "Fuck. I —Uh—"

Loren smiles. His arm under me tangles in my hair and he brings my mouth to his. Because I feel foolish, I kiss him hard and desperate because… I completely meant that.

We remain entwined until I'm no longer feeling like an idiot, just riding his fingers and kissing him. Because I haven't told him I want to get off, he's just playing. Lightly brushing my prostate and stretching my hole as we kiss.

It's the moment between us like this that I crave. The things we share, unspoken.

"Do you really?" he asks.

I nod, keeping my eyes closed. "It's too soon to say that, right? To feel that way? I mean, it's only been like a couple months but it just feels like a lifetime. I feel you everywhere. I *want* to feel you everywhere. To feel you more than I think is possible."

Loren rolls us so I'm under him, pressing his fingers deeper inside me, and our dicks together. I definitely feel him more now. His mouth moves along my jaw, my neck. I groan as I let myself go under him.

"I have something," he whispers.

"What?"

"Will you let me pleasure you now? Can I make you come?"

"I'm not ready," I whine.

"You don't want to be done," he says, and I nod. "I won't make it quick. Promise."

"You can do whatever you want to me, Loren."

He smiles. "You say that, and I'm going to carve my name into your skin."

I shudder at the low rumble of his voice. I'm not sure I'd be opposed to that, but I don't say it out loud.

Loren gently disentangles us and moves to the side of the bed. He returns thirty seconds later with a… something. He settles between my legs and holds it out for me to inspect.

It looks like a combination dildo and plug. But when he shows me the other end, there's a hole in it. It's maybe six inches, not thick, but there's a bulge exactly where it's going to hit a prostate. The way the ends curl up, I think it'll also press against my taint.

Bringing my gaze back to Loren, he grins.

"I can't grow my dick, but I think I can give you more and still be inside you," he tells me.

"Just so we're clear, I love your dick the way it is," I promise.

He grins. "I'm very glad about that."

"So…" I start, looking at this thing again.

"It's called a fuckhole sheath," he says, amused. "I put it inside you like a plug and then fuck into it inside you."

I shiver. A trickle of pleasure runs down my spine. "Yes. Do that. Be, uh, slow, though."

Loren nods. I watch as he lubes it inside and out and then asks me how I want him. This man!

"Just like this," I whisper. "I want to look at you. We've never had sex like this before."

He smiles and my stomach flutters.

After his four fingers were inside me, this isn't anything to write home about. Until the bulb at the base. I shudder when it settles into place.

"No condom," I say, already panting.

Loren had just picked one up. His eyes meet mine and I think he might argue. My cheeks burn. But he tosses it away and reaches for the lube instead.

"Come here," I whisper, when he lines his cock up.

He leans over, resting his weight on his forearm so he can still reach what he's doing and look at me.

"You can tell me you want to use a condom. You know that, right?"

His tongue peeks out as he licks his lips. "We will never use one again if that's what you want. It's habit more than anything; I'll happily cream inside you, Oakley."

I shiver. We got tested, just as I told him we would, though I think he was definitely asleep for that comment since he was amused the following morning when I reminded him. Dutifully, he brought me to the clinic and we went through the whole ordeal, including the lecture about safe sex, which he remained completely entertained by. We also listened about all the new drugs on the market to protect against some things, which Loren thought was funny since there's a lot more than just one or two fatal communicable diseases in the world, so why are they picking and choosing which to create drugs against.

His mind is an interesting place to be.

However, we've always worn one after that. Including once we got our results back. I thought that's just how he was comfortable.

"Do that," I whisper. "I always want skin on skin, if that's okay. I never plan to be with anyone else again, so… I think we're safe."

The heat in his eyes, the way he looks at me like he's going to eat me alive, it makes my head spin. To think that you could go your whole life without ever finding someone to look at you this way. Like you're the only thing that exists. The only person who's important.

"If you want," I add when he doesn't speak.

Loren's mouth covers mine. This is the most aggressive kiss he's ever given me. I wrap my arms and legs around him, pressing his body to mine so there's no distance between us. I feel his desire. His need.

Then his cock is pressing into the thing in my ass and my breath catches. It catches and doesn't release as he spreads me wide, pressing the bulb into my prostate. Holy fuck. Holy fuck!

He's slow, just as I told him to be. His mouth doesn't leave me, licking open mouth kisses all over my skin as I cling to him. I swear, I can somehow feel this stretch, his dick, *everywhere*.

I jerk and jolt as he continues to enter me. Deeper and deeper. I think he's gained a few inches as he makes room in my body for him.

"Loren," I groan.

"Is this the kind of more you need?" he asks.

Tears sting my eyes and I'm ready to write it off as a side effect of the overwhelming invasion that's taking over my body. But really, it's because he's done this just for me. He found a way to give me more of him.

"I love you," I whisper, voice trembling. "So damn much, Loren. Please, please don't ever leave me."

"Never," he promises, burying himself deep. I can't take a breath as my body shudders around this thing in my ass. His dick, specialized. The constant pressure against sensitive nerve bundles has me nearly vibrating. "At the risk of sounding psychotic, I'm never letting you out of my life, Oakley. I will never let you go. You're mine. I will kill anyone who tries to get in the way or tries to take your love from me."

His threat is very real. Remembering that he's killed two men for me makes me shiver.

"Loren," I gasp. "Slowly, okay? I don't want to come yet."

He nods. It's a very strange sensation to know he's pulled out of me and still feeling full. And then to feel that full feeling expand and send a wave of pleasure through my body has my head spinning.

I need... more. I need his voice.

"Tell me more," I whisper. "Tell me you'll kill people to keep me."

"I will kill everyone," he murmurs, his teeth skimming my neck.

He's got me tight in his arms now, which makes movement a little difficult, but since we're aiming for a snail pace orgasm, I'm not about to let him go anywhere. Besides, this feeling is something I don't ever want to lose.

"No one will touch you again, Oakley. No one will kiss you. Absolutely no one will touch this dick or this ass. You're mine. All of you. Only I get to please you now. You only get to come on me—on my dick, my chest, my face, my back. I don't care. You can cover me in your cum. But *no one* will ever touch what's mine."

"You'll kill them."

"Brutally. I'll tear them to pieces until they're unrecognizable. I'll burn them alive and listen to their screams, carve their skin with acid, run their limbs through a wood chipper, bury them alive."

His thrusts become snaps of his hips, making my eyes roll. "I. Will. Kill. Anyone. Who. Touches. You." Each word is punctuated with a hard jab of his hips as if he brands each word into me—physically and verbally. His words echo in my head. Embedding there.

He'll kill for me. That's how much he loves me.

"Tell me you love me," he demands. "I need to hear it again."

"I love you," I say, digging my nails into his skin. "I love you. I love you. I love you."

I'm so fucking sore when we're done, but I think that's the *more* we both needed.

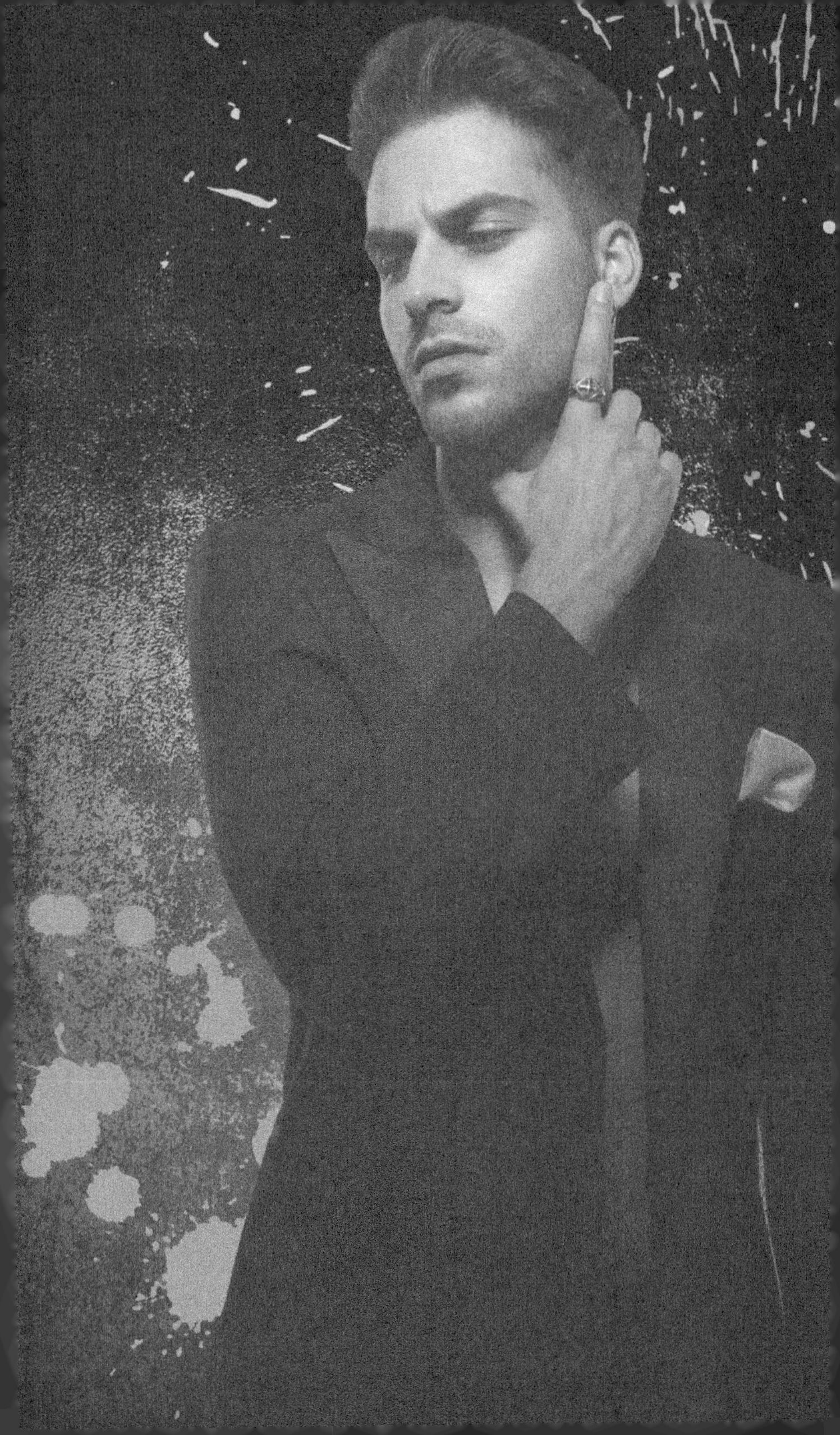

31
LOREN

After a few hours, the tension in my body finally leaves. It happens less and less with Oakley, but it's stupidly frustrating when I wake up and feel like I'm about to come undone because I'm being touched. I've even taken to looking up ways to desensitize myself to this. It's never bothered me before. Everyone needs their personal space, so I've always been able to maintain that distance.

But I don't want to keep any distance between me and Oakley. I want to touch him all the time. That's a little difficult when I cringe away because my skin feels too tight.

Heading downstairs toward the front door to retrieve my boyfriend from his friends' house, I pause when I think I hear his laughter. Since he left my room hours ago, I assumed he actually left. This was the very first morning that I didn't walk him across the street because he assured me he didn't need that much close watching.

I feel like I should have been praised for the effort it took not to watch him cross the street through my bedroom window.

When I think I hear his laughter again, I turn for the hall and follow the sound. The distinct noise of a video game reaches me first as I approach.

I'm really not good about sharing my things. It's a very weird thing for me when my family is concerned because I'd give them anything, and yet, I'm strangely possessive of everything that's mine. Even something stupid like a pen. Or my favorite butcher knife I use to carve people with.

Yet, when I stop in the doorway of the living room to find Oakley with the triplets, laughing and holding a game controller in hand, the strange flurry of warmth and butterflies inside me *isn't* that same feeling of needing to take back what's mine so they can't have it. Instead, I stand there and stare, perplexed by the feeling I'm unaccustomed to.

Oakley's hair has mostly fallen out, the curls framing his face. His eyes shine with mirth as he stares grinning at the screen. His legs are tucked under him and he has a pillow in his lap as he leans forward.

His entire body shifts when he manipulates the controls, as if the angle of his body will help his character on the screen.

"Noo," he calls out, laughing and drawing out the word as Imry says, "That's shit," and Avory adds, "Asshole." Of course, this only makes Ellory laugh maniacally.

My brothers are very important to me. I'm also quite possessive and protective of them, especially Avory and Ellory because of our childhood. It's not that I just don't like to share Noah or Oakley, I don't like to share my family either. I didn't think I'd like having the different spheres of my life blend together.

But watching them play games and laugh together? I'm overcome in a way I was not expecting at all. Dinner with them was one thing. I was there. I could still keep possession of all the people in my life separately.

This is different. They'd been playing games without me. And I really kind of maybe love it. So weird to find that perhaps I want them to find friendship together.

Oakley drops his hands to the pillow and glances at the door and gives me a wide smile. He brushes his hair back and that big smile turns shy.

Licking my lips, I step into the room. My brothers watch me in silence as I round the big cushy chair where Oakley is so I can reach him. As I've seen him do too many times to count, I tuck the wayward strands of his hair behind his ear.

"Feeling better?" he asks.

With the absence of the tight, itchy feeling on my skin when I brush my fingers along his jaw, I nod.

"Want to play?"

I shake my head.

"Want to sit with me?"

For a minute, I just look at him. Study his face. His shining eyes. Beautiful smile. Such kindness and softness in this man. I'm surprised when I realize I don't want to interrupt them with my presence.

However, I've been away from Oakley for a few hours now, and I'm definitely over that. So I nod and kneel on the couch to sit beside him. He moves the pillow from his lap and shifts while reaching for me to pull me into him.

I lean back against him, my back to his chest, and wrap his legs around my stomach. He laughs and we wiggle and arrange pillows for a few more minutes until we're comfortable. When we've settled and his arms come around my chest with the controller in his hand, I can feel my brothers watching.

They're sitting on the couch beside the big chair we're in. Ellory and Avory are sitting much like Oakley and I are—Ellory in Avory's lap. That's how to tell them apart. When they sit like this, it's always Ellory in Avory's lap. I think I once witnessed it the other way, and they immediately switched, saying it was too weird.

Imry is on the cushion beside them, leaving the cushion closest to us empty.

"I thought you were going home," I say to Oakley.

"I was, but then they asked if I wanted to play a racing game, so I stayed." He presses a kiss to my head, and I try my damnedest not to smile. "Is that okay?"

"Yes."

"You're not going to get mad that we borrowed your boyfriend without asking?" Ellory asks.

"Not this time, but I make no promises for next time," I answer.

I don't have to look at them to know that I'm receiving huge triplet smiles. Maybe they can feel how differently *I* feel about this one thing. I don't hate it at all.

"Ready for the next cup?" Imry asks, changing the subject.

"Yep," Avory and Ellory respond together while Oakley nods.

I spend the next hour or so right there. In Oakley's lap with my hands brushing the soft skin of his legs. He's always clean-shaven and his torso and even his arms are so smooth, I'm kind of fascinated with the hair on his legs.

Absently, I run my fingers through it, up and down his calves, while I let their laughter and teasing jabs dull to background noise. Comfort. Oakley presses a kiss to my head every so often. His arms tighten around me sometimes. He hugs me, rocking us from side to side between races.

The confusion and surprise that I'm *not* upset at sharing Oakley remains floating around inside me for a bit, dulling a little more as each minute passes and I simply enjoy this moment. I want more of these moments where I can be a spectator and Oakley can do his thing with my brothers, but I'm still here to feel him.

I'm surprisingly relieved that they get along when I'm *not* present. There's comfort in that, even if I can't quite wrap my head around it.

"There you are."

We all turn to the doorway to find Voss standing there. He's looking as perplexed as I felt when I first stood in the door.

"You don't even like video games," he says to me.

I shrug. "But I'm not playing. I'm watching."

Voss shakes his head. "Can I talk to you for a minute? I'm sure they'll recap what you missed."

"We will," Oakley says, kissing the side of my head and then unwrapping his limbs from around me.

Already, I hate the loss of his touch, but I swing my legs over the side of the chair and move toward my brother. We continue down the hall to our makeshift conference room, where he shuts the door. Dad's there, but then, I think he uses the room as an office, too.

"I need a favor," he says.

"I'm not loaning you Oakley."

Dad looks up from whatever he's been working on while Voss just blinks at me.

"I'm not even going to ask why that was your first assumption. I don't want to borrow your boyfriend, Loren."

I shrug. "Just putting it out there."

Dad chuckles and returns his attention to his work.

Voss shakes his head. "Okay, thanks for that clarification. I'll keep it in mind. However, I'd actually like to talk about my friend, Enoch Zayn. Are you familiar with him?"

"He's a rockstar's kid," I say, shrugging.

"He's an old friend from college. We roomed together for three years. You even visited a few times," he tells me.

"I won't ask to borrow your friend. I have my own."

The way he looks at me makes me want to laugh. I was entirely serious about Oakley, though I suppose I knew that's not what he wanted to ask. This time, I'm just pulling his leg, though. It's fun to give your brothers a hard time. Why have brothers otherwise?

He pinches the bridge of his nose and decides to ignore my comment. "He's being stalked. This guy has gone so far as to break into his house while Enoch's home, attack him with a butcher knife, and hit him with his car, which resulted in a broken arm. Enoch has a security detail now, but he's afraid. This guy is still hanging around."

"Where are the authorities?" I ask.

"Not doing their job," Voss says, frowning. "It's Vegas. Apparently, there are more important things to do than protect someone from a man who has literally caused injury."

"Hmm."

"He was really scared when he called me, so I told him I'd take care of it."

I nod. "Sounds good."

"You like to play dumb sometimes," he deadpans.

Grinning, I shrug. "I'm retired."

"You're not retired. You're on sabbatical, and I really need this favor."

"Ask Myro."

"Loren, we're not going to let anything happen to Oakley," he promises. "They're on winter break right now, so he's staying here with us anyway, right? He's completely safe. And I promise you, no one will borrow him while you're away."

"I'm not—"

"Please," Voss says. "This guy is showing up everywhere. He had a hunting knife last time Enoch ran into him in public. *I'm* afraid for him. I know how important keeping Oakley safe is to you. It's important to me to keep Enoch safe. You can trust us to keep Oakley safe while you're helping me."

I stare at him and try to determine why it matters so much. After college, I've never even heard him mention Enoch. Besides, why does it have to be me? Why not Myro?

"You'd do the same for Noah," Dad says. "Enoch is Voss' Noah."

Well... I suppose that changes things. Studying my brother, I think that maybe I'm getting a little better at reading people. I can identify that he *is* worried. His concern looks a lot like Oakley's.

"I'll see if Oakley is okay staying here with you," I say.

"We can spend time next door if he wants to stay with his friends too," Voss offers.

"They have a rule about not bringing strangers into their space," I tell him. "Besides, they're not all back home yet."

"We're not strangers and I think we're all friends at this point. They're here all the time."

"I'll ask him if he minds."

"Do you plan to tell him you're going to kill someone?" Dad asks. "What have you told him about your contracts?"

"We've had this discussion. You know what I've told him."

"He thinks you've only killed for him," Voss says.

I nod, shrugging. "He knows I'll do it again too."

Voss sighs. I'm not sure why that bothers him, but based on the way he presses his lips together, I'm sure it does.

"He likes to hear that I will," I add, in case he thinks I'm just announcing it and making Oakley uncomfortable. "He asks to hear it when we're having se—"

"Don't!" Voss blurts out suddenly, holding up his hand to stop me. "I really, *really* don't want to talk about your sex life or know anything about it."

Dad chuckles, subtly shaking his head.

"I've heard yours," I say, frowning. "Remember those times you invited me to your college dorm?" I know he does. He just reminded me I'd been there.

Now Dad laughs.

Voss covers his face. "Honestly, Loren," he mutters. "Please, just do this for me. I'm begging you. This guy is unhinged. I'm sure he's going to kill Enoch if it carries on much longer. *Please.*"

I sigh. "Fine. I'll ask Oakley if he's okay to be on his own for a few days."

He nods. "Thank you. I'll send you the information."

For a minute, I study my brother. "Do you love Enoch?" I ask.

Dad looks up again.

Voss drops his hand from his face and frowns. "In the same way you love Noah."

"I don't love anyone, remember?"

He gives me an amused smile. "I think we all know that's shit. Stop hiding behind it. But in the way you're asking, no. He's a good friend of mine. I'm not into guys, which I think you know, since you seem to recall my sex life just fine."

Shrugging, I turn to the door. "Neither was I. Besides, I didn't say guys. As in plural." I open the door and step into the hall. "I asked specifically about Enoch."

I don't receive an answer as I walk back to the living room. My phone pings as I step in, no doubt from Voss with the information I need. They pause the game so I can retake my seat.

"What happened?" Oakley asks.

"Another contract," I share, feeling the triplets look at me. "Voss begged. It was worth seeing."

Oakley grins.

"It means I have to leave for a few days," I admit, and his smile falls. "Will you stay here with my brothers? Sleep in my room? They'll keep you safe."

Oakley looks at the triplets. The three of them nod. My boyfriend turns a confused expression on me. "Why do you have to leave to deal with a contract?" he asks.

"Sometimes they require field research," Imry says before I can answer. "Is Myro going with you?"

I shrug, shaking my head. "Silly for us both to go, isn't it? If he's going, then I don't need to. Voss still never said why he wanted me instead of Myro, though I asked."

"We'll go with you," Avory says.

My eyes meet Imry's. Usually, it's him who's with me. Not his two-thirds. But… yeah, I kind of want him to stay with Oakley. I nod. "Sure. But we're not sharing a room."

"Could totally give you lessons," Ellory mutters, unpausing the game.

"I promise, I don't need lessons. Oakley and I have a very healthy and satisfying s—" His hand suddenly claps over my mouth, making the triplets cackle. I look up and he's bright red.

"Why do you do that?" he asks, trying to bury his face in my hair.

Glancing at my brothers, I find them grinning. I smile behind Oakley's hand and don't miss the fact that Avory and Ellory are comfortable enough with Oakley that they don't mind hinting about their relationship in his presence.

For a reason I don't quite understand, this makes me really, really happy.

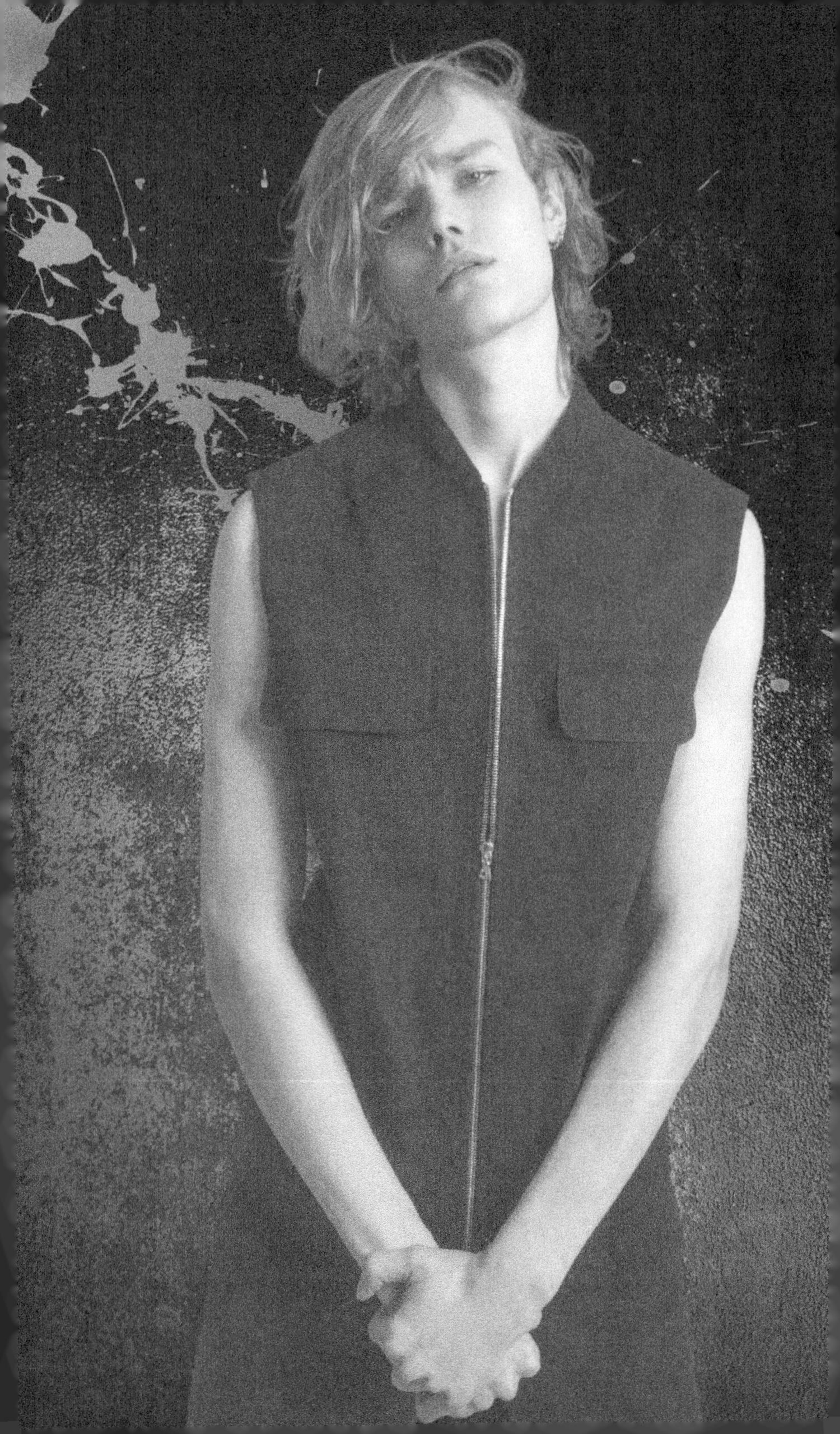

32
OAKLEY

THE FIRST TWO days that Loren is gone, I stay at his house. It should feel weird, right? I'm practically a stranger. At the very least, I should feel slightly awkward with his father.

But… it's not. I can feel that they're still careful with me, testing the waters to make sure they don't inadvertently make me uncomfortable, but otherwise, I feel like we've been friends a lot longer than a few months.

It's hard to believe so much has happened since September. I'd barely begun school when Daniel/Jason showed up in my life. Then there was Loren, the serial killer, and then *really* Loren. And now, it's like I've just never left his place.

It's weird and lonely sleeping in Loren's room alone. Yet, I'm sure I'd rather be here than completely alone across the street. At the Van Doren's, there are people here. Four others with the triplets and Myro right down the hall. I can hear them moving around to some extent, and I take a lot of comfort in it.

The first night alone in Loren's room felt very… intrusive. This is his personal space. There's the urge to look around, open drawers, and snoop into all the nooks and crannies. I even go so far as to text him to ask if I can. I swear, I can hear his amusement in the text he sends back, which confirms that I can look wherever I want.

I don't, but having permission makes me feel less like an invader.

The first night makes me realize how much I've come to really love sleeping with Loren. The way his arms wrap around me. How I can feel his body everywhere. Feel his breaths on my neck and his heartbeat against my back.

At least I can still smell him on the pillows and within the blankets.

Late on the third afternoon that Loren's not here, I head home. Well, to home number two. Or maybe that's home number one since I lived there first. Anyway, I head across the road to the home I live in with my best friends.

Unsurprisingly, Voss and Imry follow me across. Brek, Levis, and Briar are home and when Levis texted, I said I'd be right over.

Stepping inside, I smile. They don't seem at all bothered to find Voss and Imry coming into our space. I didn't think they would. They enjoy the Van Dorens.

"Okay so tell me how Christmas was," I say by way of greeting, curling up in my usual chair.

"Normal for me," Brek says. "I'm never going to be the child they wanted, but they love me despite my shortcomings."

Imry and Voss give him surprised, disgusted looks. "What does that mean?" Imry questions.

Brek shakes his head. "My family likes to pride themselves on being number one in everything, with awards and accolades and shit. From academics to sports to careers." He shrugs. "I've never lived up to their standards."

"Which is stupid," Briar insists. "You have a 3.9 GPA and a job offer."

Brek shrugs again. "I spent the week listening to how Sally was invited to speak at a conference in India for her research. Ryan graduated high school having broken the academic record in Rhode Island. Little Suzie Michael can now ride a two wheeler and she's barely three. 'Oh. Honey. How's college going?' I hear as an afterthought once they've made it clear that all my cousins —even my three-year-old cousin—have outdone me everywhere."

"That's shit," Voss says.

"Yeah, well." Brek shrugs once more. "That's my life."

"What's the job offer?" Imry asks, changing the subject back to something other than Brek's father.

"There's a local real estate agent, Zaiden Nyles, who I've met on campus a few times—he's teaching a course on real estate—and we've been talking. He offered me an entry level job once I graduate where I can learn and prep hands-on for the real estate course. When I become licensed after the test, he'll give me a job as an agent."

"That's awesome," Voss says. "Your parents weren't excited for you?"

"I didn't tell them," Brek admits with a bitter chuckle. "Not only is that not utilizing my degree, but it's also entry level with no prestige."

"No offense, but your parents sound like assholes," Imry says.

Brek waves them off. I know it hurts him, even though he's pretending it doesn't right now. He's lived with this his entire life, so he's become a bit desensitized to it. He knows what's going to make them happy, which is nothing he manages, and what's going to earn him mock pride that sounds more like 'oh, that's nice, dear' than actual congratulations.

It's never even mattered what's important to Brek. He *is* smart and he *is* driven. He's accomplished some really impressive things in his educational career, but they weren't at the very top; so to his parents, they were nothing better than merit awards received by everyone who simply shows up and puts in the time.

I've always been really glad that Brek is an only child. I can't imagine how miserable his life would be if his parents were constantly pitting him and a sibling against each other for who's the *better* Holleran child.

"What about you?" Brek asks, looking at Briar. We know that means he's had enough with the conversation.

"As you, normal. We show up, act like we're close for family, and then go our separate ways after exchanging generic gifts that we all inevitably return," Briar tells us.

"I'm not sure if that's pleasant or tragic," Imry says.

Briar chuckles. "Honestly, we're just really different. Siblings likely couldn't be more different then we are. There's no ill will. We weren't shit to each other growing up. We just literally have zero in common. Believe me, we've actually tried over the years —of our own desire. The most we can pull off is faking interest in what the others talk about so we've kind of just let our relationships simmer, I guess. We love each other. We'd show up if someone needs something, but overall—we're just not friends."

"Yes, tragic," Imry affirms. "I don't mean this to sound mushy, but I can't imagine not being close to my brothers."

Voss nods, frowning. "Built in best friends."

LOREN

I grin, hiding it behind my knees. That's how me and Dylan were growing up too.

"That's corny," Briar says, grinning. "I love my family, but I'm cool with our relationship. Yeah, it might be nice to have 'built in best friends' but there are worse situations to have with siblings."

"Speaking of which," I interject. "I haven't heard from Haze. He doing okay with Oren?"

"He's coming home tomorrow," Levis says. "He just called me yesterday to ask for a pickup from the airport. He says it's been good for them both, but they're still working on building their relationship, so more than a week is a little much for the first visit."

"I'm glad it's been good, though," I say.

Levis nods. "Definitely. For both of them."

We've never actually met Oren in person, though we've seen him from afar. Everything we know has come from Haze over the guilt-ridden years and out of fear for his brother. Otherwise, we don't know Oren at all.

The more Haze told us growing up, the more afraid we became for him. As much as we'd have loved to become heroes and somehow rescue Oren from the fate he found himself in—yes, we talked about it often—our selfish focus was on making sure Haze was safe and relatively unharmed.

A moment of silence settles around us before Levis continues, "We don't celebrate Christmas, but we celebrated the New Year. Everything was fine and my mother sent me home with a whole Osechi Ryori to share with you."

"Yes!" Brek cheers, grinning.

"That's... New Year's food, right?" Voss asks, tilting his head as if he were trying to recall.

"It is. Three layered lacquer boxes filled with different, traditional foods we eat on New Year. My mom and sister make several to give to friends they've made here in the U.S.," Levis tells us.

"That's awesome," Voss says, grinning.

Levis nods. "It's really awesome that I get to eat it twice this year." He looks at me. "What about you? How was your first Christmas without your family?"

I huff. "I'm still salty that my parents wanted to travel instead of being with me and my brother, but it was great. You don't really know what is actually a family tradition until you experience someone else's family Christmas."

"Loren spoiled the fuck out of him," Imry teases, smirking.

I flush. "I don't understand how he managed to buy all that without me knowing. He never leaves my side!" I don't miss the way Brek tries not to scowl.

"Online. The man rarely sleeps. The guest room has been filling with boxes for the past month," Voss shares, chuckling.

"But yeah, it was great," I admit, glossing over it when I'd love to say more but want to avoid Brek's attitude. "Mom and Dad called and showed me their chalet and strange tropically decorated tree. I talked to Dylan for a while, and Mom promised we'll all get together for my birthday next month."

"That's something," Levis says.

"I want to hear what Loren got you," Briar says, apparently ignoring the way Brek is becoming sour.

LOREN

"My favorite thing was the black throw pillow that said, 'fuck it, just get naked.'" Imry laughs. "The look of horror on Oakley's face!"

"Oh no," Voss interjects. "You misremember. The look of horror was when Loren, witnessing Oakley's blush, said he thought that one was more appropriate than the one that read 'Taint Tickler.'"

I press my hands to my face to hide the way it's turning red as Briar and Levis laugh. Through the cracks in my fingers, I can see Brek scowl. Once again, I change the subject.

Over the next few hours, we continue to talk and catch up. As long as the conversation stays away from Loren, Brek is pleasant enough. I have to change the subject abruptly like three times before the others seem to catch on and stop bringing up Loren. From the way Voss and Imry eye Brek, I think they finally realize why I'm doing it.

However, I've apparently gotten too comfortable in this 'avoid the subject of my boyfriend' ruse, because the next time he's brought up and I turn the conversation elsewhere, Brek says, "Why do you keep doing that? What's so bad that even *you* don't want to talk about *your* boyfriend?"

While I intend to ignore him and move the conversation along, Voss interjects, "He's changing the subject because you constantly get a dick up your ass every time my brother's name is mentioned."

"Voss, don't," I say, warily.

"I do not," Brek defends. "We can talk about his lack of—"

"Don't you fucking finish that," I snap and sit forward. "You know what? I'm done with this conversation with you. You don't want me to talk about Loren, but when I don't you get pissed off that I'm not. There's no making you happy and quite frankly, I'm tired of trying. When you're done being a dick, let me know, Brek, because right now, I have no interest in being around you." Getting to my feet, I head for the stairs and stomp up them, Brek's look of surprise staying with me.

As if he doesn't know he's been a fuckhead for months! Whatever.

I'm stomping around my room when I turn to find Imry in my doorway. "You okay?"

"I don't know what his problem is. Loren makes him uneasy and therefore, I should act like he's a pariah or some shit. I'm over it."

"The longer you're with Loren, the more you're going to find people are very black and white with him. They either love or hate him. Most of the time, their inability to understand why he's different makes them hate him."

"It's shit," I mutter, dropping onto my bed with a huff.

"It is. Loren doesn't seem to care much, which isn't surprising. His ability to care about such things is absent." He grins. "But it bothers me and my brothers. We protect him from the outside world as much as we can, as does Dad."

I smile. "I don't think he knows that."

Imry's smile lingers. "He doesn't. Mostly because he doesn't know how to recognize that we do. But when you love someone, you innately want to protect them. Just as you did tonight with Brek."

Sighing, I fall backward and close my eyes. "I'm just so damn tired of Brek's attitude. He's been weird since Daniel/Jason and yeah, I get it. My judge of character maybe needs some work, as does my self-image, which I think is really what made me ignore all of Daniel/Jason's red flags. But fuck."

LOREN

"In his defense, Loren has a whole lot more red flags than Daniel did," Imry admits, amused.

I snort. "Oh, I know. Maybe they're a different shade of red, though. Like… burgundy."

Imry laughs. "You sleeping here tonight?"

"Yeah. That okay?"

"Of course. You have a spare room in this place?"

"Downstairs across from Levis by the front door. But there's only one."

"Well, I asked about it, therefore it's mine. Sweet dreams, sunshine. See you in the morning." He closes my door behind him.

Refusing to give any more attention to the mood Brek put me in, I decide to go to bed. It's already nine, so that's plenty reasonable. I move through my bathroom and then strip from my clothes before climbing into my bed. Before I turn off the bedside lamp, I text Loren.

ME
Going to bed. Hurry home.

LOREN VAN DOREN
Good night. See you soon.

ME
I'm across the street. Pick me up tomorrow as soon as you get in?

LOREN VAN DOREN
Okay.

Even in my irritation, I fall asleep relatively quickly, but I'm woken up by my bedroom door opening. It's still dark out so I'm slightly disoriented when I turn around. In my sleep, I imagine it's going to be Loren. But it's Brek.

He hovers over the side of my bed.

"What?" I say groggily.

"I'm sorry," he whispers. "For being such an ass."

I huff. "You want to tell me why you've been an ass, or am I just going to accept your apology and go back to sleep?"

I can barely make out the curve of his lips as he smiles. He climbs onto my bed and I move over to make him room. As he settles, I close my eyes. We can talk with my eyes closed.

"I've been jealous," he says.

"That makes zero sense," I mutter. "You don't even like him."

His inhale is loud. "We've grown up with Honey Bee, Levis, and Briar always having partners. You, Haze, and me... we were always the three that didn't. I know you and Haze had circumstances around why you didn't but..." His voice trails off. "I guess I didn't expect that the only people I could actually imagine being, uh, *like that* with were the five of you. Not that I entertained the thought much, mind you, but the knowledge that the *only* people I ever found attractive were you guys kind of messed me up. So now that you have someone and have practically moved out, and Levis is talking about marrying this girl, and Honey Bee has mentioned getting her own place after graduation more than once... I'm having a really hard time adjusting and accepting it all."

I'm not surprised by most of what he said. Brek has *never* been good at change. He hates it. Gradual change he can roll with more easily, but big things have always sent him into slight panics. In just five months, there's going to be a lot of change triggered by graduation.

LOREN

"So you're taking it out on me. More specifically on anything having to do with me when Loren's concerned.".

Brek sighs. "I'm jealous," he repeats.

"I realize you think that's supposed to clear this up, but I'm not seeing the connection quite yet."

"I don't want you to be with Loren."

"Okay, that much I've figured out," I say, chuckling.

"Jesus, Oakley," he mutters and shifts on the bed. I open my eyes when he does. I have like ten seconds to register his words and what happens directly following. *"I want to be with you. I love you."*

Then his mouth is on mine.

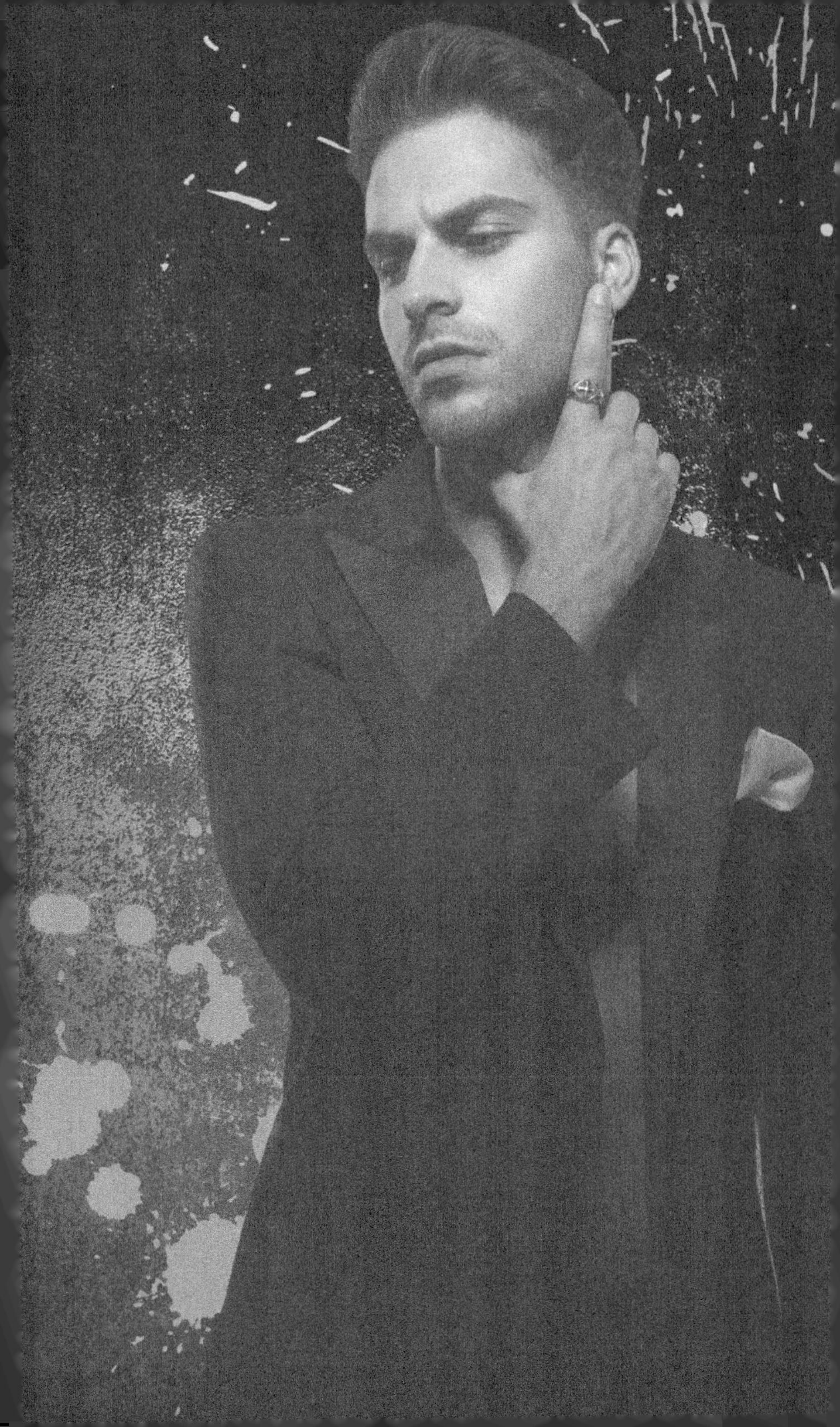

33
LOREN

HIS NAME IS REUBEN TRUDEL. After reading through the entire contract Voss sent me, I can see that it's not only Enoch's situation that's called attention to Reuben. He has a medical history of schizophrenia, untreated. The police have been called on him time and time again for unstable and threatening behavior. He quite literally has told those around him that he hears voices, and they tell him to do bad things.

In reality, this man is a ticking time bomb. He has the makings of a mass killer. Unsurprisingly, the police have done nothing to prevent this man from becoming a public danger. It should be on their hands if he commits murder. There are no less than half a dozen pages of Trudel being reported and the police either blowing it off or making a less-than-cursory check on him.

The police have literally been handed a threat *before* he graduates to murder and yet… what are they doing about it?

For the first three days in Vegas, I track Trudel's movements. I learn his behaviors and habits. Observe how he interacts with those around him. Witness his personality disorder in person.

I'm fascinated by the amount of characteristics that we share. I don't hear voices, but it's almost impossible to miss the fact that Trudel does.

On the third day, I hunt. The stalker becomes the stalked as I bide my time to take him down. Voss was right to be afraid for Enoch. His security detail is kind of shit. We'll have to talk about that. I'm sure Van Doren Technologies has a security company and there's no way there'd be holes in their perimeter if they were here.

My brothers cut off Reuben from invading Enoch's house more than once. In less than seventy-two hours! Like, what are these security bitches even doing? One is on his phone all the time. That much I've seen.

Useless.

"He's a danger to himself too," Avory observes when he returns from blocking Enoch's path and rerouting him. "He's bleeding at his hairline where he cut himself with the edge of his knife while scratching an itch, I think."

I appreciate that it gets dark early this time of year. It means I don't have to deal with the extra challenges that daylight presents.

The first opportunity we get to corner Trudel comes around six in the evening. He's just outside Enoch's gated community. The gates are a joke, though. Sure, they're manned where vehicles move in and out, but the gate that surrounds the community is holey at best. For the past three days surveying the area, we've yet to see a single patrol around the actual perimeter.

Maybe the gate itself is supposed to be secure enough to be a draw for the residents. If it were me and I was promised the security a gated community is supposed to offer, this wouldn't cut it.

Then again, I have no problem running my knife through an intruder's throat. But that's just me.

Conveniently, this community is located right on the edge of the city. It takes me and my brothers no time to disarm Trudel and wrap him in duct tape before shoving him into the plastic- three-tarp-lined trunk of the rental. Then we head out toward Red Rock Canyon.

Trudel doesn't make much sound. The crinkle of the tarps are more in timing with bumps and turns than with him actually moving around. He didn't put up much of a fight. Maybe he wanted to be caught.

We drive ninety miles into the desert. While my brothers construct a grave, I drive my knife through his neck and watch him suffocate while he bleeds out. He stares at me. There's something familiar in his eyes. Something I recognize. I wonder if it's the similarities between us.

The three of us deposit Trudel into the grave, tarps, plastic, duct tape and all. I even leave the knife in his neck. We stop for take-out on the way and then at a truck stop where we change and shower, throwing everything we have in the dumpster.

There are cameras, sure. But there's no blood on us. The only reason we're throwing away these garments is in case Trudel's hair stuck to us. Otherwise, this was a clean kill. Besides, once someone finds him, he'll likely be well on his way to decomposition. By that time, the car will likely have been sold by the rental company, the dumpster's contents covered within a landfill, and we will be nowhere near Vegas, already with no ties to Trudel and no reason for anyone to look at us.

Okay, we'll be more than 400 miles from Vegas.

Not that I'm concerned at all about the police *actually* noticing that this guy disappeared. They didn't pay any attention to him while alive, a threat and freely walking around with a knife in his hand. They were practically waiting until he actually killed someone before he mattered.

Avory and Ellory stay in the car while I walk through the broken gate of Enoch's gated community, frowning toward the front gate as I walk across the drive like I belong here. Useless. These people are useless.

As are the now *absent* security details at his front door. Shaking my head, I knock.

A minute later, Enoch opens the door.

Enoch looks like any other rockstar's child that you could imagine. He's wearing black pants, somewhat formfitting, a loose tank tucked in, and a leather belt filled with rivets. There are two chains around his neck, a wrist filled with bracelets, and his hair is dyed black, falling just past his chin in fluffed curls. He has a sharp jaw and gray blue eyes.

"Loren?" he asks.

He doesn't look particularly scared.

"Hi," I answer.

Enoch looks around before stepping backward into the house and allowing me inside, shutting the door behind me. "What're you doing here?"

"Is your house bugged?" I asked.

His eyes widen and he looks around, slightly horrified. "No?"

I frown. "A couple things—one, this gated community is shit. I walked right in, unnoticed. You should move. Two, your security team is also shit. They're nowhere in sight." I can see his fear come alive in his eyes. "Three, talk to Voss about all of that and installing cameras, interior and exterior. However, I suggest moving somewhere that's *actually* secure first."

Enoch nods. "Okay."

"Four, your stalker situation has been nullified."

His eyes widen. "Nullified... What does that mean?"

I smile and don't answer.

"Uh, oh... Umm, thank you?"

He's rather mousy for a rockstar's son. "You're welcome. Call my brother tomorrow." I turn to the door and pause. "Do you love Voss?"

"What?" he asks, eyes wide once more. "I... no. I mean, he's a good friend so, yeah, but no. I don't *love* him. Why? What has he said?"

I nod. "Lock your doors, Enoch."

Once again, I walk through his 'safe' neighborhood uninterrupted and climb back into the car. There's a flight in an hour so I have Avory and Ellory drop me off at the airport while they remain on the morning flight. I'm not about to stay an extra night away from Oakley if I don't have to.

The flight is less than an hour and a half. I'm out of the airport and in a cab by 12:30 am and headed to my house. As I step inside, I glance at the house across the street where I know Oakley is. My desire to go there immediately is strong, but I decide to take a shower first. Just in case I didn't clean under my nails well enough.

Not that it truly matters. I was not only wearing gloves, but I didn't get near his blood.

Trudel is how most of my kills go. They really aren't personal. I don't feel anything specific when I stab them, usually in the neck, but sometimes the heart or lung, depending on how long I want to see their lives fade away. Once I tried the gut, but sepsis takes a while, so I went for the neck in that one too. There's not even a thrill as I watch them die. It's just... pleasant, I suppose. I enjoy it.

Occasionally our contracts come with a request for a specific kind of death. Depending on how Myro interprets the damage our target caused, he sometimes tells me what they want. Not that I don't have the entire contract as I get ready for the job. It's that I rarely care what it says more than identifying information. Myro tends to tell me when I should make a death long or painful or kill them in some particular fashion.

My shower is short, just making sure I'm clean. Then I dress and head across the street to retrieve my boyfriend. The door is locked, as it should be, and while I could go around to the back and break in through the sliding door as I have in the past, I decide that maybe I should just knock. If no one answers, *then* I'll break in. Seems reasonable.

I'm pleased to find that Imry answers. He smiles and takes a step back. "I had a feeling you'd show up tonight."

"Did you?"

"When Ave said that you were targeting just after dark? Yes."

"Why stay longer than I have to?" I ask as he shuts and locks the door behind me.

He chuckles. "Voss is on the couch. He's butthurt that I took the spare room, but he's snoring so I don't think he's that uncomfortable."

I glance into the dark expanse of the house beyond the entry. Sure enough, I can hear Voss' snoring. I think I'd suffocate him in his sleep if I had to hear that every night.

"Everything go okay?" Imry asks.

LOREN

I nod, shrugging. "Enoch needs to move and hire actual professionals. Voss is not taking care of his friend."

He grins. "Oakley went to bed three hours ago. You going to take him home?"

"Yes. His friends have a weird rule about boyfriends and girlfriends spending the night."

"I'm impressed that you choose to respect that."

"Why? I don't want to put Oakley in a compromised position."

His smile widens. "That's why I'm impressed."

Yep, that didn't clear it up. So I nod and head for the stairs, keeping as silent as I can so I don't wake others. His texts throughout the day said that Levis is home, who sleeps in the bedroom downstairs, and then Briar and Albrecht. The other two are still out of the house.

I'm surprised when I hear voices from Oakley's room. At first, it's only his voice that I hear asking, "Okay, that much I've figured out." I'm ready to write it off as he's talking in his sleep but then a voice answers.

"Jesus, Oakley. *I* want to be with you. I love you."

I open the door as Albrecht's mouth lands on Oakley's. Everything inside me turns cold. The edge of my vision darkens as possessive anger surges through me. I'm across the room in three strides, ripping Albrecht off Oakley and forcefully tossing him across the room.

He lands with a loud *thunk* against the big chair I used to sit in to watch Oakley sleep. I turn, hands fisted, to reach for him again when Oakley jumps on my back and wraps around me.

"Don't," he says. "Please, don't hurt him."

"He kissed you," I growl, taking another step toward Albrecht.

The overhead light turns on and for a moment, I'm blinded by the sudden change.

"Please," Oakley begs. "He's my best friend. He's confused. Please let him go."

I'm shaking. His request is nearly unheard as I tremble with fury.

"I love you," he whispers, his lips pressed to my ear. "Don't kill my best friend."

Reaching behind me, I grip his thigh.

"Brek, get out of my room," Oakley orders.

Albrecht doesn't move for a solid thirty seconds, but then he's scrambling to his feet and tripping over himself to get to the door. The rest of the household is standing there, Imry gripping Levis' arm since he's holding his wakizashi as he stares between us.

In the door are Briar and Voss.

"Take him home," Imry whispers.

There's still black smoke licking at the side of my vision. Gripping Oakley's arm, I haul him around to the front of me. He comes with a yelp and then laughter as I catch him. He's in nothing but some sexy little underwear, which only ignites my fury further because not only did Albrecht touch him, but my Oakley was practically naked in bed.

"Take me home," Oakley murmurs, his fingers trailing through my hair. "Please."

I reach for a blanket and wrap it around him before heading for the door. Without a word, they split to let me through.

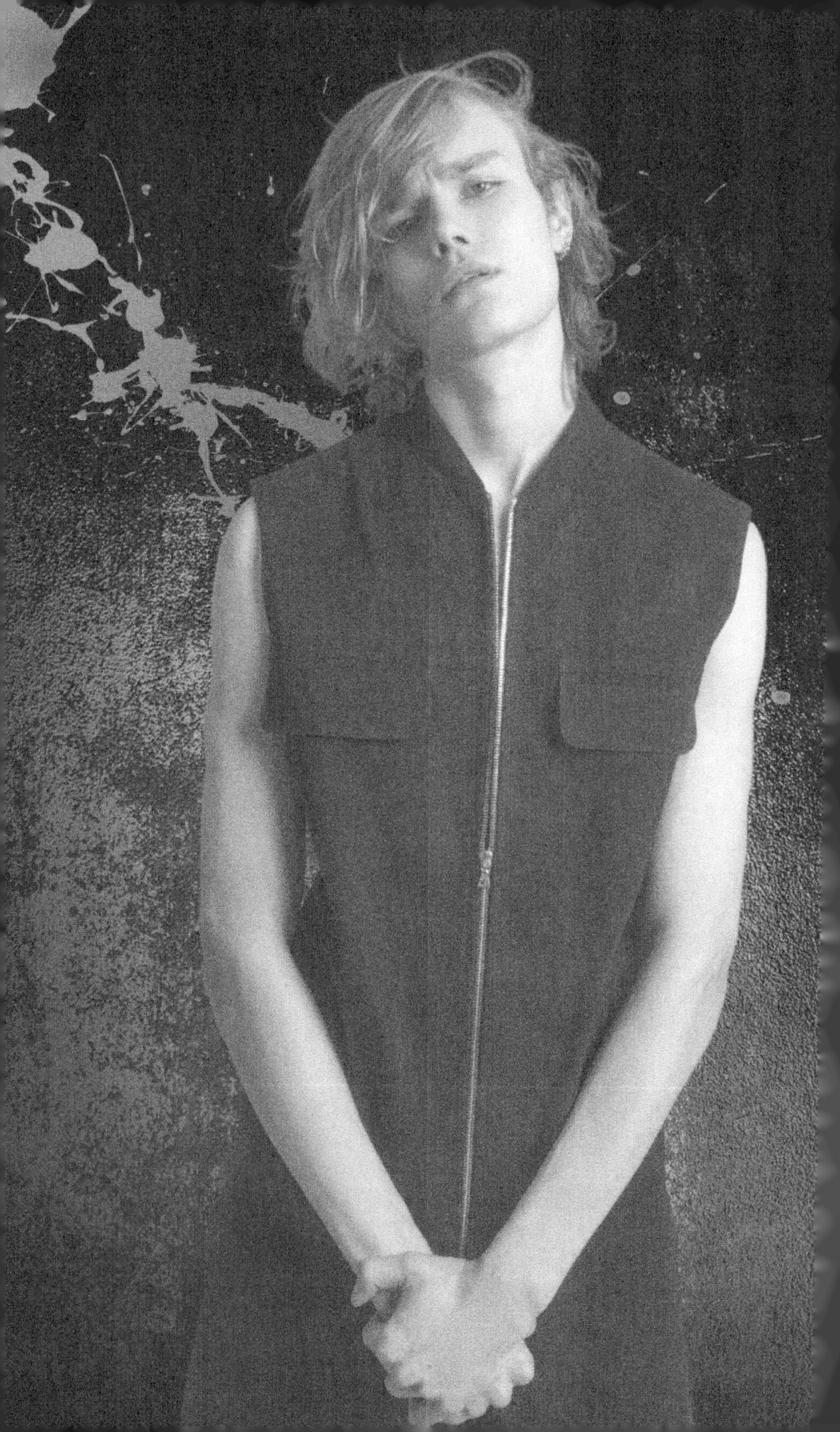

34
OAKLEY

He's shaking. The look of fear on Brek's face swims through my head as I cling to Loren. Frozen in fear as he looked upon the face of what I assumed was the killer Loren. I couldn't see Loren's face. He was so quick and silent I didn't know he was there until Brek suddenly vanished, then landed against the chair on the floor.

I'd been so disoriented and shocked by all the things Brek said and did, it took me precious seconds to even register the looming shadowy mass that was Loren Van Doren stalking toward Brek as he cowered in the dark.

Loren is still shaking when he steps into his house. He moves silently. I'm actually rather impressed with the level of silence he manages right up until he shuts his bedroom door.

There's a light on over his desk and I absently wonder if I left it on. Though I don't remember turning it on at all. When I realize his hair is damp, I think he must have come here first before coming next door.

If he'd waited maybe thirty more seconds, I'd have had Brek off me. I'd been so stupidly surprised by his admission and then shocked when he actually kissed me that I kind of just... froze. Deer in headlights kind of shock.

I'd have handled it. I'd have slapped him.

But Loren was there.

He doesn't set me down once we get to his room. The blanket he picked up and wrapped around me is covering me well and while I want to call attention to this sweet, attentive gesture while he's clearly struggling to keep himself under control, I recognize that now's not the time.

"I promised that I'd kill anyone who ever touched you again," Loren says, his voice dark. Venomous. "Anyone who *kissed* you."

"He's confused," I whisper, keeping my arms tightly around him. "Brek doesn't like change and he's scared of losing everyone in one fell swoop when we graduate. He didn't mean it."

I can feel his frown more than see it since I'm tucked into his neck.

"How do you not mean a kiss?" he asks.

"Please, trust me. And *please* don't kill my friends."

"They're not allowed to touch you," he growls.

"That won't happen again, Loren. I swear."

I can feel the way he's shaking. It moves through me in a low vibration. Like the earth under our feet is filled with tremors. I need to do something. But I'm not sure what.

Unhooking my legs, I slide down his body and stand on the floor. Cupping the sides of his face, I pull his attention to me. I can see exactly why Brek looked so scared. My Loren isn't home right now. I'm not sure even Loren is aware of the mask he wears all day. Because this man is barely recognizable.

LOREN

"I love you. I love you, I love you, I love you, I love you." I repeat it as a chant until he blinks several times and stops shaking.

"You came home early," I say, hoping to distract him. "Was your contract done early?"

Loren gives me a curt nod. It's jerky and I know he's still struggling.

"I'm glad you're here. I hate sleeping without you."

His eyes hood. Then I think about what he walked in on and flinch.

"Take your clothes off," I whisper.

Loren's hands tighten on me, but he takes a step back and undresses. I watch as he does, unveiling his body for me piece by piece. He's so sexy. Beautiful perfection.

He stands naked before me, and I press my hands to his stomach. When he flexes, I can see the distinct lines of his abdominals. Toned, hard beneath my palms. His muscles jump at my touch, and I wonder if he needs to not be touched right now.

"What do you need?" I ask. He glances at the window and I turn him so he can't see it. "Look at me, Loren. Stop thinking about him or I'm going to be offended you're thinking of another man right now. Tell me what you need."

His perfect dark eyebrow rises. Distract him with something outlandish? I'll try anything.

"I don't know," he admits.

"How about if we get into bed," I suggest, "and you touch me. Want to do that?"

Loren licks his lips, his gaze flickering down my body. He nods. I sigh in relief and shove my underwear down so I can step out of them. I make a point of stopping at the nightstand to grab the lube and ensure he sees me tossing it on bed before climbing on.

He hovers where he is, rocking slightly, and I wonder if I'm going to have to launch myself on his back again to keep him here. I lay down and spread my legs. His eyes drop and again, he licks his lips.

The fact that he's still thinking about killing someone right now tells me how very mad he is.

"Come here," I whisper.

He sways and I practically sob in relief when he actually comes toward me. Loren hovers over me like a predator, his eyes nearly glowing in the dim light. I swallow.

"Did I tell you how much I love what you did with your bed?" I ask, knowing damn well I have. Many, many times over. "I love that you did this for me."

The corner of his mouth lifts slightly and I know he's trying to let me pull him from his murderous mood.

"Know what else I love?"

"Me," he answers without pause.

"Definitely you. But I also love when your whole weight is on me. When you hold me down and fuck me slow and deep and hard. I love to bite you and let the hint of the bitter taste of your blood touch my tongue. Can we do that now?"

He comes down on me and I shimmy around under him so we're lined up properly. Though his weight means I can't quite reach the lube, since he's holding me down. Loren grabs it and he pushes a hand between us so his fingers can reach my hole.

His eyes never leave mine as he works me open. Carefully. That's never changed no matter how many times we have sex. The way he's always so damn careful with me brings tears to my eyes.

It isn't long before he's pushing inside me. "Take my hands," I grunt. "Hold them under me. Don't let them go."

Loren does as I tell him to, so I'm bound by his hold.

"Now fuck me hard."

He does. I'm not sure if it's the angle with my calves on his shoulders and him holding me in place with my hands under me, or the intensity of his mood, but every violent thrust makes me whine-grunt. That sound that's high pitched as a result of the motion when he shoves the air from my lungs by means of my ass.

"I love you," I say, because I can't keep words in. As much as I'm usually babbling how good he feels, tonight the only words that come out of my mouth are that I love him.

It drives him on and his thrusts are harder and harder. My entire body feels like it's going to unravel by the time I practically shout that I need him to come. He shoves deep, dropping his face into my neck, bending me in half. Raising my head, I sink my teeth into his neck as I jerk and jolt through my own orgasm.

Then his weight comes down as we both fall from the orgasmic high. He lets go of my hands and wraps me tightly in his arms.

"Promise me something," I say. He grunts in acknowledgement. "Promise that you won't kill my best friends."

Loren doesn't answer. For a long time, he remains silent. His voice is quiet when he answers, "I promise not to kill your best friends *if* they don't fucking touch you again."

"They won't touch me like that again," I swear.

He sighs but his muscles are finally relaxed. "Oakley?"

"Yes?" I ask, nearly asleep again.

"I like your teeth in me."

I grin, shifting under him so I can bite him again. He sighs and I swear, he falls asleep as I dig my teeth into his flesh until my jaw aches.

OVER THE NEXT SEVERAL DAYS, I can't find Brek anywhere. He avoids me to the point where my friends know when I'm about to walk in the door because Brek will literally get up in the middle of a conversation and practically run.

He doesn't run anywhere that I can corner him, though. He leaves the house entirely.

After a week of this, I'm frustrated and hurt.

I push Loren into his room and place my hands on my hips. "I need you to stay here," I say. He looks at me amused. "I'm not going to leave the house, but I need you to stay here in this room. Promise me?"

"Why?" he asks.

"Because I need to talk to Brek, and he sure as hell isn't going to talk to me with you around."

His smile is less amused now.

"I swear to you, he won't touch me. But please, stay here. Promise?"

It takes me nearly an hour to get his promise and trust that he's going to keep it. Then I leave and head to find one of his brothers. Literally any one of them, I think. I come across Voss first.

He looks up from where he's cooking over the stove and gives me a smile. "Weird seeing you alone," he teases.

"I need some help," I say, and his expression immediately turns concerned. Before he can get the wrong idea, I continue, "I need someone to convince Brek to come over here and then lock him in a room where he can't escape so I can force him to talk to me."

Voss chuckles. "Done. Give me ten minutes."

I watch as he finishes preparing his meal, washes the dishes, and then sticks it in the warming drawer before tossing the towel on the counter. "Be right back."

The front door opens and closes a minute later and I can see him through the window walking across the street. Glancing at the warming drawer, I muse that his food will be ruined by the time he gets back. That rubbery overdone texture that you find at buffets.

Wandering to the back room, I watch out in the window as the landscapers move through the yard alongside the construction crew that's finishing up with details. It still looks like a mess, but it's not as bad as it had been. I can almost see it coming together.

"Oakley."

I spin around at Voss' voice, startled.

He grins. "Come on."

"You got him here already?" I ask.

Voss nods. "I think he wanted to be caught." He winks at me and opens a door down the hall. I'm not even sure what this room is, having never gone down this particular hall before.

Brek turns around when the door opens and frowns when he sees me step inside. Voss grins and backs out. I lean against the door so Brek can't run. He could jump through the window if he wanted, but I don't think he's going to do that.

He sighs, his shoulders sagging.

"Ready to man up and talk?" I ask.

The bemused smile he gives me says that he's not entirely sure he wants to. However, he also nods.

"I'm sorry," he starts. "I shouldn't have kissed you."

"Just so I'm clear, are you apologizing because you're scared of Loren or are you actually sorry?"

His smile is a little bigger this time. "Both."

"He's not going to hurt you," I say with confidence.

"I'm glad *you're* convinced of that."

I sigh. "Listen, yes, Loren was definitely going to hurt you that night. You can't honestly think that someone else wouldn't respond in the same way, under the same circumstances. You *knew* I have a boyfriend and chose to disregard that, and quite disrespectfully kiss me. Uninvited. Unwelcome. Without permission."

Brek looks like he's lost at least a couple inches of height by the time I'm done with how he hunches in on himself.

"So, yeah, Loren was mad. As he had every right to be. Had the situation been different and he'd *not* shown up, I'd also have been pissed and slugged you as soon as I registered what the fuck you were doing. Either way, the house was going to wake up and someone was going to be standing murderously over you. That was a really shitty thing to do, and while I still want a better explanation, understand that nothing you say can excuse it."

"I'm sorry," Brek repeats. "You're right. Completely and entirely. I don't actually have anything else to add to that. I was wrong. I crossed a line. I've just been so afraid of losing everyone, you specifically, that I… acted rashly."

"You don't believe that you're in love with me, do you?" I ask.

The way he gives me a sad smile, I think maybe he does believe it. But I don't. I know Brek and he periodically latches on to one of us harder than the others, especially when he feels that they're slipping away.

I cross the room and wrap my arms around him, hugging him fiercely. "You're not," I insist quietly. "No matter where I go or who I'm with, you're always going to be my best friend. No one will change that. Nothing will come between us. It's been over a decade, Brek. We've all been through *a lot* and look at us! Despite this right now, we're just as close as we've ever been. Closer, even."

He eventually wraps his arms around me.

"I love you. So, so much. I'd be so damn hurt if I lost you. But you need to accept that I love Loren. I'm staying with him, Brek. I know you can't see beyond your fear and hurt, but he treats me so well. Legitimately too. Not like Daniel/Jason."

Brek scowls, shaking his head.

"I love that you're scared for me and want to protect me, but I promise, I'm happy. I'm with him by choice and for the right reasons." Granted, some of the things I love might be a little twisted, but I don't need to offer that information at this juncture. "I really, really need you to stop being an asshole. Okay?"

He nods. "I know."

Taking a couple steps back, I rest my hand on his chest. "Your girl is out there, Brek. I promise."

With a sigh, he shakes his head. "Maybe. I don't know. I don't do well talking to other people."

"You do fine," I say. "Sounds to me like you've been talking to the real estate guy just fine."

The corners of his mouth tick up. "Yeah."

"You pick up on a vibe and when a person jives with you, you *do* allow yourself to get close. There's nothing wrong with being picky, Brek. No matter how picky you are, I know the right person will come along and you'll recognize it, even if it doesn't happen right away."

He nods again. "Thanks for your vote of confidence."

"You're welcome. Want to play video games? I think I can get the triplets downstairs and we can race."

Brek grins. "Yeah, okay. Sounds cool."

"And you can be in the same room as Loren without being a tool," I add.

He's less enthusiastic about it, but he still agrees. Which I take for the win it is.

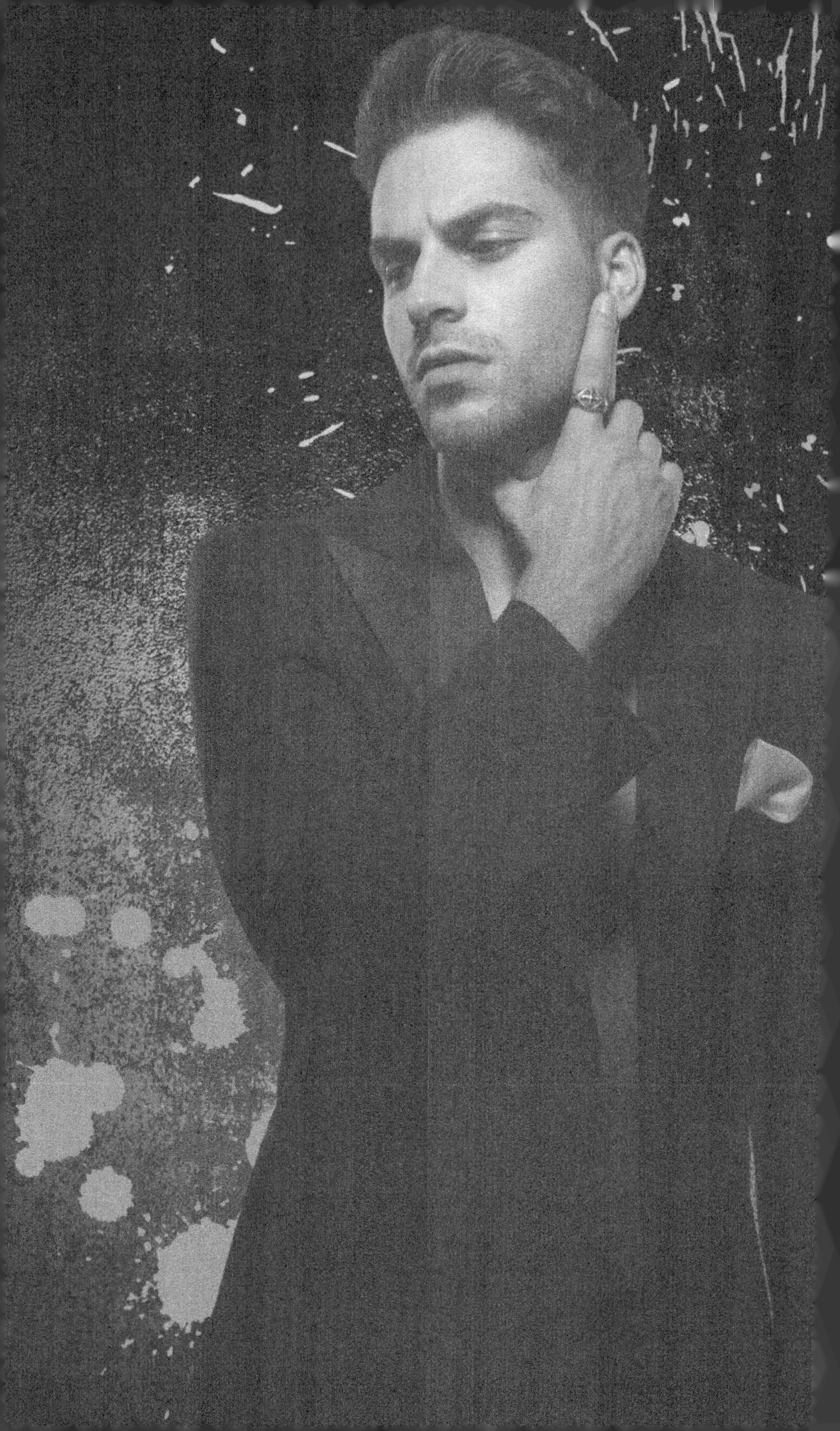

35
LOREN

W E'VE BEEN LYING in bed for the past hour, mostly only casually touching. Well, kind of. School starts next week and he's feeling stressed about graduation. Unsure what he *should* do, as opposed to what he *wants* to do. And when he's stressed, he likes his hole messed with and his dick suckled.

I don't have his dick in my mouth because he also wants to talk, so he's pressed to my chest, arranged in such a way that I have one of his arms trapped under my body and the other locked above his head while I finger him, and we alternate between lazily making out and talking.

Most of the time, this situation leads to 'more' once he's driven to frustration and needs to be filled beyond my capability. That's when we take out the toy that stretches him extra wide while I fuck him. I've recently bought something for his cock, too; but I'm saving that for another day. A day when maybe even the bulbous stretcher toy doesn't quite hit the mark he needs.

Right now, he's content. The stress isn't on his shoulders as heavily as it will be as the end of the semester approaches. Besides, I've been toying with a decision.

However, I'm trying to be more mindful of my decisions, especially concerning the two of us, those deserve conversations and Oakley needs to have an input. So I need to figure out how to approach it while not letting it sound like I've already made up my mind.

Which I have. And I'm not changing my opinion. So we'll have to see how this new strategy of talking it through before I make it happen works.

Oakley pulls his lips from mine and sighs. They're red and swollen. I love this look on him. He's so damn sexy.

"I love this," he says.

"Keeping your hole stretched?"

His cheeks pinken. "Yes, but I mean laying in bed with you like this."

"Hole stretched and restrained," I try again, keeping my smile hidden.

He huffs. "Yes," he says, firmly, "but I mean—"

"Our bare skin pressed together. Hearts beating against each other. Sharing the same breathing space. So close that I can see the different shades of brown that make up your eyes. Keeping a piece of myself lodged within your tight body so we're quite literally a single unit. That's what you like?"

His lips are parted as he stares at me. I can feel his breathing shiver through him. His head bobs slightly. "Exactly all that," he whispers. "I've never had this before. It's so… just…" He shakes his head. "I can't even put words to it. How good it feels."

I nod. "I feel the same way. Exactly everything you just said—me too."

"I guess maybe we are sharing a lot more firsts than I initially thought."

"I guess so," I agree.

"So on that note, can we talk about another first that neither of us has had?"

"You're adorable thinking you have to ask first."

He grins. "So we have sex the same way all the time."

I frown. "I'm quite certain we're rarely in the same position twice in a week."

Oakley laughs. "Sorry, that's not what I meant. I mean that your dick is always in my ass. Right?"

"Yes. Last I checked, we enjoy that."

He laughs again. "We do. A lot. But... what if we tried it the other way? With my dick in your ass? Would you consider it?"

I glance down our bodies where our hinting chubs are pressed together. "Your dick is much bigger than mine."

Oakley rolls his eyes. "It's really not. You feel that way because you're the best boyfriend in the world and will keep my cock in your mouth for over an hour when I get stressed. I'm sure it feels a lot bigger than it is."

"We're going to have to agree to disagree on that."

"Or if you really want me to prove it, we can get a soft tape measure and I can show you I'm right. But if this is your way of saying you're not interested in that, I'm definitely cool with that."

"It's something you want to do."

He doesn't answer. I think he's figured out by now that if he says yes, we're going to do it regardless of how I feel about it. He's recently been very careful choosing his wording. Something we both know I don't miss.

"If you're open to it, then maybe I might be interested in seeing if we like it," he says slowly. As if he's trying on each word.

I stare into his pretty eyes and wonder whether I might like fingers up my ass as mine are up his right now. I can't deny how much he enjoys it. Not just in these moments, but any time I get him ready to be fucked. Or even just when I'm sucking his dick. He likes to be fingered.

"We can talk about it," I concede.

"Some guys don't like it," he says. "If you want to try it, I need you to promise—and not break that promise—that you'll tell me whether you do or not. Okay?"

"I promise."

He gives me a shrewd look, not at all believing me.

"My turn," I say.

Oakley grins. "I mean, you already have your fingers in me."

I push them in a little deeper, enjoying the way he shudders. I'm only marginally fingering him. Slowly working his hole without any true intent behind it. It's not meant for pleasure. I internally think of it as maintenance. Emotional maintenance. He needs to feel the evidence of a physical connection. He wants there to be a way that I'm constantly inside his body—my fingers, my cock, my tongue. I think beyond his sexual need, it answers a deeper, hungrier emotional need.

We don't talk a lot about our pasts from before we met. I think we're saving it for a rainy day. But I've gleaned some things over the last few months, and I know that he's as touched starved as I am averse to touch. It's only my craving to possess this man that has me overriding that most days.

And his emotional starvation is just as vast. Outside of the love of his friends, he's a very lonely man.

"Yes," he breathes out.

"You need to move in with me."

He laughs, his hips rocking on my fingers a little. "I'm already here all the time," he says.

"Yes," I agree, staring at his face. His eyes are mostly closed. His breaths are coming a bit more rapidly now as he moves against me. "But I want you to bring all your things and move into my room. Permanently."

Oakley grins. There's a quiet moan in the back of his throat.

I smile. "Pay attention."

His smile is beautiful. "I heard you. You want me to move in."

This is the part where I'm biting my tongue because I'm truly not giving him a choice. I will definitely pack all his belongings myself and bring them here while he's otherwise occupied.

I nip his chin. "Tonight," I insist.

He moans, his hips rolling a little more urgently. Horny boyfriend. "If I get you off, will you pay better attention?"

Oakley laughs. It's one of the sexiest sounds I've ever heard. "Sure, but, Loren?"

I roll him onto his back and bear down on him. "Yes?"

"You and I both know you're going to move me in regardless of what I say right now. Right?"

"I appreciate that you know me so well," I respond, pressing my fingers deeper into his ass, this time intentionally garnering a response. He shivers, bringing his free arm up to meet the other I have pinned so I'll take them both. "So why aren't you giving this proper attention?"

"I already live here," Oakley says with a little shrug. "Put your dick in me and let me fuck myself on you, Loren. We can talk at the same time."

I roll my eyes. We both know that's likely not going to happen.

Pulling my fingers from his ass, I apply lube to my dick. I'm going to miss the days when he doesn't have to go to school and we can stay in bed all day. Only measuring time by how many minutes pass between orgasms.

"To your balls," he orders when I press the crown of my dick to his hole. "Right away. Hard. Okay?"

If I hadn't been fingering his ass for the better part of an hour, there's a chance I might not have complied with that demand. I get that he likes it hard. So do I. But there will never be a time under any circumstance that I will *actually* hurt this man.

Bracing myself on the bed, I shove in. My gaze remains locked on Oakley's face. He makes the sweetest, choking sounds as his body nearly bends in half as he arches so dramatically. So sexy. I think this man could keep me hard far longer than what should be biologically possible.

I adjust so I can comply with what he wants. Keeping myself still so he can work himself on my dick.

"I already live here" Oakley resumes our conversation, his voice a mixture of groans and the hottest breathy sounds I've ever heard. "My space in the other house is just a storage room."

"Then let's empty it. I want you here. I want this to be your only home."

"Okay."

"Do you want that?"

He grins, rolling his hips on me. "Yes. I want to be wherever you are. I want to be here every day. I want to come home with you. I want to do my homework while I ride your dick. I want you to latch onto me with my cock in your mouth and your fingers in my ass while I study for tests—all tests. Or any time I'm stressed. I want you to fill me with your cum every single time you orgasm. I want it all."

Jesus that's... that's. Overwhelming. In a good way.

True to my man's form, he doesn't stop talking. When he's enjoying himself like this, he babbles, but up until this point, it's always just been sexy talk. How good I feel. How much he loves that I killed for him. The kinds of things that I think are probably pretty typical for dirty talk.

It's probably a good thing he doesn't require me to move much because I'm hanging on his every word.

"I don't care where we live, Loren. I'm with you always. I want to be here, yours. I don't ever want to leave. I want to have kids with you—like eight. We're going to spoil the fuck out of them. I want to marry you and then remarry you every year on our anniversary so everyone can see—including you—how much more I fall in love with you every single day."

"What else?" I ask when he pauses. There's no filter right now. Oakley simply word vomits his wants as he works up to his orgasm. And I listen raptly. Committing everything to memory. "Tell me everything you want, Oakley. Everything."

"I want to eat your ass. I want to make you feel good in every way. I want to spend weeks, months fingering you until you're ready to ride me. I want to make you feel so good. So good. Just like this. Just like you make me. I really hope you'll like it too.

We don't have to switch often because I'm totally a whore for your cock, but I want to sometimes."

I grin because I knew that's what he wanted.

"I want to graduate this year," he says through a loud moan. "I want to spend my life here, with you. Making you happy. That's the career I want. I want to raise our babies and want you to come home to me cooking naked for you. I want you to never get tired of this. Fuck, I'm going to come."

I'm slightly disoriented at his last words, trying to figure out how that fits into the cooking naked and raising our babies and his concern that I'll get tired of this. It isn't until he cries out and I realize he's coming on my dick that he'd been talking about what was happening right now.

His jaw clenches as his muffled sounds fill the room. Any part of my body should be between his teeth right now so he can bite me like he likes. As I like.

"Keep holding me like this," he tells me between pants. "Fuck me until you get off, Loren."

I do, staring at this man's face the entire time. Letting his words play on repeat in my head. All the things I learned. All the things I'm going to make happen for him. I fuck him as I stare into his eyes and he stares back, moaning and squirming under me. He doesn't look away now.

We're more than connected with my cock in his ass. There's something else spanning between us. Growing. Strengthening.

When I come, my entire body shudders. I swear, I can feel the pleasure course through every nerve ending, as tingles run from my toes to my scalp. I'm nearly hyperventilating by the time I empty inside him and drop onto him. He 'oomphs' and because I still have his hands, he wraps his legs around my waist, instead. Holding me to him.

"Do you want to keep living with your family?" he asks when a few minutes pass.

I nod. "Is that okay?"

"Yeah."

Sighing, I brush my lips over his neck. "I'm going to give you everything you want. Everything. Every last thing you just said you wanted."

He laughs quietly. "Except the switch thing. I can't control what I'm saying like that."

"Including the switch thing. We can set a future date and work up to that. Like your graduation when you officially become my househusband. *Then*, we'll celebrate with *you* fucking *me*."

Try as he may, I don't miss the way he moans. Yeah, that's happening. I don't even care how much I may or may not like it. Oakley gets whatever the fuck Oakley wants.

"I love you," he whispers.

I smile and close my eyes. "Everything," I murmur. "It's all yours."

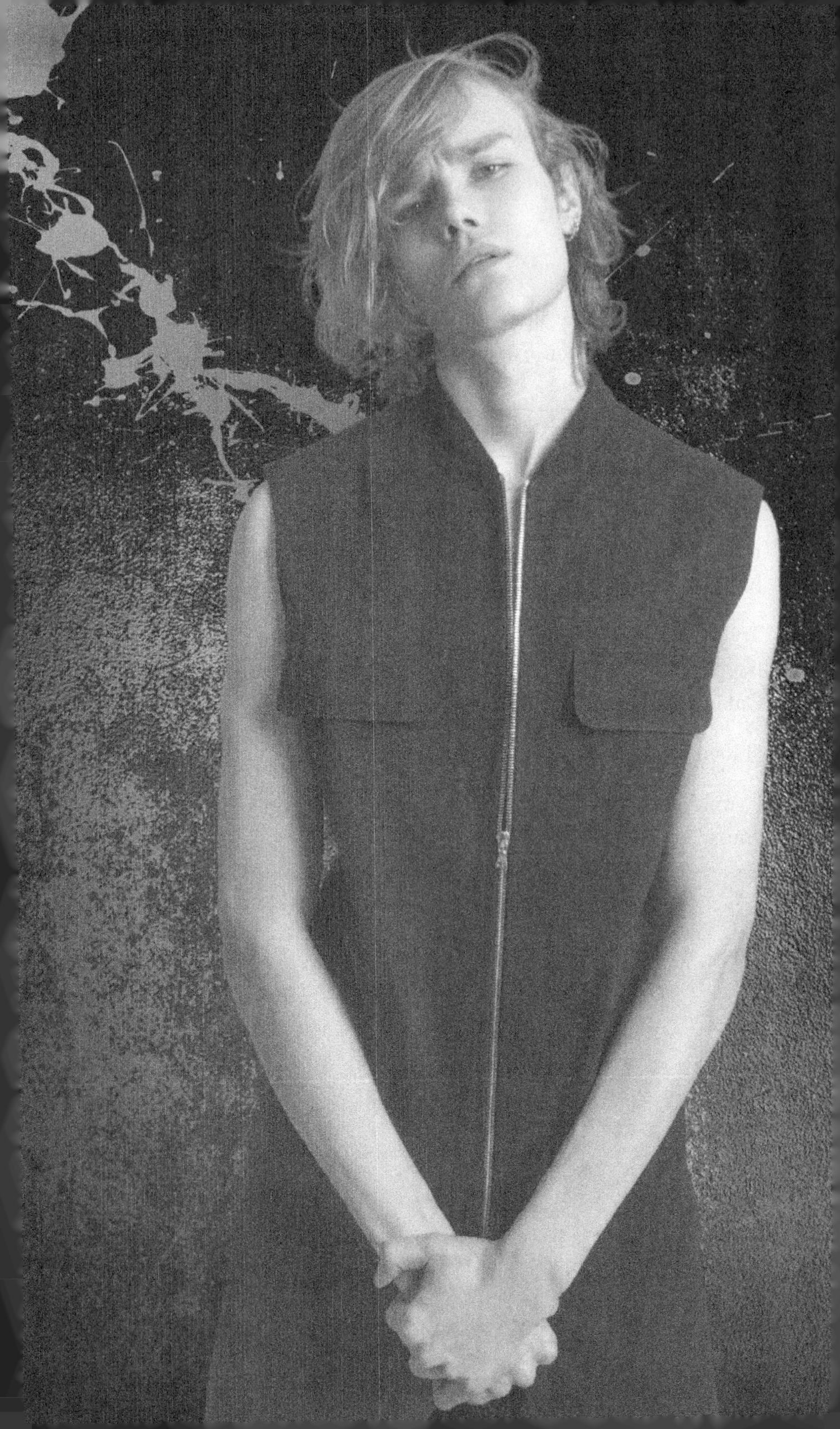

36
OAKLEY

Three months later - April

Between Voss and Talon, I'm learning to cook. Not necessarily well, but I'm trying. However, it's Imry who's teaching me how to bake. I'm much better at baking. I think it's the structure and precise ingredients that help.

Loren doesn't claim to be closer to any one of his brothers over the others. Or say he has a favorite but secretly, I think he's closest with Imry. That might be why I am too. We spend a lot of time together when I'm not with Loren or they're not tending to one of Loren's contracts.

I'm at least 40% convinced that 'contract' is a code word for something, though I've yet to truly figure it out. Which is fine.

It's been three months since I officially moved in. I kind of thought there'd be some growing pains and awkward moments, if not between me and Loren, then just in general because I'm brand new to their household. But most of the time, it feels like

I've always been here. They treat me like part of them. Without getting sappy, I couldn't have ever dreamed up a better family to move into.

I spread the frosting over the top of the cookie and push it aside. As I'm picking up the last one, Imry adds another batch of cooled cookies to my tray. I'm not even sure why we're making so many, and yet, they just keep coming.

From the fresh batch, I slide a frosted one to Honey Bee, one to Haze, and after adding extra frosting to a third, I slide that one across the cool stone countertop to Brek. His eyes flicker to mine and I receive a crooked smile before he returns his attention to his book.

He's still convinced that he's in love with me, and while I don't mean to invalidate how he feels or pretend to know his feelings better than he does, I really do think he's just hanging on as tightly as he can because everything is changing so quickly.

In just under a month, we graduate. *Nothing* will be the same then. Levis is talking about marrying the girl he's seeing, Honey Bee has been out every night for the past seven weeks with the same guy, even Haze has said he's met someone he might be interested in. Then there's me, who's moved out. I'm not sure what Briar's plan is, though.

I keep hinting that I think Brek might benefit from talking to a therapist or something, because he has mad anxiety right now and it's only going to get worse. But he brushes it off, assuring us all that he's fine. Maybe while he has finals to prepare for, he can distract himself, but it won't be long before he achieves this goal, and he's forced to face the next part of his life.

"You need to study?" Imry asks.

Glancing at him over my shoulder, I shrug. Even if I failed these classes—all four!—I'd still have plenty of credits to graduate.

LOREN

Not that I'm going to fail them. However, I study much better when Loren and I are... connected. I call it study time and Loren seems more than happy to suckle my dick with his fingers lodged in my ass until I'm finished whatever work I'm doing.

My ability to concentrate under those circumstances is rather impressive. It's like he sucks everything out of me, and I only have the ability to focus on a single thing. Which should be the way he touches me, but that turns into background comfort more than anything. I *feel* him, but I don't feel him. It's hard to explain, even internally to myself, but it's just right for me.

"Nah. I'll study before bed tonight." When I can reward myself with a well-earned orgasm after. I leave this out, though I have no doubt Loren would have voiced it.

"You feeling good about your classes?" Honey Bee asks.

I nod, licking the frosting off the back of my hand. "Yep. Dunno what I'll ever use the information I've gathered from them for, but they're some of the best I've taken to date."

"I can't believe you're really graduating to stay home," Haze says, chuckling.

"But I'm graduating on time," I point out. "If we went with my indecisive first through eighth plans, I'd probably be in school for another decade."

"You love school," Brek says. His voice is quieter these days. As if he doesn't necessarily want to be heard.

"I do and I might still take classes. But I really am wasting time and money without having an established goal."

Every last person in the kitchen responds with some form of 'you're not' and I laugh. "Okay, *to me*, it feels like I am. I want to be working toward something and until I figure out what that is, I'm just going to spend my days with Loren."

I don't think any of my friends approve of my plan moving forward. The Van Dorens seem as excited for this next step as if I were becoming president of the world, but my friends want more for me. Sometimes, I wonder how I'd feel if one of them were in my situation. Would I be disappointed that their only ambition in life was to tool around the house of their partner?

It's not that I don't *want* to do something, it's just that I don't know what that something is. What I know for sure is that I don't want to dread going to work every day. I want to enjoy my life and since we spend the better part of sixty years working, I need it to be something I love.

That's not unreasonable. The thing is, I'm only twenty-two. How the hell am I expected to know what I want to do with the rest of my life when I've barely begun to live it?! It seems rather unfair to put that kind of pressure on people.

I glance up when I hear the front door open. My heart races because I imagine it's Loren. He's gotten better about leaving me at home as long as it's under the condition that I don't go anywhere without him. Not even with my friends unless Levis will be bringing his wakizashi, which he can't because it's illegal to walk around with a sword.

My friends get frustrated, but I still have the scars on my neck to remind us that I was nearly murdered. I'm more than fine staying with someone who will kill any would-be murderer.

Loren steps into the kitchen and immediately meets my eyes, like we're drawn to each other. I grin and his smile is swoony. He comes around the counter and pulls me against him, kissing me breathless.

When he backs up, I notice that he has something in his hand. Before I can truly process what he has or what he's doing, Loren has the box open, my hand in his, and he's putting a ring on my finger. My eyes widen, jaw dropping as I stare at him.

LOREN

"The officiant will be here momentarily," Loren says.

"Officiant?" Honey Bee repeats.

"Woah," Imry says. "Hold on." He pulls Loren back a step, laughing. "This is one of those moments when you *ask* him, not tell him. You need to talk about this *before* making plans."

Loren frowns. "We have talked about it. A lot." His gaze flickers to Imry for a minute before settling back on me. "You always say you want to be married before you graduate. So I'm making that happen."

"Yes, but..." My voice trails off. "What about my family? We need to plan a wedding. They don't just happen."

"What's to plan? I have rings and now the person who makes it legal will be here momentarily. It was a rather simple plan."

Imry laughs and claps my shoulder. "You will always have your hands full."

"What about Noah?" I ask. "Don't you want him to be here?"

Loren tilts his head slightly.

"We can't just get married now. Where will we do it—the kitchen?" I ask, feeling slightly hysterical.

He looks around. "It doesn't really matter where. All that matters is you."

My breath catches and the panicky feeling that had started to take over melts away. This man has never said the words 'I love you,' but he still manages to tell me every single day how much he loves me.

Trying to not be a sap, I blink the tears that start to form in my eyes. I step into him and wrap my arms around his neck, bringing my forehead to his. "I love you. I want this. But... I need some time to plan a wedding. I want my family here. I want you to have Noah here. I want it to be beautiful and a day we're always going to remember."

"I will remember it. The day I made you my husband," he disputes. "The day you change your name to Oakley Van Doren. The day everyone will know you're mine and I will never let you go. It will never be a day I forget."

"Oh my god," Honey Bee mutters. "He makes it impossible for me to stay mad at his presumptuous decisions."

"It's not presumptuous," Loren insists, frowning. "Oakley tells me he wants to be my husband before graduation every night while I'm fuc—"

I slap my hand over his mouth, cheeks burning. "Fucking Christ," I mutter. "Stop doing that."

I can feel his smirk under my hand. About half the time I know he does this without understanding it's inappropriate. The other half, he sure as fuck knows and does it to make me squirm.

Haze is smirking, sitting back on his stool with his arms crossed over his chest. Honey Bee is still smiling that begrudging smile because she hates to love how sweet Loren is to me. But Brek is trying very hard to find happiness during this moment.

Loren turns his head, making my hand fall away. "I'm sorry. I suppose we should have talked in more depth about it."

Sighing, I kiss him lightly. "I really, really love that I can say I want something even in passing and you just make it happen. It's the sweetest, most romantic thing and you constantly leave me breathless. But this one thing, I really think I need some time to get some details worked out first."

"Okay," he says. "How is Friday?"

"This Friday?" I ask.

Imry laughs as he moves cookies around.

"Or... next Friday?" Loren tries.

He really doesn't understand the process of putting a wedding together. To him, the only thing that matters is the two of us.

"Uh," Voss says as he steps into the kitchen, "there's a lady at the door saying she's here for the wedding?"

Loren kisses my nose. "I'll tell her to come back... in two weeks?" he hedges. If you didn't know him, you'd think he was being pushy. Really, he's just trying to figure out what I want. How long I need. What's the soonest moment he can give me exactly what I've been asking for.

I laugh.

"Tell her you'll call her to reschedule," Honey Bee suggests helpfully.

"Hmm," Loren hums as he takes a step back and turns to leave the room. I watch him go, my heart racing. The further he gets, the more I think that maybe he's right. The *most* important aspect of marrying him is him.

"Wait! Loren!" I call and throw my towel on the counter to race after him.

He's already at the door when I nearly slide into his side. "I've changed my mind. I want to do this now."

"You do?" he asks, amused and unconvinced.

"Yes," I say, eyeing the woman at the door as I turn into Loren. "You're right. You and me. That's what matters. And I do want this before graduation. So let's do it now. Okay?"

He smiles. "Yes. Right here?"

I laugh. "No. Uh... backyard?"

Loren nods.

"I'm going to change into something not covered in flour." Looking at the woman, I say, "Do you have a little bit of time? I need like twenty minutes."

"Of course."

"Okay good. Thank you. I'm going to change. Get your family and my friends and I'll meet you in the backyard. Okay?"

There's a soft look on Loren's face. A small smile as he looks at frazzled me. "Take your time," he says, pressing his lips softly to my jaw. "Take a breath. Everything will be perfect. I promise."

I take a breath and nod. Yeah, okay.

"Go. I'll meet you in the backyard in twenty minutes."

Biting my lip, I nod. There's a part of me that wants to drag him upstairs just to have him there. Loren never gets frazzled. He's this constant beacon of calm and steady. You know, unless he's ready to kill someone who kissed me when they shouldn't. But his quiet, sure presence always helps to put me at ease.

Heading up the stairs, I move through the shower quickly and then stand in the middle of the closet and look around. What am I supposed to wear?! I don't have anything appropriate for a wedding. Not even to attend a wedding, never mind be one of the grooms.

"Don't overthink," I tell myself and slip into one of Loren's favorite pairs of underwear. I choose fitted dark pants and the nicest shirt I have. I pull my hair half up, making sure that some of it falls loose around my face because Loren loves when it does.

I'm jittery and shaking by the time I come downstairs. The house is silent as I walk through to the back door. Beyond the pool paradise, Loren's family and my friends are waiting for me. I'm surprised and breathless when I see flowers everywhere.

Taking a deep breath, I step outside and am met with Honey Bee as she places a crown of flowers on my head. "He's planned more than he let on," she whispers and hands me a bouquet. "The only thing I was able to suggest that he hadn't thought of was getting your parents and brother on video. His friend is there too. I think Daddy Jalon also called his brothers in video."

"It's a good thing I don't wear makeup," I whisper back as she links her arm with mine and walks me toward the small crowd. "I already feel like ugly crying."

"He's pretty intense when he's giving orders. He knew exactly where he wanted the flowers and which were pulled for your bouquet."

The way my heart pounds makes me worry I might pass out. He did this. Loren did this *for me!*

I've always loved the way he looks at me. Intense and focused, as if I'm the only one who exists for him. Everything about him is breathless.

Honey Bee kisses my cheek and lets me go as I close the distance between us. Loren's smile is small, sweet, absolutely sexy, and all for me. "You're beautiful," he murmurs, and my knees nearly buckle.

"You did this," I whisper.

His smile spreads slightly. I'm not at all surprised that Loren places his hands on my hips and pulls me close before giving the woman a nod that she could begin. I don't know what she says. I barely register the fact that there are people among the flowers as I stare into Loren's dark eyes.

I repeat words when I'm prompted. I say I do when prompted. Once again, I'm taken by surprise when Loren produces more rings from his pocket so we can exchange rings when the time comes.

I'm only barely holding it together when we're given the okay to kiss as a married couple. I nearly jump in his arms and press my lips to his. He holds me tight, claiming, as if daring the world to try to take me from his arms.

This is the exact place I want to stay forever. In the arms of Loren's obsessive love, knowing that he has and will kill for me.

WANT MORE LOREN AND OAKLEY?

Newsletter extra

Thank you for reading about Loren and Oakley. If you're not ready to be done with them, you can sign up for my newsletter where you'll have access to another scene in *Hockey 101* when my next newsletter is sent. Access to this story will be granted once my newsletter goes out once a month so please be patient. There will also be an extra scene in my patreon, where you'll find a whole lot of other goodies, including N/SFW art from this story soon!

Are there other characters that piqued your interest as you read this book? You can read more about them in my other books or those to come!

You can find Oren's story in **Coach Stare Down**.

WANT MORE LOREN AND OAKLEY?

If you'd like to read about Loren's friend, Noah, you can in **Lucky Shot**.

For every planned book in this series, you've met the main characters! Yes, all of Oakley's friends are with Loren's relatives. Can you guess the pairings? You'll see many more characters that have passed through these pages in more books to come! You will also get to meet some of Daddy Van Doren's brothers in various books/short stories so stay tuned for them.

There are also characters that you'll see in other series, too. This world just gets bigger and bigger with each book I write and each character that waves at me from the pages. Sometimes those flags are white and other times they're red. We totally met a red-flagged character in this book! Maybe two...

Make sure you take a peek in the pages that follow for a glimpse into what you can expect within the books I've mentioned (and the next one to come in the **Van Doren** series)!

AUTHOR'S NOTE AND ACKNOWLEDGMENTS

Okay, so... first things first. *As of right now,* I have seven books in the Van Doren series. Yes, seven. I'm sure you can figure out that we have five men in Oakley's friendship group, including him. And there are six brothers in the Van Doren household. I've given you a freebee with Oakley and Loren (haha). I'm dying to see who you're pairing up. I'll give you a single hint - one brother gets Honey Bee. Yes, permanently. There is no best friend's boyfriend trope in this series. No cheating. One brother remains straight and no, I will not be writing that story.

Reuben Trudel isn't an actual person (obviously) but his backstory is based on an actual case of a mass shooter that was local to me and my family, who permanently injured some close family friends and killed a bunch more. He needed help. The police knew he needed help. The medical facilities knew he needed help (though their hands are tied by law as to how long and in what manner they can keep someone). But this man didn't get the help he needed and ended up on a shooting spree.

The thing is, the man Trudel is based on didn't go on a *killing* spree. He wasn't trying for their deaths. He wanted to hurt people. He had a very high profile background. He knew how to shoot to kill, what weapons to use to do so, etc. His shots were very specific. His aim was spot on. He had no intention of killing masses of people - he wanted people to hurt like he did.

The man Trudel's backstory is fashioned after was eventually found - *after* the damage he caused and days *after* he killed himself. Yes, days. The tragedy of his story isn't just that he was able to hurt and kill so many people but that he was denied the help he needed for *years*.

The image of Oakley has changed over time as has part of this storyline. At first glance, I saw him as a soccer player, kind of tall and lean and Loren was going to be a teammate. But that was almost a year ago and clearly, things happened. I saw a truer vision of Loren in **Lucky Shot** and as I got to know the Van Dorens, it became clear that these boys are going to be full of bloody fun.

And then the connection between **Coach Stare Down's** storyline and Oakley's and all the why's kind of fell into place. Let me tell how *obsessed* with the Van Doren's I became while writing Loren's story. I've probably rearranged the order of release half a dozen times as I wrote and I'm still not convinced that I'm going to write the next one first.

All this to say, I hope you love Loren and these characters as much as I do!! Are you ready for more Van Dorens?

BOOKS BY CREA REITAN

MM NOVELS/SERIES

For Puck's Sake

Shiver

Starting Line

Lucky Shot

The Crease

Wingman Score

Coach Stare Down

Stick Lessons

The Defending Goal (2024)

For Your Love

For Your Time

For Your Heart

For Your Mind

For Your Forever

Van Doren

Loren

Noah (2025)

Rainbow Dorset University

Collide (2024)

For I Have Sinned

POLY TITLES

Harem Project Novels

House of Daemon

House of Nereus

House of Aves

House of Wyn

House of Igarashi, 1

House of Igarashi, 2

House of Agni

House of Kallan

House of Malak

House of Darkyn (2024)

Sweet Omegaverse

Alpha Hunted

Knot Interested

Omegas of Chaingate

Get Pucking Knotty

INFECTED FAIRY TALES

Wonderland: Chronicles of Blood

Toxic Wonderland

Magical Wonderland

Dying Wonderland

Bloody Wonderland

Wonderland: Chronicles of Madness

The Search for Nonsense

The Queen Trials

Veins of Shade

Finding Time

Neverland: Chronicles of Red

Neverwith

Nevershade

Neverblood

Nevermore

Hellish Ones Novels

Blood of the Devil

House of the Devil

Brothers of Eschat

Unsolicited

Equipoise

Paranormal Holiday Novel

12 Days

Satan's Touch Academy

A Lick of Magic

A Touch of Seduction

A Touch of Darkness

Fae Lords

Karou

Immortal Stream: Children of the Gods

Mortal Souls

The God of Perfect Radiance

The Hidden God

The God Who Controls Death

Gods of the Dead

Gods of Blood

Gods of Idols

Gods of Fire

Gods of Enoch

Gods of Stone

Standalones

Wrecked

Hell View Manor

Stroking Pride (A Sons of Satan Novel)

A Tale of Steam & Cinders

Terror

Haidee (A Ladies of MC Novel)

Silent Night (2024)

ABOUT THE AUTHOR

Crea lives in upstate New York with her dog and husband. She has been writing since grade school, when her second grade teacher had her class keep writing journals. She has a habit of creating secondary, and often time tertiary, characters that take over her stories. When she can't fall asleep at night, she thinks up new scenes for her characters to act out. This, of course, is how most of her meant-to-be-thrown-away characters tend to end up front and center - and utterly swoon-worthy! Don't ask her how many book boyfriends she has...

When not writing, Crea is an avid reader. Her TBR pile is several hundred books high (don't even look at her kindle wish list or the unread books on her tablet). Sometimes, she enjoys crafting; sometimes, exploring nature; sometimes, traveling. Mostly, she enjoys putting her characters on paper and breathing life into them. Oh, and sleeping. Crea *loves* to sleep!

Note - Crea is an Amazon exclusive author. If you're reading this ebook anywhere other than through Amazon, it is a pirated copy and has been stolen! Please don't add to that.

THANK YOU

I hope you enjoyed Loren and Oakley's story. Every red flag needs a happy ending, right? Wait, that's not how the saying goes... Never mind. Stay tuned for book two - *Noaz*.

Would you be so kind as to take a moment and leave a review? Reviews play a big role in a book's success and you can help with just a few sentences.

Review on Amazon, Goodreads, and Bookbub

Thank you!!

Crea Reitan

PS - If you find any errors, spelling or the like, please do not use your kindle/Amazon to mark them. Amazon's algorithms pull the book! Instead, please reach out to me on Facebook at https://www.facebook.com/Crea.Reitan or via email at LadyCreaAuthor@gmail.com. Thank you!!

Made in the USA
Middletown, DE
19 September 2025